For Colton
Thank you for believing in me, even when I didn't.

CONTENT WARNING

Still Chosen: Another Unwanted Adventure contains many elements I hope you enjoy. However, it also contains a few things that some readers may be sensitive to, including death of a friend, drowning in backstory, freezing to death, violence, grief, abandonment, and gaslighting.

STILL CHOSEN

ANOTHER UNWANTED ADVENTURE

STEPHANIE G OLSON

PROLOGUE

It was over. I'd won.

Zaletor the Eternal Emperor and pawn of the disgraced goddess Kalexia was dead, and all that remained to show he'd ever existed was a crown and an ugly black robe. The room still echoed with the beautiful sound of the crown clattering to the floor.

"Phoebe!" Tristan burst in through the wreckage of the door. His arms were covered in scratches, and his red hair was plastered to his forehead with sweat and blood, but his face held only relief. That expression vanished when he saw the gaping wound in my abdomen. "No!"

I don't know if he whispered or screamed the word, but he rushed to my side just as my knees gave out, catching me as I crumpled to the floor.

"Hang on," he cried. "Mercury will be here soon. They'll fix this."

I gasped as he pressed a hand against my side. I knew there was nothing Mercury could do, but I didn't argue. My trousers clung uncomfortably to my legs, sticky with the blood pooling around us.

"It's finished." I ran my hand down his smooth cheek, finding it pleasantly warm. Or my hand was freezing. Noticing the fallen crown and robe for the first time, Tristan sucked in a ragged breath, his olive skin going pale. When he looked back at me, his eyes were shining. Skies above, he was gorgeous, even with the frown that crumpled his face.

"You should have waited for us. We could have helped you."

I smiled, even as the world started to fade at the edges of my vision. "And share the glory of victory? Never."

His mouth tightened. Tristan always could see through my bravado, but I wanted to go out on a high note. I wanted him to remember me like this, sassy and unbroken. It was definitely getting colder, and I struggled to focus. I'd kept my secret from him long enough.

"Don't be angry. But this is what was meant to happen," I said, doing my best to memorize the hazel green of his eyes. They were the only things I could see clearly. "Mercury told me on day one I had to be willing to die to stop Zaletor. It was the only way."

"That Ethereal son of a bitch!" Tristan growled. "How could they ask that of a teenager?!"

I had no answer. My breath was coming fast and shallow, and I knew it was time. But I felt ready. He would be okay. They all would.

"Please," I mumbled, not even sure if he could hear me. "Tell the others . . . they are . . . the best family . . . I could have . . . asked for."

Darkness had swallowed everything except Tristan's eyes, and even they were starting to blur.

"I love you."

Not exactly original, as far as last words go, but oh well.

1

———————

20 Years Later

I had never liked to dwell on the past; there were too many ghosts. But since the entire kingdom held a yearly celebration to honor the exploits of my childhood, thinking about the past felt like all I ever did. Especially at this point in the year, when planning was in full swing.

The event was known as the Commemoration Festival, and it was celebrated in every city across Bearnel. There was feasting, dancing, and a grand parade through the capitol. People looked forward to it all year.

Well, *most* people. For me, the festival was something to be endured. I would spend the day shuffled from event to event with a smile plastered on my face. I'd be on my feet for hours greeting diplomats or entertaining priestesses before leading the parade from my carriage. If I were lucky, I'd be able to get a few hours' sleep before overseeing the guests' departures the following morning. It was exhausting, and I hated how everything was designed to put me on display. I wished I could do away with the whole spectacle. But one thing I'd learned in the last twenty years was that my happiness often had to be sacrificed for the joys of others.

After all, a queen's first duty was to her people.

Since the citizens of Bearnel loved the festival, it was my responsibility to ensure that everything ran without a hitch. If anything was less than perfect, I was the one people complained to. It was in everyone's best interest that I oversaw the details personally. Hence why I was taking slow breaths through my nose to smother my growing annoyance at the two people in front of me.

One of them, an elderly woman in a crisp black tunic, regarded me patiently. "With all due respect, Your Majesty, we have two whole months. That's plenty of time to finalize decorations for the dining hall."

Vena was the castle's Steward and responsible for the day-to-day operations of the staff. Her grandmotherly appearance contrasted with her practical, straightforward nature. Normally, I found her candor refreshing. Today, however, I felt like I was speaking to a wall.

"I understand that it may feel that way," I replied, keeping my tone light. "But we need to have contingencies in place for if something falls through, and that takes time. Most guests consider the closing banquet the highlight of their visit. I will not risk another wilted centerpiece incident."

Vena grimaced, deepening the wrinkles around her eyes. "That was seven years ago."

I couldn't help but tap my foot under the table. "And yet I still hear comments about it."

Her lips pursed. Before she could argue, I shifted my ire to the man across from her, who had been watching the exchange with ill-concealed glee.

"Mayfield, why was there a drafted proclamation on my desk about tax increases?"

As the Royal Secretary, Mayfield ensured my decrees were carried out by the mayors of the major cities. The opposite of Vena in every way, he was a reedy man, with a long face and meticulously combed hair. He was the type of person who preferred to use twenty words when six would do. I considered him to be a horrid sycophant, but a necessary evil.

"Your Majesty, as it is the twentieth anniversary, the events for this year's festival must be larger and grander than any prior. Which requires more funds."

My face remained impassive. "According to yesterday's treasury report we are more than capable of hosting an event for the citizens without additional resources."

"Perhaps here in Glassleaf the money is readily available, but the major cities will all be hosting celebrations of their own. We must increase taxes temporarily to facilitate this. Half of the money will be sent back here for our central celebration, while the other half will be used by the mayors for their celebrations." He gave what I assumed was intended to be a remorseful shrug. "We cannot deny anyone the right to celebrate The Great Victory."

I could practically hear Vena's teeth grinding, but I ignored her. "And we won't. But I will not risk bankrupting my citizens for mere extravagance. If something is out of budget, it must be deemed unnecessary." My tone left no room for argument as I leveled my gaze at the man. "There will be no tax increases."

Mayfield's expression turned stony as a flush appeared on his cheeks, but he dipped his chin in acknowledgement. With the matter settled, discussion turned to arrangements for the parade.

When the two of them got into a battle over when each of the visiting dignitaries would arrive, I took a moment to breathe. As inconspicuously as possible, I pulled a slip of paper with my daily schedule out of my pocket. Today's dress was a deep burgundy velvet with silver embroidery along the high neckline and wrists. It was moderately comfortable, as far as dresses went, which made it one of my favorites. My eyes darted over the tiny script, and I held in a sigh when I saw that I would be having lunch with the representatives from the Citadel. As the religious order devoted to serving The Goddesses, the priestesses always treated me not as a queen, but a divine miracle blessed by The Goddesses themselves. Their worship was, to put it mildly, exhausting.

After that, I was expected at the docks for the dedication of a new ship, and then I had back-to-back meetings with the leaders of the military and the merchant's guild. Finally, a formal dinner was scheduled with some visiting emissaries. The paper said where they were from, but it didn't really matter. The exact people may be different from day to day, but my schedule was always the same. And, as always, there were no breaks.

Vena cleared her throat, and I looked up to find both of them looking at me.

Crap.

"If you could repeat that?" A queen did not apologize, even when she was definitely not paying attention.

"Certainly, Your Majesty," Vena replied. "There will be more delegates visiting this year than usual, to mark the anniversary. It seems many of them have already been promised lodging." The glare she shot at Mayfield said everything I needed to know about her opinions on that. "As such, we were thinking some of the guests could be housed in the main castle, to ease their stay."

Mayfield shifted in his seat at the word "we".

"It's a fine idea," I said, "but there aren't any guest rooms in the main castle. Are you suggesting we put cots in the library?"

"No, Your Majesty." Vena's smile was patient. "But perhaps some of the, uh, vacant bedrooms would be put to use."

Oh.

Something in my face must have changed, because Vena pushed on. "I know everyone would prefer their presence at the festival, what with it being an anniversary and all. But it's been years since the rest of the family has come for the Commemoration Festival, and if we could put those rooms to better use—"

I held up a hand, and silence filled the room. They both were staring at me, which wasn't unusual, but this time their eyes were filled with pity. I kept my voice neutral.

"I understand your request. I will add it to my list of things to consider and will give you my answer next week." I pushed back my chair, and they stood as I did. "Now, I must leave you to prepare for my luncheon with the representatives from the Citadel. Please inform the Council of my updates to tomorrow's meeting agenda. I won't have us going off track again."

They both bowed and murmured their understanding. I strode from the room as the old grief coiled in my gut. To hell with the schedule. I was taking a break.

The Commemoration Festival had always been tedious. There were hundreds of details to organize and contingencies to plan for. But this year I'd found it more difficult than ever. The emphasis my advisors were placing on the anniversary was meant to show how far the nation had come. Instead, all I saw was everything I'd lost.

The castle was a bustling hive of people, but I walked calmly through the halls, nodding politely to anyone I encountered. I'd told the castle staff long ago they didn't need to bow to me every time we passed in the hallway, but they did it anyway. I took a left at a fork in the hallway, knowing it would lead me to a less used part of the castle. The door behind me clicked closed and like magic, the activity around me ceased, the only sound the dragging of my heavy skirt on the plush rugs that covered the polished wood floor.

While Vena was the expert on activity within the castle, I knew the building's layout better than anyone.

When Zaletor had taken power two hundred years ago, he'd slaughtered the ruling family. The castle had sat empty during his reign, as he'd preferred to rule from the safety of his tower in the Eastern Plains. When I was named queen, it had taken months of repairs and cleaning to make the structure habitable again. I'd spent that time exploring, familiarizing myself with the castle's secrets and even adding a few of my own.

Those were good times.

Hall after hall vanished beneath my feet as I tried to clear my head. Vena was right, of course. The rooms in the main castle were sitting empty, and they were easier to access than those in the guest wing. The maids cleaned them every few days to keep the dust from taking over, and the bedding was changed monthly. Just in case any of them showed up.

Which, of course, they wouldn't. Did I really expect one of them to simply drop in out of the blue, ready to stay? Then why did it feel wrong to even consider opening up their rooms?

I walked aimlessly, absorbed in my thoughts until I realized with a start where my traitorous feet had carried me. I lingered outside the study, a place I normally avoided at all costs. The room held a few books, and assorted weapons hung artfully on the walls. A wooden dummy was tucked into one corner, displaying my old armor. It was still polished to a shine and now seemed hilariously small. But the room's main feature was an enormous painting that stretched across the back wall. I stepped forward, drawn to the painting like a moth to a flame.

There we were. All five of us.

My family.

Only Becca and Tristan had been related by blood, but we'd been a family, nonetheless.

I swallowed past the lump in my throat as the memories clawed their way up.

Everyone had been captured so perfectly: Jax with his dark curls and a big, dramatic smile on his face. The golden hilt of a sword was visible at his hip, and his chest was puffed out with pride. Becca was giving her cheekiest grin, her auburn hair a stark contrast to her black clothing. She looked ready to vanish into the shadows at any moment by merely pulling up her hood. Alto stood behind Becca, close enough to touch. His golden hair was a messy halo above a soft smile and intelligent brown eyes. And to the left, next to me as always...

I looked away from Tristan's face. That was too much.

I looked instead to my own face, soft with youth and hope. My hair was short, barely to my collarbone, and such a dark brown it looked black against my pale skin. I don't know how the artist had managed to get my eyes the perfect shade of purple, but they glimmered bright with joy. I never learned if their amethyst hue was intentional, a mark from The Goddess' indicating my status as their Chosen One, or simply a chance anomaly. Either way, they were my most recognizable feature. My left hand clasped tight to Tristan's, while my right arm was thrown over Becca's shoulders.

The only one who didn't look right was Mercury. They had been summoned back to the Ethereal Plane almost immediately after I'd vanquished Zaletor, so we'd had to describe their form to the artist. The results were...mixed. The height, wings, and coloring were correct, but Jax kept insisting Mercury had always had a giant human nose. Eventually, the artist had given up and merely painted the Ethereal's face as a smudge.

Thinking back on that day now, I wanted to smile at the fun we'd had. But I couldn't.

A table sat beneath the painting, empty, save for a single, ever-burning candle. A candle that had been there for the past thirteen years.

Right beneath Becca.

In my heart, I knew Jax and Alto would never attend another Commemoration Festival. As for Tristan, well, it was best not to think about him.

Shaking myself out of the fog of the past, I fled the study. With conscious steps this time, I made my way to my room at the other end of the castle. My suite was one floor above the four empty rooms. Next week, I'd tell Vena that three of the rooms could be given to guests who needed them. But not Becca's.

When I entered my room, I locked the door behind me. It was a formality, as at least six people had the key to get in, but it felt like the right thing to do. I crossed the elaborate space to a washbasin, wanting to splash my face in an effort to pull myself together, when a barely audible rustle sounded behind me. I stopped as the hair on my neck rose.

My heartbeat faster, but I kept my expression calm and crossed to my dressing table.

"You might as well come out," I said, reaching up and removing my earrings. They were delicate silver leaves, matching my dress' embroidery perfectly.

Nothing happened.

My heart raced. It had been years since there had been any type of assassination or kidnapping attempt. Unbidden hoarfrost spread down my fingers, my magic ready to surge forth at a moment's notice.

My eyes widened a fraction as I held up my hand. I forgot

that happened whenever I got scared. It had been so long since I had anything to fear.

Returning my focus back to the room, I took in a breath to shout for the guards.

"It *is* you!" came a familiar voice.

Startled, I spun to face it, and a blast of ice shot across the bedroom.

Mercury deflected the ice with ease, sending the shards crashing into my writing desk. Their tail twitched in amusement.

"You've really gotten sloppy."

2

———

My brain couldn't process the reality of what I was seeing.

Mercury's form had always been a strange sight. But in the twenty years since I'd last seen them, I'd forgotten just how striking they were. Standing nearly three feet tall, the Ethereal resembled a winged cat, with fur like liquid silver that constantly fluctuated in a mercurial fashion that inspired their name. Most of the time they were solid, but they could shift into a gaseous form at will, becoming a living mist. The shadowy, bat-like wings sprouting from their back appeared to be made of smoke.

All of this was impressive, but it was their eyes that took my breath away. Looking into Mercury's eyes was like looking into the universe. They had no iris or pupil. Instead, each eye was a solid blue-black and filled with flecks of light burning like stars. I still had dreams about those eyes, though my memories did not do them justice.

While I may have forgotten a few small details, I knew

Mercury looked exactly the same as they had twenty years ago, as though not a single day had passed for them.

"You're here." The words fell stupidly out of my mouth. I wrapped my arms around my chest, squeezing my elbows and fighting the overwhelming desire to rush over and hug them. To prove to myself they were real. But the Ethereal had never been a fan of physical contact, and they'd never understood the human need for hugs. "You came back."

They studied me, with only shifting star-flecks to indicate where they were looking.

"What's wrong?" I asked, sensing some hesitation.

They cocked their head. "You look so different."

The Ethereal was an angelic entity, serving as a messenger for The Goddesses. I knew they were immortal, but I had never considered that they might not comprehend things like aging.

"I'm older than when you were here last. By twenty years."

Mercury gazed at me critically. "Yeah, I know. But you're larger than when I last saw you."

My jaw clamped shut and I felt my cheeks burn.

"And what happened to your hair?" they went on, gesturing with a paw at my elaborately braided chignon. "It used to be all dark, right? Why are there some gray parts now?"

Somehow, in the years since I'd seen Mercury, I'd forgotten how much I could hate them.

"That is not an appropriate—" I forced myself to take a breath. "I was *sixteen* the last time you saw me. Developing a stomach and thighs is completely normal. And hair turns gray due to age and stress. It's a miracle it didn't happen the first time you were here, considering how much of a pain in my ass you were."

They stalked forward on silent feet, still assessing me in an infuriating way. "Hmm. Weird. I'll take your word for it. But why are you wearing a dress? You hate dresses. That's the main reason I didn't recognize you."

It was true I hated anything with a skirt when I was young. It just got in the way, and I'd always have to wear a belt or pouch to carry my things.

"I have to wear dresses now," I replied, running a self-conscious hand down the front of my gown. "I'm the queen. The queen has to wear dresses."

Their face scrunched in confusion. "I thought the queen did whatever she wanted. Isn't that the whole point of the job? Can't you just decree 'no dresses for the queen' and that's that?"

"I—well, it's not that simple."

Stupid Mercury.

They waved a dismissive paw. "You know what? It's not important. You're the queen, you're larger, and you wear dresses. Good catching up. Now, let's go! We've got work to do!"

My head was reeling. Was this actually happening? Had the stress finally broken me? Was I dead, and this was the underworld?

I plopped down onto the bed before I could collapse to the floor.

"No! Don't sit! I said we've got to go! Where's the rest of the group? Some of them were useful. And where can we get you a horse? I remember you can't move very fast without a horse." They were practically bouncing with excitement.

"This can't be happening." I pressed my hands against my eyes to block out the nightmare in front of me. "This must be some sort of dream."

I felt the bed shift as Mercury jumped up beside me. A large, heavy paw rapped against the top of my head.

"Are you having trouble hearing me? Isn't that another human thing about aging?"

I waved them off. "I can hear you just fine. I'm trying to decide if you're real or merely a figment of my imagination."

With a flop, they lay down beside me, their furry face turning impish. I'd forgotten how damn expressive they could be.

"I understand. I'm sure you've missed me terribly. But I can assure you, I'm very real. And we very much need to go."

"I don't know what's going on, but I can't go!"

Mercury's ears flattened, their eyes flicking to the door.

"I see. I can break that down, no problem. How many guards are outside? I'll kill as many as I can while you—"

"I don't mean it like that! I'm not a prisoner here," I insisted, though the claim felt somehow false. "I'm saying I can't go on a random adventure with you just because you showed up out of nowhere. I have things to do here: duties and responsibilities."

Their silvery essence churned.

"You have a *duty* to The Goddesses! Your *responsibility* is to keep evil in check. Those are the things you're meant to be doing."

And just like that, I felt sixteen again. The fate of the world was on my shoulders and my life was barely my own. But my feelings of self-doubt were quickly replaced with fury.

"First of all, as far as I'm concerned, The Goddesses can shove it," I stated, ignoring the look of outrage on their face. "Second, what evil? Zaletor is dead! The kingdom is at peace! Everything's been running smoothly for decades!"

Mercury stood up on the bed, making themselves taller than I was sitting down, and glared at me.

"Oh, really, Miss 'I'm the queen and I know everything?' Then *why* have there been surges of dark energy in the Eastern Plains?"

My anger was snuffed out like a candle. "What?"

"Oh yeah! For months now! At first, they were small. Barely even blips in the Ethereal Plane. We didn't think much of it, assuming someone had discovered some trinket or relic from Zaletor's reign and was messing around with it. But *this* time is different! Whatever it is, it's been getting stronger and pulling more energy from my world over to yours. It's gotten bad enough that The Goddesses want you to put a stop to it."

At that moment, someone could have punched me in the stomach and it would have been more comfortable.

"How can that be? You told me before that Zaletor was only able to become as powerful as he was because he made a deal with The Dark Lady. She's been imprisoned by her sister Goddesses for her treason, and Zaletor is dead. If no one else is able to make that type of deal, *how* is someone that powerful?"

"These are all excellent questions," Mercury said, leaping down from the bed and crossing to my open closet. "Good thing we will have plenty of time to talk it through with the group while we travel. Is it cold out right now? Let's get your coat."

Frost coated my fingers again, spreading to the bedspread beneath me in sparkling tendrils. My heart was racing so fast I worried I was going to be sick.

"No."

There was a crash as something tipped over in my closet.

"Oops. That looked expensive. Did you say something?"

"I said NO!"

A silver feline head poked out from the doorway. "What do you mean 'no?'"

"I mean, I'm not going. If some new evil is growing in the world, find someone else to deal with it. I did my part twenty years ago. I let you and The Goddesses upend my life once already, I'm not going to do it again. So find someone else."

With a burning glare, Mercury stalked out from the closet.

"That's not how this works. They call. You answer. End of story."

The sheer command in their statement, like I was still a child to be scolded, had me seeing red.

"Listen, you little goblin, I answered their call. I did their bidding. And I *died*. Whatever is happening now is terrible, and I agree someone needs to put a stop to it. But it won't be me. The Goddesses chose a champion before, they can do it again. I'll even tell them everything I remember about—"

Mercury laughed, the sound a hissing cackle.

"You're not getting it, Phoebe. You're '*the chosen one.*' Not 'the girl who was chosen that one time to do one thing and then was done.' You are the only person on *earth* who has been blessed with all four magical abilities. That's not something that can be done a second time. If someone needs to face the new evil in the world, *you're it*. AND," they pushed on, sensing my intent to interrupt, "if it turns out Zaletor is somehow behind this, you and your friends know better than anyone how to beat him!"

"It. Can't. Be. Zaletor. I killed him. He's gone."

"All of him?"

"Yes! He vanished in a plume of ash, leaving only a robe and an ugly crown behind. We burned the robe, destroyed his tower, and gave the smoldering ash pile the finger. And the instant he died, all the souls he was using to power his stone creatures were released, so there wasn't even anything to hunt down!"

"And you destroyed the crown?"

My mouth snapped shut.

Shit.

"We...um."

Mercury's eyes bugged out. "Um??"

Double shit.

As queen, it had been ages since I'd had to explain myself to anyone. I didn't like it. Especially since the little imp had a point.

"Listen, we *tried* to destroy the crown. But the damn thing couldn't be melted or crushed or shattered. We did the best we could."

"And *what,* exactly, was the best you could do?"

"We managed to pry out the stone and hid the two pieces separately so no one could ever find them. The crown is here with me. I kept it close so I could make sure it never fell into the wrong hands."

As I spoke, their claws dug deep into my comforter. A rattling growl sounded low in their throat as they exhaled a breath, but their voice was chillingly calm. "Okay. It's probably fine. We'll check on the crown, *then* we'll leave for the Eastern Plains. Where did you hide it?"

I held my tongue about the whole "leaving" thing. At least until I'd proven the crown was still safely hidden. "It's in the catacombs beneath the castle. And I'm telling you, it's still there."

"Son of a bitch."

My curse echoed through the dank tunnel as the torch in my hand illuminated the hole in the wall. The hole that was normally covered by a loose cobblestone. The hole where I'd stashed Zaletor's crown all those years ago.

The hole that was now empty.

Mercury was pacing in a small circle beside me, their tail lashing in frustration.

"Okay Okay Okay Okay. When did you see it last? That can help us narrow down when it went missing."

"I suppose it *has* been a while." I held the torch to the hole again, in case I'd missed seeing a glittering crown in the impossibly narrow space.

They stopped pacing. "How long is 'a while?'"

Maybe I had the wrong hiding hole. I was sure I'd put it directly across from the tomb of Sir Richard the Nimble, because teenage me had thought "Nimble Dick" hilarious. But maybe I'd pulled the wrong stone. I began frantically searching the wall for any rocks that would come loose.

"Phoebe," Mercury said, their voice turning firm. "How long has it been?"

With a grunt of frustration, I pressed my forehead against the cold stone wall.

"Thirteen years."

"WHAT?!"

I flinched as their shout reverberated around me. "I forgot about it, okay? I had a lot of other things going on. Like running a kingdom."

"How. Could you possibly. Forget. About something like this?!" Each phrase was punctuated with anger. I could see they were close to losing it. "It's bad enough you didn't finish the job and destroy it!"

"Give me a break!" I spat back, beginning to lose it myself. "I was *sixteen*! Despite the responsibility you and The Goddesses gave me, I was still just a stupid kid! And I was exhausted! So, yes. I hid the crown and called it good!"

Truthfully, I *had* planned on checking on the crown more frequently. The day I placed it in the hole in the catacombs, I'd made a vow to myself that I would check on it once a month, to make sure it was safe. But once a month had turned into once every three months. Then six. Then once a year. Until eventually I stopped coming. I'd think of it from time to time, but it never seemed important enough to make a trip down here. And my days were so full, on the rare instances I had some time to myself I didn't want to spend it in the dark, depressing catacombs.

And, if I was being honest, I didn't want to look at the crown. I had enough reminders of my "great victory" throughout the castle. I didn't need one more.

Still, this was very, *very* bad. Even though Zaletor was dead, someone had his crown. It was a relic, a symbol of his reign, and I knew better than anyone that symbols had power.

"So," I began, putting the stone back in the wall. "What are you going to do now?"

It was like watching a tiny silver explosion.

"What am 'I' going to do?!" Mercury shouted. Their wings flared as their large paws stomped at the ground. "No, Phoebe! We! What are 'we' going to do?!"

"I already told you I'm not going to—"

"*You* are the one who didn't destroy the crown! *You* are the one who lost it! *You* are the one who has been telling everybody Zaletor is dead but can't explain the dark energy occurrences! Face it, *Your Majesty*, you need to stop what's going on, if not for the safety of the world, then for the safety of your own skin! Because what is everyone going to say if you are wrong?"

My heart might have stopped.

I was positive Zaletor was dead. I'd swear it on my life. But the crown had been my responsibility, and I'd failed at that pretty drastically. And while *I* knew it couldn't be Zaletor, other people would grow suspicious if the same terrible things started happening again. It's not like I'd ever been able to produce a body to prove my claim. If rumors spread that he was back, people would panic. Besides, no matter who it was, someone was pulling a dangerous amount of dark energy into the world. If left unchecked, that could rip a hole in the universe.

Damnit. Mercury was right.

I needed to find out what was going on. In person and attracting as little attention as possible.

"Ok," I grumbled. "But we're leaving the castle my way."

3

I knew the Council and castle guard would never allow me to leave by myself. Even with the kingdom at peace, it was unheard of for the queen to go anywhere outside the castle without a full escort.

Luckily, I'd been daydreaming about ways to escape for years. I'd never planned to follow through on any of them, of course. It was merely a way I'd developed to pass the time during particularly boring events or meetings. Sometimes it was an epic escape through windows or secret tunnels only I knew about. Other times, it was as simple as walking out the front door in a cloak, never to return. Now, I was able to pick the very best scenario for this particular situation.

Mercury would have preferred the option of leaving immediately without saying a word and fighting anyone who tried to get in our way. But they'd agreed to my plan, mostly because I'd vowed to chain myself to my desk if they didn't.

I'd instructed a page to gather the members of my Council, Mayfield, Vena, and the representatives from the Citadel, mostly because they had undoubtedly already arrived. I arranged to have all of them meet me in the throne room at once. To pull this off, I was going to need to sit in the big chair.

The throne had been presented on my seventeenth birthday, when I was crowned queen, and was an artistic masterpiece. Made from a brick of solid white marble, it had been carved with life-like depictions of flames and icicles, and a winged cat supported each armrest. When sunlight streamed into the upper windows of the throne room, it glowed like a beacon of hope.

It was also the most uncomfortable thing I'd ever placed my backside on. The armrests were too wide for me to reach, and even at five-foot nine, my feet dangled above the ground. I was told putting any type of cushion or pillow on the marble seat would "ruin the visual effect", which meant I had to shift every few minutes to keep my legs from falling asleep. It had been unpleasant when I was young and spry. Now, sitting in it was pure torture. I always walked away with an ache in my lower back that took days to ease.

But everyone else loved it and saw it as a symbol of my reign. So, several times a week, I climbed up the footstool required to reach the damned thing and placed my queenly ass on that instrument of pain. And everyone else was happy.

Now, with Mercury hiding behind the dais in mist form, I sat imperiously in my throne while the group assembled. As the two dozen or so people filed in, I watched them cast curious glances at each other, trying to determine what was going on. Several advisors shifted nervously, which wasn't surprising. The last time I'd called an impromptu meeting like this was to inform them my wedding was canceled. That had been a decade ago.

Once everyone was present, I cleared my throat.

"I've called you all here to inform you of a recent development."

Everyone looked at me with rapt attention. I kept my head high.

"I have just received a vision from The Goddesses."

Shuffling and murmuring. One of the Citadel priestesses let out a small gasp.

"In light of the twentieth anniversary of The Great Victory, they have commanded that I make a pilgrimage to the Eastern Plains to make an offering in their name. I will be leaving at once."

Four people started talking, but I held up a hand. When they fell silent, I nodded permission to the tall barrel of a man who served as the head of the Royal Guard, Captain Inniual.

"This is obviously joyous news, Your Majesty, and the will of The Goddesses must be obeyed. However, we need more time to prepare. If we wait a week, perhaps two, I will be able to assemble a proper escort and vet the inns we can stay at along the way."

"None of that will be necessary," I said, "as the Royal Guard will not be joining me. Nor will there be any official escort or security from the palace."

Inniual's mouth dropped open. I prepared for the argument that would ensue, but the High Priestess jumped in first.

"I must say, Your Majesty, this is truly a glorious day and a most wonderful honor." The ancient woman's face was flushed with joy as she clasped her hands before her. "We have always known The Goddesses smile down upon you and bless your leadership. But it is important for us all to remember the sacrifice you've made for the safety of this kingdom. Upon returning to the Citadel, I will draft a proclamation at once to inform everyone far and wide of your—"

I interrupted, unable to listen to her drivel on for ages. "You will do no such thing. The Goddesses were quite clear that this is *not* a journey for Queen Phoebe, Light of Bearnel, but a task for Phoebe Blessed-Heart, vessel of power. I must be reminded of my own humility and the grace bestowed upon me. The people of Bearnel will not be informed of my journey until *after* I have returned. I have no doubt that if they are aware I am traveling among them, they will feel the need to aid me, thus negating the whole purpose."

The High Priestess looked crestfallen. I was sure she'd been drafting the proclamation in her head before she'd even spoken. But she merely nodded, unwilling to challenge the will of "The Goddesses."

"Your Majesty, please," Inniual pleaded, "I understand this is a holy undertaking with some restrictions imposed, but I cannot in good faith allow you to travel the kingdom alone!"

Finally, I thought. Now things would go a lot more quickly.

As if on cue, Mercury's Voice echoed through the throne room.

> *"She won't be alone! I will be with her, as is my sacred duty."*

They materialized on the throne beside me, standing atop the massive armrest with wings spread wide and face stern. There was a collective gasp from the assembly below and everyone immediately dropped to their knees. The priestesses all gaped at Mercury, eyes shining with tears, while everyone else looked at the floor, likely considering themselves unworthy to gaze upon the Ethereal.

Mercury ate it up. Every bit of it. Knowing no one was currently looking at me, I rolled my eyes at the display.

Showboating little prick.

"Yes," I stated, trying to get things back on track. "As you can see, my faithful friend Mercury has returned to mark this occasion with me and to ensure my well-being. I will be as safe as can be and will return before the Commemoration Festival."

Everyone nodded. What else could they do? No one would dare question whether the Ethereal could keep me safe.

"Secrecy is of the utmost importance. Until I return, the citizens of the city, including the castle staff, will be told that I am sequestered in prayer. If that fails, tell people I'm sick. Nothing deadly, but something inconvenient enough to keep me in my rooms. Just...think of something. In the meantime, you are to continue preparations for the festival."

Mayfield cleared his throat, stepping forward. His face was tight as he bowed.

"This is marvelous, Your Majesty, but I would be remiss in my duties if I didn't beg you to stay. There is so much to be done before the festival and your people need you here."

Heat burned in my chest, like the stirring of embers. "Your opinion has been noted. But I'm leaving."

"Of course," Mayfield bowed again. "In that case, would it not be best to establish a temporary ruler while you are away?"

I could see half the Council roll their eyes, while the other half looked terrified at the prospect of Mayfield being placed in charge.

"That won't be necessary," I said, ignoring his crestfallen look. "The Council will continue to operate as a unit to make decisions. And, Vena, you may prepare three of the unused rooms in the family quarters for our guests who need them. But Becca's will remain sealed."

"Of course, Your Majesty. An excellent compromise. It will be done." She bowed, but the twitch of her lips suggested she'd already guessed as much.

I tried to keep the nervous excitement from my face. I probably failed. But everyone bowed in acknowledgement as I rose from the throne and made my way out of the room, Mercury hot on my heels.

I was leaving the castle.

I was going on an adventure.

My stomach flip-flopped and I nearly fainted with worry.

This was a terrible, dangerous idea.

What if the citizens of the kingdom discovered I was gone? Maybe making an official announcement was safer. And what if whatever was out there turned out to be more than I could handle? It certainly wasn't Zaletor, but *something* was drawing dark energy. I could still take Captain Inniual's suggestion. We could gather a few guards, just enough to ensure my safety, and travel in comfort. This excursion was likely a wild goose chase, after all. What harm would it do to take a few precautions?

Becca's face rose unbidden to my mind, her hair tangled and eyes vacant.

That was all it took for my resolve to harden. Traveling alone and in secret was the best course of action. It was my only hope of stopping whatever evil had sprung up without drawing attention, even though it made me hyperventilate.

As I walked, Mercury caught up with me. "I think that went well."

"As well as it could have." I squeezed my hands into fists to keep them from shaking.

"All that's left is to round up the rest of the group, find some horses, and we're on our way!"

Ice wrapped around my fingers and my heart, but I didn't break my stride.

"There's no need. Let's gather some supplies and go."

"Really? None of them were at that meeting, so I assumed

they were out doing things and we'd collect them on our way out."

I shook my head while keeping my focus on the hallway ahead. "It's just you and me this time."

Mercury was silent for a moment, and I braced myself for what I knew was coming.

"Why is Becca's room sealed? And why is everyone else's room unused?"

"We can talk about this later. There's still a lot to do before we leave." I'd hoped this conversation would wait until we were out of the castle.

In a flash of mist, Mercury appeared directly in front of me, blocking my path and forcing me to halt before I collided with them.

"What aren't you telling me? What's going on?" Their face, normally so mischievous and jovial, was pinched with worry.

I glanced around to make sure we were alone. None of this was a secret, but it still felt like a private conversation. Realizing where we were, I gestured to a nearby door.

We entered the study. The lights were low, giving the space a solemn, mournful feeling. Or maybe that was just me. I closed the door behind us, sealing us in.

Mercury looked around, smiling at some of the junk on the shelves they undoubtedly recognized, then their starry eyes turned to the portrait.

"Ugh! Why do I look like that?"

I hung back by the door, hugging my arms across my chest. "You weren't here, so we had to describe you to the artist as best we could. Jax kept giving suggestions."

They shook their head. "Remind me to pose for a new portrait when all this is over, because this will not stand."

I couldn't bring myself to smile. I could only wait while

their eyes fell on the candle beneath Becca. Their ears sagged as understanding hit, and their wings drooped to graze the floor.

Though I felt separate from my body, a pang of guilt still cut through my chest. "It was thirteen years ago. She was in charge of the entire navy at that point. We'd had reports of pirates along the southern coast, so she took a fleet to put a stop to their raiding. She didn't come back."

"The pirates?"

"A storm. She'd finished up with the pirates and was on her way back. Every ship went down. Hundreds of lives were lost." Even now, more than a decade later, my throat closed up as the words came out. When was the last time I'd spoken of it?

I couldn't bring myself to share that we'd searched for her for days. I'd prayed to The Goddesses that she'd be alive despite all the other bloated bodies we passed, but if we'd found her body, I'd at least be able to say goodbye. But we'd never found her, alive or dead.

"I'm so sorry, Phoebe."

Unable to resist, I walked forward to stand beside Mercury beneath the painting, gazing up at Becca's beautiful face.

"Things weren't the same between us after that. Jax and Alto couldn't stand to be here when she wasn't. And Tristan, well, we handled Becca's death very differently. There had already been fractures between us, but losing Becca caused a rift that couldn't be repaired. In the end, they all left."

Tearing my attention away from the painting, I found Mercury studying me. It was impossible to tell what they were thinking, but I had a feeling I wasn't going to like it. I turned back to the door.

"I'm going to pack a few things. There's a secret exit from my closet that leads down to the west gardens. We'll use that to get out of the castle unnoticed, then purchase a horse and more supplies along the way."

I could feel their eyes still on me as I opened the door.

"You're not the girl you were," they said. I couldn't tell if they were speaking to me or merely making an observation.

"No. That girl is long gone."

4

———

I'd forgotten how much traveling could take a toll on the body. I'd barely reached the Arts District, not two miles from the castle, and I could already feel the ache in my knees. When this was over and I returned to the castle, the first thing I was going to do was command all the hills in the city to be leveled.

I had no doubt Mercury saw my struggles from their vantage point among the rooftops as they traveled along as a mist. And they were almost certainly judging me for how slowly I was going. The sooner I got a horse, the better. But I wanted to get to the furthest edges of the city before I risked interacting with anyone.

It was a sunny afternoon, and the Arts District was relatively quiet. Clusters of people gathered to watch performers or artists set up along the street, but it was nothing compared to the hoards that would flood the area in the evening, eager to catch the latest play or visit the ever-changing galleries. At least I didn't have to worry about being jostled about, I thought, lifting my already filthy skirt to step around a suspicious looking puddle.

It had been years since I'd had cause to wear trousers, so I'd had no reason to keep track of them. Apparently, every pair I had owned had vanished. I suspected the tailor. Not that any of my old pants would have fit me, but still. I couldn't go unnoticed traveling the kingdom in my gowns, so I'd stolen a simple linen smock from a maid's closet.

I wished I'd taken some shoes as well, because my feet were already aching in my stiff leather boots. They were well made and probably would be perfect for such a journey, but they were brand new and not broken in. Vena had them made for the Harvest Festival the previous fall, but the entire event had been canceled due to bad weather. I didn't leave the castle much, and I'd had no reason to wear them since.

At least my cloak was appropriate. It was a dark brown with fleece lining and no added decoration or embellishment. It was a bit heavy for spring, but would be comfortable to sleep on at night, and I'd be glad for the extra warmth if the weather turned. And it was voluminous enough to swallow me completely, hiding my face from view.

The only other things I carried were a pair of daggers, one on each hip, a day's worth of food, and a pouch of coins and jewels. It was far more than I would need, but I wanted to be prepared. Besides, despite my desire to hurry and travel unnoticed, I liked the idea of staying at nice inns more than sleeping on the ground. Anything else I needed I would have to acquire as I went or make do without. It would be a good experience for me, having to work for things again.

As I neared the end of the block, I saw an arc of flame extend toward the sky. The representatives from the Citadel had started performing early in an attempt to draw people into their next show. My stomach did a flip, but I kept walking. The city had changed a great deal since my youth, and I didn't want to risk getting lost by taking a side street. I kept my gaze forward, but from the corner of my eye I could see a woman in a bright red costume standing outside the Citadel Theater, spinning a ball of fire on her fingers while she shouted to the street.

"Come one! Come all! Get your tickets now for the greatest display of singular Gift performers Bearnel has to offer! Witness and be amazed at the various miracles bestowed by The Goddesses!"

The woman threw the ball of flame high into the air, and with a wave of her hand, exploded it like a firework. The few people who had stopped to watch gasped and clapped. I resisted the urge to pull my hood down over my face and hurried past.

The term "singular" had been added to the title of all of the Citadel's Gift performances out of deference to me, which I thought was nonsense. Since I was literally the only person to wield more than one Gift, much less all four, I was very much the minority. But the High Priestess who'd come up with the idea would not be swayed, insisting it was a way to honor the Goddess' blessing. The Citadel sponsored the theater under the guise of showcasing the talents of Gifted who were skilled enough to perform. That was clearly bullshit, because if it was really about showcasing all the Gifts, they'd have a Specter.

The ability to control an element to some degree, what the Citadel affectionately called Gifts, was relatively common. Ignis and Terra, fire and earth wielders, were seen the most frequently, though the majority could do no more than light a candle or make a hole in the ground to plant a seed. Nothing compared to the woman now casually throwing fireballs in the square. Someone who could control water, known as an Aqua, was found less often, and occasionally presented as a Glacies, who wielded ice. Still, everyone knew at least one person who possessed one of The Big Three, as I liked to call them.

But the rarest of all Gifts, and by far the most feared, was the control of soul essence. The official name for this Gift was Anima, but everyone always referred to soul wielders as Specters. Able to see and communicate with the spirits of the recently deceased, Specters should have been considered the most valuable of all Gifted. But thanks to Zaletor, or more specifically, Zaletor's right-hand man Broin, Specters were feared and distrusted by everyone, including some members of the Citadel. Broin had been extremely powerful, and he had done unspeakable things in his master's name. While it was still considered a Gift from The Goddesses, the Citadel preached that soul magic was intended as a reminder of humility and never meant to be used. Most Specters kept their Gift hidden, and it was nearly impossible to find someone willing to teach how to wield it. Needless to say, the Citadel Theater did not employ any Specter performers.

I tried to smother the indignation that bubbled up as I continued down the street. Everyone wanted to forget that it was my Specter Gift that had put an end to Zaletor all those years ago. A Gift I wouldn't have even known how to use if it hadn't been for Becca. She was the only Specter I'd ever met who didn't fear her Gift, which is probably why she was the most powerful one the world had ever known.

A flash of mist from the roof beside me brought my mind back to the present. If anyone had been paying attention, they'd have noticed the small cloud was moving against the wind, revealing it for what it truly was: Mercury.

Air belonged to the Ethereals, and that element was theirs alone to control. I knew from experience my companion could create a gust of wind strong enough to launch a grown man across a room. Mercury was the only Ethereal I'd ever met, but common lore said they came in every conceivable shape and size. The only thing they all had in common was wings.

I wondered if they were all assholes, too.

The streets became busier as I entered the Merchant District and I had to focus on not bumping into anyone. I stuck to the sides of the road, both to avoid being crushed by carriages and to keep to the afternoon shadows. My hood made surveying the street more difficult, but it was a risk I'd have to take. My face was well known to the citizens, many of whom gathered to wave at me any time I went outside the castle walls, and if anyone got close enough to see my eyes all hope of secrecy would vanish. However, if I got far enough away from the castle, where I would never normally be, I could be over-looked as someone who merely looked similar to the queen. Since I lacked an escort, it was possible.

But even from the depths of my hood, I noticed the person trailing me.

Despite my life of luxury these past decades, old instincts never die, and the sound of someone moving in time with my steps cut through the din of the crowd. I didn't want to glance back, in case drawing attention to it caused a further scene, but my mind raced. Was it someone from the Castle Guard, disobeying my order to stay behind? Or someone else who had seen me leave and was concerned for my safety? These options were both possible, but doubtful. The mystery figure also kept to the shadows, though not as successfully as I did, and the occasional slap of bare feet on stones told me a great deal about their livelihood. No, this wasn't an official tail. This was someone looking for trouble.

Conscious of the possibility that this was an intentional decoy to distract me from the real threat, I kept my pace even, not bothering to reach for either of the daggers at my belt. With my magic and Mercury, I didn't feel my life was in any danger.

Still, I'd clearly been marked as a target, and I had no idea how long this mystery figure would be willing to tail me.

I slowed my steps. It would be better to force the confrontation now than be followed through the entire city. Moving toward a nearby vendor stall, I paused, pretending to consider the table of fine pottery pieces. I kept my distance from the table, not wanting to seem too interested, and there were a handful of other customers in front of me, so the shopkeeper paid me no mind. But my pursuer saw an opening.

I waited, knowing exactly what move they were going to make. It would have been easy to avoid it, but I was curious to see how skilled they were. And if I was still any good, myself.

The person in front of me stepped to the side, forcing me to step back to avoid hitting them, and that's when the attack came. There was the slightest shifting of my cloak.

Faster than an adder, I spun.

A shrill yelp filled the air as my hand closed on a too-thin wrist that was a hair's breadth from my purse. The would-be thief struggled against my grip.

"Lemme go!" the girl yelled, twisting like a feral kitten.

She looked about ten, with a cloud of curly red hair. She might have had freckles, but her face was so dirty it was impossible to tell. At the sound of her yells, the people in front of me at the pottery stall turned to look.

Shit. If people noticed a pickpocket in their midst, they'd summon the city guard. It would turn into a whole thing. I needed a way out.

"Mary!" I scolded, pitching my voice higher. "I told you to wait for me at home!"

Whatever the girl had expected me to say, that wasn't it. Her angry expression twisted in confusion. The pause was enough for me to start dragging her away from the curious faces.

"Just wait till your father hears you've been avoiding chores again. You'll get a tanning, you can be sure of that!"

To my relief, the onlookers turned their attention back to the table. A pickpocket was a threat, but a naughty child was none of their business.

I didn't know if the girl realized I'd just saved her from being apprehended or if she was simply too shocked to fight back, but she hung her head in shame as she allowed me to pull her down the street.

Once we were a block away, I released my grip and continued walking. I expected her to take off the second I let go, but to my surprise she followed after me.

"Wait up!" Her feet slapped loudly against the cobblestones as she raced to keep pace.

I frowned, wanting nothing more than to shoo the child away. Instead, I turned down an alley, finding it blessedly empty aside from crates and rubbish. When I was sure we were out of earshot from the street, I faced the would-be thief. Studying her now, I could see the threadbare tunic she wore was three sizes too big, tied at her waist with a length of twine, while her trousers were too small. She was thin, but not the gaunt thin of someone who's starving. And so very, very dirty.

"You shouldn't be stealing," I said, crossing my arms beneath my cloak.

The girl scrunched her face in a scowl. "I gotta eat somehow. The wealthy folks don't even—"

"No, I mean *you* shouldn't be stealing. I heard you coming three blocks back and your lift technique is sloppy. The first lesson of being a thief is be invisible. You must not have been doing this long, or you'd have had your fingers broken by now."

Though some of the sullenness remained, the girl's eyes went as big as saucers.

"How'd you know that?"

With a grim smile, I held up my left hand.

"It heals most of the time," I said, looking at my fourth and fifth fingers. Both were at a slight angle compared to the rest. "At least, when the guards do it. For them, it's meant to be a reprimand. But if a shopkeeper gets ahold of you, you're usually not so lucky. They want you to remember."

The girl's mouth hung open, and even through the layer of grime I could see that she'd gone pale as she examined my fingers.

"Besides," I added, pulling my hand back into my cloak, "why do you need to steal? Aren't there places that will give you food and shelter?"

That had been my first act as queen: to ensure that no children would go hungry in my kingdom. I didn't want anyone to grow up as I had.

Snapping her mouth closed, the girl shuffled. "I didn't know if I could trust it. I heard stories of the old days, of kids going into a place to get food and not coming out again."

A chill that had nothing to do with my magic curled in my stomach. I suppose it had been too much to hope that old fears could be set aside. After all, the stories the girl referred to were true when I was young. It's not something people forget.

"What's your name?"

"Poppy."

"Well, Poppy, I can assure you that if you go to the kitchens around the south side of the castle, you can get a half loaf of fresh bread and four pieces of bacon every day at sunrise and a full meal at sunset. No charge. And you don't even have to go inside."

She looked me up and down, assessing.

"Your eyes look funny."

"Your face looks funny," I shot back. Maturity be damned, I was in a hurry.

Poppy's glare deepened, then transformed into a toothy smile. And damn if I didn't find myself smiling back. As much as I wanted to turn away, to end the conversation and be on my way, I couldn't go until I made sure this girl was alright. She was one of my subjects, making her my responsibility. Besides, it was like looking at myself thirty years ago.

"Where are your parents? Why do you need to steal food?"

The girl shuffled again, her eyes glued to the cobblestones.

"Ma died a few weeks back, and Da's ship doesn't return until fall."

I swallowed thickly, my heart aching for her. "I'm sorry to hear about your mother. Isn't there anyone who can take you in until your father returns?"

A shrug was her only reply.

"Alright. Go to the Citadel here in the city. Tell them your story and they'll take you in and care for you until your father comes back."

She gave me a wary look. "The priestesses? Won't they make me say prayers and stuff?"

"Not if you don't want to. The priestesses cannot force you to pray. But you will probably have to do dishes."

The girl stuck her tongue between her teeth as she thought. "Where do you live? Can I come with you?"

"I'm leaving the city as soon as I can get a horse, and I can't look after you where I'm headed." The girl started to protest, something about not needing to be looked after, but I shook my head. "This is not a debate. And if you're thinking of following me, don't."

Her expression became too innocent, proving she was considering just that.

"Don't make me take drastic measures to keep you here." I held up my hand again, this time willing a thick layer of ice to coat my fingers. It was an effort to hide my grimace at the amount of energy it took when it wasn't fueled by adrenaline.

At least the display had the desired effect. Poppy's mouth popped open and her eyes went wide again.

"You're a Glacies!"

"Shhhh!!! Keep your voice down!" I hissed, shaking the ice from my fingers. "Yes, and I'm on a very important mission. So if you try to follow me, I'll freeze you to a wall. Understood?"

The girl nodded, bouncing on the balls of her feet.

"I never met a Glacies before! Are you cold all the time? Or do you never feel cold?"

Great Goddesses above, I was glad I'd never had children.

"Enough. I need to go. Go to the Citadel and stay safe."

With a heavy sigh, she nodded. "Alright. But hey! If you need a horse, I know where you should go!"

Ten minutes later, once I finally got the girl to stop talking, I headed back out into the street. I watched Poppy head off in the direction of the Citadel, her pockets now heavy with coins. I knew it wasn't enough, not even close, but it was the best I could do. And I'd needed to do something.

After all, I'd spent most of my young life on the streets.

I could still remember winter nights pressed against the bricks of a bakery, knowing the hot stones were the only thing keeping me alive, and the beatings for not being fast enough when I picked a pocket. But there was so much more I knew I couldn't remember. My life of ultimate luxury since becoming queen wiped away all but the worst experiences from my memory.

The world had improved since then, but clearly not enough.

5

———

After the incident with Poppy, my progress through the city had gone much smoother, but there had still been several miles to cover. The crowds of the Merchant District had given way to residential streets and taverns, but that was where I had the most to fear. Even in a time of peace, people noticed strangers in their neighborhoods, especially strangers who were trying to move about unnoticed. I'd been forced to push my hood back slightly and slow my gait, lest someone think I was a burglar.

By the time Mercury and I arrived at Bortran's Inn, the sun was low in the sky.

The large building sat directly at the city's edge, and I made a mental note to thank Poppy if I ever saw her again. This was indeed the last outpost of Glassleaf.

Still, I hovered near the road outside the inn. The thatch-roofed building was three stories tall and bustling with activity. This could be beneficial. After all, what's one more face in a crowd of dozens? But my stomach fluttered at the thought of going inside. If I were recognized, word would spread like wildfire.

"What's the hold up?" Mercury whined.

They floated as a mist around my feet, the silvery fog writhing with impatience. To passersby I probably looked like a wraith.

"I'm thinking." Really, I was stalling, but they didn't need to know that.

"You're stalling," the mist said.

Asshole.

"I'm trying to figure out the best approach, okay? There's a lot of people inside and I don't want to be noticed."

"Just go around back to the stables and get a horse. What more do you need to think about?"

I frowned. How had I gotten so bad at this?

Without comment, I maneuvered around the side of the building and found the stables, which were almost as large as the inn itself. The smell of horses and dung hit me before I got to the door, flooding me with memories from a lifetime ago.

"Wait out here," I whispered, "an indoor mist will be too distracting."

They grumbled in protest but floated toward a copse of bushes along the side of the building. Bracing myself, I slipped inside.

The space was large but far quieter than I'd anticipated. A boy was sweeping out a stall at the front, and I could hear a soft humming from somewhere further back. There were already a few lanterns lit and from their soft glow I could see stall upon stall of dozing horses.

The stable hand looked up as I entered. "Can I help you?"

The mysterious humming continued, the voice gruff but in key.

"I need to buy a horse," I replied. My heart sank as the stable hand shook his head.

"Sorry ma'am, no horses available for sale. If you can wait a night or two, we might be able to manage something, but not on such short notice. Though you could ask around inside. See if anyone is willing to sell." He nodded toward the inn at this last bit, indicating the crowd I'd heard earlier.

I scowled as an unusual feeling of failure settled over me. Why had I thought this would be easy? I couldn't even make it out of the city according to plan. How in the hell was I going to get to the Eastern Plains? Frustration bubbled in my gut, and it took a second to realize this was the first time in decades anyone had said "no" to me. There was no discussion or negotiation about logistics or optics or how to make it work. Just... "no." I didn't like how much it unsettled me.

"Thank you," I said, reminding myself to be polite. It wasn't the stable hand's fault, after all. "Is it alright if I sit for a minute to think?"

The boy shrugged and continued sweeping, so I moved to a pile of straw bales and plopped down. The sharp straw stabbed into my legs through the thin fabric of my skirt, but it still felt good to sit after so much walking.

I couldn't wait two days to *maybe* get a horse. And I certainly couldn't walk into a crowded inn to negotiate. An ache crept up the back of my neck, and I could feel the chill starting in my fingertips.

"Long day?" a deep voice asked.

I looked up to find a man and horse standing a few feet from me. In my gloom, I hadn't heard them approach. Now I realized the humming had stopped, so this must be the mystery person from the back of the stable.

"The longest," I grumbled, keeping my fingers tucked beneath me.

He was tall, with chestnut hair and a trimmed beard, and his hazel eyes crinkled as he smiled. His jacket was a collage of leather pieces sewn together in a haphazard design, but the result was somehow beautiful. The garment was worn and scuffed in places, likely from years of service.

"Where are you trying to get to?"

My jaw clenched instinctively, and I stood, brushing the straw from my skirt as I eyed the door. Seeing my reaction, he held up a hand.

"Forgive my prying. I forget my manners sometimes after being in the wilds. Your business is none of mine."

"The wilds?" I cocked my head. My wariness hadn't abated, but I studied him curiously.

He nodded. "I'm a trapper by trade, which means long weeks with no one to talk to but Boss." He ran a hand down the neck of his horse, the gesture affectionate, and the animal nudged him in response. The dark bay stallion was so large, I knew most people would have stumbled, but the stranger was clearly used to such tactics and held his ground.

"See?" he smiled, rubbing the horse's nose. "No manners. He probably learned it from me."

I found myself smiling. Something about him set me at ease.

The horse perked his ears toward me. With two steps he was at my side, and I held out a hand for him to smell. The sparse hairs of his nose tickled my skin as he investigated, then turned his attention to my bag. I'd thrown back my cloak when I'd sat down, and the horse nudged at the sack slung over my shoulder. The stranger stepped forward, intending to pull the animal back, but I laughed.

"You're the second pickpocket I've encountered today," I told the horse. "And by far the most successful."

I raised my eyes to the man in question. When he nodded, I

pulled an apple out of my sack and held it out. The horse took it happily, devouring the fruit in three bites, and promptly nosed my bag again.

I chuckled, stroking its head. "Boss indeed. You are aptly named, my friend."

Looking up, I found the man studying me, a small smile on his face.

Averting my eyes, I stepped back.

"Well, you are clearly on your way. I wish you luck on your travels."

I turned toward the door, but the man called after me.

"I'm Kitt, by the way."

Hesitating, I glanced back. But rather than wait for me to offer my name, the trapper plowed ahead.

"Boss and I are headed north, if you're looking for company. I know I already exposed our lack of manners, but neither of us snores, and Boss knows all the best inns."

I studied his face, looking for any hint of deception or malice. My time as queen, plus my childhood on the streets, had made me an expert at assessing people's intentions. I could tell when someone wanted me for my power, my influence, or my body just by the look in their eyes.

Kitt's eyes held only kindness, and an earnest desire to help. It made me hesitate, consider, but only for a moment.

"I appreciate the offer. But the journey I'm on must be made alone."

After all, there would be no way to hide my identity or the purpose of my quest from a travel partner. Not to mention the Ethereal that traveled with me. As kind as this man was, he would only slow me down. And while my instincts told me he could be trusted, they had been wrong before.

Kitt's brow furrowed in thought, his hand on the horse's neck, before he nodded to himself.

"Alright then," he said, returning his eyes to me, "but you were looking for a horse. So, take Boss."

My jaw dropped. I stared, waiting for him to laugh at the joke, but the seconds ticked by.

"I—thank you, but I can't do that."

"Sure you can. He's all tacked up and everything."

"I'm sure you need him to do your job."

Kitt scratched his chin. "Well, I've been considering taking a vacation anyway. It's clear whatever errand you're on is of the highest importance."

This was insanity. I couldn't take this man's horse! All my years of eloquent speeches and managed emotions went out the window as I sputtered objections. Kitt had the audacity to smile at my struggles before casting a quick glance over his shoulder. The stable hand had vanished to the back of the room, likely sweeping the stall Kitt had just vacated. Facing me again, Kitt's smile softened.

"Please, I know this is odd, but a stranger once helped me and all they asked in return was that one day, I pay the kindness forward. Today is that day."

I hesitated. Again, the gentleness in his face threw me off balance. I didn't want to trust him, but for some reason I did. And I did need a horse...

Sensing my wavering, Kitt brightened. "How about this, you can meet me in Linipa whenever you're finished with your errand. I can wait a few days here for another horse, then we can swap whenever you arrive."

Linipa was a large city in nearly the direct center of the country. It was a two-day ride from here, and three from the ruins of Zaletor's tower on the Eastern Plains.

I opened my mouth to argue, but a shimmer of mist wisped past an open window. My time was up.

"Alright," I said. "There's an inn across from Linipa's Citadel called the Leather Shoe. I'll meet you there in six days. And... thank you."

Kitt nodded again, and after giving Boss a final pat, held out the reins.

It wasn't until later, when I was far from the city, that I realized he'd never asked for my name.

Mercury waited to corporealize until we were well outside the city limits. Thank The Goddesses their appearance didn't startle Boss. Though, considering how easily the giant horse had taken to me becoming his temporary master, I was beginning to think very few things could startle Boss. Maybe as a trapper's horse he was used to animals darting out of nowhere. But I was willing to bet none of those animals cursed like the Ethereal now flying alongside me.

"What took so damn long?! All you needed was a horse!"

"It got complicated," I shot back, readjusting my seat. "There were none for sale by the inn, so I had to buy some man's only horse."

I'd insisted on giving Kitt money, telling him to use it to purchase a new horse when some arrived. He'd resisted, but I'd pointed out the new horse would become mine when we traded in Linipa, so it was perfectly fair. The problem was, I had no idea how much a horse would actually cost, so I'd just given him a handful of coins. He hadn't argued at least.

"You could have just killed him and taken the horse, but at least we're finally on the way," Mercury grumbled.

Their wings trailed smoke with each beat, and every once in a while, they'd place their feet firmly in the air, as though landing and jumping off from an invisible platform. Despite my frustrations, my heart swelled at the sight as my present and past collided. I'd asked Mercury about the movement years ago, curious if the jumping helped the Ethereal fly. Mercury had merely shrugged, the only time I'd seen them shy, and stated that it made flying more fun.

I smiled at the memory. It was something I'd forgotten, a seemingly inconsequential moment. But now, watching them glide beside me, I cherished it.

Seeing my wistful stare, Mercury scowled.

"What?"

"Nothing."

I turned my focus to the road ahead. The area outside the city quickly became farmland in this direction, a boring landscape of crops stretching out for several miles. But as I gazed over Boss's ears, all I could see was the world waiting before me. And I was eager to meet it.

6

———————

An hour and thirty-four minutes.

That's how long I made it before deciding I should turn back. Kitt was probably still at Bortran's. I could return Boss and get back to the castle before midnight.

"We should have waited to leave until tomorrow," I grumbled. "I could have gotten one last night of comfortable sleep, and we would have started our journey in daylight." The sun had set shortly after we'd left the city, and while the roads were safe enough at night, I didn't enjoy the prospect of traveling in the dark. "We should turn back. We're not too far from the inn. We could start fresh tomorrow and—"

"No," came Mercury's reply, somewhere to my left. The night sky was overcast, and their form was difficult to track without the moon or stars. "If you turn around now, I'll never get you back on this road. The horse is plenty fresh, and he has no trouble walking at night, so we'll continue on."

I slumped back into the saddle. They weren't wrong, but they didn't have to be so imperious about it.

We'd spent most of the trip so far in silence. Despite my occasional flashes of memory bubbling to the surface, I found myself at a loss for what to say. I had no idea how time passed in the Ethereal Plane, if it passed at all. Was Mercury the same entity I'd known years ago? Had their life, or I suppose, their *existence* changed after what happened with Zaletor? They certainly seemed as frustrating and belligerent as ever.

Either way, *I* had changed. The headstrong girl who would charge into a room, yelling sassy one-liners, blasting ice shards first and asking questions later, she was gone. She died that day on Zaletor's tiled floor. I was the person who came back, who had to clean up the mess and sit on the throne and learn to be silent and rational because the world around me was healing.

And I was tired.

"Let's stop for the night." I pulled Boss to a gentle halt. My eyes had adjusted enough to know we were in a somewhat wooded area. It would be a rough night, but at least we'd have cover.

Mercury's voice floated around me. "No. We travel through till sunrise, then you can have a two-hour break, then it's back on the road! Just like the old days!"

I gave a harsh laugh as I climbed down from the saddle. "Good luck with that."

It took all of my concentration, but a small flame burst to life in my hand. I heard Boss snort with surprise, but the stallion didn't shy away from the sudden magic. I exhaled, straining from the effort, and the fire grew to the size of an apple. Good enough, I decided, leading Boss off the road and into the trees.

Mercury was protesting, loudly and with curse words. I maneuvered through the sparse forest, careful not to light any bushes or low hanging branches on fire, until I found a clearing big enough for Boss. It was far enough from the road that we wouldn't be bothered by other travelers and the ground was relatively flat, so it was perfect. I looped the reins around a tree, clumsily as I only had one free hand, and began kicking aside dead leaves and debris until I reached the earth beneath.

Keeping the flame going took most of my focus, but I laid my free hand on the ground and willed a small divot to form. Something just large enough to hold a firepit.

Nothing happened.

Gritting my teeth, I tried again, picturing the outcome in my mind.

The ground remained unchanged, but the fire in my hand quivered.

"Shit," I panted, and resorted to digging the hole with my traitorous free hand.

When I deemed the pit large enough, I scooped in leaves and twigs. Holding my breath, I lowered my small flame and watched the fire catch. The clearing glowed with light, and I scrambled around to find sticks large enough to feed the flames, a feat made easier by the use of both hands. Finally, after what felt like ages, the fire burned cheerily of its own accord and I flopped back onto the ground, sweat beading on my brow from the effort.

"Well," Mercury said, strutting into view. "*That* was the most pitiful display of magic I have ever had the misfortune to witness."

"Fuck off." Not a queenly response, but I was exhausted.

They cocked their head. "When was the last time you used more than one ability at a time?"

While the Citadel and priestesses referred to elemental control as Gifts, Mercury had always called it an "ability" or merely "magic." For them, "Gift" implied that The Goddess had intentionally chosen some people over others, when in reality it was entirely chance. The Goddesses had created all of humanity with the latent ability to wield the elements as a way to help them survive the chaotic world, but as time had passed and the world became safer the magic had begun to fade. It was something in the blood, the Ethereal told me once, something that could go dormant and arise as needed. I had been the only person The Goddesses had actually "Gifted" with intention, to fight the new evil that had arisen, but the Ethereal still didn't like the term.

Learning this, seeing how much of what the Citadel preached was misunderstood, biased, or, in my particular case, completely fabricated, had forever impacted my view of the religious order. It gave people hope and helped those in need, but my vision of its ultimate authority on all things concerning The Goddesses had been shattered. Still, I hadn't been willing to shatter it for everyone else.

I watched the fire in silence as Mercury studied me.

"Phoebe," their voice was too calm. "When was the last time you used *any* of your abilities?"

I let my silence be my answer. In truth, I didn't know how many years it had been since I'd done anything other than party tricks for visiting ministers. A chunk of ice here or a flash of sparks there. I couldn't remember the last time I'd used Terra, as the pit before me clearly showed. And as for my Specter ability, well, everyone else liked to forget I had that, so I had learned to forget about it as well.

"Skies above! Why didn't you keep up your training? The Goddesses told you that you might be called upon again!"

A muscle in my jaw twitched. "I didn't think they were serious. It's not like I heard from them ever again or had you around to explain their cryptic bullshit."

The Ethereal bristled at my disrespect, but I didn't care. The memory of those four melodic voices speaking in unison still haunted my dreams.

The fact was, magic didn't help me rule the country. That took intelligence, patience, and empathy. I didn't have time to practice magic. Hell, I barely had time to sleep. So, I'd focused my energy on what was most important. I'd never even considered that I might need to use my full abilities again.

Pushing myself up, I began untacking Boss, which was both necessary and an excuse to turn away from Mercury's wrath. The saddlebag revealed an extra blanket and supplies to care for the horse so I dug out a grooming brush, hoping the conversation was over.

But for Mercury, it was just getting started.

"Fine. You don't want to talk about how you, the most powerful magical creature to currently walk the earth, after yours truly of course, have become too lazy to even create a hole in the ground. That's fine. Let's move on to another topic, shall we? What happened between you and Tristan?"

My stomach lurched, but I kept my focus on the horse. *That* conversation was not going to happen.

"I admit, I'm no expert in human affection. But the last time I saw you, you two seemed stupidly happy and were talking about spending your lives together."

I whipped around, grooming brush still in hand. "The last time you saw me, I had just *died*. It's safe to say I wasn't at my most rational."

Mercury's eternal eyes narrowed. "That's the second time you mentioned dying. Are you still upset about it?"

"Am I—yes! Of course I am! I'm pissed off that my death was *required* to defeat Zaletor. How could The Goddesses have asked that of a child?!"

"Wow," Mercury sat down, wings folded tight. "Okay, first of all, as I explained the first time, your life had to end as payment for The Goddesses' involvement in bestowing multiple abilities upon you. The universe requires balance, and what they did, no matter how necessary, was a big no-no. That's how dire the situation was. Second, yes. You died. But you came back! You're welcome for that, by the way. Now stop holding onto the bad and focus on the good!"

"How am I supposed to focus on—what do you mean, "you're welcome"?"

"Who do you think suggested the loophole that your death could be temporary and still restore the balance? Who do you think made the case that you were special, beyond the abilities you'd been given, and you deserved to live a full and happy life?"

My anger flickered but didn't extinguish. "*You* had them bring me back?"

Their ears flattened, and I could see the fury glittering in their eyes. "That's right, and a fat lot of good it did!"

"What's that supposed to mean?!"

"It means, what have you been doing with your life the past twenty years?!"

The fire at my feet flared to match my temper. "How can you even ask that? This world is so much better than it was! The people are happy and safe and—"

"The people can shove it! What about you?"

"I'm fine," I argued, after pausing a second too long.

"Bullshit! When was the last time you had fun? Or did something spontaneous?"

"Why do you even care?" My fists trembled at my side as I tried to control the emotions that were begging to erupt.

Mercury's body glittered in the firelight, giving me a clear look at how they struggled for words. "I know it's been ages for you, but for me it's been barely a blink. So, you can imagine my surprise to find that the force of nature I knew has been replaced with—" Their inability to finish the thought cut deeper than anything they could have said. But the Ethereal continued. "I can see how it was difficult to process what happened, but you've been hiding in that castle all these years, just because you died?"

"No! Because Becca died!"

They stopped short, but my rage couldn't be contained.

"When Becca died, *she* didn't come back! The entire kingdom mourned her loss, but they were also afraid. They'd seen the five of us as a symbol of triumph over the darkness and a promise for the future. When Becca didn't come back, it was as if one of the gods themselves had died. One of their symbols of hope had been taken and they worried the world would go back to how it had been. My job as queen is to do what's best for my people and in this case, what's best is to keep myself out of harm's way. They will never have to fear like that again."

The smoke curling from their wings lessened.

"But what about the life you wanted? The life with Tristan?"

Their confusion gutted my wrath. My shoulders slumped as I considered how to phrase my feelings. "Tristan and I, we were young. We wanted different things out of life. That's the way it goes sometimes. Besides, I wasn't supposed to have a life beyond the battle with Zaletor. As far as I'm concerned all of this is just a bonus, so if I'm less than happy, that's a fair trade."

They started to say more, but I turned back to Boss.

"I'm tired. We can talk more in the morning."

The Ethereal continued to gaze at me, but they kept silent as I pulled out the extra blanket and claimed the softest piece of ground I could find. The blanket smelled of hard soap, so at least it was clean, but there was another scent. One that reminded me of moss and the sky right after a rainstorm. It was nice.

I had performed a minor feat of magic, and I felt drained. Curling up in the blanket, wrapped in the strange but pleasant scent, I willed sleep to come. Instead, all I could think about was the revelation that my second chance at life was all because Mercury had fought for me. And now, they regretted it.

A fat lot of good it did, indeed.

7

—————

That night I dreamed of my death. Not of the death waiting for me in the future, but the night I'd given my life to destroy Zaletor's. It felt like being on the verge of sleep, where you don't quite know if you're conscious, but you know you're not fully asleep.

Floating.

Peaceful.

Then, from the nothingness, came four female voices in unison.

"Well done, Phoebe Blessed-Heart. You have saved your world."

Even as a formless wisp of spirit, I'd attempted to roll my eyes.

Do you mind? I'm dead, which means I don't think I answer to you anymore. I'd like to begin my eternal rest in peace.

I didn't have a mouth or vocal cords, so I'd simply thought

the words as loud as I could. It must have worked, because they replied.

"You have defeated the evil, but there is still much to do."

Much to do?! Zaletor is gone! Not even dust was left!! Also, if you hadn't noticed, I'm rather dead *at the moment.*

"Yes. You have fulfilled your destiny and balanced the scales. Our sister, the Dark Lady, has been imprisoned. Now, as a reward, you may return."

Ugh, here we go with "destiny" again. If you think—wait? What do you mean "return?"

"Live well, Blessed-Heart. You may be called again."

Then I was hurtling to my body, like falling off a cliff except sideways.

With a gasp, I was back.

I couldn't have been dead for more than a few moments, the blood that covered me was still warm, but I felt smooth skin and firm muscle beneath the tattered remains of my shirt.

By then, the rest of my friends had made it to the throne room. When I'd taken that first gasping breath, pandemonium had erupted.

Everyone was talking at once again, but over the chaos, Mercury's awed whisper cut through. "They listened."

I didn't think to ask what they meant or why they looked so relieved, because Tristan was running his hands over my body in a very un-sexy way. When he was sure I wasn't hurt, he pulled me to my feet and tenderly pressed his lips to mine. I returned the kiss with enthusiasm, putting every ounce of love into it, until everyone around us shifted with discomfort.

"Do you two mind?!" Becca yelled, crashing into us with her arms thrown wide. "We're all glad you're okay, Phebs, but I'd rather not watch you suck face with my cousin for the rest of the day."

I grinned. I decided I'd never stop grinning. Throwing my arms around her slight shoulders, I hugged her fiercely. "Tough luck. It's what you're going to watch for the rest of eternity."

"Don't touch that!" Mercury snapped, breaking us out of our revelry.

I looked up to see Jax standing above the crown, as though he'd just been bending over to grab it.

"I wasn't going to nick it, I just wanted a look." Jax shoved his hands in his pockets in a not at all suspicious gesture.

Unconvinced, Mercury frowned. "It needs to be destroyed. The robes too. Every bit of Zaletor must be wiped from the earth."

I rolled my eyes. I'd come back from the dead and the stupid Ethereal couldn't even give us a minute to celebrate the fact that we'd all just *saved the world*. Typical.

Becca pulled away, crossing to join Mercury in their analysis. With a longing look in his eyes, Alto followed.

Taking advantage of the momentary privacy, I turned back to Tristan and slipped my arms around his waist. "Dying was as far as I'd planned things out. What happens now?"

He smiled, and it was the most glorious thing I'd ever seen.

"I guess we live."

The sun had barely begun to lighten the sky when a paw started smacking my face.

You've slept enough. Let's go!"

Smoldering hells, if I could kill them, I would.

"Good morning to you too," I snapped, dragging myself into a sitting position. In my peripheral vision I could see leaves tangled in the nest that was my hair, but that was the least of my concerns. Everything hurt: my head, my muscles, even my bones. I'd lain for at least an hour last night, consumed by my thoughts, before sleep had finally claimed me. Now I grimaced at the effort it took to merely stand. Goddesses above, maybe it would have been better to keep traveling all night.

At least Boss looked rested, which made sense as he'd barely had to do anything yesterday. I found a sparse clump of grass for him to have a quick breakfast and made a mental note to stop for water as soon as possible. And for some pants, I added, looking down at my stained skirt, which had done nothing to keep me warm. The night had gotten colder than I'd anticipated, and once the fire had gone out, my cloak hadn't been enough.

Thankfully, Kitt's extra blanket had been perfect. In the daylight, I could see it was beautiful, made from deep burgundy threads woven with a few off-white stars around the border. A warm, durable blanket made for someone who spent many nights out in the wilderness. Brushing off the leaves and debris, I folded it carefully, giving it an extra little pat as I tucked it safely away in the bag.

Once I'd saddled Boss and had everything ready, I took a few minutes to stretch my screaming limbs. It had taken that long for me to be able to stand up straight without effort. Birdsong filled the air, and I pitied the poor creatures who were forced to witness what I knew was a very undignified spectacle. I hissed and grunted, reaching first for the sky, then the earth, twisting carefully to the left and right. The whole time, all I could think of, aside from how much pain I was in, was my soft bed and the warm bath that would have been waiting for me in the castle. To say I was feeling less than optimistic about the rest of the journey would have been an understatement.

Finally, I felt capable of climbing onto the horse. But as I turned to lead Boss back to the road, Mercury appeared in front of me.

"Fill the hole."

Their voice was edged with command. It wasn't the official Voice the Ethereal could use, the one that could command armies and make even the bravest person quake with submission, but it was close. I blinked, looking back at the cold fire pit.

"Why bother? The fire is long dead. A hole in the forest isn't going to hurt anything."

"It's not about the hole. It's about you. Your magic skills are pitiful."

I glanced at the hole, remembering how I'd strained the night before. "You're the one who made a big deal about needing to get moving. My magic is fine. I'm a little rusty, that's all."

I started to walk around them, but they blocked me again.

"You've gotten used to your cushy life. Fine. But we are walking into a potentially deadly situation. Something powerful has been accessing dark energy, and while I think very highly of myself, you shouldn't have to rely on me to keep you safe. From now on, any moment you are not eating, sleeping, or taking a shit, you're training. Now. Fill. The. Hole."

I stared at their silvery form, torn between anger and shame. They glared back at me, unblinking, and I was suddenly aware the forest around us had gone silent. Every bird had quieted, and even the breeze had stilled. The only sound was from Boss shifting in discomfort, watching our standoff with wary eyes, ready to bolt at the first hint of danger.

"Fine," I grunted, turning to the fire pit. "For the record, you were infinitely nicer about this process the first time."

They didn't balk. "The first time, you were a scared, lonely child who had been abandoned by her family for being too powerful. I didn't want to overwhelm you. Now, you're a powerful, lonely adult who's been abandoned by her family for being too scared. You don't need nice. You need truth."

I hissed a breath, hardly believing what they'd said. My aches and pains were suddenly forgotten as rage slithered through my veins.

"How *dare* you say that to me?"

Their tail swished silently on the ground. "Oh, does the truth make you angry? Imagine that."

There were no words to express how much I hated them. Fury boiled my skin and I felt like I would burst from the pressure. I hadn't felt like this in years. I felt...

Powerful.

My eyes narrowed.

"Asshole."

They smiled, fangs shining in the morning light, as I held my hand over the hole. It still wasn't easy, and I could feel sweat forming again as I strained, but my anger pulled my power forth along with it. With excruciating slowness, the pile of dirt beside the hole crumbled and filled the empty space.

I trembled from the effort, but after a few moments the ground before me was flat and whole, with only a patch of fresh dirt to indicate anything had ever been amiss.

"Excellent," Mercury said, "now we can leave."

My anger still simmered, but I couldn't deny the results. Taking Boss's reins, I grappled with how frustratingly correct Mercury had been about my magic.

"So I'm starting from square one." It wasn't a question.

Mercury laughed. "Great Goddesses, I wish! At least when I found you, you were moderately skilled with your ice magic. This time, we're starting at square zero. There is no square. And we don't have a lot of time, so I hope you're feeling rested."

8

We arrived at the village of Stenomar shortly after noon. Never in my life had I been more relieved to see a cluster of buildings. It meant food, pants, and most importantly, a break from the exhausting training.

I had spent the entire morning with one goal in mind: create a sphere of ice and keep it hovering beside me.

Sitting atop Boss, who alternated between a walk and a trot, I'd cursed with effort. Mercury had chosen to start with ice, as my Glacies ability had always come easiest, since it was the first of my Gifts to have manifested. But it was taxing, and I struggled to remember even the most basic techniques. The spheres I'd created were often too large, making them heavy and unwieldy, and covered with lumps and pits that affected their balance. Half the time the stupid things crumbled in my hand before I could even get them aloft. I strained, remembering when I'd been able to craft a perfect ice sword with barely a thought.

Yet somehow, creating the spheres was the easy part. If I managed to create one solid enough to hold together, I still had to hover it next to me, which required constant focus. Perhaps if I'd been training in an empty room without any distractions, I would have fared better, but I was on the road. The world around me offered constant distraction, whether it was Boss shifting as he moved, the traitorous wind trying to throw the sphere off course, or the arrival of another traveler. If my thoughts strayed for even a moment, the magic faltered. And every time the ball fell, crashing to the ground with a disappointing crack, I had to create a new one. As such, the road between where we'd made camp and the village was littered with shards of ice, and my pride, slowly melting in the morning sun.

When we had crested a small hill and saw the cluster of buildings in the distance, I'd nearly cried with relief. Mercury had been doubtful.

"Is it even worth stopping? It hardly looks large enough to have the supplies you'll need."

"You just want me to keep training," I glared. "Stenomar is small, but there will be a stretch of market stalls. I'll be able to find some things at least."

When I'd first become queen, I'd felt it was important to learn as much about my kingdom as possible. To me, this had meant knowing the name of every city, town, and village in the realm. It had taken years of pouring over maps, and I'd driven my advisors mad with constant questions about places they'd never even heard of. Everyone around me, including my friends, had seen it as an interesting but useless skill. But I'd done it.

Not so useless now, I thought with a strange sense of satisfaction as Stenomar spread before me. Like shifting through a pile of documents, I scanned my brain for the information I wanted, pulling it forth with more ease than a ball of ice.

The village had a consistent population of only about three

hundred people, but it was located at a vital crossroads, meaning it welcomed a steady stream of travelers. It would be easy to blend in. But only, of course, if I could get Mercury to wait for me outside the city.

That argument went on for nearly a mile.

"I'm sticking with you," repeated the curl of mist conspicuously floating alongside Boss. There were more travelers on the road by this point, and I was constantly maneuvering to block the mist from view. "It's the only way to keep you from bolting back to your precious castle."

I gritted my teeth. As much as I missed the comforts of my beautiful cage, Mercury had proven just how useless I'd become. If a great danger emerged to terrorize the kingdom, I was in no shape to defeat it. The training was torturous, but I couldn't claim to be doing what was best for my people if I turned away from it now.

"I'm not going to turn around, and I won't be gone more than an hour. But I need to buy supplies and it will be difficult to do that when everyone I encounter is terrified of the midday fog that follows wherever I go. You can wait for me at the north end of the city."

An older man driving a cart in the opposite direction shook his head at me as we passed, muttering something about people who talked to their animals. I ignored the slight, running a hand down Boss's neck, but made a mental note to keep my voice down.

Mercury made no such concessions. "I can't risk it. Besides, why does it matter if people see me? Hells! They'll probably give you things for free as thanks for allowing them to look upon my glory!"

I was beginning to think my teeth would be nothing but nubs by the time I returned to the castle. "How about this, you go wait for me at the north entrance, or I'll turn around right now! It's that simple."

The mist halted, hovering still. "You wouldn't dare."

"I guess we'll find out!" I called over my shoulder.

Boss kept walking. I braced for further arguments.

"One hour," they hissed, "then I start walking through town singing the bawdy songs Jax taught me."

I knew it was a threat, but I couldn't help but smile at the thought. "Deal."

With a soft grumbling, the mist floated off to the left, presumably to skirt the town.

I was more or less unprotected without the Ethereal's presence, but I took a moment to appreciate the silence.

Entering the village proper, I found the main road was lined with several inns and taverns and shops of every kind. There were dozens of carts, each with a different type of food, and a pleasant mixing of smells filled the air. Glancing down a side alley, I could see the village quickly became residential, with signs and fences to deter travelers from wandering past the main road. It was after noon, but there were still clusters of people at the food carts waiting for their midday meal.

It was a cloudless day, so I kept my hood back, aware that concealing myself would only draw more attention. Fortunately, I was a mess from my night on the ground. Every time I thought I'd picked out the last leaf from my hair, I found another one, and my face was lined with fatigue. As long as I kept my eyes down, no one would realize I was their beloved queen. Climbing down from Boss, I surveyed the stretch of shops, weighing where to start.

The general store was located at the village's halfway point, and I was pleased to find it well stocked. I left Boss hitched to a post outside, and I could feel the horse's eyes on me as I paid for a large bag of apples. Then I found a food cart selling jerky and dried fruit and bought some of that as well.

Pants proved more difficult to procure. While it wasn't uncommon for women to wear trousers, I needed a pair that were comfortable and wouldn't fall to pieces after a few hours in the saddle. This meant enduring the nightmare of trying them on.

I found a shop with colorful banners hanging from the upper windows indicating a tailor's residence. Most places would only have clothing that was made to fit, requiring the customer to wait hours or days for the finished garments. Luckily, this shop had a selection of trousers and tunics premade and available for sale. Imitating a Tealian accent to avoid suspicion, I explained what I needed. The kindly woman behind the counter stared at my body for a few moments, her gaze uncomfortably critical, before selecting a handful of options for me and ushering me to a curtained area at the back.

Tucked in the small closet of a changing room, I scrambled to try things on as quickly as possible. I knew the space was private, but voices from the street beyond carried through the thin walls, making me feel exposed.

"I heard Grady's horse got loose again. I swear, that animal is smarter than he is."

"Mary got more fancy ribbons delivered from the city! We need to get there today before she sells out!"

"Price of grain went up again. Where's Glassleaf get off with all these tax increases?"

I started, my attention snagging on the voices beyond.

"It's the way of the world," came a second voice, "it happens every festival season. Don't know why it still surprises you."

My fingers fumbled at the ties on my pants. The taxes were raised every season? That couldn't be right.

"Well, this year's been worse than ever. You know whose fault it is, don't you?"

The second voice sighed. "Yes, Murphy, you've told me many times. Though I can see by your face, you're about to tell me again."

I held my breath, preparing for the condemnation about to come my way.

"The fuckin' Council, that's who! I swear, someone needs to make sure that group of fools is doing their jobs. From where I'm standing, they don't do anything but sit around all day, thumbs up their asses, and make our lives harder."

"What?" I cried, then slapped a hand over my mouth.

If the mystery speakers had heard my outburst, they didn't tie it to their conversation because the second voice went on.

"You only complain so much because you're young. You were barely out of diapers when Her Majesty saved us, so you don't remember how much worse things were before. It's why you'll never hear me complaining."

"Hey now! I'm not making any complaints toward Her Majesty! I just don't like the thought of those Council fools taking advantage of her kindness!"

I couldn't believe my ears. The second man sounded genuinely outraged at the mere suggestion his companion might speak ill of me. I pressed my ear to the cloth, anxious to hear more, but the voices trailed off. My mind reeled at the conversation, until I realized the pants I'd been trying on had fallen around my ankles.

Perfect.

A minute later, I exited the small changing area with my prizes. The woman was standing at the counter mending a shirt and smiled at my approach.

"All to your liking?" She nodded to the pants I was wearing.

"Yes, thank you. I'll take these as well." I held up a second pair of pants and a tunic.

Setting her sewing aside, the woman gave me the total price. I fished the coins out of my pouch.

"We don't get many visitors from Tealia," the woman smiled as I handed over the money.

Which was exactly why I'd chosen the country across the sea as my cover. Keeping my eyes downcast, I nodded. "Visiting family for a few weeks. The seasons here are lovely."

"Only a few weeks? You should stay for the festival at the start of summer! The whole country will be celebrating the anniversary of our queen's Great Victory!"

My cheeks hurt from holding my smile in place. "I'm sure it will be a grand occasion."

She began folding my new clothes, taking the time to brush out every crease. "Oh yes. The big event is in the capitol, of course, but everyone in town pitches in for our local festival. It's a nice way to show our respect and gratitude."

I wished my Terra magic was stronger, so I could make a hole to swallow me.

"It seems like you love your queen very much."

Holding my clothes like hostages on the counter, she sighed. "It's true, though, between you and me, I still haven't forgiven her for denying us a royal wedding. What a lovely bride she would have been."

In an instant, my discomfort turned to anger as my fingers went cold.

"Maybe she'll find love again someday," I ground out.

But the woman waved it off, leaning back enough to free my clothes. "If that boy Tristan wasn't good enough, no one is. I'm sure she's committing herself to a life of piety, like those priestesses do."

Of course. Because if I didn't love Tristan, I couldn't love anyone. In that moment, I was sure that if I'd wanted to, I could craft a perfect ice sphere. And hurl it at the woman's face. Reaching out, I swiped my new clothes from the counter. If the shopkeeper noticed the temper in my voice or the ice at my fingers, she didn't say anything as I fled the store without another word.

Fifteen minutes later, Boss and I emerged from the village cantering down the road.

"Cutting it close," came a voice to my right. "I was doing my vocal exercises."

I kept my eyes forward, ignoring the mist beside me.

"Is everything alright?"

Everything was terrible. The citizens of Bearnel were so grateful to me for stopping Zaletor, they refused to blame me for tax increases. Granted, they were tax increases I didn't authorize, but I couldn't investigate them until I returned to the castle. Oh, and they were still holding on to my failed teenage love.

"Fine," I lied. "Everything's great. Let's get out of here. I don't want to stop anymore."

In mist form the Ethereal had no face to tighten in doubt or eyes to glitter with concern, but I could still feel them assessing me as we left Stenomar behind.

9

———————

Somehow, my skill with magic got worse as the afternoon turned to evening. The ice I crafted was too brittle, and it would shatter before I could even attempt to float it beside me. Finally, a sphere exploded in my hand, sending shards of ice directly at my face.

"I'm done for the day!" I fumed, wiping my stinging cheeks. "It's not worth losing an eye over."

To my surprise, Mercury didn't argue, and we rode on in awkward silence.

As the sky turned pink, making the grassy hills around us glow like an ocean, we set up camp. Even Mercury agreed it was wise to not enter the Eastern Plains at night. The road had borne no signs of recent travelers since we'd turned east, which was no surprise considering what lay a few miles ahead, so I didn't bother pulling Boss far from the road to camp. I stomped down a few of the lush green blades, which promised to be an infinitely more comfortable bed than last night's forest, though it meant less options for firewood. Boss certainly didn't complain, lowering his head to eat with a happy snort.

At least someone was enjoying our little adventure, I thought as I brushed him down.

"You're only struggling with your magic because you've been moody all afternoon."

I turned to see Mercury lounging on the grass. In the light of the setting sun, their silver body turned a striking rose-pink color. It would have been beautiful if it weren't for the "I'm about to meddle" look on their face.

"I haven't been moody!" I could hear the whine in my voice as I said it but refused to back down. Stuffing the brush back into the saddlebag, I staked Boss's lead to the ground so he wouldn't wander too far, then collapsed onto the crushed grass.

"Your emotions have always affected your magic. Anger gives you power, short lived though it may be, joy gives you precision, fear makes you overcompensate, and sorrow makes you lose focus. You've been a little storm cloud ever since you stopped in that village and now you can't do anything. What happened?"

"It's—"

"Don't say it's nothing!"

I heaved a breath, thinking of how best to put my feelings into words. "For the past two decades, everywhere I go, people know who I am. They fawn over me and bend over backwards to make me happy. It's been so long since I interacted with someone who didn't know who I was—since I could learn what people really think of me."

Mercury frowned. "Do they not like you?"

"It's worse than that! They WORSHIP me! They talk about me like I'm some divine being! I knew people felt that way back when I was young, but I thought it would be different further away from the Capitol. I'd figured people had moved on. I'd *hoped* they'd moved on."

I flopped back onto the grass, looking up at the sky. Boss

gave a snort, and the soft crunch of paws on grass told me Mercury was coming to sit beside me.

"Listen," they said, "I want you to be happy more than anyone. But it doesn't seem like such a bad thing to be loved by your people."

I sighed. "It's too much. The real me can never live up to the version of me they've all created. They cling to my 'great victory' as if that's the only accomplishment I'll ever have. If the people I'm supposed to help and protect can't move on from what happened, how can I?"

Mercury was silent for a moment, which was something I thought was impossible.

"I think—"

Before I could learn what they thought, Boss reared up. His snorts and cries filled the air and the only reason he didn't bolt across the plains was the rope I'd staked to the ground.

Leaping to my feet, I scanned the area and saw a figure stumble over a nearby hill. The sun was setting directly behind them, and I held up a hand to shield my eyes.

"Are we on someone's property? A farmer, perhaps?" Mercury asked, squinting.

Boss whinnied, pulling at the tether in fear.

Something about the stranger was making the horse panic, but I couldn't see their face. The figure lurched forward, erratic and stiff, progressing down the hill toward us with a slow determination.

"If we are, the farmer's drunk."

With a shock, I realized Mercury was still in their true form. I opened my mouth to tell them to change, to avoid being seen and blow our cover, when they inhaled deeply, searching for any traces of magic on the wind. With a snap of their wings, the Ethereal's back arched.

"Gladiator!"

My mouth went dry and I could feel the blood leave my face.

It couldn't be true, I thought, looking back to the figure descending the hill. Zaletor's stone minions had all perished when he had.

The Dark Wizard had been a master Terra, even before the Dark Lady had imbued him with additional power. He'd created an army of stone soldiers, each statue crafted in his own image, down to the dimple on his chin. And each one was brought to life with a soul his Specter Broin had ripped from an innocent person. The soldiers, which we'd called Gladiators, had been formidable opponents, enforcing their master's rule across the realm. But they had all crumbled to dust upon his death, releasing the souls trapped inside. Which had been a blessing, since hunting down and destroying all ten thousand of them would have been nearly impossible.

My heart raced in my chest as the sun set behind the hill, allowing us to see the figure clearly. I braced myself for the fear, the flood of memories, and—

"Uh, Phoebe? What the fuck am I looking at?"

"I—I don't know."

It was...disgusting?

Instead of a solid statue with perfect human features, the creature that shuffled down the hill appeared to be made of living mud. There was no face that I could see, and the limbs were gangly, dripping sludge onto the grass with each step. It was still a hundred feet away, so it was difficult to judge the height, but I doubted it was much taller than I was. Its arms lashed out at the grass around it, like it was angry at being touched. And even from a distance, I could see there was something strange about its eyes.

"Can you remove the soul powering it? Like when you were young?"

I shuddered at the memory but shook my head. "I'd have to touch it. Which looks like a really bad idea."

Besides, even though I'd used it to defeat Zaletor, Anima had never been my strongest Gift. It didn't react to my emotions the way my other abilities did, and I hadn't practiced in years. I hadn't felt the need without Becca around to make me.

My mind raced, looking for any tidbit to explain the monster making its way toward us. "There's only one, right? The two of us can easily—"

As if they were summoned, three more creatures rose over the hill.

"Oh shit." I scrambled to Boss, who was still panicking. The horse reared again, and I had to spin to avoid getting kicked in the face.

"That's going to be a problem," Mercury cried behind me. I whipped back to see there were now a dozen monsters pushing toward us. The one in the lead was closing in rapidly.

There wasn't time to saddle Boss. I grabbed the saddle bag, which held my money pouch and Kitt's blanket, and left everything else in the grass. I knew the saddle and gear were expensive, but they could be replaced. Speaking as softly as I could, I tried to calm the horse enough to mount. The stallion's eyes rolled at the scent of magic carried on the wind, and he reared again.

"This isn't going to work," I panted, dodging a hoof. "He's too afraid. Even if I can get on, I'll fall and break my neck without a saddle!"

"Then we're going to have to run." Mercury stood with their wings flared wide, and I knew they were planning an attack. The only thing stopping them was fear of spooking the horse further.

"But if he gets loose, we'll never catch him!" Despite the

approaching danger, the thought of telling Kitt I'd lost his precious horse sent an ache through my heart.

Mercury's tail flicked, but they tore their eyes away from the approaching threat to focus on the horse. Then their Voice was echoing through my bones.

"Hear me. You will keep yourself out of danger, but you will wait for us over the hill. When it is safe, you will return to us."

I watched the animal's skin shudder at the words, but for a brief moment he stilled. It was just long enough for me to lunge down and rip out the stake that tethered him to the spot. The instant the tether was free of the metal rod, Boss turned and bolted up the hill behind us. I wished he could have taken me with him, but I knew I would never have been able to keep my grip without a saddle. And while Mercury's power allowed them to command, they couldn't convince anyone to put themselves in danger. Telling the horse to stay close by was the best option available.

I was so focused on making sure Boss made it to safety, I didn't see the shot coming. With a wet smack, a fat glob of clay struck the ground inches from my left foot, splattering me with grime.

Stumbling back, I looked up to see the closest creature raise its arm.

"Run!" Mercury yelled, and I scrambled up the hill after Boss. The Ethereal bounded alongside me, though they could have flown ahead with ease. "Here's the plan: once we crest the hill, you sprint around to the left while I distract them from the right. If you vault over one on the outside, you can land in the middle of their group and—"

"I can't do that!" I panted. The very notion of vaulting over someone, let alone a disgusting creature, was simply beyond comprehension. "What's next, a backflip?!"

"If it would help! You used to be able to do a backflip!"

Even with danger at our backs, I gave an exasperated grunt. "I used to be able to do a lot of things. Right now, it's taking everything I've got to simply run up this damned hill!"

Mercury grumbled beside me, but the stupid suggestions ceased. My lungs burned as I clawed my way up the incline. Every place my hand or foot landed was instantly covered in frost, the lush grass dulling in the twilight.

I was halfway up the hill when Mercury screamed, "ROLL!!"

Without pausing to think, I threw my body to the side, rolling through the grass right as another clay missile hit the spot my head had been a heartbeat before.

"They're speeding up," Mercury announced as I tried to scramble back onto my feet. "Hang on to the ground as best you can!"

Even though it had been decades since I'd heard it last, the Ethereal's instruction to "hold on to something" instinctively had me gripping the earth in a panic. Digging my fingers deep into the soft soil, I felt my Terra magic rise up in response to my fear. Unfortunately, just like Mercury had said it would, my magic overcompensated, and I found my arms trapped up to my elbows in the ground.

"Shit!"

"Good enough!" Mercury nodded.

The Ethereal raised their shadow wings and, in one fluid motion, beat them forward. The blast of air went outwards across hills like a wave. The grass rippled in frenzy, hundreds of blades coming loose and whipping into the air. I felt myself being pulled back by the draft, my trapped arms the only reason I wasn't tossed across the field. Turning, I watched the monster at the front, who'd been just about to hurl another clay ball, splatter backwards, becoming just another smear of mud on the grass. Six more of the creatures were similarly destroyed.

But the remaining five were further back, and the strength of Mercury's attack had lessened by the time it reached them. The gust had toppled them all, but once the wind died out, their half-solid bodies began taking shape again. To my horror, three that had lost larger pieces merged into one giant monster, and they all continued their pursuit.

Mercury was panting, wings drooping nearly to the ground. I knew a blast like that would have taken tremendous strength, and even the Ethereal was not without their limits.

I tried to push up to my feet, determined to use the opening Mercury had given me to escape.

My arms remained buried in the earth.

"Are you kidding me?!" I hissed through the grass at my face. I could hear the distant squelch of steps as the monsters kept pressing forward.

The hardened earth held my arms at an awkward angle, so I shifted myself to my knees to get more leverage. Clenching my teeth, I pulled with all my strength, but the ground held me firmly in place. My breaths came in quick gasps as I tried to wrench myself free.

Quicksilver paws stepped into my line of vision.

"Told you."

"Would you stop analyzing my magic and get me out?!"

"I can't! You're afraid, and your magic is trying to protect you! You'd be able to control this if you'd been practicing."

I pulled so hard my shoulders burned. Tears rolled down my cheeks, brought on by the pain or panic. It was no use.

Mercury sat beside me, brushing the grass out of my face with a gentle sweep of a paw. Their tone became soft. "You need to let go of the fear."

A part of me knew they were right, but the sound of the creatures was getting louder. Had they sped up? I turned to check, but a smoky wing blocked my vision.

"Don't worry about them. Take a deep breath. It's only you and me."

"It's not, though! I can't believe I finally left the castle for the first time in years only to die in a fucking field!"

The earth around my arms pressed tighter. A sob escaped my throat.

"What did I say to you the first time we met? Do you remember?"

It was hopeless. I was as good as dead.

"Phoebe," Mercury insisted, batting me on the head, "do you remember?"

The insolence of the action startled me, and the memory cut through. "Of course I remember. I thought you were a hallucination."

"What did I say to you?" Their voice was calm and velvety, like we didn't have a care in the world.

Laying my head on the ground in defeat, I gasped for breath.

"You told me that I was this powerful for a reason. And if I learned to master it, I could help a lot of people, including myself."

"Exactly. And for all I harass you, you are still powerful. Look at this! Yesterday you could hardly fill a hole without bursting a blood vessel. Now, you've crafted a hold so solid it may as well be stone!"

My body was trembling so hard it hurt, but I focused only on their words.

"It's okay to be afraid. But that fear isn't helping you right now. So take a deep breath, and let it go."

Squeezing my eyes shut, I inhaled as much air as I could,

ignoring how the grass tickled my nose. The earth that held me smelled musty and rich, and I let it flood my senses. I held the breath for a few seconds, then slowly hissed it out through my teeth.

"Again," Mercury instructed.

I visualized my fear leaving my body with each exhale, letting it take shape and crouch before me like a goblin.

"You're not bad," I whispered, "but I don't need you right now. Please let go."

The ground vibrated with each step the monsters took.

In my mind, the fear goblin evaporated, leaving me alone and safe.

The earth trapping my arms crumbled to loose soil, freeing me instantly.

I—I did it.

"Oh, thank The Goddesses," Mercury exclaimed. The soft voice was gone, replaced with panic. "I didn't have another plan if that didn't work!"

They stepped back, and I realized the ground around me was smattered with clay balls, some smashed deep into the ground. Mercury must have been deflecting them the whole time without me noticing.

Exhaustion dragged me down like an anchor. Rolling, I found the giant conjoined monster less than twenty feet from me. This close, I realized what had bothered me about its eyes: there were none. Instead, the creature had two gaping holes that glowed with a dark light, which were currently focused on me. My arms ached from being trapped, but I threw them out in front of me, calling my Glacies power forth. An icicle the length of my hand formed, shooting out toward the creature.

It missed. By a lot.

"How have you gotten so bad at this?" Mercury cried.

I shot another icicle. This one lodged into the creature's

shoulder, which would have been impressive except I'd been aiming for its head. I doubted the monster had organs to puncture, but it stumbled backwards at the force. Using the opening, I resumed racing up the hill, though much slower this time. But it didn't matter. I was almost at the top. All I had to do was get far enough ahead to call for Boss.

"Stop!"

I froze, unsure why Mercury had instructed me to halt, until I heard the crunch of footsteps in grass.

This time, it was coming from the other side of the hill.

I was trapped.

The giant monster behind me righted itself, not even bothering to remove the icicle stuck deep in its body.

"Fire! Phoebe, use fire!"

I knew I was drained, that even the adrenalin in my system wasn't enough to perform miracles, but I threw out my hand anyway, screaming in rage and defeat.

An enormous arc of flame shot down the hill, incinerating everything in its path. It was blinding in the dying evening light, and I flinched back with a gasp. Even with my eyes squeezed shut, I could feel intense heat radiating past me with a vengeance. I waited, praying I wasn't about to be engulfed in flames, until the heat subsided.

Cracking my eyes open, I saw the monster before me had withered, crumbling into dust. The remaining monsters slowed as their forms began to harden, baked in the heat of the incredible flame.

Mercury turned to me with awe in their eyes. "That was amazing! I didn't know you had it in you!"

"I don't have it in me," I stammered. "I didn't do that."

Following the line of scorched grass, we looked upward to see a figure standing at the top of this hill.

10

Even in the near-darkness, I could see that the young woman standing at the crest of the hill had murder in her eyes. Fortunately, those eyes were trained on the remaining monsters who were again attempting to climb the hill. Their movements were even more erratic than before, and chunks of hardened clay broke off them with each step. She formed a fireball with a wave of her hand, her dark brown skin alight in the glow. Tight black curls billowed around her in the breeze, and her full lips were pinched tight with concentration and rage.

Mouths agape, Mercury and I exchanged a glance.

Ignoring us, the stranger marched down the hill toward the remaining monsters. The grass around her wilted in the heat of her flames.

"Do we try to help?" the Ethereal whispered.

I looked at the woman's squared shoulders and raised chin. "I think she's got it covered."

When she was thirty paces from the creatures, the woman threw her arms forward and unleashed with a scream. A wall of flame larger than any I'd ever seen cut a path through the grass, drowning out her voice and engulfing both monsters, burning them to nothing in the span of seconds.

She kept going long after the monsters were gone. The grass was too lush for the flames to spread far, but smoke filled the air. I covered my nose as my eyes burned, but I refused to lower my gaze from the stranger. Her power was staggering. She didn't even look winded, neither from the magic nor the climb up the hill.

She finally waved a hand, snuffing out the lingering flames on the hills. The sun had set and darkness had swooped in, and without the flame, I lost sight of the Ignis in the smoke.

"We need to find Boss," I whispered to Mercury. "Can you locate him from the sky?"

"Of course. But what are you going to do?"

"I'm going to go say hi. And I don't want you to give us away."

"Alone? What if she wants to hurt you too? She could *definitely* kick your butt."

"Thank you for that vote of confidence," I grumbled, knowing they were correct. "But if she meant me harm, she'd have let the sludge monsters finish me before she blasted them off the face of the earth."

"Humph. Fine, but be careful." With that, Mercury took off.

I stumbled down the hill toward where I'd last seen the Ignis, moving as quickly as my drained body could manage. I didn't even feel strong enough to create a flicker of flame to see by. So when I reached the bottom of the hill, coughing loudly with each gasping breath, I nearly ran directly into the stranger.

She was still standing over the charred stretch where the final monsters had been, though nothing remained of them now except the faint glow of embers in the grass. I took several steps back, giving her space. It took all my willpower not to brace my hands on my knees.

"Thank you for saving us—er—me."

Her expression was unreadable, but her posture remained tall and defiant. She appeared to be a few years younger than I was, but there was a hardness in her eyes.

Unsure if she'd heard me through my wheezing, I tried again. "That was amazing. I've never seen anyone control Ignis magic that way."

The only response was the rustling of the grass around us and the occasional crackle of embers. To my relief, the breeze began clearing the smoke from the area, and my breathing eased. I could see the woman's eyes narrow as she studied an arc of blackened grass. It curled slightly away from the rest of the blast.

Chewing my lip, I tried one last time.

"Are you alright? Do you know what those things were?"

"You shouldn't be here," the Ignis said, still glaring at the deviating patch of burnt grass. Her voice was light and musical, at odds with her rigid posture. "It's not safe to travel near the Eastern Plains alone."

"I, uh, I'm looking for information. This is going to sounds strange and I can't tell you who I am, but—"

She finally turned to face me, summoning a ball of flame to her hand. While it was a far cry from her show of power moments before, it was enough to light the space around us.

"I know who you are. The flying silver cat kind of gave it away."

In a flash, Mercury was beside me, their wings spread wide. "I'm no cat!"

The stranger took a single step back, her eyes wide with shock. She quickly mastered her features, but something lingered in her eyes. Doubt.

"You really are the queen? The one who defeated Zaletor."

Mercury jumped in, their chest puffed with pride. "She is. But she has many other notable and impressive accomplishments and should not be defined by only one of them."

Glancing up at me, they gave an encouraging nod and what could only be described as a smile. I was torn between the desire to hug them or shrivel into a ball to die.

The Ignis glanced between us. "Um, okay then. Are you injured, Your Majesty?"

I winced. "No, and please, call me Phoebe. This is Mercury. Thank you for saving us."

Mercury muttered something about how they didn't need saving, but I ignored it, watching the stranger expectantly.

"My name is Vanessa," she conceded, "but I prefer to be called Ness."

"It's nice to meet you, Ness," I smiled. "Your power is incredible. The way you destroyed those things, it was perfect!"

"Almost perfect," she muttered, glaring back at the dead grass.

"Uh, well, you're still the strongest Ignis I've ever seen. It's so lucky you happened by when you did."

She shifted, and her guarded expression slipped as she sucked her teeth. "Actually, that was no coincidence. I didn't know if I could defeat the whole group of them at once, so I was following them, waiting for an opening."

"You used us as bait!" Though their voice was angry, Mercury looked upon the woman with a new respect.

"More like a distraction." Ness shrugged. "I circled around to this hill thinking I'd catch them unawares when they chased you over the top, but you struggled more than I anticipated."

I forced a laugh, feeling my cheeks grow hot. "Yeah, you could put it that way."

Ness's lips tightened, as if she was suppressing a smile, and I wondered if she'd heard me struggling with my magic before cresting the hill.

Mercury placed himself between us, demanding our attention. "Listen, I'd love to rehash how you saved Phoebe's ass, but not here. Those soggy creatures weren't something I've seen before, but they had an aura of dark energy. I don't want to be here if more show up, looking for their fallen friends. Boss is back toward the road, grazing happily, so I suggest we join him."

"If you need a place to stay, my village is a day's walk from here to the north. The creatures were just there, so there's quite a bit of damage being cleaned up, but I'm sure you'd find a warm welcome."

I frowned. "What do you mean they were there? Is that where they originated??"

Ness shook her head, her eyes darkening. "I don't know where they came from. They came and went last night under the cover of darkness."

Mercury pushed at my hip with a paw. "Horse. Road. That way. Walk."

I considered the rage in Ness's eyes and thought of those monsters wreaking havoc on my people. More than anything I wanted to go to the town, to survey the damage and help in any way I could. But we couldn't spare the time. And the odds were high that answers lay in the direction we were headed.

"Thank you, but at first light Mercury and I need to head into the Plains, and the best access point is from here." I gestured toward the direction of the road.

The light in Ness's hands flickered. "No one goes in there."

Mercury bounded into the air, hovering before us at eye level. "We need to leave. You've got ten seconds before I send you flying." With a final glare, they soared ahead toward Boss.

"We should listen," I sighed, moving to collect the saddle

and supplies from where they lay. By a stroke of luck, they had been spared from Ness's attack. I nodded my head toward the hill behind me. "They're undoubtedly tired from that blast, but they'll do it."

Following my nod, Ness seemed to notice the splatters of sludge monsters on the opposite hill for the first time. Her eyes went wide.

"Five seconds!" the Ethereal called.

Ness and I hurried to follow.

After collecting Boss, who appeared to have forgotten all about the danger and followed along tame as a lamb, we found a new place to camp for the night. It felt wrong, waiting to move on after an attack, but it was still wiser than entering the Plains before morning. We set up in silence, everyone exhausted and unsure what to say. Ness kept her light going as we went, and she created a campfire once we had settled into our new spot. We'd all agreed having a fire was preferable to getting attacked in the dark, even if it made us a target. Besides, it allowed me to study the Ignis from the corner of my eye.

Fire was a difficult Gift to master due to its fickle and hungry nature. I'd seen many expert wielders with fresh burns on their arms or face from a maneuver gone wrong. It was considered a worthy cost, providing a balance to a magic that could easily destroy.

The woman across from me had three scars on her forearms, one on the left and two on the right, but they were all small and faded. There were a few fresh cuts on her face and arms, but I attributed those to the monster attack in her village. Somehow, this woman had become the most powerful fire magician I'd ever seen with barely a mark to show for it.

"What?!" she finally demanded. "You're staring at me like I've got three heads!"

I started, realizing I wasn't so much watching her from the corner of my eye after all.

"Sorry! I'm just—how are you so powerful but not covered in scars?"

She gave a harsh laugh. "You do realize that's an extremely inappropriate question?"

"Yes, but I still want to know."

"I practice," she shrugged.

I waited, but she gave no further explanation. "That makes no sense! The act of practicing fire magic is what causes scars!"

The fire burned brighter. "I learned from my mistakes and adjusted, okay? And speaking of things that don't make sense, why are you going into the Eastern Plains?"

I leaned back, hoping to dodge the accusation in her voice. "I have business to attend to. Queen stuff."

Ness was undeterred, and apparently she took my insistence to call me by name as an open invitation to question my decisions. "Without guards or scouts? What could possibly be so important that you'd risk it?"

"That's none of your business."

"Well, my magic is none of *your* business."

"Question," Mercury said, coming to sit between us, "I thought the danger of the Eastern Plains was due to Zaletor. His magic and creatures and the like. But he's been gone for decades. Is it truly still dangerous to enter there?"

Ness and I looked at each other, both still simmering, but I sighed. As someone who lived on the region's outskirts, Ness's opinion would be more accurate than mine, so I held out a hand indicating she should answer the Ethereal's question. She frowned, but her tone was significantly calmer as she faced Mercury.

"There have always been stories. People talk about the terrors that roamed the Eastern Plains as if it were yesterday. Anytime a calf dies or a hailstorm destroys the crops, people blame the Dark Wizard. Parents still tell their children the Gladiators will take them away if they misbehave, things like that. But there hasn't been any actual activity...until recently."

Mercury and I both leaned closer, enthralled.

"People have seen lights glowing far out in the Plains, though no one is ever brave or foolish enough to go see what they are. Then, last night, those creatures marched into town and began attacking anything and everything. We fought off a few of them, but the others left as suddenly as they'd arrived. I don't think anyone was killed, but I can't be sure. I went after them as soon as I found their trail."

I remembered the way the creatures had dripped mud and dirty water as they moved. It would have been an easy trail to follow.

"It's clear you have a lot of anger toward them. Was a friend or family member injured?"

"No, it's not that." Her anger seemed to evaporate, and she pressed her lips tight together. Skies above, she was trying not to cry. I waited patiently, and even Mercury kept their mouth shut.

Ness took a deep breath. "I have—*had* a glassworks shop. I saved for years to buy it, and I spent months making it perfect. I heated most of the glass with my Gift, but I had a little kiln for the days I was tired or distracted. It was my dream come true. I spent thousands of hours creating everything from functional dinnerware to delicate works of art."

Tears brimmed in her brown eyes, clinging to her long lashes.

"They destroyed everything in a matter of minutes. They

knocked down a wall, and then the kiln exploded. And that was that. My dream is gone."

I stared into the fire, unsure of what condolences to offer. I couldn't imagine what it would be like to have everything you'd work for ripped away. Yes, the shop was a place, not a person, but the wound was still too fresh, the mourning too deep, to bring up such a thing now. And while the mayor of the region would be able to ask for funds to rebuild, the townspeople would prioritize fixing homes over shops. Keeping my mouth shut, I gave her the space to collect herself.

Mercury decided to go with a different approach.

"You're telling me you followed a dozen monsters for a full day toward the Eastern Plain, *alone*, before finally blasting them all to ash, just to get revenge over a destroyed glass shop?" Their voice was incredulous.

Ness looked at the Ethereal, the steel returning to her eyes, and nodded.

There was a beat of silence as Mercury gazed at her.

"Well, you are officially the most badass human I've ever met. You should come with us!"

"What?" Ness and I spoke at the same time.

"Think about it. There's clearly someone wielding some dark energy out there. Even if it's not 'you know who,' someone is stirring up trouble. Since you're still, shall we say, 'a work in progress,' we could use some extra muscle to help us out! And you," they turned to Ness, "you might get to blast more monsters! Wouldn't that be fun?!"

"Our mission is one of utmost secrecy," I reminded them, casting an apologetic smile at the Ignis.

"Oh please. She's already seen us together, destroyed a bunch of animated clay monsters, *and* you've told her where we're heading. Something tells me our secret is blown."

Mercury and I looked at Ness.

"You think Zaletor is back from the dead, and you're going to fight him again," she offered with a shrug.

Mercury crowed with triumph.

"We don't know anything for sure!" I exclaimed. "We're simply getting more information. But if it is true, you don't seem very concerned about it."

Ness shrugged again. "I don't really remember much from that time. I know things were terrible and people lived in fear, but mostly I remember the celebrations once you killed him. Everyone was dancing and crying, and because my Gift hadn't presented yet, Mama told me I could be anything I wanted when I grew up."

I considered this, how someone only a few years younger than myself had been able to live a carefree life, all because of what my friends and I had done. What I'd been willing to sacrifice.

Sensing my hesitation, Mercury continued. "You don't want to get the old gang back together, but what happens if we get where we're going, and you can't handle it on your own?"

Guilt and grief made my insides go cold.

"I can handle this on my own," I insisted. "Besides," I turned to Ness, "you don't want to come, do you?"

Ness paused, considering, and her gaze went to the dirt on my forearms from when I'd been trapped in the earth. "I don't want to intrude, but you do seem to be struggling with your magic. I can't in good conscience let you go into danger unprotected."

I saw it again, the hint of wariness in her eyes, and I realized what it was. She was disappointed. If she traveled with us, it would be out of pity. My cheeks burned with embarrassment, but I sat up straighter.

Mercury's head tilted in confusion. "What's the harm in having her with us?"

I couldn't send another person on a dangerous mission only for them to not come back. But I couldn't explain all that in front of Ness. And they were both looking at me like I was crazy.

While they might not have known my thoughts, Mercury clearly saw me struggling. "It's the right choice, Phoebe."

I chewed my lip, but sighed in resignation.

"What if I pay you to be my escort? It will only be for the next day or two, just until we leave the Eastern Plains, and with any luck it will be extremely boring." The arrival of the monsters had me shaken, but I still held on to my belief that Zaletor was dead and this was some sort of copycat.

A new interest glowed in Ness's face. "How much?"

"If you help me, I'll pay to rebuild your glass shop. Immediately."

I didn't know if I had enough in my pouch to cover all the expenses, but I had enough to make a down payment, and I could get the rest when I returned to the castle. I'd already planned to ensure the town was rebuilt using funds from the castle—The Goddesses knew we had enough—but I'd make sure Ness's shop was a priority.

For the first time since I'd met her, she smiled. It was small, hesitant, but the hope was undeniable. "Deal."

I offered a hand, and we shook on it.

As she settled in for the night, I found Mercury staring at me with a bemused look on their face. I cocked an eyebrow, curious what they were thinking, but the Ethereal merely smiled before curling up beside me.

11

Everything I'd seen so far of the kingdom had been lush and green. This was partially due to the season, as spring was in that fleeting time of bloom without a hint of summer's heat. The other factor was me. Or rather, my defeat of Zaletor, who had gripped the land in near-perpetual darkness for two hundred years, causing the world to wither. Since it had been so long since I'd traveled outside the capitol, it was wondrous to see the changes, to see everything look so alive.

The exception to this flourishing of life was the Eastern Plains. A vast space at the foot of a towering mountain, its barren rocks and scraggly brush piles looked exactly as they had twenty years ago, and it made my stomach turn. Even Boss hesitated when we veered down the dusty, unused road I knew would lead us there. Apparently, whatever vitality Zaletor had leached from the earth was gone for good.

Because of this, the whole region was uninhabited. At least, that's the reason my advisors gave. But I knew that even if this were the most fertile soil on earth, no citizen of

Bearnel would want to live in the shadow of Zaletor's mountain.

Mercury said they could sense dark energy as we approached, like ozone before a storm. They said it wasn't fresh, but lingered from all those years ago when vast amounts had been pulled through on a daily basis. Now it hung in the air, marking the area for what it was: tainted.

"It's more like a desert than a plain," I muttered as we stood looking out over the hell we were about to enter. "It's a shame we can't burn the whole thing to the ground."

Ness, who had been quiet through the morning's travel, came to stand beside me. "I've always wondered what type of glass this sand would make. But I've never been brave enough to try."

"It's for the best," Mercury said, "nothing good can come from here. Now let's go."

As they flew ahead, scouting for dangers, I glanced at Ness. She still stood tall, but now that we were here, I could see the hesitation in her face.

"You're not bound to me, you know," I whispered, "you can turn back at any point."

Her gaze snapped to mine. "We made a deal. I'm not backing out now."

And that was that.

It was a half day's walk to the site of Zaletor's tower. The plan was to get there as quickly as possible, then get out. Even if everything went right, it would be well after dark by the time we returned to the grasslands, but none of us wanted to stay any longer than necessary. The only positive aspect to this leg of the journey was that my training was paused. Mercury needed all of their focus to scan for any threats, even though it was nearly impossible for anything to sneak up on us. The wispy brush provided no cover, and the earth was perfectly flat. Even the road we walked on was barely differentiated from the landscape around it, the ancient cobblestones now covered with enough dirt to hide it from sight.

But we didn't truly need the road. Our destination rose before us in the distance.

The Dead Mountain was a single, craggy peak jutting from the earth. It looked out of place surrounded by the flat wasteland because it was. The mountain wasn't a naturally occurring landform; Zaletor had made it, ripping the earth upward, then constructing his tower at its base. I glared up at the mountain, even as I pushed back at the memories that came with it.

The tension among our group was high. Ness and I both walked, not wanting to burden Boss further now that he carried both our packs, and it didn't take long before my feet began to ache.

"So," I said, looking to distract myself from the pain, "were you born in Beeson? Or just had your shop there?"

She paused, startled, before resuming her pace. "I never told you I came from Beeson."

"I know, but that's the only village within a day's walk of where you were. Unless you were traveling much quicker than I calculated, in which case you were likely coming from Roseland. But Roseland is more a textile-based town, so I'm betting on Beeson. It's one of the country's top exporters of oils and potions, so glass bottles would be in high demand."

Ness stopped again. The expression on her face was almost concerned. "How do you know all that?"

I shrugged, but continued walking. I'd stopped feeling self-conscious of my hard-won assortment of knowledge years ago. "I made a point of learning about the people of this country. It seemed like something a queen should do."

The sound of her steps resumed as she caught up to me. "I

don't disagree. I'm merely surprised you followed through. Most people wouldn't."

Glancing over, I found Ness studied me closely, the barest hint of admiration showing in her eyes. *That* made me self-conscious. When I looked away, she loosed a breath.

"No, I wasn't born in Beeson. I moved there after completing my apprenticeship five years ago. Like you said, the area has a need for bottles and jars, so it seemed like a good place to set up shop."

A muggy breeze swept past, blowing more dirt over the road. There were no birds here, and the ghostly rattling of dried branches was the only sound aside from our steps and Boss's occasional snorts of displeasure.

"You moved there without knowing anyone?"

"I wanted to make a fresh start." There was a sharpness to her tone that told me she was finished with the topic at hand.

Fair enough. I was prepared to continue the trek in silence, when she cleared her throat.

"Is it true they're impervious to harm?" She nodded to where Mercury flew ahead of us. "I know the stories and all, but that part always seemed far-fetched."

"For all intents and purposes, Mercury is. I think there are things that can hurt them in the Ethereal Plane, but not in our world. They don't talk about that much, I think to be superior, but I've seen that infuriating creature take a crossbow bolt to the chest." I swallowed, remembering the terror I'd felt seeing the projectile hurtle toward them. "It shattered on contact. They didn't have a scratch."

"That's incredible. And all Ethereals are like that?" The Ignis shook her head. "I suppose it's for the best that their world is separate from ours."

"No kidding. But Mercury is special; as the Messenger for The Goddesses, they're the only one who can pass between worlds. They can even teleport from place to place here in our world, though they avoid it unless absolutely necessary, because of the dark energy it uses. Oh, and their Voice, which allows them to command. It's extremely loud."

With a flourish, the Ethereal looped in the air and descended, landing beside us on the road.

"I'm also devilishly beautiful and have exceptional hearing. If you're going to talk about all my great qualities, at least let me be part of the conversation."

"Ah yes," I nodded, "they're also a colossal narcissist."

Ness's face darkened as she eyed the preening Ethereal. "You can use dark energy? I thought it was bad?"

"It is, here in your world," Mercury explained, "but in the Ethereal Plane it's a natural force that flows through everything. Like a current of power connected to all things. When that power is pulled from my world into yours, some of your world's energy is sucked back in return." They waved a paw, gesturing at the desolate wasteland around us. "So it really should be avoided."

We reached the base of the mountain hours later. The earth rose up so suddenly from the surrounding plains, it was easy to imagine the entire thing had been dropped from the sky. At Mercury's direction, we traveled along the base until we arrived at a large crevice that curved inward. It wasn't a tunnel, as the sky was always visible overhead, and I knew from my last time here that the crevice stretched almost a mile into the mountain before opening into a large clearing. Still, even looking at it made me feel like I was suffocating.

The opening was unadorned. From a distance, it blended in perfectly with the surrounding rocks. But I knew this was the entrance to the Dark Wizard's lair. I could feel the tainted power drawing me in, even as my feet refused to move. I heard Mercury land beside me.

"Tell me again how much I need to do this," I whispered, unable to rip my eyes from the gaping maw of the mountain.

"*We* need to do this, if only to confirm there's nothing there."

I felt the barest hint of a wing brush my arm. I managed to blink, breaking the mountain's hold, and looked down at the Ethereal.

"I'll be right beside you every step of the way. Just think about how much you can rub it in my face about how right you were if there's nothing there."

Swallowing hard, I managed a smile. But my hand still trembled as I tugged Boss's reins, leading us into the mountain.

The sounds of the plains silenced as we moved into the crevice. It was like stepping into another world. A terrible world.

"How is this possible?"

I turned at the question and found Ness gazing around at the sheer rock walls rising up around us, the gray sky still visible overhead. She had a hand on Boss, gripping the saddle tight.

"The Dark Wizard was a powerful Terras," I said, returning my focus to the path ahead. "Long before we were born, he raised this mountain and the tower within it out of the earth, crafting both as he saw fit. The surface above is razor sharp, making it nearly impossible to scale, so this crevice is the only way in or out. It's why every army who tried to overthrow him was defeated."

"And why the six of you were able to sneak in," she realized.

I nodded, though she likely couldn't see it. "With the additional power he received from the Dark Lady Kalexia, he assumed no one would ever be able to defeat him. By the time I was born, there hadn't been an army large enough for him to consider a threat for nearly a century. In his arrogance, he had only two Gladiators guarding the mountain's entrance."

Getting in had actually been easy, but we were all so anxious throughout the journey it had seemed much more difficult at the time.

"The lingering dark energy is getting thicker," Mercury said, their quicksilver form churning. "We're almost there. The tower should be around that bend."

I remembered how the Ethereal had bristled at the energy in the air all those years ago. "We're lucky the bastard didn't blast a hole through the world, with all the power he drew from the Ethereal Plane."

"I've never understood why the Dark Lady gave him so much power," Ness muttered. I wondered if she was talking to alleviate her nervousness, as I had done out on the plains. "I remember the priestesses saying her eons of existence had made her cruel, but there must be more to it."

"She was bored," Mercury ranted, their ears flat. "While her sister Goddesses were content to spend eternity in peace, leaving the universe to exist in independence, Kalexia was restless. She opted to stir up trouble rather than sit still. That's the real reason she gave Zaletor near limitless power, simply to see what would happen."

Ness grappled with this startling reality. "She wasn't trying to destroy our world by opening pockets of dark energy, siphoned from the Ethereal Plane?"

Mercury snorted. "No, but I can see why your Citadel went with that story. It sounds much more nefarious."

I was worried the poor Ignis would have a breakdown if Mercury shattered any more long-standing beliefs, so I cleared my throat.

"In my opinion, it doesn't matter why she did it. The fact is, she did, and she was imprisoned. She can't hurt anyone again." I gestured ahead. "There's the yard."

They both fell silent as we reached the path's final curve. The open space of Zaletor's fortress would be concealed until we rounded that bend, but it didn't matter. I knew what we would find: a large, empty space. I could see the moment so clearly: I'd laugh with relief, but pretend it was a laugh of triumph. Mercury would act like they knew it would be empty the whole time, insisting they were merely doing their due diligence in checking. Ness would gaze around in awe, feeling the weight of the space even if she couldn't understand its full significance. And finally, we'd collect ourselves and leave. Mercury and I would formulate a new plan, and Ness would daydream about her new glass shop as we walked out, leaving this empty, dead space behind us, never to return.

That's what would happen, I decided. With a deep breath, I stepped confidently around the bend.

And froze.

"No." The word tumbled out of my mouth.

The height of the mountain walls meant the entire clearing was cast in shadow. But there was no mistaking the cylindrical tower that punched up from the ground at the far end. A single window was placed at the very top, looking down on the world with mocking haughtiness, and a lonely candle burned in the sill.

"Get over here!" Mercury cursed from the rock wall's edge. "Stay out of sight!"

I did no such thing. My memories surged forth, and this time I didn't stop them.

I could still smell the smoke, still feel the dust as it clung to the sweat on my skin. If I'd used magic, I could have leveled it all myself in a matter of minutes. But since I had defeated Zaletor alone, I'd wanted my friends to get the closure of destroying his stronghold. We did it together; I brought the main structure down, Tristan burned the furniture, Alto crumbled the smaller pieces, and Becca and Jax used hammers. It took three days, but we'd demolished all traces of the tower.

Now I gaped at the impossible tower, tucked like a parasite into the rock walls of the clearing. The single candle glowing in the top window mocked me with its presence. My brain struggled to comprehend how it could still be here when I could see the scouring marks on the surrounding walls from where we'd ripped it down.

"It's not tall enough," I realized. The marks on the wall stretched a good two dozen feet higher than the tower structure. "And weren't there more windows than just the one? This isn't the same tower!"

"Well, he must have rebuilt it. Phoebe, I'm begging you—wait!"

But I was already running. A smart person would be running back out of the chasm, putting as much distance between themselves and the danger as possible. I ran forward, straight to the tower.

But the terrain was different than I remembered, and I quickly slowed my pace, gasping for breath. What had been a flat stretch of rock was now filled with craters and mounds of various sizes. I had to tear my gaze from the tower to keep from falling into a hole. Each time, I expected to look up and find the whole thing had been my imagination. But each time, the tower loomed closer.

Mercury glided in front of me, blocking my path.

"Stop! What if he's in there?!"

"He was *dead*, Mercury! I'm telling you; he was dead!" I was shaking, from anger or fear, and my magic roiled beneath my skin like snakes. I didn't need to hold up my hands to know there were icicles on my fingers.

The Ethereal continued blocking me, their star-flecked eyes bright with worry. "Okay, I believe you! We'll figure this out, but please take a breath before you hurt yourself or Ness."

She had hung back by the clearing's entrance with Boss, but hearing her name, Ness stepped forward. The Ignis didn't appear to be afraid, but her wary gaze swept over everything in the clearing assessing for threats. Including me.

I swallowed and took a deep breath in through my nose. It wouldn't do any good if I burned myself out before even stepping inside. My magic calmed slightly, but I could feel it lurking inside me, waiting to be of use.

"Someone has definitely used dark energy here recently," Mercury said, studying the tower. "But I don't sense anyone drawing it now. Not like, well, not like last time."

As a creature of the Ethereal Plane, Mercury could feel when dark energy was being pulled into this world. Zaletor had used it constantly, like a powerful river flowing into his body. Mercury's ability had given my friends and me a huge advantage because we had always known where the Dark Wizard had been. If he had somehow survived, he was currently elsewhere.

The candle in the top window flickered enticingly.

"I need to know."

Mercury blew out a breath. "I suppose we've lost the element of surprise, anyway," they conceded. "But we go slowly. And you stay beside me at all times."

I nodded, just as Ness reached us.

"You don't have to come with us," I told her. "It's likely a death sentence."

Her eyes were wide, but she shook her head. "I'm with you."

I wanted to command her to leave for her own safety. But I knew that would be futile, so I gave her a tight-lipped smile.

"Alright then. Let's see who's home."

12

If I hadn't figured out from its exterior that this wasn't the original tower, its interior would have given it away in an instant. Gone were the shadowy alcoves I'd ducked into to avoid detection, or the labyrinth of corridors I'd had to memorize to find the central chamber. Even the elaborate tile mosaic, which Zaletor's crown had chipped when it fell, had been dug out of the ground. Now, the tower was a single, massive room. A crude set of stairs spiraled up the length of the structure, presumably leading to the window we'd seen. The only furniture was a battered table and chair pushed to one side and a cot opposite the door. This tower was a shadow, a pale imitation of what it had been.

But it was still here, which meant someone had built it.

For reasons I couldn't explain, I found the new, sparse approach terrifying. The open room made a surprise attack from the enemy impossible, but I still hesitated to step in more than absolutely necessary.

"Why would anyone rebuild this?" Though their voice was hushed, Mercury's words echoed through the empty space. I looked up, following the sound, then quickly returned my gaze to the floor as a wave of dizziness swept over me.

"I'm more worried about the 'who,'" I breathed, trying to regain my balance. "I don't know any Terra alive powerful enough to have done this."

"What about the Dark Lady?" Ness offered, wandering about the room. "Maybe she escaped and gave power to someone new."

Mercury shook their head. "The Goddesses ensured she could never be freed. They each used a small piece of their own essences to entomb her inside a prism. And since The Goddesses cannot be killed, they will keep her sealed for all eternity."

We all fell quiet at the thought. Considering Zaletor's actions, the Dark Lady's punishment seemed appropriate. Still, the idea of being trapped for eternity made me nearly as dizzy as the height of the tower.

Ness cleared her throat. "Well, whoever was living here has been gone for weeks." She kicked at a pile of rubbish next to the cot, sending an empty food tin rolling across the floor.

I ran a finger through the dust on top of the desk and hummed my agreement. There were a few pieces of paper scattered on the floor, but they were all blank.

"There's nothing down here, so that just leaves…" I risked a glance up again.

Though the clearing outside had remained in shadow, it was still brighter than the interior of the tower, and the window high above glowed like a beacon. The thought of climbing all those steps made me nauseous, but they had to lead somewhere. I shakily approached the bottom stair, breathing rapidly.

"I got this," Mercury said, stopping me with a wing. They took off, flying along the stairs around the tower, and were quickly out of sight. Still, my stomach rolled at the idea of going up *and* around that quickly.

Deciding there was nothing left for me there, I hurried outside, ignoring a confused look from Ness. Gulping down air, I pressed my back against the tower. The stone was cool, and the sensation would have been soothing if it weren't for the wrongness of it all. I slid to the ground, ignoring how the uneven stone of the tower pulled at my shirt, and pressed my forehead to my knees.

"Not a fan of heights?"

I didn't look up at Ness's question, only shook my head against my knees. I heard her sit beside me, but she didn't say anything more. It was only when my stomach had settled that I leaned my head back.

"When I was a kid living on the streets of Glassleaf, the ability to move quickly through the city was paramount. The other street kids always insisted the rooftops were the best way to get around, but every time I tried, I'd get dizzy and freeze. I spent years figuring out the quickest routes that didn't involve climbing buildings."

I swallowed, unsure why I was telling her all this. But she didn't interrupt, and my heartbeat was slowing down, so I continued.

"My coronation parade was almost canceled because I was too afraid to stand on the float. Becca held my hand the entire time, even though I was definitely crushing her fingers." I smiled at the memory I'd somehow forgotten. "Anyway, I was able to overcome some of it as the years went on, but great heights still make me dizzy."

Ness was silent, and I felt a rush of embarrassment at my babbling. I was about to push myself up when she spoke.

"I'm afraid of cows."

I blinked. Her tone had been reluctant, so I waited, giving

her the choice of whether or not to say more. She cleared her throat awkwardly.

"When I was seven, I got trampled by a panicked herd. I got lucky, just a broken arm and a bunch of bruises, but I still have nightmares about cows with razor-sharp hooves."

Suddenly, I wondered if the scars I'd seen on her arms were from her accident instead of magic gone awry. If that was true, it meant Ness had always possessed an unparalleled level of control. But I held back my questions, trying to show her the same level of courtesy she'd shown me. We sat in silence for another minute before Mercury emerged from the tower.

There was something in their mouth.

The Ethereal dropped a scrap of paper on the ground beside me, but I made no move to grab it. Shifting their wings, they said, "The candle is ever-burning. It's impossible to tell how long it's been there, but this was tucked underneath it."

I thought back to the ever-burning candle at the castle, beneath the image of Becca, and nodded. When I still didn't touch the paper, Ness reached across me and grabbed it.

"The Holy One Has Returned," she read. "What does that mean? Is it talking about you? Because you returned here?"

I was too tired to panic. Too drained to scream or smash things. Mercury stayed quiet, waiting for the explanation they knew was coming. I took a breath, filling my lungs to the point of bursting, then hissing it out through my teeth.

"It's not talking about me. In our final confrontation, Zaletor referred to himself as Kalexia's holy instrument. He said it was her will that he rule over the earth."

I let the truth settle into me, even as I said it out loud.

"It's possible Zaletor is alive."

Only Boss was excited as we made our way out of the crevice and back into the Eastern Plains. In his mind, our journey was done, and we were returning to safety. I envied him.

Mercury, Ness, and I hadn't spoken much since leaving the tower. I'd burned Zaletor's note in my hand, not wanting to leave it for anyone else to find, but the words haunted my steps. I knew it was possible someone else had written it, but it felt too reckless to hope for that.

We reached the edge of the Eastern Plains while the moon was still rising. Once the rocky dirt turned to grass, we stopped.

"Are you alright?" Mercury finally asked.

I'd spent the last few hours considering that very thing, and shook my head.

"I failed. All these years, I truly thought I'd killed him. What are people going to say when they find out? I let them make me queen, but it's all been a lie."

"Not a lie," Mercury insisted, "just...an unknown error."

I wanted to roll my eyes, but fear sat like a stone in my belly.

"Mercury, what if Zaletor is alive because I didn't die? What if, by bringing me back, we enabled him to come back too?"

It was all about balance, after all. But the Ethereal shook their head.

"This is something else. Maybe he'd been sustained by stolen souls for so long that he was able to avoid true death, and he's been clawing his way back to life ever since."

I tried to believe them, but the guilt was consuming me. I could only nod my head.

Ness, who had been busying herself setting up camp and pretending to ignore us, paused. "I thought he was immortal?"

"That's what he wanted everyone to think," Mercury said. "In truth, he discovered a way to keep himself alive using the souls of others."

I sighed, rubbing my temples. Ness knew so many other secrets, what was one more?

"It was his deepest secret. An extremely powerful Specter can pull the soul out of a living person, killing them. Zaletor's Specter, Broin, was strong enough to not only rip people's souls out, he could put them into others, extending their lives. That's why they took so many prisoners alive.

"Broin put the souls of people without magic into the statues Zaletor made, creating Gladiators. He put the souls of Gifted wielders into the two of them, keeping them alive and unageing for two centuries. They kept it secret to preserve the 'Goddess-Blessed Immortal Emperor' image Zaletor had crafted."

This had been the fate of Tristan's brother, Marcus. Tristan's quest for vengeance was what had led our paths to cross.

"Realizing this was the key to defeating them. Becca killed Broin in a Specter battle for the ages, while I used my own Specter gift to pull out the trapped souls from Zaletor's body. He aged two hundred years in an instant. Afterward, we decided to keep the truth behind his immortality to ourselves. We didn't want any other Specters to try what they did. Besides, people feared Specters enough as it was; I didn't want to add to that."

It all sounded so simple now, but it had taken us months of fighting and planning to get into that tower.

"Where did he get the wielders?" Ness asked, interrupting my memories.

Anger cut through my exhaustion as Mercury and I glanced at each other. "People turned them in," I replied. "It's easy to forget that there were those who supported Zaletor, who helped enable his rule. There was a whole secret organization tasked with kidnapping and supplying captured wielders to the emperor. Anyone with an abnormally powerful Gift was a target."

Or any level of Specter, I thought, picturing Becca's smiling face.

Ness cursed. "That's horrible. What kind of person would do such a thing?"

I'd always wondered the same. But now I had more distressing things to worry about. Mercury's suggestion that Zaletor had escaped death because of his years absorbing soul magic was terrifying, but I frowned, remembering the sludge monsters and the imperfect tower.

"If your idea is correct, he must still be building up his strength. Those monsters weren't nearly as dangerous as the Gladiators I remember. I don't think they even had souls inside. They were too reactive and stupid. And we still need to consider that it might be some sick copycat."

"Whoever it is, you'll be able to handle them," Ness stated as she shook out her blanket. "Even if it is Zaletor, you beat him once; you can do it again."

She stretched out on the ground, relaxing in the soft grass, as though it were that simple. The conviction in her voice was startling, especially considering how all she'd seen me do so far was fail. It was...nice. I pulled a few coins out of my pouch, tucking them into my boot for the trip back, and tossed the bag toward her. It landed near her blanket with a musical jostling of metal.

"The downpayment for your new shop," I explained, when she looked up in confusion. "I can send you more when I get back to the castle, but we've returned safely from the Eastern Plains. Your promise has been fulfilled."

Ness stared at the pouch beside her, her full lips pressing together tightly, then shook her head.

"I can't take this yet. I remember you explicitly said that if I helped you, you'd pay for my glass shop. Well, you're clearly still in need of help." She tossed the pouch back to me, her aim much better than mine, and snuggled into her blanket. "I'll take the money when you don't need me anymore."

Part of me wanted to argue, to insist it was too dangerous and that she should return home rather than risk getting hurt. But how could I prevent her from following me or telling others what was happening unless I kept her close?

"What do we do now?" Mercury asked, sitting beside me.

I considered the options.

The rational thing would be to return to the castle immediately, mobilize the military, and send them out to find and fight the threat. It might be difficult to find a lone dark magic user, but if we sent out a message to every city explaining that someone was using dark energy to create mayhem, and there was a possibility Zaletor was alive, everyone would be on the lookout. If he was out there somewhere, someone would see him.

It was the smart, safe thing to do.

But I chewed my lip.

Once that message went out, there would be no taking it back. Yes, someone had stolen the crown from the castle, was creating monsters, and was using dark energy for unknown purposes. But if I told people Zaletor was back, everyone would panic. People would be suspicious of every Specter alive, and rational thought would be lost. Then if it turned out the culprit was someone else, it would all have been for nothing. No one would ever trust me again.

And if, *if*, he was alive, the last thing I wanted was people trying to fight him alone. Zaletor had defeated full armies during his reign, and even if he wasn't to full power yet, there was no telling the harm he could do. Part of why my friends and I had been able to defeat him the last time was because we were a small group, keeping our actions secret. My magic was getting stronger, albeit more slowly than I'd like. But now that I had a goal, I would work harder. I wouldn't risk the lives of others when there was still a chance that I could finish this before anyone found out. Then I could return to the castle and act like none of this had ever happened.

And you don't want the world to know you messed up.

The thought wormed into my brain unbidden, and I shook my head to clear it.

"Now we head to Linipa. It's a two-day trek to get there, so we'll have plenty of time for magic lessons as we go."

Mercury's eyes narrowed. "Is this about returning that guy's horse?"

The image of Kitt's smile made my chest tighten in a strange, pleasant way, but I shook my head.

"We'll do that too, because we promised, but there's someone else in Linipa we need to find. If Zaletor is back, even at a fraction of his normal power, there's someone we need to talk to."

13

The only friend I had kept in contact with was Alto. I hadn't seen him in person for a decade, but we traded messages two or three times a year. Mostly pleasantries, and I'd long ago given up asking when he was next coming to visit the castle, but I'd always read every letter with care and responded as quickly as I was able. My hope was he'd also stayed in contact with Jax and would know where to find him.

I still hated the idea of bringing my old friends into this mess, especially since our relationship was currently...complicated. But they both had skills and knowledge that would be of use. I explained all this to Mercury and Ness as we sat in the grass outside the Eastern Plains. Mercury nodded when I finished laying out the plan.

"And with any luck, one of those two can tell us where to find Tri—"

"I think we'll be good without him," I glared.

For the two days of travel it took to get to Linpa, Mercury passed the role of magic tutor over to Ness, who took to the job with gusto. She instructed me to create a ball of flame, then make it grow and shrink as she commanded. Every time I tried to make the flame grow, the ball refused to get any larger. And every time I wanted it to shrink, it extinguished. Finally, she stopped me.

"You're worrying too much. Imagine the warmth of your own body. You create it without even thinking. All Gifts come from within, but being an Ignis means your ability is a part of you more than others. So don't fear it, because it's all coming from you." She considered for a moment, then brightened. "For the rest of the morning, don't create any flame. Just think about your own body heat. We'll start there."

As it turned out, thinking about flame was much easier than creating flame. But her words were never far from my mind as we shuffled along with a crowd toward the city.

Unlike the other large cities in Bearnel, Linipa was completely surrounded by an imposing stone wall. It was a holdover from Zaletor's time, when Gladiators and other terrors could attack at any moment. The citizens had constructed it, hoping it would keep them safe. It didn't, not when the Dark Wizard could make monsters capable of flight, but the wall's mere existence helped some people sleep better. There were no threats to the city anymore and the gates weren't guarded, but I remember hearing they were still sealed every night, out of habit and memory.

We arrived on a warm, windless afternoon. Since we were entering the city on the eastern side, we'd meet with Kitt first. Once we'd returned Boss and collected the new horse Kitt had hopefully acquired, we'd continue south through the city and to where I knew we'd find Alto. It was the obvious plan based on the city's layout, but I was glad to be seeing Kitt first. I found myself excited to see the trapper again, even though it would only be for a few minutes.

"Tell me about Alto and Jax," Ness said as we approached the gate. "You are so different from what the stories say, in all the best ways of course, so I'm curious if the same is true of them."

I noticed that she'd specified those two, leaving Tristan conspicuously out of the conversation. We walked with the flow of people headed into the city, with Boss in between us. Mercury had crammed their mist into one of the packs so as to stay with us unnoticed. Normally I wouldn't talk about my past with so many people around, but no one was paying attention to us. Everyone we passed appeared tired and occupied with their own thoughts, making Ness and I essentially invisible.

"Alto was quiet. He's a Terra, but his true power always lay in his intelligence. He's a year younger than me, so he was fourteen when Becca and I found him. While the more powerful Terras were taken to the tower for Zaletor to—well, those with weaker gifts were forced to work in his mines. We'd liberated the work camp, freeing the Terras enslaved there and cutting off Zaletor's access to steel and gold. Most of the Terras had fled, anxious to return home or hide in the mountains near the sea. But Alto had wanted to help. I admit, we were skeptical at first, because of his youth and rudimentary magic, but it quickly became clear that he was a brilliant strategist.

"And whatever you've heard about Jax is probably true. He was a thief we, uh, *encountered*, early on. To this day, I've never seen a better swordsman, nor a person more in love with himself. Be warned that whenever we find him, unless he has changed drastically, he *will* hit on you."

Ness laughed, the first true laugh I'd heard from her, and I smiled at the sound.

"Thanks for the warning," she smirked. "When was the last time you saw either of them?"

My smile faded.

"It's been years. They were both infatuated with Becca. She never returned either of their affections, and they'd both understood that, but it was still difficult for them when she died. Jax adopted a few bad behaviors and left rather than address the issue, and Alto said he needed to get away because everything reminded him of her."

I kept my face relaxed, a trick I'd picked up from years of Council meetings and discussions with the Citadel High Priestesses. It was something I'd learned to do when I was keeping information to myself. My answer wasn't a lie, but it wasn't the whole story.

Especially in Jax's case.

After we'd defeated Zaletor, Jax had adapted best to the notoriety. He'd loved living in the castle, buying expensive things and being recognized everywhere he went. But when Becca died, he'd changed. He started spending money faster than I could keep track, and he was drunk more often than not. I knew it was grief, we were all handling it differently, and his approach was self-destruction, so I gave him time.

But things only got worse as the weeks went by. I found out he'd started gambling and owed lots of people money, money he expected me to pay because I always had. Then, he had shown up to a dinner with foreign ambassadors too drunk to stand. Tristan had managed to escort him out of the dining hall before anyone else could notice, but that had been the moment I realized something had to be done.

The next day, I'd informed Jax he needed to clean up and start earning his own money. Tristan and I had come up with several options: trade ambassador, fencing instructor, speech writer. All of which would have allowed him to remain living in the comfort of the castle, but we'd made it clear that his unlimited access to the treasury was finished. I had told him I would no longer pay his debts, and that the castle would no longer provide alcohol. I'd tried to be fair, thinking that if we all took a break from drinking, it would be easier for him to do so. Despite my frustrations, Jax was still my family. And he had been hurting.

Jax hadn't seen it that way. He'd screamed that we'd turned against him, that we were putting a target on his back by not paying the debts he owed. Tristan had tried to calm him down, saying we merely wanted Jax to be happy, and that was when things had truly turned ugly. In his anger and hurt, Jax had asked why we bothered to care about his happiness when we didn't bother with our own.

"You think I don't see it?!" he'd shouted, "The two of you don't even speak anymore unless you're fighting or you think someone's watching. I can hear you, you know, up in your rooms arguing."

I could still remember how my hands shook with the effort to keep the ice at bay. I'd told him to stop talking, mostly because I was struggling to keep my emotions in check, but he'd taken it as a challenge.

"*Everyone* is talking. About how Tristan sleeps in his room instead of with you. They all seem to think it's the grief, that Becca's death has driven you apart, but I know it started long before then. That it's the ice in your veins that—"

I'd never know what else he would have said because then Tristan had punched him. The sound of fist hitting flesh had been more painful than my friend's words. Like the final thread holding a tapestry together snapping apart.

Jax had spit a glob of blood on the floor, and left.

I had called off my wedding a month later.

A week after Jax left, a letter had arrived. It wasn't signed, but I'd recognized the sloppy handwriting. It had only two words: "I'm sorry." At that point I hadn't been ready to forgive him, but there was no return address, no information about where Jax was, so I couldn't have responded even if I'd wanted to. That was the last time I'd heard from him directly. I'd tried to keep tabs on him, mostly to make sure he didn't hurt himself or do anything too stupid, but he moved around so quickly, I'd lost track after a few months.

In my heart, I'd forgiven him long ago. His words had been ugly and uncalled for, and I certainly wished he'd been less of an ass about the whole thing, but I'd needed to hear the truth. Tristan and I hadn't been happy, but we'd both been prepared to live our lives that way because we'd thought it was best for the kingdom. Jax's accusations had made me see that we weren't fooling anyone and that trying to force the issue would only cause greater problems down the road.

Still, I kept all of that to myself, not wanting the pity or indignation that Mercury or Ness might feel. But as we walked, I felt the pack shift beside me, and wondered if it was Mercury's way of letting me know that they were there for me. Even if it was a coincidence, I took comfort in it.

"I can't guarantee either of them will be particularly happy to see me," I finished, "especially with the news we're bringing. But they're family. The only family I've got."

The gate came into view ahead of us, and we were forced to slow our pace as people funneled into the city.

"Family is a tricky thing," Ness said. I couldn't see her face, but her tone was serious.

"Where is your family?"

Ness was quiet for a moment. I wondered if she wouldn't answer.

"My parents have a ranch to the southeast, near Carscia. When my Gift presented, it was clear I was more powerful than the average Ignis. But they wanted me to be better. They made me practice every day. 'Only perfection will do,' my mother always said. They told me The Goddesses had given me extra blessings, and I needed to be worthy of them. That I should show my gratitude by devoting my life to them and becoming a Priestess when I came of age. I did the training; I honed my gift. But I had a different dream. My parents were… less than pleased with my decision. I haven't spoken to them since I left."

Much like my answer, Ness's response seemed like it was leaving several things out. Still, I grimaced. I couldn't imagine putting the pressure of perfection on a child, especially on one with such a dangerous gift. Perhaps her parents felt they were keeping her safe. But I remembered Ness's face when she saw that a blast of flame had gone awry. Aiming for perfection, even now. I wondered how many of her scars were invisible.

"I'm sorry," I said, "it must have been very difficult for you to leave like that. But I'm glad you found a path that brings you joy."

"Sounds like you and Phoebe had opposite problems when it came to parents," Mercury grumbled from the pack. I glanced around, anxious someone may have heard the disembodied voice, but no one paid us any mind.

"I thought your parents died?" Ness looked at me over the top of Boss's saddle, her brows furrowed. "They say you were an orphan on the streets because your parents died before your Gifts presented."

I stiffened as Mercury's voice came again, this time edged with anger. "Why would people say that?"

Shit.

"There are too many people around to have this conversation," I evaded. I knew exactly what the Ethereal would say if they knew the truth about what the Citadel had done.

Unfortunately, that turned out to be the wrong thing to say.

"Now you *have* to tell me!" the pack hissed. It shifted again, startling Boss. The stallion paused, tossing his head.

"Fine fine fine!" I whispered, soothing the horse. "But you have to promise to stop scaring the horse!"

The bag stopped moving, though I noticed Mercury made no promises to remain calm, and soon Boss resumed walking. Steeling myself, I took a breath.

"The Citadel decided it was better to say my parents died. The fact that they abandoned me when they found out I had more than one Gift never sat comfortably with the Priestesses."

"They abandoned you?" Ness's eyes were wide as she gazed at me.

"More like discarded!" I could hear the rage in Mercury's voice, though the pack remained blessedly still. "And the Citadel had the nerve to say they died?!"

I couldn't help the small smile that crossed my face. Though it had been years since I'd heard their familiar rant, I was well aware of Mercury's feelings about the people who birthed me. The wounds from my abandonment were long-since healed, but I still remembered those days vividly.

Ness still stared at me in confusion, and I recalled she had been too young to remember how bad things had been under Zaletor.

"Nowadays, Gifts are considered a blessing. But during Zaletor's reign, they were seen as potential threats. Most people kept their Gifts hidden for fear of being taken to work in the mines, or worse. When I manifested my Glacies magic at six, my parents were surprised, but they said it would be easy to hide. Then, a few weeks later, I got angry and lit a tablecloth on fire with my bare hands. They explained it away, thinking it was impossible for me to also have Ignis magic. But when I blasted apart a stone wall because my favorite toy was locked on the other side, they knew I was...different. And they were afraid. We didn't know I was Goddess-blessed at that point; they simply thought I was dangerous. Without waiting to see if I had

Anima as well, they dumped me on a street corner in Glassleaf and never looked back."

Ness's mouth hung open. "Why didn't the Priestesses take you in?"

I waited a moment as a man with a cart hurried past, then shrugged. "There were no Priestesses. Back then, the Citadel was ruled by Zaletor's cronies. They acknowledged the existence of all five Goddesses, but they described Kalexia as the most powerful and Zaletor as her instrument. They kept tabs on all Gifted people who came to their door, and many were whisked off to the Tower, never to be seen again. I wasn't the only orphan child whose parents chose to leave rather than risk attention. Besides, I was different. I didn't know why, but I knew if anyone found out, they'd take me straight to him."

The pack seemed to be trembling. A few tendrils of silver curled out from inside, seething. "You let them change your origin story?"

Shame filled me, but I nodded. "I was young. After his defeat, Zaletor's leaders within the Citadel were quickly overthrown by the Priestesses, who had been keeping the original Order alive in secret for two hundred years. I think they were ashamed that people had become so afraid of Gifts that parents would abandon their children rather than protect them. They thought telling everyone that my parents had died would be a good step away from that mentality."

"And you agreed to it?!"

"I didn't know what else to do!" I countered, "And I figured that way, if my parents ever came back and tried to be part of my life again, I could claim they were liars looking for attention, since my real parents had died when I was young. I was a child, and I was hurt. I didn't want them trying to weasel their way back into my life just because they found out I was a Goddess-blessed queen."

Mercury was silent and the bag went still. I was glad they were tucked away so that I wouldn't have to read the expression in their eyes.

"Did they ever come back?" Ness asked.

I stared ahead, not seeing anything.

"No. They never did."

14

The Leather Shoe Inn was a three-story stone building near Linipa's Citadel. Its main floor was a tavern, packed with well-worn tables and chairs and a massive fireplace along the south wall, while its upper floors held guest rooms. The elegantly painted sign out front featured a boot with the sole coming off, and I smiled as I watched it sway in the breeze. I'd suggested it to Kitt as our meeting place because it was one of the few places I'd visited in person, and I was pleased to see it looked exactly the same as the last time I'd been there.

When I was named queen, my official coronation ceremony had been held at the main Citadel in Glassleaf. It was a pompous and tedious affair that I had very little say in, but it was an event for the people. After that, I'd traveled to all the major cities, where a smaller ceremony was conducted at each local Citadel. I'd spend a full day in each city, overseeing feasts and events, then be whisked off to the next. It had been exhausting.

Linipa was at the halfway point in this procession, and I'd

been nearing burnout. To blow off some steam that night, Becca and I had excused ourselves from the formal dinner under the guise of menstrual pains, changed into our real clothes, and slipped out into the city. We'd spent the entire night at the Leather Shoe, drinking with people who had no idea of our true identities, singing off-key with whatever song the minstrels were playing, and reveling in the fact that we were alive. We'd made it through.

When we'd finally stumbled back to our rooms, Becca had spun me to face her.

"You're a phoenix!" she'd slurred, squishing my face between her hands. "You're unstoppable and no matter what pushes you down, you're going to rise up again! And I fucking love you!"

I'd squeezed her shoulders, overcome with drunken emotion. "I love you too! I couldn't have done any of this without you. And you're just as amazing and powerful! You're a...a...super impressive animal!"

We'd laughed and cried and staggered our way to the nearest couch.

The following day had been rough, both because of the hangover and because of our friends. Tristan had been furious when he found out, scolding us for our immaturity and seething with frustration as we stopped the carriage four times to vomit out the door. Alto had felt similarly, but he opted to glower the whole trip instead of berating us. He'd probably figured Tristan was yelling enough for the both of them. And Jax was upset he hadn't been invited.

But I had no regrets, because that night with Becca at the Leather Shoe was one of the best of my life.

We left Boss in the stables behind the inn. Mercury wasn't pleased about staying in the saddlebag, but I pointed out that they were the one who had insisted on coming with us into the city. At least I wouldn't have to worry about anyone stealing anything. As much as I didn't want anyone to learn of Mercury's presence, I rather liked the idea of a robber opening the saddleback to discover the Ethereal grinning up at them.

Considering the amount of people we'd seen entering the city, I wasn't surprised to find the Leather Shoe packed full of patrons. The tavern had a cheerful atmosphere, and I wondered if there was some occasion for the crowds and the festive feel. I gazed around the room, seeing many tall, bearded men but not the tall, bearded man I was looking for.

I counted the days in my head since I'd met him in Glassleaf. We'd agreed to meet here in six days' time, and I was a full day early. Had he not arrived yet? Or had something gone wrong, and he hadn't been able to get another horse? My heart began to race as all the possibilities filled my head.

Oh Goddesses, I'd never even told him my name!

"You came."

I turned toward the deep voice behind me, finding Kitt's gentle face grinning, and smiled with relief. He was dressed in a linen tunic similar to my own, the patchwork jacket presumably discarded due to the hot weather.

"You sound surprised. I promised I'd be here. Boss is safe and sound in the stable out back."

His grin widened at the horse's name, but the look in Kitt's eyes was still one of astonishment. He looked me over, but there was nothing lecherous in his gaze. It was more like he was checking me for injuries or missing limbs. We were standing near the doorway, undoubtedly obstructing traffic, and when the door opened again, I had to step out of the way, closer to Kitt. The familiar scent of moss and rain filled my senses. The smell of the burgundy blanket, which had comforted me these past few nights, had been the smell of him.

I knew this wasn't the right place to tell him, but I couldn't wait a moment longer.

"Kitt, I can't thank you enough for lending me Boss. He's amazing, and he made a world of difference on the road. And I'm sorry I never told you my name back at Bortran's but, well…"

He stepped closer, chest nearly pressed against mine, and whispered, "It's alright. I know who you are."

I tilted my head back to see his face. "You do? Since when?"

"Since the moment I saw you. You're a rather recognizable person, if someone bothers looking."

His smile was genuine and warm, but it was only through sheer willpower that I kept my own smile from faltering. Of course he knew who I was. He'd given me his damned horse! A cherished companion and essential for his livelihood. A person wouldn't do something like that for any old stranger. Obviously, he'd picked up on my desire for secrecy and humored me. That's all.

My face burned with humiliation even as I tried to think of a clever response, when I felt a nudge at my back.

Oh right. I cleared my throat, shoving my feelings down.

"Ness, this is Kitt, a trapper and the kind stranger who let me borrow Boss. Ness is a friend I've made on my trip."

Even as I said the words, I hesitated. Had I overstepped? Did Ness think we were friends, or was babysitting me merely a job for her? Three hells, why couldn't I do anything right today?!

But Ness smiled and held out a hand.

"It's nice to meet you. Boss is a very fine horse, as long as any apples are hidden away."

Kitt chuckled with agreement, and they shook. My shoulders loosened slightly, but when he suggested we retreat to the stables, I practically ran out the door.

As soon as Kitt walked into the space, a loud whinny filled the air. Boss stood in one of the stalls, and he'd shoved his head out of it as far as it could go. The smile on Kitt's face as he rushed to the horse could have lit up a room, and he whispered words of thanks and relief.

Hovering by the doorway to give them a moment, I found Ness staring at me with a glint in her eyes.

"What?"

"He's cute," she said, smirking.

"I mean, I suppose." I shifted my feet, looking anywhere but at her. Or Kitt.

Her mischievousness melted. "What's the matter?"

"Nothing. I guess I'm tired from all the travel. I've been reading into a lot of things lately."

When Boss had settled, Kitt returned. "Thank you for taking such good care of him."

It was his eye contact, I realized. Kitt looked everyone in the eye and gave them his full attention. That's why I'd misjudged our last meeting so badly. Still, as I gazed into his eyes, the color of fresh soil and honey, I smiled back. "Thank *you* for letting me borrow him in the first place. Otherwise, I'd probably barely have reached Stenomar by now."

Ness began removing our gear from Boss's stall, being extra careful with the pack that held the thankfully silent Ethereal, while Kitt showed me to the dappled mare he'd purchased with the money I'd given him.

"Her name's Rosie," he said, then smiled and held out a small purse. "And there was quite a bit left over from what you gave me. I'm guessing it's been a while since you've purchased a horse."

"She's perfect," I said, ignoring the joke. The mare's coat shone, and her legs were long and muscular. She would be the perfect companion for the rest of our travels. Though I'd sorely miss Boss, who was currently craning his head around the stall to see the newcomer.

"Don't worry," I whispered to the stallion, "you're still my favorite."

Kitt regarded me from the corner of his eye. "Where are you heading next? Some big adventure, I hope."

"Actually, I've got a few more questions to answer, then I'll return to Glassleaf."

His contented smile dissolved. "Sounds serious. If there's any way I can be of help, let me know."

"Oh," I started, "well, I appreciate the offer, but you've already done so much and—"

"You could come with us," Ness called. I gaped at her, but she tilted her head. "As a trapper, he could come in handy if we need to, you know, find something. *Or someone.*"

I could see her reasoning, though the glint of mischief had returned to her eyes. But I shifted uncomfortably. If Kitt came along, he'd find out about everything. And then he'd judge me for failing and he wouldn't look at me so kindly anymore and why did I want him to look at me so badly? And *why* did my companions keep inviting strangers on my quest?!

Kitt didn't move, waiting for a verdict. Skies above, he was willing to come along if I let him. That realization caused a fluttering sensation in my stomach.

"I can't—I can't in good faith invite you along until you know exactly what we're doing. Then, you can decide if you truly want to join us."

The stable was busy, so I ushered him into the stall where Boss was munching loudly on hay. As succinctly as possible, I explained what Ness and I had found out in the Eastern Plains, our plan to find out who was truly behind the attacks on nearby villages, and my fear that I may not have succeeded in vanquishing Zaletor. The words poured out like a confession, but I kept my chin high and my words clear. As I spoke, Kitt's warm expression grew stony, but there was no blame in his eyes.

"And one last thing," I said, gesturing to my pack, "Mercury has returned and is helping me. If you come with us, you'll be subject to their constant criticism and snark."

A misty paw emerged from the bag's flap and waved.

Kitt remained motionless, though he visibly swallowed at the evidence of the Ethereal. I waited for him to back out, to come up with some excuse to not come. I prayed that when he did, my face wouldn't convey my disappointment. Ness leaned against the stable door, waiting.

Finally, Kitt nodded. "I'm in."

Ness grinned and even Boss knickered. But I stared at the trapper in disbelief.

"Why?"

He shrugged. "Spring is a slow time for me, so it's not as though I have something better to do. Besides, it seems like you could use some help."

My mouth hung open in shock, but I shook my head, focusing.

"I can pay you for your time. I would hate for this to impact your livelihood."

He gave a noncommittal nod. "I have a few more errands to run here before I can leave. I hope that's not a problem."

"Of course! I mean, that works out well. I have someone in town I need to see, and I'd prefer to have that reunion alone. But there will hopefully be four of us, then."

We all agreed to meet up back at the Leather Shoe at sunset. I was still reeling from my good fortune, to the point that I almost forgot the gravity of the meeting I was about to have.

15

———

Ravenwing Book Store sat nestled between buildings in a quiet section of the city. It was a charming little structure with a thatched roof and a hand-painted "Open" sign visible in the plate glass window. It was as welcoming as a store could be.

But I'd been outside for ten minutes, trying to work up the courage to enter. It was twilight, and I had let Mercury take mist form beside me. I did my best not to step through them as I paced.

"Maybe we don't need the two of them after all," I reasoned. "Last time, it took all of us to learn Zaletor's secrets and gain entrance to the Tower. But I defeated him on my own."

"That's true," Mercury said. "And then you died."

"Right. And then I died. I would like to avoid that this time."

"This was your idea, you know," they prodded.

I didn't even have it in me to respond with a sassy comment. They were right. And if I didn't go in now, they'd never let me live it down. Squaring my shoulders, I stepped forward. A tinkling bell sounded as I pushed open the door, and I held my breath as though I was about to jump into a freezing pool of water and not a bookstore.

The interior was bright and cozy, and every available surface was covered. The bookshelves along the walls showed no empty spaces, while maps and globes filled assorted tables. It was exactly as I'd pictured it based on Alto's letters. Alto had never married or fathered children, at least as far as I knew, so the bookstore was his whole world.

"Just a moment!" a voice called from an unseen backroom.

I picked up a nearby book. It appeared to be a collection of poems from a land far to the south. I flipped through the pages, barely seeing the words, until I heard footsteps.

"Sorry about that!" A middle-aged man with thinning blond hair emerged from behind a bookshelf. "How can I—"

He froze.

His face was leaner than the last time I'd seen him, and its boyish roundness had given way to a square jaw. His clothes were loose on his frame, as though he'd lost weight at some point but hadn't bothered to get a new wardrobe. Even from across the room, I could see his fingers were stained with ink. There was also an ink smudge on his chin, as though he'd tapped it in thought without realizing.

An uneasiness filled my stomach as a muscle in Alto's jaw twitched. But I smiled weakly. "Hello, Alto. It's good to see you."

"Phoebe!"

From one instant to the next, he'd rushed forward. It was my turn to freeze as he threw his arms around me. No one ever touched me at the castle, and his forwardness took me by surprise. But once I realized what was happening, I returned the hug with force.

"I missed you," I muttered into his shoulder.

A loud, conspicuous cough sounded beside us.

Alto raised his head, then jumped back.

"What, no hug for me?" Mercury preened. Then added, "That was a joke. Do not hug me."

"Mercury! What are—I thought we'd never see you again!" Alto's smile was enormous, but his eyes were full of questions when he looked at me.

I swallowed, knowing I was about to shatter his happiness.

"We need to talk."

〜

"That's not possible," Alto whispered, "he's dead. You killed him."

We sat in the storage room of the bookstore. He'd closed up early so we wouldn't have to worry about customers interrupting while I explained everything that had happened the last week. His face had leached of all color as I'd described finding the Tower and the note inside.

The shame I felt at his words was like a knife in my gut, but I shook my head. "I thought I did, but I might have been wrong."

The wisp of Mercury's wing brushed my back in support.

Stunned silence filled the room, pressing in on all sides, until Alto shook his head in disbelief. "Why did he wait all this time?"

Mercury answered for me. "We don't know. And we don't know what he's planning. But he's started drawing dark energy again, so it's only a matter of time before he makes his move."

"How can he draw dark energy?" Alto's face twisted with confusion. "You took his crown."

I looked at Mercury to see if they knew what Alto was talking about, but the Ethereal's brow was furrowed. "What does that have to do with anything?"

Alto glanced between us, considering, then moved to a dark wood cabinet in the corner of the room.

"A few years ago, I began researching more on Zaletor's origin," he explained, pulling a small silver key from his pocket. "I figured most of what we were taught as children under his rule was propaganda, and I wanted to know the truth. There isn't much, probably because people were too afraid to write about it, and what exists is mostly speculation, but I've collected everything I could find."

He unlocked and opened the cabinet, revealing two small shelves filled with books. Unlike the books in the main part of the store, these were darkened with age, and the room quickly filled with the smell of old paper.

"Why would you want to know more about Zaletor?" I asked, staring at the books. I couldn't say why, but I was afraid to touch them.

Alto looked to the floor. "I'd hoped it would help with the nightmares. I'd tried everything else, so I figured if I knew more about the boogeyman, he would be less frightening."

My chest tightened, and I fought the urge to hug him again. Alto was still strategizing, still looking for clever ways to overcome his enemies, even when they only lived in his memories.

"Anyway," he shook his head, banishing whatever thoughts had arisen. "Everyone knows he was born a Terra and made a deal with the Dark Lady to become more powerful. But three texts refer to the crown as the source of this additional power. The Dark Lady crafted it herself and gave it to him when he became her servant. Zaletor used it like a conduit to boost his Terra Gift to previously unknown levels, pulling the energy from the Ethereal Plane. One of the books theorizes that it could do even more than that, like heal small wounds or allow Zaletor to teleport."

Mercury's silver form was churning. "But I didn't sense

anything from it. If I'd caught even a whiff of dark energy from it, I'd have brought the damn thing back to the Ethereal Plane with me rather than leaving it with you teenage idiots!"

"It's a conduit," Alto shrugged, "so maybe it doesn't give off any energy of its own. When it's not actively drawing power, it's just a crown." He looked at me. "But you took it when you defeated him. Where could he have gotten another one?"

I felt like my own soul had been removed. This couldn't be real. We couldn't have screwed up that badly. Looking down, I found Mercury watching me, and I could tell they were thinking the same thing.

Alto looked between us, sensing the shift in mood. "What's going on?"

Praying I wouldn't vomit from guilt, I forced myself to say, "The crown is missing."

"What do you mean, 'missing?'"

"I hid the base of the crown in the castle crypts. I was the only one who knew where it was, but when Mercury showed up, we went to find it and it was gone. Zaletor must have taken it."

The idea that he had been in the castle, right below my feet, was too much.

"Why didn't—" Alto started, then pressed his fingers to the bridge of his nose. He took a breath, frustration radiating off him. "What happens now?"

"I have to make this right. Zaletor is back, and he's hurting people. But it seems he's not at full strength yet. The tower was hollow, and the new Gladiators are barely solid."

Alto shook his head. "Why would he start stirring up trouble if he's not at full power? Why would he start attacking villages with half-formed soldiers when all it does is alert you to his presence and give you time to stop him?"

"Maybe that's the point," Mercury said, "he wants you to know he's back and you failed."

I flinched, but I couldn't disagree. "But why now? Alto's right. Why not wait till he's too strong for me to stop him?"

"Unless there's more to it than simply defeating you." Alto raised his fingers to his chin as he thought through all the possibilities, leaving another smudge of ink. "What if he wants to humiliate you? Destroy your image?" He looked at me. "Isn't the Great Victory festival coming up soon?"

The bottom fell out of my stomach. "It's the twentieth anniversary this year. The festival is going to be bigger than ever."

"Zaletor was always one for theatrics. The real attack will be at the festival. It's the perfect time to reveal himself. He doesn't have to be at full power, he just has to be *alive.*"

"And everyone would see the truth: that I failed."

Failed. The word echoed through my head with each beat of my heart. *Failed, failed, failed.*

"For all we know, the muddy Gladiators were a practice run. He might not have anticipated that Mercury would return and sense the dark energy being used." Alto finished.

Mercury nodded. "But no matter when he plans to attack, now is the time to stop him." He turned to Alto. "That's why we're getting the gang back together."

"Most of the gang," I clarified, "but it's true. If you, Jax, and I work together, we can find Zaletor and stop him before he hurts more people."

And before anyone else finds out, I thought, but kept that to myself.

"What do you say? Will you help us save the world again?"

The slight color that had returned to Alto's face as we talked vanished before my eyes. His shoulders curled in, making his already baggy clothes appear to swallow him. He looked at me, then to Mercury, and finally to his cabinet of books.

"No."

With trembling hands, Alto closed the little cabinet, locking the history of Zaletor away.

"I'm sorry," he said, facing me, "I can give you supplies and all the knowledge I've learned, but I can't—I can't do that again. My place is here."

It was probably for the best that I already felt hollowed out from the information he's shared about the crown. Otherwise, the rejection would have hurt more.

"If Zaletor returns, all of this ends!" Mercury cried. "Won't you fight to protect it?!"

Alto was trembling now, and the fear in his eyes cut through my numbness and broke my heart.

"Stop," I told Mercury. "It's alright. We'll figure it out."

The Ethereal bristled and opened their mouth to say more, but something in my face must have convinced them to think better of it. With a final huff, they turned and marched out of the storage room.

Alto looked close to tears, so I walked over and took his hand. As much as I wanted his help, wanted to reconnect to this piece of my former life, I wasn't going to force him. And it was clear he'd made up his mind. So, we stood together for a moment.

"I always wish Becca was still here, but now more than ever," I whispered, unable to keep the words inside. "The thought of trying to defeat Zaletor without her is almost unthinkable."

For an instant, something flashed in Alto's eyes. It was an emotion I couldn't read, but it was gone before I could even be sure. I wondered if I'd said the wrong thing, but he gave my hand a gentle squeeze. "Every day I think about what could have been. She was the best of us all."

I nodded. I wanted to stay and talk more, about anything and everything, but time was of the essence.

"I'll take whatever information you have. I don't suppose you've stayed in contact with Jax as well?"

"I know where to find him. He would probably be up for another adventure."

I forced myself to smile, even as the disappointment swirled inside.

"What sort of trouble has he been causing?"

Despite the lingering fear in his eyes, a rare, sly smile spread across Alto's face.

16

"You've got to be kidding me." I gaped as we stood outside a brightly lit theater in the city of Narism.

I'd said the exact same thing the day prior when Alto told me where to find Jax, and even then, I hadn't entirely believed it. But here was the proof: a giant poster with my old friend's face on it.

As the star of the show.

When I'd returned to the group alone, they hadn't said anything. Ness had brushed her shoulder against mine, Kitt had given me a small nod, and that had been the extent of it. I'd expected the brief journey from Linipa to Narisim, a large city west of the capitol, to be extremely awkward as the four of us figured out the new travel dynamic. But, to my surprise, Kitt fit seamlessly into the strange trio of Ness, Mercury and myself. Both the trapper and the Ignis were quiet and happy to respect my desire to keep to myself after my encounter with Alto.

As expected, Mercury had complained enough for both of us.

While I'd never visited Narism before, I'd heard wealthy

families who wanted to escape the bustle of Glassleaf lived there in quiet comfort. But walking through the streets, I could see everything was more extravagant than I had ever imagined. And The Russell Theater was the city's crown jewel. The grand stucco building stretched up toward the sky, and the glittering crystal spheres dotting the marquis could be seen for blocks. Beautifully painted canvas banners hung suspended from the upper windows, their corners weighted so they wouldn't flap in the breeze. The theater looked like it had stood there forever, and I was shocked that such a place could have survived Zaletor's reign.

"I admit I'm not the best at understanding human nature," Mercury said as they stared up at the brightly lit theater exterior. "But this...this doesn't seem right."

I agreed: it wasn't the fact that Jax had become an actor. He'd always been outgoing and expressive, dramatic in a way that was simply impressive. No, the issue at hand was the play itself.

"*The Great Victory*," Ness read, her face conspicuously expressionless. "The Thrilling Tale of Bearnel's Freedom. Featuring Real Hero Jax Tessian."

We loitered in an empty doorway across the street to avoid the large crowd that had already formed outside the building. People milled about, speaking in excited voices as they waited for the doors to open. I assumed that was a good sign for the quality of the performance.

"How haven't I heard about this?" Surely news that Jax was acting in a play detailing the exploits of our youth would have reached the castle. Why had no one told me?

"We have GOT to see this show!" Mercury exclaimed, bouncing up and down.

I was less enthusiastic. Sitting through a story about me, knowing that Zaletor was actually still out in the world, sounded like actual torture. But the only way into the theater was to buy tickets for the show, and the only way to find Jax was to get into the theater.

"Alright," I conceded, "we'll get tickets."

It was excruciating.

Mercury giggled maniacally for the first ten minutes, even during the somber scenes of my childhood on the streets and the startling discovery of having multiple Gifts. More than one head turned our direction to see who was being so disrespectful, and even though the theater was dark, I'd had to slide down in my chair to avoid the angry looks. But the Ethereal, tucked in the back and draped with a spare cloak, didn't even notice.

It was infuriating and humiliating, right up until the moment when their character appeared in a puff of smoke. Then it was my turn to laugh.

It was a puppet. A fuzzy marionette that looked more like a gray monkey than the elegant, feline Ethereal. Tears rolled down my face as I watched performers wearing all black prance the little monstrosity around the stage, while Mercury promised destruction upon the whole theater.

The moment of levity was short lived. I shifted in my seat as I watched my character struggle to control her many powers, which were recreated using different colored ribbons instead of any actual magic. I knew Mercury was watching me pointedly during the training montage, but I refused to look at them.

The most painful part was watching the young actress playing me hate, then fall madly in love with, a handsome sailor who was on a quest for revenge. Certain moments were more accurate than I would have liked, and I assumed Jax had given the script writers inside information. When Actor-

Phoebe opened the door of her hideout to find Actor-Tristan standing in the rain, injured and distraught, only to have him explain that he didn't know where else to go, I wanted to vomit. Meanwhile, I heard several people in the crowd actually sob.

The whole thing was overly romantic, and it gave no hint at the future falling out we would have. I couldn't explain why I kept glancing at Kitt to see his reaction. He watched the whole show with rapt attention.

At least Becca's role was done well. That made me feel a bit better about the whole thing. But not by much.

Finally, at the start of Act II, Jax appeared with a flourish.

I swear my jaw hit the floor.

He was playing himself. His *teenage* self.

Jax was a year older than me, closer to forty than thirty, and here he was pretending to be seventeen. There were a few murmurs in the crowd as he brandished his prop sword at plywood Gladiators, but it was all positive. People couldn't believe they were seeing one of their heroes in the flesh, regardless of how ridiculously out of place he looked among the young cast.

As the show went on, I had to acknowledge his acting skills were excellent. But I was so distracted by the floppy wig he wore, likely to conceal gray hair or baldness, that before I knew it, we were at the dramatic finale. Except in this version, Actor-Phoebe used an ice sword to cut off Actor-Zaletor's head, killing the Eternal Emperor once and for all. There was no mention of the Dark Wizard using the souls of the Gifted to stay alive, so at least Jax had kept something to himself.

Also, I didn't die in this version, just vanquished a villain and achieved a "happily ever after" for the five of us. It felt... unfulfilling somehow. At least to me.

But the theater erupted with applause. People stood to cheer, and some tossed roses at the actors' feet. Jax received the biggest applause of all and made a point of coming out for an encore, bowing low, with a grin wide enough to see from the back of the room.

No one noticed us slip from our seats and into the empty hallway.

Despite the grandness of the theater, it was surprisingly easy for the group of us to sneak backstage, with Mercury as a mist between us. Stagehands bustled about to reset everything for the next performance, and no one even glanced in our direction as we hurried down a set of stairs to a hallway of dressing rooms. Thankfully, the space was empty, as the actors were resting between shows, and we proceeded down the line of doors till we arrived at one with Jax's name and a glittering gold star, which I noticed was significantly larger than anyone else's.

I raised my hand to knock, but like when I had stood outside Alto's bookstore, I hesitated. Did I have any right to take Jax away from all this? What if he rejected me, too? I could still remember the way his voice had cracked when he'd screamed at me years ago.

"Jax and I didn't part on good terms," I whispered to no one in particular. "What if he won't talk to me?"

Pushing me gently to one side, Ness stepped forward and rapped her knuckles on the door.

"I'm not taking notes, Reginald!" Jax shouted through the door. "My performance was exceptional, and I'll not hear another word about it!"

"Actually, we're fans," Ness replied, "we'd like an autograph."

There was the distinct sound of someone tripping and a muffled curse, then the door whipped open.

Jax stood framed dramatically in the doorway, still wearing his costume. The wig I'd been fixated on during the show was hastily placed on his head, his gray curls poking out the back. He held a quill still dripping ink.

"Of course!" he grinned, his eyes going straight to Ness. "I always have time for my adoring fans. Especially ones as beautiful as you. You really shouldn't be back here, you know, but it can be our secret. Now, do you have something for me to sign? If you need, I have—"

"Jax!" I pushed forward, demanding his attention.

He was patting his pockets, looking for something to autograph, when he finally looked at me. His gray eyes went wide.

"Hi," I whispered.

Without a word, he slammed the door in my face.

I was too stunned to be angry or surprised. The silence in the hallway was deafening.

Then, the door wrenched open. Jax's nose was pinched tight as he shoved a finger in my face.

"You've got a lot of nerve, showing up here like this," he snapped. Ness reached out and lowered his finger, but Jax didn't seem to notice. "How *dare* you?!"

"I'm sorry," I stuttered, "it's just—"

"Five years. *Five years* I've been writing to you, *begging* you to come see my show. Every year people ask me, "Oh, Jax, is this the year?" And every damn year I say, "Maybe!" And you've *never come.*"

"You've written to me? But I didn't—"

"AND NOW," he bellowed, "here you are, sneaking down to my dressing room in between performances like some sort of—of—*unimportant person*! Ugh, I bet no one even saw you come down here. At least tell me you haven't seen the show yet! If you sat in the theater like some sort of commoner, I will never forgive you!"

"Hang on!" I hissed, pushing him back into the privacy of the dressing room. There were open drawers and boxes blocking any semblance of a path, but I managed to make it far enough into the room for all of us to fit. "You're mad because I came here and *didn't* make a big deal about it?!"

Someone shut the door behind us, which was good because Jax resumed shouting.

"No, Phoebe, I'm FURIOUS because you came here and didn't make a big deal about it!" His face crumpled and he flopped dramatically onto a cot in the corner. "I was supposed to get all the credit for you showing up! All the prestige! But now, everyone will think it was just a fluke! If they even believe me at all!"

I couldn't decide if I wanted to laugh or scream at him.

"Enough!" Mercury insisted, materializing between us. "We don't have time for this!"

Jax's jaw dropped, then a giddy smile spread across his face as he sat forward.

"Mercury! Dear friend! You've returned! This is perfect. Forget everything I said a moment ago! Your presence will be even more noteworthy than Phoebe's! Everyone will be so impressed!"

Under normal circumstances, Mercury would have preened at the lavish attention. But even they'd had enough of Jax's ramblings, and they shoved a large quicksilver paw over the man's mouth, silencing him.

"For the love of all things magical and holy, stop talking."

Jax started, stunned at the gesture. Ness stifled a laugh

"I am going to remove my paw, and you are going to remove that dead animal from your head and have a conversation with us like a normal person. Understand?"

Jax's cheeks flushed, but he nodded. When Mercury removed their paw, Jax stiffly pulled the wig from his head, running a hand through his thinning gray hair, and straightened.

"Well, I suppose I was a bit...*emotional* just now. You're here, and that's what matters."

I was here, here to tell him that our "Great Victory" was a terrible failure and we'd been inadvertently lying to everyone for the past two decades. That the play he cared for so much was false propaganda. I hesitated, cursing my own roiling emotions.

"You've been doing this show for five years?" Ness asked, moving the conversation along with expert precision. I noticed she'd hung back by the door, whether to give us a semblance of privacy or to keep her distance from Jax, I couldn't tell, but I gave her a grateful nod.

"I don't even need to look at the script anymore," he grinned, "I know everyone's lines by heart. Our director, Reginald, has been suggesting I transition to more of a production role, but I know he's simply jealous of my fame. Probably worries I overshadow the rest of the cast, which is fair. Most of them are new this year, and they're still finding their footing. This is only our first week, so a few stumbles are to be expected, but with my helpful tutelage I think this year will be the best yet! I heard they've already added more performances in honor of the anniversary and all."

As he rambled, I took a moment to survey the dressing room. It was large, probably larger than the others, based on the placement at the end of the hall, but it felt small due to all the clutter. There were old playbills and posters scattered around, many of which bore Jax's signature. The dresser whose open drawers I'd nearly tripped over was bursting with clothes, many of which showed signs of repair. A semicircle of clean floor had been established next to a rack in the corner, which had more lavish pieces hanging from it. I recognized a few of them from the show and assumed this was where Jax kept his costumes. The cot Jax sat on was rumpled with blankets and pillows, and a small wood box beside it held a book and various trinkets.

"Jax," I interrupted, "are you living here?"

His face froze in a smile, then he laughed. "Isn't it marvelous? I don't have to worry about being mobbed by fans after every show or forgetting something at home."

Now that I paid more attention, the room had the distinct scent of body odor, though it wasn't overwhelming, so at least Jax was doing his laundry regularly. I saw a small rubbish bin in the corner half full of paper food wrappers and crumpled sketches. But it wasn't the presence of these items that surprised me; it was what was missing. There wasn't a single bottle.

"So will you and your beautiful friend be staying for the next show?" Jax winked at Ness.

With Alto, I'd laid out all the facts clearly and in order of discovery. I'd guessed he would be skeptical, and I knew clear logic would be the key to convincing him that the Dark Wizard had returned. Even though he'd declined to help me, my assessment of how best to break the news had been correct.

Jax would need a different approach.

"Zaletor is trying to destroy the world again," I blurted out.

Shock, disbelief, fear, and a myriad of other emotions flickered across Jax's face in rapid succession. I held my breath, unsure what I'd do if he refused to help as well. Jax had no Gift, but his skill as a fighter had saved us many times all those years ago. True, he was older now, but judging by his movements on the stage, he'd kept up his sword work.

Finally, Jax's features settled into grim determination. "What are we going to do?"

We.

At that one word, a weight lifted off my shoulders.

"We're going to stop him," Mercury said. "He's not up to his full power yet, so we plan to destroy him before he does anything catastrophic. But time is of the essence."

"Right," Jax nodded, "I need ten minutes to pack my things, and another twenty minutes to talk to Reginald." He leaned toward Ness and said with a conspiratorial whisper, "I'm guessing it will take that long for him to regain consciousness after I tell him I'm leaving and another ten to pry him off my ankles, since he'll want me to stay. But my understudy could use a few weeks in the spotlight. He's never gotten to perform, you know, as I've never missed a show. Poor lad will probably crack under the pressure."

My head spun, and his ramblings didn't help.

"You're truly willing to come with us? After everything—even knowing the dangers?"

Jax's eyes locked on mine, and, for an instant, his mask of bravado slipped away.

"This is our responsibility. I have many things to atone for in life, and I won't shy away from them now."

My heart swelled at the frankness of his words, and for a moment I saw not the swashbuckling actor or the grieving man who'd screamed at me. I saw my brother.

"Besides," Jax grinned, "once we succeed, they'll write a new play about *this* adventure! I can see the marquee now! 'Starring Jax Tessian: The Two-Time Savior of the World!' Then I can play myself on stage for the rest of my life!"

17

When I'd first set out from Glassleaf, I'd made it an hour and thirty-four minutes before second-guessing my decision to leave. Jax only lasted twenty.

The trip though the city had gone surprisingly smoothly. Jax had embraced his role of "disguised celebrity," and we'd slipped out of Narism on the western road. But once the crowds were gone and there was no audience, he assaulted us with a barrage of complaints, with the occasional question thrown in.

"We should be taking a carriage. Sneaking through the countryside like this is so undignified. Far beneath someone of my rank. And yours, I guess. And where is your retinue of chefs and porters? We could be traveling in style and comfort!"

We were several miles from the city, and the sun was close to setting. Still, the whining persisted.

At Mercury's instruction, we had headed toward the sea. They didn't specify why, so I assumed they felt the pull of dark energy. They walked beside me, their ears flattened in irritation.

I smiled. "You're the one who originally suggested I get everyone back together, remember?"

They snorted, but before they could reply, Jax gave a loud sigh.

"Surely we'll get another horse at least? You cannot possibly expect me to walk the whole way."

"You're riding a horse right now!" Ness cried. Even her calm demeanor was fracturing under Jax's behavior. Sure enough, he sat atop Rosie as I led the mare. Boss carried most of our supplies, and Kitt and Ness walked beside me.

"Let's stop for the night," I decided. I'd hoped to keep traveling for as long as we could stand, but if I didn't do something soon, Ness would barbeque the actor before we went another mile.

"Stop?" Jax raised himself, scouting ahead. "There isn't an inn for miles yet."

"This is going to be a very long trip for you," Mercury crooned. Their grin revealed sharp front teeth. The sword master's face fell as we pulled the horses off the road. He let out a brief sputter of indignation, but I blocked it out as I scanned for the best place to bed down. The area we were in was mostly farmland, and we found a stretch of open pasture that promised a more pleasant night's rest than the rocky hills ahead. Based on the vegetation and some well-honed instinct, Kitt said there was likely a river or stream nearby. We found a spot not far from the road and Ness, Kitt, and I began setting up camp, while Jax, who insisted he'd pulled a muscle climbing off the horse, sat and critiqued.

"Was he always like this?" Kitt whispered as we untacked the horses. I'd noted he'd dropped his bag and blanket next to mine by the fire. It may have been a coincidence, but something about it still made my stomach fill with butterflies.

"He was always a bit dramatic, though I admit he seems to

have grown unbearable. With any luck, he'll tire himself out soon, and we can have some quiet."

"I can hear you!" Jax called from where he had plopped down next to the fire.

I gave him my sweetest smile. "I know."

He narrowed his eyes at me, then turned to the trapper.

"Tell me something, Kitt," he said, spitting out the name like it had a foul taste. "Why exactly are you along on this important journey? How is any of this your problem?"

I shot him a glare, but Kitt was unfazed.

"The fate of the world seems like everyone's problem. I think it was providence, meeting Phoebe at the inn."

While it wasn't dark yet, I hoped the fading light hid the blush I felt rising on my cheeks.

But Jax grunted. "Sounds like a pretty convenient excuse to me."

Kitt's easy smile faded. "Not that I need to explain myself to you, but I assure you, my only goal is to help however I can."

"Actually, as I am Phoebe's brother and friend, you *do* have to explain yourself to me."

"Enough!" I called, glaring at Jax. He kept his eyes on Kitt.

Alright, I decided, it was time.

"Kitt, why don't you and Ness see if you can find the stream you mentioned. The waterskins are still half full, but I'm sure the horses could use a drink."

They both agreed without question, possibly understanding the conversation that was about to happen, and Mercury gave some excuse about stretching their wings. Soon it was only Jax and me in the camp. Jax opened his mouth, likely to complain or accuse, but I jumped in first.

"What is your problem?"

His face was incredulous. "*My* problem?! I'm trying to look out for you! What do you even know about that guy?"

"I know he helped me when he didn't have to. He's a good person, and I trust him."

"Did he know who you were when you met?" He took my silence for an answer and threw his hands in the air. "Clearly, he was trying to gain your favor."

I rolled my eyes. "I doubt that. But even if he was, he's been incredibly helpful!"

"He probably just wants in your pants!"

"Maybe I want him in my pants too! Did you ever consider that?"

The fire flared brighter at my outburst, and Jax pursed his lips. "I'm just saying that no one besides the two us would ever agree to come on this surely suicidal journey without expecting something at the end. Hells, Phoebe, even Alto chickened out! And he knows the score! Assuming we somehow survive this, Kitt's going to want something out of it, you mark my words."

"What about Ness?" I shot back. "I notice you've conveniently left her out of this. All the suspicions you're throwing at Kitt apply to her as well!"

"Ness is different." Jax waved.

"Because she's gorgeous?"

"I—because she's—it's not the same!"

Ice itched at my fingertips, but I kept it at bay. "Let me make one thing clear: the only ones who need to be on this journey are Mercury and me. The rest of you are here because we believe you can be helpful in some way. But make no mistake, Jax, if I feel your attitude outweighs your helpfulness, I will send you back to Narism without a second thought. AND," I held up a hand to prevent him from interrupting, "as far as I'm concerned, you don't get an opinion in my love life ever again. I still consider you my brother, but after everything that happened, I'm not sure we're friends."

This last struck him like a blow, but I held firm. After a moment, Jax cleared his throat.

"I am sorry for what I said that day. Truly. I know I said this before in my letters, but I hope—I hope your decision to call off the wedding wasn't because of me."

Ness's fire settled to a pleasant crackling flame as my shoulders slumped. "I did call off the wedding because of what you said, but it was because you made me realize that staying with Tristan wasn't going to help the kingdom after all. Not when everyone could see how miserable we both were. And I never got any of your letters, which is a whole other problem. I didn't even know where you were until Alto told me."

"It seems someone in the castle didn't want us keeping in touch," Jax mused.

A new heat crackled inside of me at his words, one fueled by suspicion and rage, but I pushed it aside.

"One problem at a time," I said. There was no point worrying about what could happen when I returned to the castle while chances were still high that I never would. Either through my own demise or because people found out I'd failed and removed me from power, my days as queen were likely limited.

"Well, in light of this horrifying information, I suppose I can no longer be mad at you for not sending presents to *my* wedding." He gave me a crooked grin, and I saw the olive branch.

"You got married?"

He nodded, looking at the fire. "Twice. It didn't work out either time. I'm sure it will come as a complete surprise to you to learn that there are some people who think I'm a bit much."

I chuckled. "I'm shocked. You need to stop hitting on Ness, by the way. That kind of thing may have passed for charming when you were younger, but you're probably ten years older than she is. It's creepy."

To his credit, Jax nodded. "In my head, it was endearing. But you're right."

The moment stretched between us, until I found myself saying, "I am sorry for telling you to leave."

He shrugged, not meeting my eyes. "You were right to kick me out. I was in a freefall and would only have done something stupider if left unchecked." Jax swallowed. "I haven't touched a bottle since that day. Not a single drop."

I didn't know how to respond, so we sat in companionable silence for several minutes as the sky grew dark. A slight breeze stirred the cornfield beside us. The happy crackle of the fire was the only other sound, even though there was no wood to fuel it. I marveled at how Ness was able to keep it going, even at a distance.

"We're going to need him, you know," Jax muttered, picking at the grass around him.

"I told you, Alto refused. And I can't—"

"I'm not talking about Alto." He gave me a pointed look.

The calm I'd felt a moment before evaporated, replaced with frustration.

"Absolutely not."

"I bet he's kept up his Ignis training, making him extra useful, and he'll feel just as responsible as we do to stop all this."

I clenched my teeth. I was so angry, it felt like the earth was shuddering beneath me. "We are not bringing him into this, Jax."

"I know this is not a comfortable scenario for you, but—"

The earth burst apart as a boulder struck the center of our campsite.

I heard Jax curse, while I leapt to my feet. I had been so

engrossed in our argument that I hadn't noticed which direction the attack had come from. I couldn't see anything outside the ring of our small fire, but I felt the earth shudder with approaching steps.

Stupid, I hissed at myself, *never let your guard down!*

A whistle cut through the air, and I turned to see a rock the size of my head hurtling straight toward Jax. Throwing out a hand, I willed the earth to protect him. There was a ripping sound as a wall of dirt rose up around him, just in time to absorb most of the blow.

"Great Hells!" Jax cried as the rock clipped his shoulder. At least it didn't hit his head, I thought, as I resumed my search for the attackers.

There was a noise to my left, and I whirled around to see an enormous monster emerge from the pasture. It was twice as big as the ones I'd encountered outside the Eastern Plains and just as disgusting.

"What is that?!" Jax's face was pale as he scrambled to collect his sword from where he'd deposited his things.

"A Gladiator," I replied, trying to calm my breathing. Though ice was my go-to weapon, it had done little to stop the monsters before. Instead, I focused on the earth, solid beneath my feet, and on the fire crackling beside me.

The hiss of a sword being drawn sounded behind me, and then Jax was at my side.

"It looks different than I remember. Please tell me that's not what they always looked like?"

"Zaletor isn't at full strength. This is the best he can do. For now."

And apparently the giant creature was already learning. Instead of hurling its own mud at us, it dug a pumpkin-sized boulder out of the ground and lobbed it into the air. It arced toward us, but the Gladiator's aim was too far to the right. Still, as the rock crashed into the ground, I knew that it would have dealt a death blow to a person.

The creature reached the edge of our camp, and Jax raised his sword to meet it.

"Be careful!" I called, suddenly struck by the reality of the danger I'd brought him into.

Undeterred, Jax darted forward and slashed across the creature's leg mid-step. The limb dropped to the ground with a splat and the creature toppled forward. With an elegant spin, Jax sliced through one of its arms, then used his momentum to hack off its head. With a splatter of muddy water, the monster collapsed. Jax puffed for breath, but his face glowed with pride as he surveyed his fallen foe. But his expression was short lived, as the monster redistributed the mud from its torso to form a new arm and leg. It didn't bother with a head.

"Watch out!" I yelled. We both dove out of the way of its wildly swinging arms.

Crouched near the firepit, Jax panted beside me. "Phoebe, darling, I hate to admit it, but we could use some assistance."

Right. I could scream, but if Mercury, Ness and Kitt hadn't heard our commotion already, I doubted it would do any good. I focused on Ness's campfire.

Imagine the warmth of your own body. You create it without even thinking.

Adding my own magic to Ness's, I willed the small campfire upward. With a blast of heat, it grew into a pillar of flame ten feet high. Jax yelped and shielded his eyes, while the headless monster slowed. Its body hardened, not completely, but enough to hinder its movements.

"Jax, now!"

With his eyes averted, Jax advanced on the creature. Sweat beaded on my forehead as I split my focus, keeping the pillar burning high while forming ice at the creature's feet, holding it in place. With a few expert strikes, Jax removed the legs and arms from the creature's torso.

Then it was over.

"Phoebe?!"

I looked up as Mercury careened into the campsite. They must have left Ness and Kitt behind to get here right away, and now they hovered in the air, surveying the trashed camp and clay chunks.

"A visitor," I ground out, unable to maintain the pillar of fire any longer. I lowered it to the size of a large bonfire and hoped it was hot enough to cook the clay pieces. "Bigger than the other ones."

Mercury studied the creature's feet, still frozen to the ground, then grinned at me.

"You used multiple gifts! And you didn't pass out!"

I gave the Ethereal a thumbs-up, too exhausted to quip back.

The creature's torso lay discarded by the fire, its dismembered limbs surrounding it. While I wanted nothing more than to roast it beyond recognition, I rallied the last of my strength, crouched down, and placed a hand on the creature's stomach. Mercury and Jax fell silent, waiting.

Even though I was exhausted, I willed my pulse to slow and remembered what Becca had taught me years ago. It took a few moments to center myself properly, but when I did, a firm tugging sensation started in my gut. I gasped as the Specter power buried deep inside me stirred. All magic came from inside the body, but unlike the other gifts, which came from the wielder's hands or feet, soul magic came from the stomach. With the old Gladiators, I used to be able draw forth the trapped soul from them in the form of a dazzling golden mist. But now, nothing happened.

"There was never a soul here," I whispered, wiping grime from my hand onto the grass. "It was merely a puppet."

Jax grunted as he began moving the other pieces closer to the fire. "So someone is out there, pulling the strings?"

I nodded as he dropped the head beside me. Its eye sockets were the same dark pits as those of the creatures outside the Eastern Plains. Unsettled, I shoved the blasted thing into the fire. I stood, barely, then collapsed onto the nearest blanket, pulling my knees up to my chest to stop them from trembling.

Jax dropped to a seat beside me. His face was red from the effort and the heat. "That sucked."

"At least we didn't need any help," I joked, very much wishing someone had been around to help.

Jax flopped back onto the grass. "Yup, we're a couple of mighty warriors."

Before I could respond, a rasping chuckle rippled through the campsite.

"Oh, yes," the voice dripped with disdain, "what an impressive display of talent."

The bottom fell out of my stomach as I whirled to see a figure standing at the edge of our camp. He was shrouded in flowing black robes, his face hidden behind gauzy folds, but a familiar golden crown glittered on his head.

"Hello, Phoebe," Zaletor taunted.

18

"It seems we've both seen better days," he rasped. His voice was weak, but the malice in it was all too familiar.

My blood went cold as my mind struggled to accept what I was seeing. Even with the evidence of his return mounting, I'd still held out hope our current enemy had been some imposter or acolyte of the Dark Wizard, bent on avenging their master. But the truth stood before me.

I'd been wrong. I had failed.

Jax shrank back, but even though my heart raced in my chest, I kept my head high as I pushed to my feet. Somehow, the shame of my failure overshadowed my fear, and a single thought crystalized: I would not fail again. Standing before the resurrected Zaletor, I refused to cower or cry. I didn't know if it was his weakened state, or the fact that I'd been a child the last time I'd seen him, but Zaletor the Eternal Emperor seemed smaller than I remembered.

But that didn't change the dark energy rippling off him, and I was almost drained.

Thunder rumbled from the depths of Mercury's chest.

"You should have stayed dead, wizard." Their wings flared in warning.

"And you should have stayed out of it!" Zaletor snarled. With a wave of his hand, he thrust two stalagmites from the ground and ripped them free to float in the air beside him. In a blink, they were hurtling at me.

Mercury batted the missiles aside with a gust of wind, and I heard them crash to the ground outside the ring of firelight. They sent another blast toward Zaletor, but he raised a wall, shielding himself. I sent a wave of ice spikes, hoping to impale him where he stood, but I was exhausted, and the spikes simply shattered against Zaletor's earthen wall. My head throbbed with effort, and I hissed in pain.

"Pathetic! Had I known how weak you'd become, I'd have killed you ages ago! All that time hiding in your glittering castle has made you soft, child."

I sucked in air through my teeth, trying to rally any element to help save us, but it was no use. I was spent. Jax still trembled beside me, his sword lying at his feet.

"How does it feel, Phoebe Blessed-Heart? How does it feel to know you failed?"

He pushed the wall that had been protecting him toward us. Mercury's wind slowed it enough for me to grab Jax and roll out of the way, but it was too close.

"How does it feel to know you deceived so many people? To have them all worship you based on a LIE?!"

I don't even know what happened next, but Mercury flared their wings, and something crashed outside the firelight. They were panting now too.

"You have no true power. You couldn't even save your friend. The pretty one who died at sea. How utterly worthless you are!"

"That's enough!" I yelled, choking on the dust in the air. Each word he said was a knife to my heart.

"Oh no, Blessed-Heart, it's not nearly enough."

Two stone slabs crashed together where Mercury was standing, and even though I knew they were impervious to damage, I screamed. Such devastation might not kill them, but my friend could still feel pain.

"It won't be enough until I get back everything you took from me!"

He hurled another slab straight for Jax. The swordsman's eyes went wide as he watched it approach, frozen with fear. I knew I couldn't roll him out of the way fast enough this time. But I reached for him anyway.

"I'll bury you and your friends and—"

Zaletor's taunt was transformed into a scream as fire lit up the night sky. The slab of rock veered to the right, grazing Jax instead of flattening him.

I hadn't seen Ness creep up, but suddenly she was behind Zaletor, throwing everything she had at him. Her white-hot flames were so strong, I had to turn my face away.

"Come on!" Kitt yelled, suddenly beside me. His calloused hands pulled me to my feet, and we both hauled Jax. We were scrambling back away from the flames, when Zaletor's screaming stopped abruptly. Lowering her hands, Ness let her fire die out.

With a mighty shove, Mercury burst from beneath the pile of rubble. I rushed to them, scanning their body for injuries.

"I'm alright," the Ethereal promised, brushing me with a wing.

My heart still raced as I got to my feet. Smoke burned my eyes, but I refused to close them for even a moment as I approached the charred crater.

Zaletor was gone.

"Is he dead?" Jax's voice trembled, his eyes locked on the spot where Zaletor had stood.

Mercury shook their head, sending up a cloud of dust. "He teleported out. I felt the dark energy."

Ness moved around the scarred earth to stand beside me. She didn't look winded at all, though her eyes were wide as she stared at the earth.

"I should have moved in faster. I was trying to stay quiet, to avoid being seen, but if I'd moved in faster, I could have hit him harder. He wouldn't have gotten away."

I was so exhausted and shaken, I almost laughed. "If you'd approached any faster, he would have noticed, and you'd have lost the element of surprise. You did wonderfully."

She gave me a half-hearted smile, but as she turned to fetch the horses, I could see her face was serious. Unconvinced.

"Are you alright?" Mercury whispered. Kitt was helping brush the dirt from Jax, but he looked up at the question.

Physically, I was fine. I felt like I could sleep for three days straight, and my body was sore from the effort of using so much magic at once. But I knew they weren't asking about that.

I considered, and maybe it was the depth of my shock, but I nodded. Zaletor's words still echoed in my head, and I couldn't help but agree with him. I had lied to everyone, unintentionally, but it was still a lie. I had to fix it, no matter the cost.

"We need to train harder."

Mercury nodded and turned their attention to the road. "We need to go. I don't know how he found us, but we can't stay here."

There was no argument from anyone on that point. Thankfully, Kitt and Ness had managed to give the horses a quick drink before my emergency signal had gone up. The two of them jumped into action gathering up our supplies while I checked on Jax. He hadn't moved since Kitt and I had helped him stand, and now he stared stone-faced at the smoldering crater where Zaletor had last stood.

"You'd told me he was back. I *knew* this was how it would go, and I still...I think I made a mistake in coming with. What use do you have for a washed-out fighter who freezes at the sight of the enemy?"

His words, so full of pain and humiliation, were mirrored in my very soul. Though weariness pressed in on me, I took my brother's hand.

"I won't hold it against you if you want to return to Narism. What we're facing—no one should have to deal with this level of evil in their lifetime. And you and I are doing it twice. But for what it's worth, your presence here tonight wasn't a mistake. That monster would have killed me otherwise."

Jax squeezed my hand, the ghost of a smile on his lips. "You would have been fine. That thing was barely a threat compared to the Gladiators I remember. For all his ranting about how far we've fallen, Zaletor isn't doing too great himself."

"That's why I'm sure we can win," Mercury insisted, suddenly beside us. "He's half the monster he used to be. Even with his stupid crown and ugly robes."

I tried to be bolstered by the Ethereal's confidence, but I couldn't seem to quell the fluttering in my stomach.

Kitt paused from saddling Boss, his brow furrowed. "The crown didn't look like the drawings you showed us. The ones Alto had done."

Mercury's eternal eyes snapped Kitt. "What do you mean?"

The trapper had the good sense to look uncomfortable under the Ethereal's scrutiny. "There was a big hole in the middle. I saw it when I was sneaking up, while I waited for Ness to circle around the back."

"That's how it looked when I hid it." I'd been so startled by Zaletor's sudden appearance, and the subsequent battle for our lives, I hadn't even noticed. "It was just a thick gold band because we'd—"

"Pried out the gemstone," Mercury finished, eyes wide. "Don't you see? *That's* why he's not as powerful!"

Ness stopped gathering up packs and came to stand with us. "If the crown is the source of his power, it makes sense that it would need to be complete to pull forth more dark energy."

"But if he doesn't have it, where's the gemstone?" Jax asked, a new glint in his eyes. Once a thief, always a thief.

The gemstone.

Mercury and I glanced at each other.

Oh.

Shit.

Ness saw the look on my face. "What is it?"

I let out a breath, feeling an overwhelming sense of déjà vu. "I don't know where the gemstone is."

"What do you mean you don't know?" Jax countered.

I narrowed my eyes at the hint of accusation in his voice. "Becca had it. We each hid a piece and agreed we'd never tell anyone where it was, including each other."

Jax cursed and even Kitt frowned.

"Could this be a good thing?" Ness asked, looking to each of us. "I mean, if we don't know where the gemstone is, then Zaletor won't ever find it either, right?"

But Mercury shook their head. "With the base of the crown, Zaletor may be able to sense the gemstone the same way I can sense when someone uses dark energy. He'd have to get close to it, but if he can't die then he's got all the time in the world to search. But there's a bigger issue that's worrying me."

We all shared a glance, unsure what could possibly worry the Ethereal more than the completed crown.

"I've been thinking about what Alto said, about how Kalexia herself gave Zaletor the crown. I was never able to figure out how he was able to draw so much dark energy from the Ethereal Plane." They shifted, their wings tucked in tight.

"But if Kalexia created the crown, I think she might have infused it with a piece of her own essence."

The others looked confused, but I felt the blood drain from my face. "I thought every piece of her essence was trapped?"

"The Goddesses thought so too. But it would explain how Zaletor was able to acquire so much energy. And if even a sliver of Kalexia's essence exists outside the prison, it could be used to free her."

For the first time ever, I saw genuine fear in the Ethereal's starry eyes. Hundreds of years ago the Dark Lady had favored Zaletor out of boredom, and she'd been imprisoned for it. Now, if she were freed, she'd be out for revenge.

"Mercury, if Kalexia was powerful enough to nearly destroy this world merely on a whim, what could she do if she actually put forth effort?"

The flattening of their ears was the Ethereal's only response.

My voice was barely above a whisper, but I had to know. "Could the other Goddesses stop her?"

Mercury didn't blink. "We *need* to find that gemstone."

The others nodded.

"Would Becca have hidden it in the castle as well?" Kitt offered as he resumed packing. "Maybe she wanted to keep it close too."

I shook my head. "We separated the pieces before I was officially named queen. I hid the base somewhere else originally, but I brought it to the castle when I moved in. But Becca left the city right when she got her piece, saying she knew the perfect place. She was gone for two months. When she returned, she said it was done, and we agreed never to speak of it again unless we had to."

Kitt might have paused, as though snagged by something I said, but I couldn't be sure.

"And she didn't say anything that might be a clue?" Jax pressed.

I struggled to remember, but it was so long ago. A vision of her dirty, travel-worn face blossomed in my mind. She'd returned without any money or provisions, but her air of accomplishment had been unmistakable.

"I think she said it was in good hands with a pumpkin? But I have no idea what that means."

Ness looked up from stuffing blankets into a pack. "She said she knew the perfect place. So where would that be?"

"It could be a million places!" Jax threw his hands in the air.

"There is one other person we could ask," Mercury said, their tone too measured.

I nearly dropped the blanket I was folding. "Absolutely not."

"He's her cousin! He might know!"

Jax gave me a pointed look. "They grew up together, Phoebe. He's our best shot. Plus, then he can help us with everything else."

"You don't know what you're asking me to do!" I tried to shout, but it came out as more of a gasp. Hells, after everything else, *this* is what made it hard to breathe?

Mercury sighed, their expression softening. "Yes, I do. Jax told me about what happened. He told me everything."

I shot a glare at Jax, who didn't even have the good grace to look ashamed.

"I know it will be painful," Mercury went on, "and more than a little awkward. But the *fate of the world* is at stake. Would you truly risk the existence of every life on this planet just to avoid talking to your ex?!"

I chewed my lip, considering. "I mean—"

"Phoebe! We *need* to find that gemstone, no matter the sacrifice."

I groaned. There was that word again. Sacrifice. Hadn't I already sacrificed enough?

"We don't even know where to find him," I exclaimed. It was my last hope to get out of this.

"Sure we do," Mercury chirped. "Alto told me. On the off chance you changed your mind, he told me Tristan was the captain of a ship that docks out of Salt Wind in the western ports."

I thought my eyes would pop out of my skull. The western ports. The goblin had planned this all along. Seeing my rage, they merely shrugged.

Kitt cleared his throat. "We don't all have to talk to him. If we just need to know about the gemstone or Becca's hiding places, Jax and Mercury can go talk to him while Phoebe, Ness and I wait somewhere nearby. They can come get us when they're done."

We all stared at him. If he wasn't across the fire with several people in between us, I'd have thrown my arms around him in relief.

"That's an excellent idea," Ness said, claiming a side.

Goddesses save me, this was going to happen.

"Fine," I conceded, "we'll go find him. But don't expect me to be pleasant about the whole thing."

Mercury nodded. "I never do."

19

―――――――

If we were going to Salt Wind, we would need to get more horses; otherwise, it would take us nearly two weeks to walk there. As much as I enjoyed the idea of postponing our arrival for as long as possible, I knew we didn't have that kind of time. When I informed the group, Jax lit up.

"I know just the place! Morina is less than a day's walk, it's on the way, and it's large enough to have horses available, but small enough that we won't have to travel through a whole city to find them. It's perfect!"

"What's the catch?" Ness asked flatly.

"The 'catch' is that Mary's Tavern has the best boar stew in the entire country, and we will be stopping to eat." Jax turned to me. "Truly, it's the best stew you've ever had in your life. And I'm including anything you had at the palace. Those fancy chefs are all style, no flavor."

I exhaled sharply, remembering how he'd whined about not having those very same chefs along only yesterday.

"We need to continue traveling unnoticed, and eating in a

tavern in a small village sounds too risky. You and I are too recognizable.”

“Dearest, there is no place safer for us than Mary’s Tavern. I promise.”

I’d planned to turn us south toward a different town, similar to Linipa in size, that would be much closer and easier to hide in. But there was an earnestness in Jax’s face that I couldn’t deny, and he’d never been one to go back on a promise. Besides, the idea of a good meal after so many days of hard travel was too tempting to pass up.

“Morina it is.”

Mary’s Tavern was a small stucco building with a slate roof near the edge of Morina. While we tied the horses outside, Mercury grumpily agreeing to wait with them, Jax practically danced through the tavern’s front door.

We followed him in to find the building full with the lunch rush. The space could seat twenty people comfortably, but it held nearly double that at present. I began to feel exposed and trapped. I opened my mouth to suggest going somewhere else, when a stunning, plump woman in a green cotton apron popped up from behind the bar.

“Graces, Tessian, again?!”

To my horror, everyone in the tavern looked up. But the focus wasn’t on me. Spreading his arms wide, or as wide as possible in the cramped space, Jax swept forward.

“What can I say, Mary my love? I cannot resist your cooking. And this time, I brought paying customers!”

The woman, who I took to be *the* Mary of Mary’s Tavern, scoffed. But there was a hint of a smile on her lips.

"Some of you lot clear out!" Mary shouted to the crowded room. "Make room for the new guests!"

There was no grumbling or protests as half the assembled patrons tossed coins onto the nearest tables and filed out the front door. Most of them offered Jax a handshake or hearty slap on the back as they went. I pressed myself behind Kitt to avoid any curious eyes, taking in his moss and rain scent.

Once the crowd had thinned, Mary came out from behind the bar to greet us. Her strawberry blond hair was swept back into a bun with a few tendrils loose about her face. She studied Jax with emerald eyes, appraising.

"I'm limiting you to two bowls today," she said, poking a finger to his chest. "Last week, I barely had enough stew left for the dinner crew."

Jax smiled at her, his eyes crinkling with delight, but lowered his voice.

"Actually, I was hoping you'd consider closing for the rest of the day for a private party. A *confidential* party."

Mary's brows furrowed, her eyes darting to the rest of us before landing on me. I saw her throat bob as she swallowed, but her lips pressed together tight.

"Aye, I think I can manage that. But if I kick everyone out now, there will be questions. In a bit, I'll announce there was a spill and the stew's gone for the day. That will empty this place quicker than a house on fire, and word will spread. Til then, you lot can set up at the table in the corner or wait in the kitchens, up to you."

Jax kissed her on the cheek. "You're the best."

"Don't I know it. Now get out of the doorway!" She cast me a quick glance, then bustled away to clear the newly vacated tables. This time when she'd looked at me, there'd been wariness there.

We made our way to a large table in the room's back corner.

The remaining patrons greeted Jax warmly while ignoring the rest of us. All except one hooded figure, who approached right as we took our seats. Kitt grabbed my arm, but the figure pushed their hood back enough to show the face beneath.

"What are you doing here?" I smiled, making a conscious effort to keep my voice down.

Alto's return smile was tight with exhaustion. "I figured after collecting Jax, Mercury would convince you to visit Tristan. And since Jax would never be able to pass this way without stopping to gorge himself, I knew this was the place to wait for you."

He lowered himself into an empty chair cautiously, as though stiff from traveling or a bad night's sleep. I made brief introductions around the table. Jax finished making his rounds of the room and paused to slap Alto on the back in greeting before heading toward the kitchen. The gesture was affectionate, but Alto winced.

"Are you hurt?" Kitt asked, seeing his grim face as he rubbed his shoulder.

In response, Alto looked at me, and I saw the pain in his face, deeper than any physical wound.

"Alto, what happened?"

Bowing his head, Alto whispered, "A creature came the night you left. I tried to fight it, but...the bookstore is gone."

His voice broke, as did my heart. I knew Ravenwing had been Alto's whole world.

"I am so sorry." I reached across the table and took his hand. "It must have followed me. I never should have gone to see you. I should have left you alone and—"

Alto shook his head with firm rebuke. "It's not your fault. It's mine. I should have come with you from the start. I knew if Zaletor was looking for revenge he would come for me eventually, but I was a coward."

I could tell any protests I made to this statement would result in an argument, so I gave his hand a squeeze.

"Was anyone else injured?" Ness asked. There was a haunted look in her eyes, and I knew she was picturing her own destroyed shop and ruined village. But Alto shook his head.

"It was only interested in me. It smashed through the store, surprising me. I wasn't powerful enough to stop it." Shame clouded his face. "It only stopped when an Aqua came to my aid, washing it away."

I had more questions, but at that moment Jax and Mary emerged from the kitchen, each with a tray of food.

"As promised," Jax grinned, placing several bowls on the table. "I present to you the best stew in the world."

Mary distributed two loaves of fresh bread and several jugs of water. I noticed her flash another wary glance my way as she tucked the now-empty tray under her arm.

"Thank you for letting us rest here," I offered, hoping to set her at ease. "This is a lovely building."

Jax snorted, already digging into his food. "It had better be, considering what I paid for the damn thing."

"Oi," Mary snapped, "I let you eat for free. Be grateful for that."

Seeing all of our confused looks, Jax wiped his mouth on a napkin. "I suppose introductions are in order. Everyone, this is Mary Vaunsen, formerly Mary Tessian."

Everyone froze, and Jax preened at his expert delivery. A true actor, through-and-through.

I recovered first. "You two were married?"

Mary folded her arms across her ample bosom. "Aye, a fact you'd know if you'd been to the wedding."

My cheeks heated at the accusation, but Jax reached across the table to pat the woman's hand. "We've already discussed that, love. Turns out someone in the castle hasn't been delivering my letters. She had to track down Alto just to find out where I was."

Mary's frown didn't budge.

"I truly am sorry to have missed it," I said. "I know I can't make up for it, but if I'd known, I promise I would have been there."

A beat passed, until finally the woman shrugged. "Well, it's not like it worked out, anyway. The marriage barely lasted a year."

"And this fine establishment was my freedom gift to her," Jax declared, waving a hand. Seeing my face, he cocked his head. "You seem confused."

"Sorry, I just—seeing you two together, you seem so…"

"Happy?" Jax offered.

"Amicable?" Mary smiled.

I nodded, and Mary shrugged. "Turns out, we're better off as friends. But it's a friendship neither of us wanted to lose. So, here we are."

I waited to see if they were joking, but neither of them laughed. "You make it sound so simple."

It was Jax's turn to shrug. "It was our relationship. We ended it on our terms. It's an arrangement that wouldn't work for everyone, but it works for us."

"At least until he cuts into my profits from eating too much free food. *Again.*" Mary shot Jax a glare, then sighed. "Speaking of which, I'll get the rest of this lot cleared out so you can relax in peace."

"Thank you," I said again as she rose to her feet. "And don't worry. I'll make sure you're compensated generously for the loss in customers."

With a grin, Mary headed back to the kitchen, and I noticed an extra spring in her step.

Still marveling at the dynamic between them, I returned my attention to Jax. "You said you've been married twice. Is your relationship with your other ex the same?"

"Great Goddesses, no!" He blew air out his cheeks. "Anthony and I do not speak. The relationship went on too long, and we'd become bitter by the end. We've both moved on from it, me several times, but I doubt we will ever be comfortable in the same room. It wasn't a pleasant ending, but I did learn from it. It made it easier to recognize what was happening with Mary and end things while we could remain friends."

There was a terrible crash from the kitchen, and Mary's curses rang through the tavern.

"She certainly is an excellent friend to have," I agreed.

20

Mary's plan had worked perfectly.

The remaining tavern patrons had quickly packed up and moved on once they'd learned of the "mishap" in the kitchen. Though, I wondered if some of their desire to leave was due to Mary's mock rage, which had seemed so real I wondered if she'd been an actress herself before becoming a tavern owner. Once they'd gone, Mercury had slipped in, still indignant about being left outside. Lucky for us, they had recovered quickly as Mary fawned over the Ethereal's beauty.

We'd shared a hearty meal, and I'd gladly agreed it was the best stew I'd ever tasted, and Mary had beamed with pride. The pot she'd dropped, or thrown from the sound of it, had been empty, so there'd been plenty of food to satisfy everyone, even Jax. I'd watched, horrified and enthralled, as the man had consumed *five bowls of stew.*

As we finished eating, Mary went and purchased us three more horses. It meant draining my purse completely, but at least none of us would have to walk to Salt Wind.

An anxious knot had settled into my stomach, and while the others relished a night spent indoors, I felt filled with energy. Sitting on the floor in a corner of the dining room, I practiced floating small orbs of flame and stone until it was nearly midnight.

"Care for some company?"

Uncrossing my eyes from the effort, I found Kitt standing beside me, a bottle in hand.

My heart skipped, but I smiled half-heartedly. "I won't be much fun, I'm afraid."

"That is a matter of opinion." Kitt settled down onto the floor beside me, stretching out his legs. He was a tall man with long limbs, but I noticed he made sure to leave me plenty of room. "Would you like some wine? I realize I've never asked if you like the stuff. There's also ale and water."

I smiled at his concern. "I like white wine; red upsets my stomach. Though..." I glanced at where Jax was leaning against the bar, regaling Ness and Mary with an overly dramatic retelling of the opening night performance of *The Great Victory*.

"Jax is the one who gave me the bottle, if that's what you're worried about," Kitt said. "And it appears to be a white."

Hearing his name, Jax glanced over at me and winked.

Scoundrel, I smiled. A peace offering, then.

Rather than asking for a glass, I tipped the bottle back. The wine was like sunlight on my tongue, the perfect mixture of tart and sweet, and it pooled comfortably in my belly. I savored the taste as I passed the bottle back to Kitt.

"I can't get over it," I said, watching Jax resume his story with an arm thrown around Mary's shoulders. "It's wonderful, don't get me wrong! But...I'd never have put 'Jax' and 'emotional maturity' in the same thought."

Kitt took a sip, his eyes crinkling. "It's always nice when you learn that life still holds surprises. Though Jax strikes me as someone who's never done what was expected of him. It makes sense that his view on relationships is no different. Something we can all learn from."

I took the bottle back and raised it. "I will drink to that." A pleasant warmth began spreading through my limbs, and I sighed.

"Speaking of relationships," Kitt began, "I realize Jax's play probably embellished a lot of details. But there's something I have to know."

Instinctively, I froze. But a smile tugged at Kitt's lips, and I gave a tentative nod. The smile remained, but Kitt narrowed his eyes in mock suspicion.

"Was there truly only one bed available when Tristan showed up at your door that night in the rain?"

I don't know if it was the wine or the ridiculousness of the question, but I burst out laughing. "*That's* what you want to know?!"

Kitt held up both hands, though one still gripped the bottle. "I'm not judging. I'm merely curious why one of you didn't choose a couch. Or the floor. There must have been other options."

Grinning, I opened my mouth and closed it, once. Twice. Kitt's own smile only grew wider with each failed attempt to explain. Finally, I sighed and grabbed the bottle in defeat.

"He was freezing, and we were teenagers. Nothing happened between us that night, but I admit the idea of someone sleeping on the floor didn't even cross my mind."

He chuckled again as I took another drink. Its warmth had encompassed my entire body by this point, and I relished the relaxation that came with it. My friends still chatted at the bar, but I no longer paid attention to their conversation. All my focus was on the trapper beside me and the bottle we passed back and forth.

"Since no one has created a theatrical production about your love life yet, I feel at a disadvantage. Have you ever been married?"

As soon as the question left my mouth, I wished I could take it back. It was too much, too personal. His love life was none of my business. Why did I even want to know?!

Kitt's grin softened, but to my surprise he didn't shrink at the question.

"Never married, though I was engaged for a time. That's something we have in common." He raised the bottle in salute before taking a drink. "Her name was Florence. She was my younger sister Hazel's best friend, and I'd known her for years. The two of them were inseparable as girls, but as we all grew older, I noticed Florence always wanted to spend time wherever I was." He smiled, shaking his head slightly. "Hazel thought it was marvelous. I was annoyed at first, thinking it was merely some girlish crush. But as time went on, I realized Florence was a kind, smart person, and I returned her affections."

I took a sip of wine, struggling to imagine the quiet, confident man before me as an awkward youth in love.

"Looking back, I don't know if we'd have made it. We had different ways of communicating and different outlooks on life. We would have had to work together, grow together. We didn't realize all that right away, of course. It takes time to know another person, and I think we were just nearing the point where we would have either grown together or ended things when my sister died."

It was a miracle I didn't spit wine all over the floor. The liquid turned sour in my mouth, and when I managed to swallow, it burned down my throat. My eyes watered, and when I blinked them clear, I could see the sorrow in Kitt's face was beyond measure as he gazed unseeing across the room.

"How did she die?"

"She'd always struggled with her health. We'd moved a few years before to be near the best healers Bearnel had to offer. They had helped, giving us a few extra years, but we'd always known things would eventually take a turn." He cleared his throat. "When she passed, Florence and I...we were grieving. Though we never said it out loud, we both knew we were staying together simply to avoid being alone. We announced our engagement a few months later."

He fell silent, staring at the fireplace. I set the bottle on the floor between us, knowing I should stay quiet, allowing him to be finished with his story only if he wished. But I couldn't.

"What happened?"

Kitt startled, as though he forgot I was there. "We couldn't grow, not smothered as we were in our grief. It wasn't either of our faults, really. I wasn't willing to put in the work to repair our relationship, to fight for it, and she wasn't either. But neither of us knew how to end it, considering all we'd been through. It was as though staying together somehow kept Hazel alive.

"Finally, one day, I realized how trapped I felt. How hollow. I didn't want to spend the rest of my life feeling that way, so I ended it."

My head was spinning, and only partially from the wine. "And Florence?"

"She was devastated. But, a few months later she met someone else. The last I heard, they're married and blissfully happy." He smiled at the thought.

It was my turn to stare out at the room, struggling to focus. The warmth I'd felt a few moments before, which had been so pleasant, was now stifling. A flurry of emotions collided in my head, and I squeezed my eyes shut.

"Phoebe, what's the matter?"

I didn't want to voice my shameful thoughts out loud. But

Kitt was right. We had this situation in common. If anyone could ever understand, it was him. I couldn't help but watch Jax and Mary banter across the room. "Do you ever envy her happiness?"

He didn't answer right away, and I dared a glance at his face. It was thoughtful, without a hint of revulsion or confusion.

"No," he finally said. My heart sank, but he went on. "I don't envy her happiness, because the life she's living now wouldn't make *me* happy. That was the whole point. But while we weren't good together, I still care for her and am glad she found the life she wanted. Now, it's my turn to find the life I want." He looked at me, and the gold in his brown eyes glinted like fireworks. "It might take a while, but that's alright. Because, when it happens, it will have been worth the wait."

My chest tightened at his words and the intensity of his gaze. Swallowing thickly, I forced a laugh.

"You're so wise. I wish I'd met you years ago."

Kitt's soft smile didn't waver. "So do I."

A flush crept up my face, but I couldn't look away. Neither of us had moved from our original sitting positions, but the few inches in between us now seemed both achingly far and frighteningly close. I couldn't explain it, but I suddenly needed to touch him. His hand, his arm, his face, anything to prove he was sitting beside me and not some figment of my imagination.

His eyes stayed locked on mine, as I raised my hand and—

Bumped the wine bottle.

With a splash, it went skittering across the room.

"Shit!" I reached out, trying to grab it, and collided with Kitt, who had lunged to do the same. Unable to stop my momentum, I crashed my elbow into his hand, crushing it into the floor. I heard him curse as he tried to pull away, so I rolled clumsily to the side. Right into the trail of spilled wine.

When I finally righted myself, covered in dirt and wine, I

found everyone had stopped to watch the spectacle. My whole face burned as I scampered over to where the traitorous bottle had stopped under a table. Mary appeared out of nowhere with a mop and bucket, and after apologizing profusely, I had nothing to do but face Kitt.

"I'm so sorry! Are you alright?"

His amiable smile returned as he took in my disheveled state, though he opened and closed his hand slowly.

"I'm fine. I can go find another bottle and—"

"No, I should get some sleep." I backed toward the stairs, doing my best to appear casual. "Thank you for chatting with me."

Without waiting for a response, I bolted up the stairs. The building had no bedrooms to speak of, but Mary had graciously allowed Ness, Mercury, and myself to use the upstairs storage room to sleep in for the night, while Jax, Alto, and Kitt took the floor in the tavern. I shut myself into the room that was barely more than a closet, cursing my own foolishness. Any tipsiness I'd felt had vanished with the spilled wine, and I thought back on the conversation with distressing clarity. I'd made an ass of myself with each word I'd spoken. Kitt's kind nature was the only reason he hadn't laughed in my face.

Skies above, what was I even doing? Zaletor had returned, the gemstone was missing, and the entire damn world was in danger! Everything depended on me staying focused. When I lost focus, people got hurt. The previous night's attack had proven that. The last thing I needed was to be distracted.

Curling onto my bedroll, I hugged my arms tight about myself, dreading the morning.

21

We made it to Salt Wind a day and a half later.

While I'd never visited before, Tristan had grown up here. He'd told me all about the home he loved, and I wasn't surprised he'd returned after leaving Glassleaf. Still, as we walked into the picturesque port city just after sunrise, I realized his stories hadn't been preparation enough.

What struck me most wasn't the weathered white stone buildings or salty ocean air. It was the sheer number of people bustling about their daily business. Shoulder to shoulder, they pushed through the market or pressed in close to the tables where fishermen set out the day's catch. The further into the city we moved, the fewer carts and carriages we passed, until the streets were filled only with pedestrians. The city was half the size of Glassleaf, but it seemed to have three times as many people.

The only pockets where crowds didn't cluster or press was near the alleys, where beggars had set up their camps. I stopped in my tracks the first time we passed a woman, clad in dirty rags and sack remnants, with a bowl in her hand and a child at her skirt. Her cries for mercy were nearly swallowed by the din of the crowd, but I heard them clear as day. I wanted nothing more than to run to her, to speak with her, but the push of the crowd made it impossible, propelling me forward with the current of people. And I quickly realized that woman was only the first of many.

I had no illusions about the inequality of wealth in my kingdom. I knew there were people who had more and people who had less. But having grown up with nothing, I'd made it a priority that everyone in Bearnel had access to the necessities: food, shelter, and aid would always be available to those in need. I'd seen the results transform the streets of Glassleaf and, based on reports from the various mayors, had assumed such was the case everywhere. Clearly, I was wrong.

Almost as shocking was that no one else seemed to care. Even my companions kept their faces forward, ignoring the cries and pleas of the people at the fringes of the crowd. There was no malice in their faces, but there was no recognition either. No shock or pull to help. As though this was something they'd all seen hundreds of times before.

Once again, I'd been ignorant to the reality of the world. Once again, someone had kept the truth from me. Once again, my people were suffering, and I had done nothing. With every step I took, my anger sharped.

As Captain of a ship, Tristan would most likely be found along the docks. But the horses made it difficult to maneuver the streets, so we stopped as soon as we found a suitable inn. Which was good, because I was having trouble controlling the turmoil inside myself.

"Are you sure you'll be able to find him?" I asked Alto as we led the horses to the back stable.

"If he's in the city, we'll find him." Alto smiled, handing the reins of his mare off to Ness. "Jax and I might only be known for what we did as kids, but Tristan's made a name for himself here. His generosity and dedication to the people of Salt Wind have made him a hero, so everyone knows who he is and, likely, where his ship is docked. That's where we'll start. We'll meet you back here in a few hours."

I held in a sigh. Wonderful.

I passed off a heavy pack to Jax, who ignored Mercury's grumblings as he slung it over his shoulder, and watched as my friends vanished into the crowd.

Ness pulled at my sleeve. "Come on. Kitt's handling things with the stablemaster, so let's go inside."

The Green Serpent Inn was crowded, but it felt downright tranquil compared to walking down the streets. Ness went to grab some drinks from the bar while I claimed a table near the back wall, shifting my dark hair forward to cover my face as much as possible. Keeping my head down was second nature now and since there was no way to stay completely out of sight, inconspicuous would have to do. Eventually, Ness plunked down a cold glass of cider on the table in front of me, and I muttered a thanks.

She slid into the chair across from me. "Have you been avoiding Kitt because something bad happened or because something good happened?"

I sighed, my shoulders slumped. "Both."

It was true. Ever since I'd humiliated myself in Mary's Tavern, I'd done everything possible to avoid him. I'd strategically placed my horse between Jax and Ness on the road, and at night, when Kitt would place his bedroll near mine, I'd pretend to fall asleep instantly. Any small talk that couldn't be avoided I kept straightforward and ended as quickly as possible. He hadn't commented, but I'd seen the confusion in his eyes grow with each interaction.

"There's just so much going on. This isn't a good time to be distracted with...whatever this is."

Ness sipped from her own glass, which I could see was filled with a dark, frothy beer. "Is there ever a good time? Danger seems to be your lifestyle. And I mean that in the best possible way."

I chuckled, the sound hollow in my ears. "Believe it or not, this is the first adventurous thing I've done in ages. My real 'lifestyle' is meetings and constant scrutiny." I swallowed. "It's not something most partners want to sign up for."

"You mean Tristan?"

I shook my head, absently tracing designs on the scarred surface of the table using the condensation from my glass. "He was simply the first. My relationships since, if you could even call them that, had to be kept secret because of public backlash."

"What? What kind of backlash?"

I recalled the shopkeeper in Stenomar who still resented me for not having a wedding, and I shrugged. "There's a lot of... judgment...when it comes to my relationships. Everyone compares any possible suitor with Tristan, or who they imagined Tristan to be. It's too much to put on a person, especially someone I care about."

"That hardly seems fair." Ness frowned. "If you and Kitt care for each other, I imagine he would want a choice in what is and isn't too much."

Shifting in my seat, I gave a noncommittal hum before changing the subject.

"There's so much poverty here. Practically every street corner has someone begging for help. Is that how it is everywhere?"

"I can't speak for everywhere, but I doubt it's like this. From what I've heard, Salt Wind operates by its own rules. There's wealth to be found in shipping and trading, but there's an underbelly that's less glamorous. And the mayor oversees it all." She considered my posture, my frown. "I thought you knew?"

"I certainly did not know." I was getting so tired of saying that. My mind swirled with confusion and anger, and for the millionth time I wondered if I'd done anyone any good in my time as queen. The people adored me, yes, but not for anything I'd done in the last two decades. I scrubbed at my face in frustration. "I should be out there with Alto, Jax, and Mercury, rather than hiding here like a coward."

"You're not a coward, and you're not hiding...well, you are hiding." She smirked at the hair still pulled over my face. "But in a 'concealing your identity' sort of way. They're simply asking about Becca's hiding places. They don't need you for that."

"Something else could happen. Jax and Mercury are both so impulsive. Alto, the voice of reason, is outnumbered. And this city is packed with people. Any number of things could go wrong, and I'm not there to keep them safe."

Ness played with the foam in her glass and shrugged. "Then they'll figure it out. All three of them are more than capable. You're worrying too much."

Her tone was so matter-of-fact that I frowned, bristling.

"Hardly. You-know-who is out there somewhere, waiting to strike, and—"

"Listen, Phoebe," Ness began, considering her words. "I understand that you're worried. And I agree there are dangers out there we all need to be cautious of. But your friends are able to look out for themselves. If they say they can handle this task, you should trust them."

She might as well have slapped me, because I lurched back in my chair.

"It's not like that," I sputtered. "I trust them! I'm just saying it would be safer for them if I were there."

"Why?"

"Because I have magic!"

"So does Mercury. And you said Alto's a Terra."

I resisted the urge to scoff. "Not a particularly powerful one."

"That doesn't matter."

"It does matter! I can do things they can't."

Ness folded her arms over her chest. Throughout everything, her expression had remained calm, even reassuring, as she'd ripped me apart. "How do you know what they can do if you never give them a chance to try? Or at least have an *opinion* about trying. It's the same with Kitt. You're making the decision for him that he can't handle life with you. You should try letting people decide things for themselves."

"This is ridiculous," I argued, mirroring her posture. Anger simmered inside me, making my skin feel itchy. "You're making it sound like I'm doing something wrong. The whole point of having all these Gifts is to use them to help people. Besides, not everyone can be as utterly perfect as you."

Now she frowned. "What's that supposed to mean?"

"It means I've been watching you, too. If you do something and it isn't exactly perfect, you get upset with yourself. That's what you were thinking when we first met, right? That even though you'd destroyed those monsters beautifully, one of your fire blasts had drifted slightly too far?"

Her face, now stony, went slightly ashen. Feeling a surge of triumph, I plowed ahead.

"And after blasting Zal—you-know-who, you apologized for not getting there soon enough. How could him teleporting away possibly have been your fault? But you took responsibility anyway. I bet you blame yourself for a million little things every single day, and for absolutely no reason. So don't come to me, saying how I'm the one taking on the weight of the world, when you're doing exactly the same thing."

"It's not the same." Ness shoved back from the table, jostling it as she rose to her feet. Both our drinks sloshed over the surface, but neither of us cared. "I'm not going to sit here and listen to this."

"Oh, so you can lecture me about my shortcomings, but when I point out one of yours, you run away? Very mature."

She stalked to the tavern's door, her posture casual, but people jumped out of the way as she moved past. I could see heat rippling off her body in the sunlight as she left.

Sinking back into my chair, I pushed my glass away. Ness was a powerful wielder, and a fine person, but she had no clue what she was talking about. Obviously I trusted my friends! They were all smart and could handle almost anything. But this was Zaletor we were talking about! He was my responsibility.

Besides, sometimes when people decided they were able to handle things, they turned out to be wrong.

An image of Becca floated unbidden into my head. The liquids that had pooled on the table froze in a heartbeat, and what remained in the glasses became solid.

Had she suffered? Was she still alive when the waves had claimed her? With her Specter Gift, had she watched all the souls of her crew gather around her in her last moments? Had she hoped, against all odds, I'd appear out of thin air to save her?

My stomach lurched, and I pushed up from the table right as Kitt arrived.

"Everything alright? Where's Ness?"

"I need some air," I said, pushing past him.

"Okay, we can—"

"I'm going by myself."

I didn't bother waiting for a reply as I left the tavern and was instantly swallowed by the mass of people. I'd probably hurt his feelings again, but maybe that was for the best too.

22

Aimless, I let the flow of humanity push me through the city. Forcing thoughts of Becca from my mind, I tried to focus on the crush of people around me. I was just as uncomfortable as when we'd first arrived, but now I endured it, embraced it. I memorized the face of every beggar on every street corner. And, most importantly, I searched for the rip that was causing all the trouble.

A city was like a piece of fabric, the threads woven together to form something solid. A healthy city was whole. True, there would always be places the threads had snared or a small patch where things had been repaired, but the fabric was always intact. Functional.

Salt Wind was a fabric with a gaping hole somewhere, a giant rip was causing all the threads to warp. The rip was affecting every thread in some way, and as a result, the fabric couldn't hold together.

So, I looked for those loose threads, the ones that would lead me to the rip. A back-alley deal, a person looking over their shoulder, an underhanded trade.

It took less than an hour.

A massive man caught my eye as he exited a shop. His clothes were ordinary, and he moved with a casual purpose, but his face looked like it had been punched from clay, and a greasy clump of blond hair perched atop his head. Despite the press of bodies, people managed to give him a wide berth as he moved down the street and into the next shop. Following, I loitered outside under the guise of adjusting my boots.

Clayface emerged quickly, tucking something into his pocket and looking smug. He continued down the street, aiming for the next building. I cast a quick glance inside the shop he'd just left, a jeweler, and saw the woman behind the counter putting away an empty purse. Her face was tight.

When Clayface emerged from the next shop, again carrying no goods or supplies, I knew I'd found the thread. Now I needed to see where it led me.

On and on it went. Clayface hit every shop for three streets. He walked confidently, as though he didn't have a care in the world. At no point did he look around or check if he was being followed. Though if he had, he wouldn't have seen me. Fueled by rage and determination, my old instincts had taken over. The crowded streets were now my camouflage, and I slipped among the people with ease.

The sounds from the docks echoed over this part of town. I expected Clayface to head to a seedy tavern or under a pier, places where illegal businesses tended to flourish. Instead, he turned down an alley and warning bells went off in my head. Following a shady figure along a crowded street was one thing, but following him down an alley was quite different. Were there exits? A waiting ambush? What if he went inside a building? I could hardly follow him then.

But I didn't want to lose the thread. Something was very wrong with this city, and I was determined to figure out what.

With the utmost caution, I approached and peered around the corner.

Empty. This close to the docks, the alley should have been filled with cargo, or at least trash, but it was clear. Practically clean. It set my teeth on edge.

A dozen yards down, the alley vanished in a right turn, blocking the rest of the way from view. Rallying my Gifts, I crept down, sticking close to the wall and listening intently.

I was nearly to the turn, when a voice came from behind me.

"What's this, then?"

I spun, nearly blasting the mystery speaker with a knife of ice, and found two men wearing forest-green uniforms standing at the mouth of the alley. One was my height, while the other towered over us both. Each wore a circular golden badge pinned to their chest, stamped with an eagle in flight.

City guards. I swallowed a cry of relief.

"Oh, good. There's a man who's—"

"Shut it!" the shorter guard snapped. His face was pinched, and he resembled an extremely unhappy weasel. "Quincy! Get out here!"

I looked at the two of them, startled by the hostility in their eyes. But a new voice yelled out behind me.

"What? I haven't changed yet!"

Turning, I saw Clayface come around the bend in the alley, fingers fumbling at the buttons of his coat.

His forest-green coat.

Well shit. Looks like I'd followed the correct thread after all.

"Who's this?" Clayface grunted. His comrade had called him Quincy, but I liked my name better.

"This mouse has been following you for the past two blocks," the tall guard sneered.

They must have been keeping an eye on Clayface as well and saw me follow him down the alley.

"Actually, it's been the last eight blocks." I angled myself so my back was to the wall, allowing me to keep all three of them in view at once. "I hope you all aren't the best Salt Wind has to offer."

Clayface turned a horrible pink color, but Weasel laughed.

"Hear that, gents? Little mouse has a death wish. Must be new to town." He elbowed The Giant. "What say we give her a warm welcome."

The grin that split The Giant's face was nothing short of terrifying, and the two of them pulled knives from their belts. Clayface must have forgotten his somewhere, but an unloaded crossbow hung from his belt. He ignored it, pushing up his sleeves and revealing arms corded with muscle.

"Wonderful." I smiled, shaking loose the tension in my shoulders. "I was looking for a way to let off some steam."

Weasel opened his mouth to make another snide comment, but I was done talking. The anger that had been building all afternoon had finally found an outlet, and I knew my best move was to attack first. Ice was normally my go-to option, and fire was easy when I was angry, but I wanted to push myself, see how my training had truly progressed. So I focused on the Gift I'd been struggling with most.

The alley floor consisted of packed dirt, and since it was free of cargo boxes, there was nothing impeding the mound of earth I summoned to sweep over Clayface. It was nowhere near the wall that Zaletor had created that night in the field, but it was enough to knock the large man on his ass. Falling back with a cry, he barely had time to register what had happened before I swept the mound over him, covering everything but his face. It wouldn't hold him forever, but at least I would only have to focus on the two guards before me without fearing an attack from behind.

I turned to find both Weasel and The Giant staring at me

slack jawed. A small cluster of people had gathered outside the alley to watch the commotion, and their faces were just as shocked.

Weasel recovered some of his composure, and a malicious glint appeared in his eyes.

"Using Gifts against a member of the Mayor's Guard is illegal." He grinned now, raising his knife. "Punishable by death."

The Giant lunged forward. The urge to freeze him in place was almost overwhelming, but I took a deep breath. Only Terra, I told myself. Just one element this time. Pressing my hands down, I opened a hole in the earth beneath them. It wasn't large enough to swallow both men whole, The Giant was so fucking tall, but the shock of it caused them to crumple together, leaving an opening.

I sprinted forward, intending to leap over the two men and vanish into the gathering crowd. But a hand shot up from the hole, catching my ankle. With a grunt, I fell forward, catching myself before I could be dragged into the pit.

Lashing out with my other foot, I smashed in The Giant's nose. He screamed in pain as I rolled out of reach, panting with effort. The crowd had grown bigger, and while everyone gave me a wide berth, a few of them cheered as I staggered to my feet.

"Watch out!" a familiar voice cried.

I whirled to find Clayface, covered in dirt and breathing hard, standing on the opposite side of the pit. He was pointing his crossbow right at my heart. I could hear the crowd scattering but kept my focus ahead, cursing myself for not paying attention.

"I wouldn't advise that," a casual voice called from behind me. It was the same voice that had warned me of the crossbow.

Even as I stood ready to fight, my knees tried to buckle. Still, I didn't take my eyes off the guard before me.

"Stay out of this, Derbeck! It doesn't involve you," Clayface sneered, his eyes leveled over my right shoulder. Weasel was already struggling to climb over The Giant. It was only a matter of seconds before they were both free.

"Believe it or not, Quincy, I'm trying to help you out," Tristan said, coming to stand beside me. Looking around, he yelled for all to hear, "I'd *hate* for Mayor Renis to have to hang you for attacking our queen."

My heart dropped. Time seemed to slow. A few gasps sounded and what remained of the crowd froze as people studied me with new interest.

Clayface scoffed, but something in Tristan's tone made him look more critically at my face. My eyes.

Weasel saw it first, and his face leached of color. "Fuck me! Quincy, put that damn thing down!"

Clayface tossed the crossbow into the pit, as though it could destroy the evidence. The murmuring quieted as people in the crowd dropped to their knees.

Shit shit *shit*!!

"Get out of here," I snarled at the guards, "and never bother these people again."

All three of them took off running, though The Giant now had a heavy limp. They made their way up the street, back toward the heart of the city, and vanished from sight. Rounding on Tristan, I glared up at his smug face.

"I really wish you hadn't done that."

He shrugged. "It was the only way I could think of to diffuse the situation. At least, the only way that didn't involve Quincy getting blown to bits. He's a worthless cheat, but it would be a horrible mess to clean up and probably only raise more ques—"

"Stop. Speaking."

Swallowing thickly, I faced the growing crowd. Whispers

rippled through it like wind in the grass. If it had been someone else who'd identified me, I could have claimed it was a misunderstanding. But these people knew Tristan. They'd take his word as gospel.

My cover was blown.

I struggled to come up with a plan. But every lie that came to mind vanished at the sight of their desperate faces. Finally, despite the fact that it would ruin my plan, I decided to go with the truth.

"I am sorry for the treatment you have received at the hands of your mayor," I said, raising my voice to carry through the small square. "I hold myself accountable for not knowing the extent of the corruption in this city, and I swear to you changes will be made."

Everywhere I looked, I saw hopeful, shining eyes. Not a single person looked at me with anger or accusation.

They should have. Smoldering hells, they should have.

Giving a final nod of my head, I turned and stalked down the street back toward the tavern. I could hear Tristan following, and the crowds parted around us, letting us pass. As he fell in step beside me, I cut him a glare.

"Why didn't you tell me things were so bad here?" I already knew the answer, but I needed him to confirm it.

A raised eyebrow was the only hint of shock he'd ever show. But I saw it.

"Phoebe, I've written to you at least a dozen times over the last few years begging for help. I even went to the castle once, but one of your advisors said you didn't want to see me."

My hands trembled as ice cracked in my veins. Keeping my steps casual, I turned down another alley and stalked to a nearby barrel filled with rainwater. I didn't even bother pushing up my sleeves before plunging both hands deep into the barrel. In a controlled burst, I released my anger into it.

The barrel froze instantly, becoming solid ice all the way through, my arms trapped up to the elbow. Tristan leaned against the building beside me, arms crossed.

"I thought you were upset with me and purposely not responding to my messages. But now I'm guessing you never received any of them."

With a slow exhale, I allowed heat to radiate out. As quickly as it froze, the water melted, and steam wafted up to my face. I didn't let it boil, though, as my hands were still inside.

"Are all members of the city guard so corrupt?"

"Those weren't city guards. Renis has his own private goon squad who report to only him."

I pulled my arms from the barrel and let them hang dripping at my sides.

"I'm sorry," I said, facing Tristan for the first time in ten years. His face had always been sun-kissed from a life on the sea, but there were new wrinkles around his eyes and forehead. His once vibrant red hair had dimmed a bit and showed a few streaks of gray, but life on a ship had kept him muscular. He was still devastatingly handsome, but seeing him now, my heart didn't race the way it once had. "I had no idea, but that's no excuse. I should have—"

"Tristan!" a female voice called.

A woman came walking toward us, a baby slung over her hip in a cloth wrap. Her prominent brown eyes were fixed on Tristan, and she paid no mind to how the baby pulled at the smooth, jet-black strands of her hair. I knew she was our age, but somehow she managed to look youthful and spry as she hurried down the alley.

"Reggie said there was trouble in the square and you were—oh!"

She saw me then, with my shoulders hunched and arms

soggy, and stopped. Pushing off from the building, Tristan moved to her, pulled by an unseen force.

The woman glanced between us. "Apologies, I didn't mean to interrupt."

"You're not interrupting at all," Tristan said. His face softened as he slipped his arm around the woman's waist, careful not to jostle the now-grinning baby. With effort, he tore his eyes from her face and back to me.

"Phoebe, this is my wife, Tennian."

23

In that moment, Zaletor himself could have appeared and blasted me off the face of the earth, and it would have been preferable to standing in that alley, meeting my ex's stunning wife. They both stared at me, him waiting for a response, her clearly confused.

Holy hells, what could I even say?

I gestured to the baby. "I didn't know you'd had another one."

I nearly grimaced at my own awkwardness. That's me, master of the spoken language.

Tennian's mouth made a perfect "o" of shock as she realized who I was.

"Your Majesty," she breathed, lowering into a deep curtsey. Any other person would have struggled to perform such an action with a baby in hand, but she made it look like a dancer's form.

"Please, there's no need for that," I said, glancing around. We were alone in the alley, but I knew word of my presence in the city would spread like wildfire. "Uh, the others will be looking for us at the Green Serpent. I suggest we make our way there.”

Confusion and curiosity mingled on Tristan's face, but Tennian shifted uncomfortably.

“I don't want to be in the way, with little Marcus and all. I should probably just head home.”

Her obvious discomfort snapped me back to sense. *Do better!* I scolded myself.

I smiled and stepped toward her. “You can do as you wish, but your presence is certainly welcome. The matter we've come to discuss is of a more delicate nature, but I know I can count on your discretion.”

The words were genuine. Even in my deepest heart I held no ill will toward this woman. What happened between Tristan and me was over long before they met, and I couldn't blame her for trying to be happy.

She must have seen my truth, because a relieved smile spread on her face.

Now Tristan was the one who shifted uncomfortably. “Who all is here?”

Clearly, he hadn't grown more patient in the years since I'd seen him. Unwilling to say anything else out in the open. I gestured toward the main road.

The reunion that occurred in The Green Serpent was filled with joy and camaraderie. At least, that's how it sounded from the pantry, where I was hiding.

Seeing everyone together, laughing and hugging, had been too much. Anxieties began to crash over me like a wave, and I was struggling to find the surface. I'd managed to excuse myself, though I doubt anyone would even have noticed if I hadn't.

My breath came in deep gasps as I tried to calm down. But it felt impossible, everything was too fucked. I tried to steady myself by focusing on one problem at a time, starting with the least confusing.

How deep did the corruption in Salt Wind go? Was it only a few guards? I doubted it. The three I'd encountered had been far too comfortable, too confident in their own authority. And the people who'd gathered to watch our fight had scattered at the sight of the crossbow, as if they'd known Clayface wouldn't hesitate to fire, even with innocents in the background.

The search for the crown's gem was top priority, but I knew I couldn't leave this place without attempting to set things right.

There was also the problem of having been seen wandering the streets. Considering how quickly good gossip traveled, I wouldn't be surprised if half the city now knew I was here. There was no way to contain it, either. Mercury hadn't been there to inspire or frighten the crowd into secrecy, and if I'd asked people not to say anything, it would only have made things worse. The sight of Tristan and I together would spark countless rumors, most of them bad.

What the fuck was I going to do?

Whatever it was, it probably meant leaving my hiding place.

Which I couldn't bring myself to do.

"There isn't time for this!" I hissed in frustration and gave my face a vigorous scrub. "Right. Fate of the world, fate of the world, fate of the world..."

Keeping that phrase in mind, I exited the pantry and found Ness leaning against the wall. Ah yes, one more thing I'd forgotten. My cheeks heated at the memory of our fight.

"How long have you been out here?"

She shrugged. "The room was getting crowded."

I took that to mean "a while." The murmur of voices echoed down the hall from the private dining room we'd been given. There'd been no point hiding our identities when our group had returned. Tristan was too recognizable, and I'd wanted to get a more private space for us to talk. Upon realizing what guests had gathered at her inn, the innkeeper had practically bent over backwards to make us feel welcome. After delivering several platters of food and drink, the staff had vanished, assuring us privacy.

I glanced at Ness, who stared back at me. Closing the pantry door, I leaned against it. "I owe you an apology," I said, and held up a hand when she tried to speak. "And an explanation.

"When I was fourteen, Mercury found me on the streets of Glassleaf. They told me I was special. That I had been created by The Goddesses themselves to defeat a great evil and save the world. But, in doing so, I would have to die."

I swallowed, feeling tired at the memory. "At that point, I'd been alone for years. I didn't have any family or friends. There were plenty of other kids on the street, but I'd kept to myself. I knew if anyone found out about my extra Gifts, they'd turn me over to Zaletor's cronies in a heartbeat. So when Mercury told me I had to die, I was angry. It wasn't fair. Why should I have to save the world when the world hadn't done anything for me? Mercury never answered. I think they could see there was no arguing with me. But they offered to train me, to help me control my Gifts. I'd lived in fear of people finding out, so I agreed. I thought if I could control my Gifts, I could hide them better. And figured once I was good enough, I could ditch the flying nuisance and live the rest of my life in peace."

Someone laughed from the dining room. The voice was muffled, but I was willing to bet it was Jax. Only he could laugh during a tale of being attacked. I smiled.

"My plan was ruined when I met Becca. She was my first

friend. Well, my first human friend. She had her own demons she was running from, but she was the first person to see all my Gifts and not be afraid. Then, one by one, the others came into my life. All of them showed me that there were people out there striving to make the world a better place, willing to do whatever was necessary to defeat the evil. They became my family, and I realized I would do whatever it took to make sure they all survived. Because I was the only one who could."

My heart ached, from pain or love or both. I struggled to swallow past the lump in my throat, knowing what I had to say next.

"When I sent Becca out to stop the pirate raids, she told me she'd be fine. That she'd be back before spring. It turned out, she could handle the pirates, but she couldn't have anticipated the storm." My eyes watered, and I resisted the urge to cover my face. "She was so strong, so capable, but she still died."

I finally faced Ness, clearing my clogged throat. "All this is to say, you were right. I don't trust my friends to tell me if they can't handle something. Instead, I try to anticipate every possible danger and take care of it all myself. When you pointed it out, I got angry and said things I shouldn't have. I'm sorry."

Ness's lips were pressed tight, her own eyes shining.

"I'm sorry too. In my head, I was telling you to make your life easier, to show you could relax a little more. But I pressed too hard. I phrased things poorly and didn't consider all the things you'd been through. Your reaction was completely understandable. Besides, even if my intent was to help, it wasn't my place to say anything."

I snorted, wiping away the tear that slipped down my cheek at her words. "Of course it's your place. You're my friend. If you don't tell me when I'm out of line, who will?"

"Probably Mercury," she laughed. Then her face crumpled.

"And you were right too. Those things you said, even if you said them in anger, were the truth."

She took a breath, steading herself. I waited, giving her the same patience and space she'd given me.

"When my Gift manifested, it was clear from the beginning I was going to be more powerful than the average Ignis. My parents were terrified that I'd hurt myself or someone else, so they told me I always had to be careful. More than careful. I had to be perfect. They said any minor slip could cause irreparable damage. I didn't want to hurt anyone, so I focused on not making mistakes. I guess at some point, that mindset started to apply to all aspects of my life."

"That's a lot of pressure to put on a child," I said.

"Yeah, well, I figured of all the people in the world, you would understand."

I smiled. "True. And your parents?"

"They always wanted me to join the Citadel. Become a priestess. They were convinced I could become the High Priestess, as if having a powerful Gift was all it took." She frowned, her eyes dimming. "But that was never my dream. I wanted to make things and build a place for myself. They never understood—claimed I was wasting my Gift—so I left."

The rage in her face when she'd destroyed those monsters now made sense. The glass shop hadn't been merely a source of income. It was a dream made real, a dream that had required the sacrifice of leaving behind the family who didn't support her. It had become a symbol of her independence, and Zaletor had destroyed it.

I held out my hand, and Ness took it without hesitation.

"I'm sorry about Becca," she said, giving my hand a squeeze. "I wish I could have known her."

"You'd have gotten along beautifully." I smiled at the

thought of the two of them wreaking havoc. Then shook my head. "If she were here, she'd know exactly what to do next."

Another laugh echoed from the dining room, snapping me back to the moment. With a final nod, I released Ness's hand. My shoulder muscles felt tighter than a bow string, and I rolled my neck around to loosen them.

"Alright. No more hiding."

Ness's large eyes swept over my face. "You good?

I exhaled, cheeks puffing out. "Nope, but I'm going in anyway."

24

Despite Ness's assertions, there was plenty of space for the eight of us in the dining room. Mercury and Jax were recounting Zaletor's attack as we entered, and all eyes turned to me. The baby was gone, and I could only assume someone had come to collect it. Tennian was pale, and Tristan's face was grim.

"It's true, then? He isn't dead?"

I nodded, unsure if I was imagining the hint of accusation in his eyes or not.

"But the crown is still incomplete," Mercury said, coming to stand beside me. "We need to find the gemstone before he does. Can you think of any place Becca might have hidden it?"

Tristan had been there when we'd pried the stone out, and he knew Becca and I had each taken a piece. In the years we'd been together, he'd never once asked me where I'd hidden the base.

Tristan thought for a moment but shook his head. "I remember she left for a few months, but she never said anything about it. And I purposely didn't ask."

My chest tightened, but I pushed the desperation away and changed tack. "When she returned from that trip, the only thing she told me was that a pumpkin was guarding it. Does that mean anything to you?"

Tristan's eyes went wide, and to my surprise, he started laughing.

"I hope that's a 'yes'" Mercury whispered.

"Pumpkin?! Great ghosts, I haven't thought about that thing in years." Tristan smiled. "Pumpkin was the name of Becca's favorite stuffed animal when she was a girl. It was a bright orange rabbit, or at least, it started off as bright orange. She took that thing everywhere she went." My heart leapt, both at his recognition of the mystery name and at the discovery of this new facet of my friend's life. Then Tristan's smile faded. "But I have no idea what ended up happening to it."

Everyone in the group appeared as crestfallen as I felt.

"Do we need to find it?" Tennian asked. Her voice was hesitant as she looked at all of us. "If it's hidden so well that none of you know where it is, can't we simply leave it be?"

I opened my mouth to explain why we felt it was important, recalling the conversation on the road days before, but Alto jumped in first.

"It *is* important. If it's out there somewhere, he'll never stop looking for it. And even if he's defeated, the gemstone could be found by someone else someday. If we're all dead and gone by then, it could cause untold destruction, even unintentionally, and no one would have the information on how to stop it." He looked each of us in the eye. "We can't leave it to chance. It's our responsibility to fix this."

The passion in his voice surprised me, until I recalled the loss of his bookshop. "We came to the same conclusion after Zaletor appeared on the road. If we face him again, we'll do whatever it takes to beat him, but since we have no idea where he's hiding or what his plan is, we need to focus on finding the gemstone."

"But what happens when we find it?" Jax fidgeted with his lapel. "We couldn't destroy the blasted thing last time."

"Last time you didn't have me," Mercury replied, puffing out their quicksilver chest. "Now that we know what the crown is, I'll take it back to the Ethereal Plane. It will be imprisoned with Kalexia, ensuring she never escapes."

Everyone nodded except me.

"First we need to find the damn thing. If Pumpkin was her childhood toy, maybe the hiding place is from that time in her life." I looked at Tristan again. "Is there any place that was special to her as a child? Or places she thought no one else knew about?"

He looked at the floor, his lips a thin line as he thought. We all stood silent, not daring to interrupt. Unconsciously, he took Tennian's hand, his thumb stroking circles along the delicate skin of her wrist. I dropped my gaze, fighting the urge to turn away.

Suddenly, Tristan looked up, a gleam of hope in his eyes.

"When we were kids, Marcus and I would spend the winter seasons with her family at Mistpoint, their estate. The seas were the most dangerous and unpredictable during that time, and our parents didn't want us out with them. When we'd visit, the three of us spent hours every day exploring.

"Then, when we were about ten and Becca was eight, she started going off on her own. Sometimes, we wouldn't see her all day. When we asked her where she spent all her time, she'd shrug and say she'd found a fun place to play. We tried following her a few times, hoping to find out where she was going, and, if I'm being honest, prove to ourselves that we were capable trackers, but we never could. She gave us the slip every single day."

I grinned, a warm feeling in my chest. "That sounds right."

"We never did find out where she was going." Tristan's smile faded, and a dark, unreadable look appeared in his eyes. "The following year, our parents decided we were old enough to go out with them during the winter. We never went back there again."

I sensed his true meaning, the revelation that likely had put an end to their visits, but pushed it aside. This wasn't the time for that conversation. Instead, I did the math in my head. "If she'd gone straight there from Glassleaf, it would have taken Becca less than a month to get there and back. She was gone for almost two."

"I wouldn't be surprised if she felt the need to take a round-about route, throw anyone following off the trail, just like when we were kids." Tristan looked at the ceiling, his eyes bright, but pressed ahead. "And remember how she returned with no horse and no supplies? I've always wondered if something happened on the road. Something that would have made the trip take longer." He exhaled. "I know it's not much, but it's the only place I can think of."

"Then it's our best place to start," I decided.

Everyone nodded in return, determination lighting each face. This felt right. Sitting with all of them, planning, working out problems. This was the feeling I remembered.

"From here, it will take us three weeks to get to the Crescent Sea," Kitt said, scratching his chin, "and that's if we don't run into any obstacles on the way."

I frowned, but before I could say anything, Alto asked, "Can you tell us where exactly the house was and what the terrain was like?"

Tristan glanced at Tennian. Some unspoken communication must have happened in that look, because she nodded.

"I can do you one better," he smiled at Alto, "I'll show you myself. Besides, with my ship, we can cut the travel time in half."

Eight different emotions battled in my stomach. Seeing Tristan again was one thing. But this, traveling with him, working together to save the world, it felt like too much. But it was necessary. We needed to find the gemstone, and he was the only person who had been to Becca's childhood home.

I realized everyone was looking at me, waiting to see how I'd react.

"Thank you. We'll take all the help we can get."

Mercury audibly sighed, while Jax slapped Tristan on the back. I felt sick.

"It will take a few hours to get the ship ready for the journey," Tristan said, "I suggest you get any supplies you need, and we'll set sail with the evening tide."

A few hours. That didn't give me much time, but if I left now, I could track down whoever oversaw the Mayor's Guard and—

There was a knock at the door. Everyone froze.

Without a word, Ness and Tristan took positions on either side of me, both Ignis holding their hands at the ready. Alto scanned the room, searching for any alternative exits, while Jax drew his sword, his normally jovial face now sharp with deadly focus. Mercury crouched in front of me, wings tucked in tight, ready to leap at a moment's notice. Even Tennian had pulled a dagger from her boot and stood beside Tristan.

Despite my thundering heart, I had to swallow past the sudden swelling in my throat. My family, ready to fight.

I looked at Kitt, who had moved forward to block the door, and nodded. Returning the gesture, he opened the door a crack, then all the way.

A messenger in a gray uniform stood waiting. Her face went

deathly white when she saw our group arrayed in battle formation.

"Your Majesty," she squeaked, "I have a message for you."

She handed a rolled missive to Kitt. The paper had barely left her fingers before she turned and fled, only to rush back to give a hasty bow before vanishing down the hallway.

Kitt shut the door, but no one relaxed.

"What does it say?" I asked, nodding to the note. My fingers were still covered in frost, and I didn't trust myself to touch the paper.

His eyes scanned the page. "It's from Mayor Renis. He heard about an incident by the docks and is inviting you to his manor to apologize in person."

"Of course he figured out where we were," Tristan grunted.

"An incident?" Mercury spun to face me. "What type of incident?"

I flinched at the accusation and worry on their face. Tristan must not have told them, then.

"I *may* have encountered some men in the street who turned out to be corrupt guards. An altercation occurred."

Everyone seemed to notice the state of my clothes for the first time. Mercury simmered with rage, releasing a string of curses that made me proud.

Tristan and Tennian exchanged another look, this one darker, before he turned back to me. "Phoebe, this man is dangerous. No one knows this city and its workings better than I do, and I'm telling you Renis is as corrupt as they come. You don't have to go."

But I smiled. "Actually, this works out wonderfully. It saves me the trouble of tracking him down."

25

―――――

A host of guards in green uniforms awaited us as we exited the The Green Serpent, presumably to escort us to Mayor Renis's manor, but I ignored them. If anything, their presence made me feel less safe than if we'd been traveling alone.

Tristan, Mercury, and Ness accompanied me while the others went to help Tennian prepare the ship. We marched through the city unimpeded, the general populace somehow condensing to make room for us to pass. Since my cover had already been blown, I kept my hood back and held my head high as we walked through the streets, not bothering to hide the anger on my face. I also told Mercury to remain in their true form as the four of us made our way through the city, a decision that pleased the Ethereal greatly. People leaned out windows and climbed onto streetlamps to watch us and, despite our circumstances, Mercury relished every moment of attention.

We made our way to a part of town that was quieter and more spread out than any I'd seen so far. The houses that dotted the street were large, surrounded by fences and walls. When we finally stopped at what I assumed was the mayor's residence, my rage nearly burst forth.

The massive building covered almost the entire block, with gardens visible from the perfectly groomed drive. The abundance was staggering, considering the poverty I'd seen in the heart of the city. But I reined in my anger, letting it simmer inside.

Not yet.

The guards halted outside the front door, bowing at the waist. I ignored them, eying the trembling steward who greeted us.

"G-g-greetings, Your Majesty," he said, bowing so low his cap tumbled from his head. He scooped it up and clutched it to his chest. "Mayor Renis is honored to welcome you to his home. Please, follow me."

I didn't move. "Where is Renis? He should be welcoming me himself."

The poor steward flinched. "My sincerest apologies. The mayor is—well—I believe he's preparing to greet you in the study."

Of course he was.

It was clear Renis thought himself above my authority. I could have pressed the issue and demanded Renis come to the door to greet me himself. But that would put him on guard. Renis seemed to think I wasn't a threat. That mistake that would cost him.

"Lead on," I instructed.

The interior of the manor was grander than I'd thought possible, making even my own castle seem plain. Every window was decorated with colored glass images of the sea. The sunlight reflected off the quartz floor tiles, turning the entire front hall into a kaleidoscope of blues and purples. As we moved into the foyer, the decor transitioned to dark wood paneling embellished with gilded-leaf furniture. More than a dozen life-sized portraits of the mayor lined the walls, and based on the thinning hair and increasing wrinkles, I suspected he had a new one painted every year. As we proceeded down the hallway, I counted three different wives over the course of fifteen years. There was something familiar about his high forehead and small nose, but I couldn't quite place it. It didn't matter.

I'd seen enough.

Not yet.

Mercury had remained by my side throughout the procession, and through the guise of adjusting the laces on my boot, I stopped to crouch down beside them in the middle of the hallway. The steward shifted nervously, but I ignored his anxious glances as I whispered a series of instructions. The Ethereal kept their face impassive, but when I stood a few moments later, nodding for the steward to continue, I could see their starry eyes twinkle with fresh mischief.

Finally, we arrived at the study, though the gilded gold chair behind the massive mahogany desk was more like a throne. But I was more concerned with the man who sat upon it.

In his mid-fifties, Mayor Ferdinand Renis was a tall man, and far less muscular than his hall portraits implied. He stood as we entered the room, though he didn't move from behind the desk. I saw his expression darken as he recognized Tristan, but when his eyes returned to me, a shark's grin spread across his face.

"Welcome, Your Majesty." Renis bowed his head, as if that were obeisance enough. "I had heard you were on a great mission, but I had no idea you would be visiting our humble city."

The steward shut the door behind us.

A single chair had been placed before Renis's desk, presumably for me, but I remained standing. Mercury took their place at my right hip while Ness and Tristan flanked me on either side. I was glad to have them with me, but I'd instructed them to stay quiet no matter what happened. This was something I needed to handle on my own.

It was time for the queen to remind people who was in charge.

Turning away from the mayor, I wandered over to a bookshelf set deep into the wall. Each shelf was covered in glittering trinkets and polished stones.

"The city is certainly humble, Renis, though your palace is anything but."

Renis chuckled dryly. "I admit I've been more prosperous than most. It's a shame I haven't had the pleasure of meeting you before now. Anyone else would look a wreck after weeks on the road, but I must say, travel suits you."

The way his voice turned velvety smooth made my skin crawl, but I continued scanning the shelf. A ruby the size of a robin's egg caught my eye, and I plucked it from between the other treasures.

"I believe you know my friend Captain Derbeck." I waved my free hand absently toward Tristan, still examining the stunning jewel.

A pause. "We've crossed paths, yes." The words dripped with disdain. Clearly, he hated Tristan as much as my friend despised him. Good.

"He has been telling me some very troubling things about Salt Wind."

Renis grunted. "With all due respect to Captain Derbeck, running a city is much more difficult and time consuming than swaggering around the docks."

Glancing up, I could practically see the heat radiating off

Tristan. But he stood firm, folded his arms across his muscular chest, and merely smirked at the mayor's insult.

"You were informed of my travels, yet not of my visit to this city. That seems like quite the oversight," I drawled, returning the ruby to the shelf. It was flawless, and the price it could fetch would feed a family for a year. Yet there it sat, a trinket forgotten among many.

"My cousin is a very busy man," Renis said.

Cousin. Of course.

Not yet.

"Perhaps too busy, if he can't even send a simple letter," I chided. "I must confess, I have found his memory to be slipping of late."

Renis laughed. "Oh, I'm sure it's merely the Commemoration Festival weighing on his mind. A lot of planning to be done, you know."

I nearly smiled.

Not yet.

"Enough of such talk." Renis rang a small silver bell, and a servant in a crisp black uniform hurried in, carrying a tray with two crystal champagne glasses. Renis took both glasses, dismissing the servant with a jerk of his head, and crossed to where I stood at the bookshelf. "A toast! To your serendipitous arrival, perhaps?"

I looked at the proffered glass, then at Renis' face.

"I'll wait to toast until everyone has a glass." I gestured to my friends. "Surely, there are more glasses on the way? Though I don't know why they weren't all brought in at once."

Renis's smile slipped, his revulsion visible just below the surface, but he recovered in an instant.

"Of course. What a horrible mistake." With a blush of frustration creeping up his cheeks, Renis held out the two glasses to Ness and Tristan. Tristan accepted the champagne with a wide grin, while Ness remained stone faced, looking the mayor straight in the eyes. When Renis's eyes fell on Mercury, he blanched.

"Don't worry about me, sweet cheeks," the Ethereal purred, stretching their quicksilver body. I noticed their razor claws caught in the rug somewhat deliberately, but Renis swallowed as he jumped away.

Rather than ring the bell to call back the servant, Renis excused himself to retrieve two more glasses. Taking advantage of his absence, I added a final instruction to Mercury's to-do list, whispering it in their ear on the likely chance we were being watched. Their earlier excitement about this new mission transcended into full-blown glee. Then, with a final wink, they vanished in a swirl of mist.

"Where did—" Tristan began, but I held up a hand. His face pinched with concern, and I couldn't blame him. Having Mercury use their teleportation had always been a last resort, seeing as how it required dark energy and had the potential to alert Zaletor to our location. But right now, I was willing to take the risk.

Renis returned with two more glasses of champagne. He must have taken a moment to compose himself, because his flush was gone, the oily smile slithering back onto his face.

"Here we are," he handed me a glass. The crystal was cool on my skin. "Oh, where is your, uh, charming companion?"

"Attending to other matters." I moved to the desk, setting my still-full glass on the glossy surface. "Speaking of which, I'm not here for toasts and pleasantries. You invited me to discuss what happened in the square."

Staring Renis in the eye, I sat back onto the massive gold chair, a spot which should have been offered to me immediately.

Renis's flush returned. "Ah, yes. How could I have forgotten? I must have been too entranced by your beauty."

Ness rolled her eyes, while Tristan visibly sneered. But they both kept quiet.

I said nothing, my face made of stone as I waited.

It didn't take long for the silence to make Renis uncomfortable.

"I've looked into the incident in question, and while I agree the situation got out of hand, I can assure you nothing untoward was happening."

"Your man was going door to door extorting shopkeepers." It was a guess on my part, a gamble, but I took it.

Renis sat in the available chair, crossing his ankles. "Tax collecting!"

"In plain clothes?"

"I believe he was running late this morning and didn't have time to change. An innocent mistake."

His casual nature made me want to break something.

Not yet not yet not yet.

"If it was so innocent, why did your other goons attack me without warning?"

"Based on what they told me, you were skulking about in alleyways. They mistook you for a vagrant and were looking out for the community. But," Renis waved a hand, "I don't deny the carelessness of Mister Quincy and his compatriots. If Your Majesty desires, will have the three of them promptly executed to cover the matter."

Renis smiled, raising his glass to me, as if it settled everything.

I returned his smile with one of my own.

Now.

"I don't see how that would help. The boldness of your guard's actions leads me to believe you are either blissfully unaware of their heinous behaviors, or they are doing so with your blessing. Either way, I want an explanation."

For an instant, I could see genuine bafflement in Renis's eyes. I wondered what Secretary Mayfield had told him about me, about how easily I could be manipulated.

Finally, Renis stood, placing his glass on the desk as well.

"I can see you've gotten a very poor impression of my city." His eyes flicked to Tristan, as if the sea captain were somehow to blame. "We will have plenty of time to discuss these concerning matters further in the coming days. You'll stay here, of course, as my honored guest. I've already had my servants prepare the guest wing for you."

There was a puff of fog in the corner as Mercury reappeared. The Ethereal had a smug grin on their face, but Renis was too absorbed in his speech to notice.

"I've also decreed that tomorrow night we will have a grand ball in your honor. It's very short notice, I'm aware, but I made it clear there would be no expense too great to prepare everything on time. All the prominent people of Salt Wind will attend, and together we will give you a better understanding of life here, since you've clearly been talking to the wrong people." He cut another glare to Tristan, then rubbed his hands together. "Now, there's much to do. A seamstress is already waiting in the guest suit to help you find a suitable gown, and—"

"Enough."

Renis stopped short at my command.

"Despite your low opinion of me, I know a great deal about this city. However, I seem to be a bit ignorant about *people*. For example, I had no idea my dear Secretary Mayfield was your cousin. Though now I certainly see the resemblance."

If I didn't know any better, I would have thought Renis was frozen. His mouth hung open as though he'd been about to speak, but all color had drained from his face. I rose from my place at the gilded chair, towering over him thanks to the dais beneath.

"I know you've been over-taxing these people. I know you've been ruling here like it's your own little kingdom and using your personal guard to enforce unfair and illegal laws. And I know Mayfield has been preventing me from learning any of this for years, all while likely taking his own cut of the funds."

Like a spell breaking, Renis stood tall. "That's preposterous! That's—as mayor of this city, I would *never*—"

I braced my hands on the table. "Renis, you are no longer mayor of Salt Wind."

Silence. Even Ness and Tristan looked shocked, while Mercury's tail flicked in anticipation.

Renis stared at me for a moment, then laughed. The hysterical, booming sound filled the small room, setting the shelves of knickknacks rattling. I waited, watching as his laughter died away.

"You cannot be serious."

"Do I look like I'm joking?" I let the glint of challenge show in my eyes.

He scoffed. "We'll see what Mayfield has to say about this."

"Mayfield is not queen." I stood tall, ice and flame in each palm. The earth beneath us lurched, causing a spider web of cracks in the tile floor. A whimper of fear escaped Renis's throat.

Smiling, I allowed my magic to dissipate. "Besides, as of ten minutes ago, Mayfield is not even the royal secretary."

That sobered him more than the magic. "What are you talking about?"

I waved a hand at Mercury, who looked like he could eat Renis alive. "My *enchanting friend* just returned from Glassleaf, where they reported everything that's been happening here.

They've also given instructions for *former* Secretary Mayfield to be detained and imprisoned for treachery, treason, and theft from the queen. All of those taxes should have been mine, after all."

Mercury's wings flared, trailing smoke. "You should have seen the look on his face when I gave the order to drag him to the dungeons. It was priceless. None of the other members of the Council seemed surprised. I think a few of them found the whole experience very cathartic, actually." They grinned at Renis. "Oh, and the sniveling rat claimed the whole thing was your idea."

Renis gaped at me, shrinking in on himself. Even Ness cracked a smile, and I thought Tristan was going to burst with righteous pride. His mirth was about to turn sour, but I let him relish in the justice of it all for a few more seconds.

"Please," Renis whispered, "have mercy."

Coward. I looked down my nose at him from the height of the dais.

"Let me be perfectly clear: this is me being merciful."

Tears filled the man's eyes. "What will happen to me?"

Here we go, I thought.

"I have a few ideas, but to reestablish trust with the citizens of this town, I'll leave that decision up to the *new* mayor."

I turned to Tristan.

His brow furrowed, but when I smiled, he blanched.

Now *that* was a face I wish I could have on a painting.

26

I put Ness and Mercury in charge of escorting Renis to the city's prison. If anyone was stupid enough to oppose them, my friends would win that fight handily. Before leaving, Mercury darted to my side.

"Everyone at the palace was asking when you'd be back. Mostly whether you would return in time for the start of the festival, though a very frowny woman also wanted to make sure you were okay."

Shit. The Commemoration Festival was only two weeks away. "What did you tell them?"

"I said, 'Sure!' Then poofed away."

"Of course you did," I sighed. "I'll figure it out."

The "frowny woman" could only be Vena. At least someone was concerned for my safety. Then Mercury left, and it was just me and Tristan. The study that had seemed so grand now felt suffocatingly small as Tristan unleashed his wrath.

"What do you think you're doing?!"

I crossed my arms as I leaned back against the desk. "My job."

"I can't be the mayor!"

"'*No one knows this city and it's innerworkings better than I do*,'" I said, doing an abysmal impression of his voice. "You have always been many things, Tristan, but you've never been a braggart. For you to have said that, you must have truly believed it. And that makes you the right person for the job."

He ran a hand through his hair. "But I don't *want* to be mayor!"

I couldn't help but smirk. I'd said the same thing about being queen. Though probably in a less whiny way. But I knew the real problem: Tristan didn't like to sit still. It's part of why we'd grown apart all those years ago. The idea of being consort to the queen, with all the events and obligations that went with it, was stifling to him. Combine that with the overly cautious and secluded nature I'd developed after Becca's death, and it was a recipe for disaster. But we all had to make sacrifices, so I played my best card.

"Then tell me, if not you, who is a better person? Who can help this city recover from Renis's rule? Who can lead it to prosperity and make it a place where your children feel safe in the streets? Because if you have any suggestions, I'd love to hear them."

Tristan paced around the room, his eyes darting about in thought. Every few seconds, he paused, considered, then resumed pacing. I took the time to do a mental inventory of all the items of value in the room. If the rest of the manor were as lavish as what I'd seen so far, we could alleviate the poverty in Salt Wind overnight.

"Is this a punishment?"

I started. "Excuse me?"

Tristan glared at me from across the room. "Did you do this to punish me?"

"Punish you for what?!"

"Because you're mad at how things ended between us?"

A choked laugh escaped me. "Great skies, I'm not mad at you!"

"You are! You refused to look at me at the Green Serpent, and you're not looking at me now!"

My eyes, which had been pointedly staring out the window, snapped to him. "Ok, fine! I'm mad! But not because we broke up. So let's just drop it."

He crossed his arms. "Is it Tennian? Because I moved on? That bullshit, she's been nothing but kind to you and—"

"It's not because you moved on, you ass!" I shouted, seeing red. "I'm mad because you *got* to move on! That people let you go out and have a new life and are happy for you!"

Tristan's rage twisted to confusion. My own anger vanished at the sight, and I sighed.

"I don't love you anymore, Tristan. I stopped loving you even before we ended things. I don't regret what we had all those years ago, but it was clear by the end it wasn't working. We weren't working."

His eyes softened and he nodded. "We wanted different things. You were just the one brave enough to say it."

"Exactly. *We* know the problems were mutual and ran deep, but to everyone else *I* was the problem. I didn't want children. I wanted to stay in Glassleaf year-round. I called off the wedding." My shoulders fell as I slumped back against the desk. "The people love me for being their savior, but they blame me for ruining our love story. Ever since, even after you married, people glare at me if I show interest in anyone. They are happier with me alone because they want me to mourn what was lost. But you got to walk away. That's what makes me angry."

He opened his mouth, then snapped it closed. With steady

steps, he crossed to lean on the desk beside me, shoulder to shoulder.

"I'm sorry. I had no idea that's why you were alone all this time."

I shrugged. "I've had lovers over the years, but it's always awkward when I have to keep them secret so they don't become the target of people's fury. Not to mention the fact that there are still shrines to my ex all over the castle. In the end, no one wants to put up with all that. And I don't blame them."

"Well, when you return, I hope things can be different. I'll make whatever statements I have to to show people how happy we all are for each other."

I frowned. "As admirable as that is, your opinion shouldn't have so much sway over my life. I shouldn't need you to defend me."

Besides, the idea of returning to the castle and the life that waited for me there made my stomach hurt. As terrible as all of this was, it felt so good to be out in the world again, having an adventure. To be free.

"I know you don't want to be mayor. But naming you will restore people's faith in the position. And if you choose to abdicate, you can name your own successor. The people of Salt Wind will trust your decisions more than they'll trust mine. What do you say?"

He swallowed, but I could see he was considering it. The idea that it could be a temporary appointment seemed to make it more appealing. Finally, he cursed.

"Alright. But only until we find someone better. And don't expect me to wear any formal uniforms."

I smirked. "I'd never dream of it."

"But you need me to go with you to Mistpoint. What happens here while I'm gone?"

"I guess you better think of something."

"Some of the people in Glassleaf will be mad when they find out."

"Oh, they already know, and I'm sure they are." When I saw his confused look, I merely shrugged. "It was all part of Mercury's instructions. They made the announcement when they had Mayfield imprisoned."

Tristan's eyes went wide. "But you didn't know if I'd accept the—you know what, never mind. Of course you had this planned the whole time."

We were quiet for a moment, but it was a comfortable silence. Possibly the type of silence that could exist between friends.

"Kitt is a good man," Tristan said, "he's the kind of person who wouldn't care what foolish people said about him." He glanced at me sideways.

I shook my head, even as I felt heat creep up my neck to my cheeks, and pushed myself up. "I am going to regret putting you in a position of power. I can tell."

We stayed the night in Salt Wind to manage the sudden transition of power.

Despite his protests about the job, Tristan took command like a pro, as I knew he would. Years spent as the captain of multiple ships had given him the presence required to lead a crowd. And it seemed he did know everything about the city.

His first act was to summon a group of city guards to replace Renis's crew, who were all placed under arrest. They were a mixture of frightened and indignant, but my presence, with Mercury at my side, was enough to deter any retaliatory action. Most were more than willing to describe Renis's corruption if it meant leniency for themselves.

All the preparation Renis had put into the ball, which was a considerable amount given the short notice, was used for a brief ceremony and celebration in the city square that evening. I publicly apologized for Renis's unchecked tyranny and officially named Tristan the new mayor. There was food and drink for all, and while I knew it was only the beginning of the reparation I owed these people, it was a start.

It was immediately apparent that Trisan couldn't leave. There was too much to do, and even with the fate of the world in the balance, I wasn't willing to risk the city falling into chaos. As much as I'd hoped he could show us around Becca's home, I was more concerned with not having a captain for the ship to get us there. Because of the vast mountain range known as The Tail, it would take a full month to get to Mistpoint by foot, even with horses. But after another unspoken conversation between the two of them, Tristan assured us we would be in good hands, as Tennian would take his place as Captain.

"She's spent just as much time aboard that ship as I have," he insisted, "and to be honest, the crew likes her better anyway."

An irrational part of me wanted to say no, to say we'd find a different route. But there were plenty of people to help with their children while Tennian was gone and Tristan was organizing the city, so there was no good reason to refuse.

"Thank you," I smiled, "we'll take any help she's willing to offer."

And that was that. With all the chaos of installing a new mayor, I'd spent most of the day with Tristan and the small group of advisors he'd called in from across the city. Aside from a brief wave across the courtyard, I hadn't seen Kitt for hours. When I was finally able to slip away from the celebrations, I found him in the private stables at the manor, where the horses would be looked after while we were gone. He was singing to

Boss as he got the horse settled and inspected the stalls for any sign of inadequacy.

Though he had started nodding off to sleep, Boss perked up when he saw me. Kitt turned, and my heart fluttered at his smile.

"I think this will do just fine," he said.

I ran a hand down Boss's forehead. He shoved his nose forward, searching for any hint of an apple. "I feel terrible leaving him behind."

"A rest will do him good," Kitt smiled, patting the stallion's shoulder. "After monsters, evil wizards, and Jax's chattering, I think he'll be relieved to have a bit of a break."

I stepped aside so he could leave the stall, but there wasn't much room to maneuver, and his chest brushed my shoulder. It was the barest hint of contact, but my breath caught at the closeness. Kitt didn't seem to notice and continued down to where Rosie was sleeping to examine her space as well. Hoping the dim light hid the flush on my cheeks, I took the opportunity to slip an apple from my pocket.

Kitt's voice rang out from the stall down the corridor. "I've already warned the stablemaster about his bad manners, but apparently you're the one I need to worry about."

"I have no idea what you're talking about," I smirked, wiping spit and apple juice on my trousers as Boss crunched happily.

Kitt's head appeared over the wall, a wry grin on his face. "He's going to get colic."

"I'm sorry. They make him so happy, and I feel like I owe him." I chewed my lip, then added, "I owe both of you."

"Nonsense. You don't owe me a thing." He gave Rosie a final pat and emerged from the stall. He must have bathed at some point, because now that he was standing still, I could see his hair stuck up in all directions. It was somehow comical and...distracting.

"I do. I owe you an apology for how I've acted the past few days. I'm sorry for pushing you away."

Kitt's cheeks reddened, and he shook his head. "No, no. I was being too forward. Your discomfort was completely reasonable."

Hells. Of course he would take the blame for this.

"It's not that. I enjoyed our conversation. And I've enjoyed getting to know you these past few days. It's just—" I swallowed.

Let him make his own choices.

"I haven't had the best luck with relationships. Everyone wants to believe my first love was my greatest love, as I'm sure you'll remember from the *theatrical production that was made about it.*" Kitt chuckled, and it gave me courage. "The truth is, the people I've cared about since then have faced a great deal of scrutiny and disrespect. It's a lot for anyone to deal with, and I hate when the people I care about are unhappy. And I find I care about you a great deal."

I straightened, knowing that if I paused, I'd lose my nerve. "I've been pushing you away because I decided all that was more than you would want to put up with. But that isn't fair to you, or to me. I want to know more about you. And I want you to know more about me, who I really am, rather than the story everyone tells. So, here are the truly important things about me: I enjoy anything with blueberries and learning about new places. I don't want children, and I despise asparagus. I've got complicated feelings about my parents, but the family I've built is incredibly precious to me. And, I think you're extremely attractive."

I was breathless from pouring out all those words at once. It was more than I'd told any prospective partner in years. And it was liberating!

Kitt only stared at me.

Unease began to build in my stomach as a tense silence filled the stable, but I waited. I'd just dumped a lot of information on him, maybe more than he'd wanted, but I didn't feel any regret. As much as I'd hoped for a positive, and more instantaneous, reaction, I couldn't blame him for needing to organize his thoughts.

Kitt swallowed. A mixture of sadness and resolve filled his face as he pulled something from his pocket.

"Phoebe, there's something I need to tell you."

In the flickering lamplight, I could see he held a gold coin. I didn't reach for it. I didn't need to. I could see the insignia stamped on it from where I stood, and it made my heart stop.

A maple leaf with a sword down its center and a rising sun behind it.

I took an instinctual step back. His comment from that morning shot through me.

"You knew we were heading for the Crescent Sea," I realized. "You knew, before Tristan said anything about where Mistpoint was."

He nodded. "I did."

If he knew where the house was, did that mean…

I shook my head. I wanted him to stop speaking before he ruined everything between us. Would it ruin everything? Kitt was my age, too young to have been involved directly, right? But what about his family? Could they have been a part of it? If they were, could I really hold that against him?

I knew the answer in my heart, and it filled me with sorrow.

He opened his mouth to say The Goddesses knows what, but the stable door banged open. Kitt and I both jumped at the sound.

"Shit," Jax hissed as he grabbed the still vibrating door. "Phoebe? Are you—oh! Sorry! I didn't mean to interrupt." He glanced between us, a mischievous glint in his eyes. "On second, thought, I can come back—"

I shook my head. "It's fine. Are you looking for me?"

Jax waved a hand, turning to leave. "It can wait."

Whatever it was, it certainly could not.

"Sorry," I mumbled to Kitt, already backing toward the door. "I should see what's going on. We'll talk later!"

Kitt's face creased in confusion as I quickly bade him good-night and hurried from the stable. I knew it was a horrible thing for me to do, to brush him off after I'd just apologized for brushing him off. But after everything that had happened already that day, I simply could not handle whatever he was about to say.

Still, the golden disk burned into my mind, and I knew it would haunt me until I learned why Kitt carried a coin bearing Becca's family crest.

27

The ship made our trip to the Crescent Sea quicker, but it was still a miserable journey. Especially for Alto and Ness, who both suffered from horrible seasickness. We were sailing against the current, and even with good winds it would take a full week to get to our destination.

I spent most of my waking hours practicing with Mercury on the deck. The wood planks were constantly covered in ice and dirt. At Tennian's request, I didn't use my Ignis Gifts, primarily to put the crew at ease, rather than from any danger to the ship. Time and again I rejected the Ethereal's suggestion to practice Anima. It felt too dangerous in such a confined space.

"Fine," the Ethereal had begrudgingly agreed. "But we'll never know what you're fully capable of if you don't *try*."

I'd resisted telling them I was fine with not knowing.

I hadn't forbidden Kitt from coming, though the image of the coin weighed heavily on me. I knew I'd have to ask about it sooner or later, but I was terrified of what his answer might be.

This wonderful feeling would be twisted into something regretful and ugly, and I was unwilling to ruin it so thoroughly.

By the fourth day, Ness had recovered enough to join Jax and me for dinner. While everyone was anxious for our arrival at Mistpoint and the search to come, the mood in the galley was jovial.

"I'd always thought it must have been fun, what all of you did," Ness admitted, picking at a slice of bread. "It sounded like a grand adventure. But now that I'm part of it, it's terrifying. How were you ever brave enough to do it as teens?"

"Easy," Jax laughed, "we thought we were invincible."

Ness looked doubtful, but I shrugged. "It's true. Even though I knew I was destined to die, I couldn't imagine dying *before* defeating Zaletor. It was arrogance and stupidity, but I can't criticize past us too much. We got the job done, after all." I considered the broken crown and added, "Mostly."

"Most teens lack a strong sense of self-preservation," Mercury added. "It's why saving the world tends to be a young person's game."

Jax grunted in agreement. "Remember the night we spent staking out a prison, waiting for that demon-man, Broin, to show up? My back aches now just thinking of crouching in that position for hours."

"How could I forget? The bastard didn't show until three in the morning. I think the last time I stayed up that late was fifteen years ago when the High Priestess insisted on doing a moonlight feast." I glanced sheepishly at Mercury. "The year after, I may have told them The Goddesses felt my presence at the event was unnecessary."

Laughter rang out through the room.

"Hells," Jax chuckled, shaking his head. "I can't believe we're actually doing all of this again."

I blew out a breath. "At least we're wiser this time...right?"

Mercury looked conspicuously at the ceiling, and I threw a crust of bread at their silver face. Their starry eyes narrowed in challenge, and before I knew it a wedge of cheese was flying at me on a gust of wind. I batted it away, cackling at the absurdity of it all.

"I've got a question," Jax interrupted, before a full-blown food fight could break out. "Why didn't my or Tristan's letters get through, but Alto's did?"

It was something I'd given a lot of thought to over the past few days, and I had come up with a theory. "Alto never asked me to leave. He would give me updates on his life and ask about mine, but he never invited me to visit or asked that I leave the castle, whereas you and Tristan were trying to get me information about the outside world. If I'd left, I would have learned just how bad things were, and Mayfield's deception would have been exposed."

Ness shook her head. "I hope his punishment is unpleasant and lingering."

"You're vicious, and I admire that," Jax smiled. He raised his glass, and Ness responded with a mock salute. Then he turned back to me. "At least once this is all over you won't have to worry about Mayfield anymore. You can return triumphant and embrace a life of ease."

He'd meant it as a lighthearted joke, but my stomach soured. Images of Salt Wind citizens on street corners and shopkeepers paying protection money flooded through me. I glared down at the table, overwhelmed with shame.

"I've already been living a life of ease, to the detriment of the kingdom. People have suffered because of me."

"Salt Wind isn't your fault," Ness insisted. Jax murmured an agreement.

"But it is my responsibility," I argued, "even though Mayfield kept me from finding out how bad things had gotten there or that my friends wanted to see me, I chose to never leave Glassleaf. That's on me. What if Mayfield wasn't the only one abusing his power? Who knows what else has been done in my name? I failed those people." I gritted my teeth. "I don't deserve a life of ease. I don't deserve their love. I don't even deserve to be queen."

The galley was silent.

"Phoebe," Mercury began, but I wasn't in the mood for my feelings to be bolstered. So I pushed away from the table and left.

The sun had gone down while I was in the galley, and as I emerged from the belly of the ship, I found millions of stars watching from above. But I didn't stop to marvel, rushing instead straight to the railing and gulping down the crisp sea air.

I couldn't do anything right. I hadn't defeated Zaletor. I'd sent my dearest friend off to die. I'd been terrible to my family. And my time as queen had left people suffering. It was hard to think of any good I'd actually done in the past twenty years.

Crouching forward, I rested my forehead on the railing. It felt better than standing upright, easier to breathe.

"Are you alright?"

The voice came from behind me, and my composure buckled. I wanted to tell him to go away. To take his stupid cursed coin and leave me in peace. Instead, I raised myself up and muttered, "No."

Footsteps sounded, and Kitt settled beside me. We stared out at the dark water and glittering stars. I felt small, insignificant.

It was as good a time as any.

"Tell me why you have that coin." I didn't bother to keep the frustration from my voice.

Kitt nodded, his eyes on the sky.

"I already told you how I recognized you that day we met in Bortran's. But there's more to it than that. I think—I think running into you there truly was fate. It was meant to happen so I could repay my debt." He looked at me now. "The debt I owed a stranger who helped me years ago."

I couldn't move. "Becca?"

"I didn't know who she was at the time. We crossed paths right after you defeated Zaletor, so I had no idea she'd just helped save the kingdom. To me, she was merely another traveler on the road." He closed his eyes, face flooded with shame. "Merely another person I could rob.

"I didn't lie about my past, but I didn't tell you all of it. When I was a child, my mother moved my sister and I to a tiny village nestled on the eastern side of the Tail. I don't remember anything about my father, if he was abusive or if he and my mother were never married, but she didn't like to talk about him. Hazel was always sickly, and while my mother worked when she could, there was never enough to go around. So I started stealing.

"I was young, not even fifteen, when I started. I didn't like the idea of hurting people, so I'd take to the woods along the road. We didn't have any inns in the area, but there was a large clearing where travelers often set up camp. I'd wait till they fell asleep, then take what I could. I knew it was wrong, and I'd only take from people who seemed like they had things to spare, but it kept us alive."

I could see that these memories weighed heavily upon him. I wanted to tell him it was alright. That I'd done similar things to survive as a child and his actions were understandable, but I couldn't. Not until I learned the extent of it.

"Then one night, a young woman set up camp. I didn't want to steal from her, what with her being alone and all, but winter was early that year, and Hazel had developed a terrible cough.

And the strange woman's clothes were quite fine. So, I snuck in as always and tried to grab her bag."

He shook his head at some memory, and I held my breath.

"She beat the shit out of me. No Gifts required."

Despite everything, I laughed. The harsh, breathy laugh of relief. Kitt chuckled as well, and it was like a spell was broken. His gaze returned to the stars, but the shame behind it was gone.

"Once I was embarrassingly subdued, she muttered something about wishing a ship could reach the Crescent Sea so she didn't have to put up with such bullshit. She asked if I had a death wish and began to glow golden with Specter magic. I truly thought it was the end for me. So, through a busted lip and broken nose, I asked her to take my sister with her wherever she was going, because she could protect Hazel a hell of a lot better than I could. That made her pause. She dropped me in the dirt and told me to explain. I was so scared and so tired of what my life had become, I told her everything. When I was finished, she packed up her camp and told me to prove it. I led her back to our house, where she saw how we were living and how sick Hazel was."

Tears rose in his eyes as he swallowed. "She gave us everything she had. A bag of coins, her horse, even a recommendation for what village had the best healers. I thought she was some sort of demi-god from the old stories, come to save us. I asked her name, how to repay her. She told me her name was unimportant. The only repayment she asked for was that if I ever encountered someone on the day they most needed help, I was to give them whatever they needed. If I promised to do that, she said, we'd be even. I swore it, and she walked off into the night. My family moved the next day, headed to the town with healers, and we were able to start over. But I saved one coin to remember the woman who saved us, and the debt that I owed."

I could tell from the look on his face he was being truthful. To Kitt, that coin was a symbol of sacrifice and hope. He had no idea what the crest really stood for.

"That all sounds like Becca," I said, even as tears streamed down my cheeks.

He smiled. "A few months later, my mother, sister and I journeyed to the nearest city for the coronation ceremony happening there. That's when I saw her, the woman who'd pummeled me and saved our lives, grinning like a devil and waving from atop the steps of the Citadel, and I realized who exactly had saved us. And beside her stood our new queen."

Kitt finally looked at me, and even in the near darkness, I could see a hint of pink on his cheeks. "That's how I knew that Becca went to the Crescent Sea. And I didn't tell you any of this when we met because I didn't think you'd believe me. You were clearly worried about being exposed, and I knew how suspicious it would all sound. Then it became this secret hanging over me, but when you said all those things in Salt Wind, I knew I couldn't keep it from you."

I gripped the railing in front of me, my nails digging into the wood. He was right. I never would have believed him that day in the stables. And if he'd shown me the coin then, I'd likely have arrested him on the spot for crimes he couldn't comprehend. But I still struggled with the half-truths.

"How is this possible? She *couldn't* have known we'd meet," I insisted.

"I don't think she did. She merely wanted me to help someone someday, and that someone happened to be you. When I saw you in Bortran's, I thought you'd had enough and were running away from it all. I honestly didn't think you'd meet me the following week."

I gaped at him. "Then why did you let me take Boss?!"

Kitt shrugged. "Because I was fulfilling my debt. And you needed to get away. But you did show up. You were clearly distressed about something, but you looked more alive than you had when I'd last seen you. That day, when you stepped into The Leather Shoe with such determination in your face, I couldn't take my eyes off you. At that moment I knew, if you'd let me, I'd follow wherever you led."

"Even if where I lead is death?" I asked, the question slipping out before I could stop it.

A smile appeared, softer than any I'd yet seen on his face, and he held my gaze as he took my hand in his. His strong fingers were warm around mine, and I was amazed at the gentleness in them.

"Even then," Kitt said, "but I still believe we will triumph. You are stronger than anyone realizes, including yourself. Not because of your Gifts, but because of who you are. You understand that there are days for justice and days for mercy. You feel your people's pain as intimately as your own, and while you have made some mistakes, you have done your best to make things right. And that is why you are an excellent queen."

I couldn't bring myself to agree with him, but when he brushed a knuckle along my jawline, I shivered. Despite my lingering irritation at his revelations, I placed my hand on Kitt's face, appreciating the softness of his beard.

"No more secrets?" I gazed deep into his eyes.

His smile was soft and open and made my heart dance. "No more secrets."

My entire body thrummed with electricity as I pulled his face to mine.

28

The shores of the Crescent Sea were craggy and gray. There were no beaches or docks to be found, so we waited aboard the ship till the tide came in. Tennian's face was grim as the two of us stood at the ship's prow, staring at the wasteland before us.

"I've never understood why Becca's family lived here," she said when I asked her if everything was alright. "It doesn't take a Specter to see this place is full of ghosts."

I couldn't disagree. Tucked into the back of a treacherous mountain range, this area had been created by a volcanic eruption centuries before. But the volcano had been silent for ages, giving the place a cold, isolated feel.

"Becca told me once it was to show their wealth. The ground is only capable of growing moss and a few sparse grasses, so all of their supplies had to be shipped in. Food, fresh water, medicine, all of it had to be brought to them constantly, a feat that would have been impossible for anyone except the richest family in the world.

"But personally," I added, "I think it was so the vile bastards could hide from the world."

Tennian shuddered beside me. "Tristan told me Mistpoint was always quiet. Even with dozens of servants, he and Marcus felt like they were in a tomb. At least they were only here for two months each winter. I can't imagine what it must have been like for Becca to be trapped here all the time."

I hummed in agreement. "I'm honestly surprised Lord Wintros allowed the boys to stay at Mistpoint at all. Becca's mother must have wanted them here, otherwise they never would have set foot in that house."

Tristan and Becca's mothers had been sisters. To hear my friends tell it, one had married for love, the other for money and power. I always wondered if Becca's mother had known prior to marrying him how her husband's family made their fortune or if it had been a shocking surprise. Either way, she'd stayed and raised Becca in this terrible place, making her just as much a monster as her husband.

Thanks to Tennian's expert maneuverings, we were able to get the rowboat nearly to the shoreline without smashing apart on the jagged outcroppings of rock. Once we were close enough, everyone leapt out to haul the small vessel onto shore. Not the most ideal way to reach our destination, but if we wanted to make it back to the ship when we were finished, we'd need the rowboat in one piece.

Once we were sure the boat was secure and wouldn't get washed out to sea, Tennian glanced at the sky. "Based on Tristan's directions, the house should be that way," she said, pointing south.

∾

We arrived at Mistpoint just before dark. While I'd never visited before, the stone mansion looked exactly how I'd always envisioned it. Jutting up three stories high, the building had few windows, with moss growing like a molding skin across the entire surface. There was a circular tower at each corner, topped with a pointed roof, and a long balcony stretched across the second floor on the front. I knew it had been vacant and uncared for since Becca left and the servants had fled. Considering the storms in this area during the spring, it was a testament to the building's craftsmanship that it was standing at all.

Seeing it now made my blood cry out in anger. I'd offered once to raze it to the ground, telling Becca all she had to do was ask. But she wanted it to remain intact, at least until nature brought it down, as a reminder of what people had been capable of.

Personally, I saw it as an insult for Mistpoint to still exist when Becca didn't.

Back on the ship, we'd all agreed it was better to spend the night in the empty house and start the search for the gemstone the following morning. However, once we stood outside the imposing shell of a manor, with the wind screaming around us, I could tell everyone was wondering if that had been the best choice.

"No turning back now," I said. I carefully picked my way up the cracked steps to the massive entrance. The salt air had stripped away the varnish from the thick wood door, and I figured it would be easy to bust through if we needed. I lifted a steady hand to the dark brass knob and wasn't surprised to find it unlocked. It took a good shove to get the door open, since it had been sitting unused for so long, but after a moment it swung wide.

Night was closing in outside, but it still felt more cheerful and bright than what waited for us inside the house. The stench of mildew and dust was overwhelming, but there was no way we'd be able to maneuver the rowboat back to the ship in the dark. Without a better option, Ness and I both conjured small flames to light the way, and we all crowded into the house.

I swallowed.

"Great Goddesses," Jax cursed, gazing around the massive entryway.

There was no denying the decay and disrepair, but beneath the debris and molding furniture, evidence of wealth still glittered. The most ornate crystal chandelier I'd ever seen hung from the center of the ceiling, cobwebs giving it the feel of a macabre cloud. The wood furniture was rotting, but the tile floors were clearly of the finest marble, and the stone fireplace dominating the east wall could fit a dining table inside. I'd thought Renis's manor had been an extreme show of affluence, but even as a carcass, the old wealth of Wintros Mansion put it to shame.

The heavy dust on the floor revealed no one had been inside in ages.

"I don't sense anything," Mercury said, their gaze drifting about the massive room. "I don't think the gemstone is here."

"She wouldn't have hidden it in the house," I stated. "If Becca came here, I doubt she even set foot inside."

Alto, normally unflappable, gazed about in shock. "Becca told us her parents had died, and I'd guessed she'd come from money, but this is beyond anything I'd imagined."

Kitt picked up a candlestick that had fallen to the ground when an end table collapsed. A brush of his finger revealed the glint of gold beneath the dust.

"How is all of this still here?" he marveled.

"And can we take it with us?" Jax finished.

Crossing the silent hall, I stared up at the remains of an oil painting high on the wall. The maple leaf crest was still visible, etched deep into the base of the frame.

"The servants didn't dare steal anything when they fled," I murmured, "not after what Becca did."

Two of the faces that stared down at me from the painting were strangers, but I still knew who they were. In Becca's mother, I recognized my friend's auburn hair and slender frame. She was beautiful and cold and even now seemed to stare down her nose at us. But I focused on her father. From him, Becca had gotten her pale skin and high cheekbones.

I hated them both, even more than I hated Zaletor himself.

Standing between them, still a child, was Becca. She looked small and withdrawn, with large eyes that I knew saw everything.

Even with her parents standing there, she looked so...alone.

I realized the others were silent, waiting. Turning, I found confused faces. Only Mercury and Tennian remained solemn. I realized Tristan must have told her, and I couldn't blame him.

Now, standing here in this hell, I felt they all had the right to know.

"Becca's parents worked for Zaletor."

No one moved, the only sound was the creak of the house and the cry of the wind.

Somehow, Jax was the first to recover. "What do you mean, 'worked for Zaletor?'"

I glared back up at the painting.

"It was a closely guarded secret, but the Wintros family had long served the Eternal Emperor, knowing there was power to be had by doing so. They did some ordinary things: managing shipping manifests, overseeing supply lines to his tower. But their real business was supplying him with magic wielders."

Ness's face turned ashen, likely remembering our conversation from the Eastern Plains, and Jax, Alto, and Kitt looked stunned. It was no secret that Zaletor had used magic wielders in his experiments, but those individuals had had to come from somewhere, and that was the part most people didn't like to think about.

"Zaletor's Gladiators could do many things, but they weren't sneaky or capable of complex planning, so the dirty work had to be done by people, and the Wintros were the head of that snake. They had a network of lowlifes all over the continent who sought out people with powerful Gifts. If someone had a Gift of any type with above-average skill, they were worth money. And Specters of any level were the most valuable of all."

"That's why you reacted to the coin the way you did," Kitt realized, looking at the crest on the frame. "You thought I was part of it somehow."

There was no accusation in his voice, but I still felt guilt as I nodded.

Jax cursed. "They just...took people?"

"If they had to," I said, "it wasn't uncommon for people to vanish in the night, their family killed if they'd put up a struggle. But in some areas, a small bounty was offered in exchange for a Gifted magician. People would turn in their friends and neighbors, or even themselves, so the money could go to their loved ones. No one trusted Zaletor, but no one knew the extent of what he was doing to people. The mines weren't a secret, but the conditions and abuse were. And to this day, no one knows what he did to the Glacies he captured."

My own ice crackled at the thought. The notebooks and diagrams I'd discovered in the tower before we'd destroyed it gave me some insight into Zaletor's sick experiments into why some people possessed the power of ice instead of water, but I'd chosen to destroy them rather than look further. The glimpses I'd seen had told me more than enough.

The others kept talking, kept asking questions, but they felt muted, distant. I used to wonder if my parents had abandoned me because it was easier than letting me be taken. If, in their own mixed-up way, they'd thought I'd have a better chance alone on the streets than growing up in a small community where gossip spread quickly. Was it easier for me to believe that? Or did I prefer to think of them as monsters?

I felt a brush against my leg and found Mercury sitting beside me. They stared up at the painting as well, but their shoulder and wing remained pressed against me, reassuring me they were there. Grateful, I rested a hand on their shoulder.

"Phoebe," Alto called, and I jerked. Based on his frustrated expression, I guessed he'd been asking me something. "What happened to her family?"

I squared my shoulders. "I never got the whole story. I don't know if Becca's parents found out about her Gift and tried to send her to Zaletor, or if she simply got fed up with living this way. But when she was thirteen—when she was thirteen, Becca killed her parents." I looked back to the painting. "She ripped their souls right out of their bodies. Then, she left."

When I finally turned around, Jax and Alto both looked like someone had punched them in the gut as they struggled to incorporate this information into the history of the friend they'd known and loved. Becca had killed when necessary during our fight against Zaletor, and again when she'd commanded the Navy, but what she'd done to her parents at such a young age was truly shocking.

And it had haunted her, even when it was the right thing to do. I still remember holding her after her nightmares. In her dreams, she'd beg their forgiveness, but her parents' souls wanted only revenge.

"Good riddance, I say," Mercury muttered.

"You knew about this?" Jax cried. "All this time?!"

The Ethereal didn't bother feigning an apology. "Of course.

When we first met Becca, she was hunting down the members of her parents' kidnapping network. She was working against Zaletor, but she had information only someone on the inside could have gotten. I couldn't risk Phoebe's safety by bringing her along without knowing more."

"Back when you were actually opposed to bringing in more help," I said, grasping for anything to lessen the tension in the room. "Unlike now, where you've invited half the continent along. Those were good times."

Mercury's smile didn't quite reach their eyes.

Kitt and Ness stayed quiet. Since neither of them had actually known Becca, I was willing to bet this revelation didn't change much for them. Jax's face was still tight with an internal struggle, but he seemed to be pulling himself together.

Alto shook his head. "I can't believe she never told me. I wouldn't have cared!"

"But *she* cared!" I countered. "It was never about any of you. She didn't want people knowing because she wanted to build her own life without that part weighing her down."

"Well, she clearly told Tristan," Alto shot back, throwing a hand toward Tennian. "Because you don't seem very surprised."

Tennian raised her chin. "She didn't. Tristan figured it out on his own." Her eyes darted to mine, looking for help.

"It's true," I nodded. "His mother had no idea what Becca's father did, or what her sister married into and undoubtedly had a hand in as well. She found out when the boys were eleven and vowed they'd never go back or have any type of contact with the family again. Which is a blessing, since Tristan developed his Gift not long after. When he and Becca reconnected in their teens, and he realized the extent of Becca's powers, he put it together himself. He told her he was happy that she'd done it and promised to keep it secret."

"He only told me before we left, in case there were some

remnants of what had happened," Tennian said. "He wanted me to be prepared."

I moved forward, claiming the center of the room. "Becca was a child, and she did what she had to do. If she hadn't, her parents would likely have handed her over to Zaletor like all the other Specters they found. She spent years atoning for their actions by helping destroy what her family had built." I met Alto's eyes. "This changes nothing."

His lips were pressed tight. Without a word, he spun on his heel and marched further into the house.

I released a breath. "We begin the search for the gemstone tomorrow at sunrise," I told the others. "Or whatever counts as 'sunrise' in this infernal place. I suggest we find the least moldy part of the house and get some sleep."

29

K itt left before sunrise, taking the warmth of his body
with him, to scout the area for Becca's hiding place
alone. I'd protested, eager to help, but he'd gently
explained that if there was any trace of Becca's movements
remaining after all these years, they'd be faint. The rocky
ground would make footprints or worn trails all but impossible.
As well intentioned as we all were, it was more likely we'd
hinder his progress than help.

Swallowing any further comments, I'd watched him go.

At least Tristan had been able to give us a general direction:
northwest. It didn't help to find her secret hiding place, and she
certainly could have intentionally misled him, but it did eliminate the south end of the valley. There simply wouldn't have
been time for her to wander that far and still be back home by
dark. It wasn't much, but it was something.

While we waited, the rest of us wandered the house. Aside
from the decay, everything remained exactly as it had been for
decades. The only exception was the library, which was in a state

of disarray. Books lay scattered across the floor, molding and crumpled, as though they'd been torn from the shelves in a panic. Perhaps some animal looking for bedding, I thought, surveying the chaos. The books' intact pages countered that idea, however, and something about the room unsettled me more than the rest of the house. I didn't linger to consider other possibilities though, especially when I realized the room was one of the few in the house with a heavy lock on its door. Who knew what kind of information the Wintros had kept sealed away?

I had no doubt Jax was stuffing his pockets with valuables, but I let it slide. Tennian spent her time flipping through the ledgers she'd found, her face grim. Meanwhile, Alto and Mercury had cleaned off the massive dining table and were discussing possible next steps. I heard murmured plans of what to do both if we did find the gemstone and if we didn't, but I could see Alto was distracted. His gaze kept drifting to the paintings on the walls. I'd heard him roaming the house in the night, trying to fill in the gaps in his knowledge of Becca. I didn't approach him, however, letting him choose whether or not to discuss it further.

That left Ness and I to train. My Glacies magic had become second nature again, nearly to the skill level it had been in my youth. Thanks to Ness, I'd argue I was an even better Ignis now than I'd been all those years ago, and I could see pride shining in her eyes as I crafted perfect spheres of flame. That left my Terra and Anima powers. Since I had no desire to see what kinds of ghosts walked the halls of the mansion, I focused on Terra. While my manipulation of the loose earth against the goons in Salt Wind had been a triumph, I was still helpless with the second aspect of Terra magic: stone. Only the most powerful Terras could wield it, and even at my strongest, stone had been a challenge.

I'd been trying to cleave a chunk of rock for nearly an hour, with zero results, and sweat dripped from my face.

"Maybe you can't use the same tactics to manipulate stone as you do loose earth," Ness suggested. Her head was propped up on her fist as she considered my struggles.

"You're the one who taught me to focus my control," I grumbled, massaging my aching temples. "To aim for perfection."

"True, but that's with material that is alive and flexible." She shrugged. "Maybe something rigid requires the opposite. Have you tried letting go of control?"

I frowned, ready to hurl the damn rock out a window instead, when the door opened. Kitt walked in, his cheeks pink from the wind. His eyes burned with excitement and pride.

"I found something."

The group of us trekked out into the wind. We walked for twenty minutes, scrabbling over the uneven terrain, before Kitt stopped.

"See that?" He pointed to the ground.

I searched, looking for whatever he was referring to, but only found the same dark, glassy rock we'd seen everywhere, with pebbles collecting in the dips of the uneven surface. Thankfully, everyone else looked as lost as I was.

"Uh, it looks like more rock," Jax offered.

Kitt's patience was infinite. "Look closer."

Ness cocked her head, pointing. "That rock looks different."

Now that she'd drawn attention to it, I realized one of the pebbles wedged into a divot of rock was rounder and paler than the rest. Kitt pried it out and held it up to us.

"This is the wrong type of rock for this area." He returned it to its place and gestured us forward. "There's another one here, and ahead there."

"It's a line," I realized, looking at the direction the mystery pebbles went in. "Or some semblance of a line?"

Kitt nodded. "The only reason I can think of for these to be here is that Becca brought them and left them behind as a trail to follow. They're subtle, and anyone else walking around would only see more rocks." He gave me a shrug. "It might be nothing."

I smiled. "But it might be something."

His return smile made my heart race. "Now that we know what we're looking for, the search will go a lot faster with all of us. Move slow, walk in straight lines, and don't move anything unless you absolutely have to. The pebbles I've found so far have been wedged in place, but there's no guarantee they haven't shifted. They've been about a dozen yards apart, so we'll head that direction for thirty yards, and if no one finds anything we'll shift to the left, repeat, then shift to the right."

I marveled at how adept he was at taking charge. It made sense, I supposed, as this was his area of expertise.

"Brilliant work!" Mercury smiled at the trapper. "I'm so glad Phoebe decided to bring you along. I knew from day one you'd be helpful."

I rolled my eyes. "Day one, you suggested I kill him to take his horse."

Kitt raised an eyebrow, but Mercury waved a paw. "I hardly remember it that way. Now, let's begin!"

The search was grueling. My eyes ached from staring at the ground for so long, and my hip hurt from where I'd slipped on the smooth stones an hour earlier. I wasn't the only one who'd taken a tumble. The light was fading, making it more difficult to see the pebbles, and we were ready to call off the search and start again in the morning when Jax cried out. His voice had an edge of excitement that told me he'd found more than merely another pebble.

We all rushed to him, stumbling and sliding, and found a crack in the earth barely a meter wide. Without hesitation, Mercury slipped inside. The rest of us waited, breathing hard from exhaustion and excitement.

"Most of us aren't going to fit in there," I panted, glaring at the opening.

I was willing to bet only Ness and Tennian were slight enough to fit, and even that would be a tight squeeze.

"Why did Becca have to be so damn small?!" Jax cursed.

Alto frowned at him, but to me he said, "Moving stone is beyond my ability. Can you make the opening wider?"

I was considering it, remembering the stone I'd failed to manipulate mere hours before, when the Ethereal's quicksilver form reappeared.

"There's a tunnel down there that ends in a door. But there's a problem."

"Of course there is," Jax grumbled.

"The tunnel has been warded," Mercury said, "I can't go in."

Warded? What had Becca done down there? I frowned at the narrow opening. The stone was freezing, leaching the warmth from my hands and knees as I crouched down. I shuddered but focused all my energy on pulling the opening wider. With a firm hand, I willed the stone to move.

But the stone had other ideas, and the only reward for my efforts was scuffed skin on my palms.

My friends shifted, the wind whipping at their hair and clothes, as I got into position to try again. I grunted, throwing my weight behind the action as I pulled at the stone.

"Shit!" I cried, falling back. My tailbone hit the ground with an unfortunate thud.

I could feel my arms trembling from the cold and the effort. This wasn't working.

Ness came to crouch beside me. "Let go of control," she murmured.

I nodded, rolling my shoulders. Everyone was silent as I crouched down and placed my hands on the slab of stone. Even with the chaos of the situation, I marveled at its smoothness. I wondered how much of that was from Becca, slipping in day after day, for years. Changing the surface slowly over time. I remembered how the ground had hardened around my arms during the first monster attack, reacting to my fear, and it was only when I'd relaxed that it had let go. I summoned that same calm now, imagining the stone was malleable and forgiving. When the moment felt right, I pushed.

The rock felt soft as clay.

I carefully pushed and pulled the earth until the opening was wide enough for any of us to get through. When I pulled my hands away, the stone became solid again. To my surprise, my handprints remained visible, the impressions deep in the rock. Slumping back, I laughed despite my exhaustion.

Jax whooped in excitement.

Kitt nodded, his eyes shining, while Tennian stared in awe.

"Nice job," Ness beamed.

Alto shook his head in disbelief. "You're learning so fast."

Even Mercury gazed at me with pride in their eyes.

Their attention made me feel thrilled and uncomfortable at the same time. "Let's go."

We slid down one by one, and I held a flame high to see what awaited us.

The tunnel was about five meters long, with a sloping floor and walls.

"This place must have been formed when the volcano was active," Ness said, gesturing to the natural rock. "Like a lava tube."

"Something like that," Alto agreed. "Becca wasn't a Terra, so she couldn't have made it."

"No, but she certainly improved it." I gestured to the walls. "This is why she was gone for so long."

Symbols dotted the length of the walls on both sides. Lines and swirls in dark paint glinted ominously in the light of our torches.

"I guess we know who raided the library," Tennian nodded.

Sure enough, a few books were scattered at the end of the tunnel, where a crude door had been set into the stone.

"Becca may have painted the sigils, but the designs themselves are old," Mercury remarked, gazing around. "And that's coming from an immortal, so it should say something. Civilizations far older than yours created them to enhance their magic." They held out a paw, then huffed with frustration. "They're also preventing me from going any farther."

"What do they mean?" Alto's eyes were wide with alarm.

Mercury craned their neck to get a better look. "Each symbol is designed to keep something out. It looks like Becca covered everything from the undead to non-human entities, including yours truly, thanks to that one." They nodded to an intricate swirl and triangle design that was repeated several times on the walls and ceiling.

"Clever," I muttered, "very clever. Zaletor's minions would never be able to get through. Maybe even Zaletor himself, considering all the souls he contained."

"Well, tough luck for you then," Jax said to Mercury as he started down the tunnel "We'll bring you the—AHHH!!"

We all jumped as Jax screamed, stumbling backwards. His shoe was smoldering, and a hole in the sole revealed an angry red welt. Ness and Kitt pulled him down, assessing the wound, while Mercury jumped in front of me.

"What happened?" they shouted, looking for threats.

"The floor," I realized, "there are sigils on the floor."

We hadn't noticed them before because of the dust and grime, but sure enough, symbols dotted the floor as well.

"Can we step around them?" Alto offered. "Or shift the rock itself to move the markings?"

"I wouldn't," Mercury muttered, their eyes darting across the floor. "This is more than a simple barrier. I don't even recognize some of these sigils. There's no telling what will happen. Besides, even the most powerful Terra can't wield warded stone."

"Could we go back out to the surface, walk until we've passed over the tunnel, then make an entrance?" Tennian suggested. "We'd bypass this altogether."

I shook my head. "Widening an existing opening is one thing. I don't think I'd be able to make an entirely new entrance in solid rock, let alone tunnel this far down. Besides, we don't know what we'd be dropping into. There could be traps down there as well."

Alto gestured back to the opening and the growing darkness. "Maybe we should come back tomorrow? Wait for daylight."

"We're here now," I countered, my frustration mounting. "Give me a minute to think."

Becca wouldn't have made the tunnel completely impassable; I was sure of it. She had to have gotten out somehow, and I had to believe she'd have left a way through on the off chance that she would need to find the gemstone again. I studied the symbols on the floor, racking my brain for any bit of helpful information. They were every possible shape and design, all abstract lines and circles. Except one.

Spaced on the floor throughout the hall were repeating designs that resembled a bird, with wings flared wide and curled at the edges. My heart stopped. The memory of Becca holding my face, drunk on mead and life, whispered to me.

"You're a phoenix," I whispered.

"What?" Kitt asked?

Not wanting to second guess, I stepped onto it.

Everyone shouted, and I tensed, waiting for the pain, but nothing happened. Not willing to relax yet, I held my breath as I jumped to the next. But by the third symbol, I smiled.

Thank you, Becca, I thought.

Finally, I reached the far end. The door was covered in webs, but there was no lock. Bracing myself, I pushed it open.

I made the flame in my hand bigger, filling the space with light, and gasped.

30

Shadows flickered all around me, and I gripped the doorframe to keep from falling back onto the sigils. Hissing through my teeth at my own skittishness, I steadied my hand enough to search the floor for traps. Finding none, I stepped forward.

"Skies above," I cursed.

I was in a cavernous room. The shadows that had startled me came from the dozens of poorly constructed tables and shelves that ringed the large space.

"What do you see?!" Mercury called.

"It's a room, filled with...stuff?"

The center was open, but every inch of wall space had been taken up. For a brief instant, I was reminded of Renis's study with its shelves full of riches. But when I approached a shelf, I realized the difference.

A shard of colorful glass. A pressed flower. A scrap of silk. A piece of driftwood with a butterfly carved into the surface.

This was nothing like Renis's room, I realized. While the assortment of objects meant nothing to me, I knew each one had undoubtedly meant a great deal to Becca. I could picture it so perfectly: her as a small child, smuggling bits of furniture that wouldn't be missed or materials to construct whatever wouldn't fit through the cavern's opening, then filling the room with things she'd collected and hoarded to bring herself joy.

These were actual treasures.

I swallowed thickly. Behind me, I could hear my friends making their way down the tunnel, mirroring my careful steps, all except Mercury. I knew the Ethereal was displeased about being left behind, but there was no other way. Stepping further into the cavern, I tried to look everywhere at once. There was so much to take in, and everything was obscured with dust. But it was all hers, and that meant it was all special.

As everyone gathered in one at a time, Ness added her light to mine, driving away the shadows.

"Great seas," Tennian breathed, "how long was she collecting things? There's a full lifetime's worth of stuff in here."

"This would have all been from her childhood," I said, "she would never have come back here except to leave the gemstone."

"I had no idea she was such a magpie," Jax smiled, inspecting a shelf with a wistful look.

"I think this is also where she practiced her Gift," Alto said. He was looking down at a pile of books and scrolls on a low table. "These are all studies on Anima, some dating back to before Zaletor's time. She must have known what she was long before her parents found out, and she brought everything here to research how to hide her secret."

I noticed everyone was keeping their voices low, as though we were standing on sacred ground. And in many ways, we were. The weight of Becca's absence had pressed down on me for years, like an oppressive coat I could never take off. And now, standing in a space where my friend had felt safe, where she'd kept all the things that made her happy in her years of pain, I found myself struggling to breathe.

A warm hand came to rest on my back, and I turned to find Kitt. His eyes were soft as he cocked his head. "Are you alright?"

I could recall so vividly the last time I'd seen her, all cocky grins and swinging hips. She'd healed so much by that time, it seemed that she was always smiling. When the report had come in about yet another pirate attack, she'd jumped at the opportunity to deal with it personally. It was clear she was looking for any opportunity to get out of the castle, as we'd all begun feeling the strain of leadership, and I'd sent her off happily. I'd assumed she'd return before the seasons changed, feeling refreshed and accomplished.

"I'm fine," I lied.

I knew he could see right through it, but he cupped my face in his calloused, gentle hand. He brushed my cheek with his thumb and nodded, then stepped back. Taking a breath, I focused on the only clue Becca had given me.

It was in good hands with Pumpkin.

There, on a shelf level with my shoulders, was a faded orange stuffed bunny. It was well loved, with a once-pink velvet nose that was now nearly bald, and a wrinkled left ear, which was probably how Becca had carried it around. But what brought tears to my eyes was the tiny locket the toy wore around its neck. It was the same silver locket Becca had worn every day I'd known her until she left to hide the stone. She'd returned without it, saying the chain broke and it had been lost. I'd offered to replace it, knowing it had meant a great deal to her, but she'd refused, saying the necklace was no longer necessary.

I knew there were portraits of her parents inside, which I'd always found strange as Becca hated her parents. She said it was motivation, to never forget. She was spiteful that way.

Steeling myself, I lifted the toy from the shelf. It was shockingly heavy to have just stuffing inside. Turning it over, I found a loose thread and pulled it free, opening a small hole in the toy's back.

Swallowing back tears, I pulled the gemstone out.

It was exactly as I remembered. The size of a robin's egg, the circular, multifaceted stone seemed to glow with every shade of red and orange. It was breathtaking, but it also made me uneasy. Before, we'd thought it merely an ornament. Now I knew what evil it was capable of.

Clutching Pumpkin to my chest, I turned around.

"I found it."

The whole room went still. Somehow, even with all our planning and confidence, part of me had doubted we'd succeed. That Zaletor would have beaten us here, or the gemstone would never have been here at all. As I looked from face to face, I could see my friends had all felt the same.

But we'd done it.

"What's happening?! Everyone stopped talking!!" Mercury's cry carried into the room, breaking the spell.

"WE DID IT!" Jax yelled, thrusting his fist into the air. Mercury whooped with joy.

"We should be ready," Ness warned, heading toward the tunnel. "I wouldn't be surprised if Zaletor followed us here and is waiting outside for us so he can take the stone."

I clutched the stone in my hand. "All we have to do is get it to Mercury. They'll take it back to the Ethereal Plane immediately. Zaletor might be powerful with the base of the crown, but he'll never be what he once was."

"Not a problem," Jax smirked, strutting toward the exit. "We can definitely handle him at half strength. I won't let him slip away this time."

Tennian followed him out. "If we leave now, we can get back

to the house, get everything packed, and be ready to return to the ship at first light. It will be treacherous, but the tides will be with us."

The others headed toward the exit, discussing the best defensive plan, but I stayed a moment longer, looking around the quiet space one last time. With trembling hands, I tucked the stuffed toy into the loop of my belt. I couldn't explain why, but I wanted it with me.

"Thank you," I whispered to the room. I prayed my words would reach her, wherever she was.

Someday, when this was all over, I'd come back. I'd study every single item and drink an entire bottle of shitty wine, remembering my friend and trying to forgive myself.

"It's surreal, isn't it?"

Startled, I found Alto beside me. His gaze was far away.

I nodded. "I hope she wouldn't mind that we found this place."

He looked more lost than I'd ever seen him, and I knew the space was affecting him as well. Giving him a moment, I turned to the door that led to the tunnel and found it closed. Odd, Alto must have closed it behind him when he came back.

No, not odd, I told myself. He wanted a moment alone, like I did. Wanting to give him privacy, I reached for the handle.

"Why didn't she love me back, Phoebe?"

I blinked, shocked at the suddenness of the question as I faced him.

"I—I don't know, Alto. We don't choose who we love. If the feelings aren't there—"

He spun to face me. "But the feelings *were* there! I know it! If we'd had more time, if she hadn't been taken from me, I know she would have seen it, too. One day, she *would have seen it*."

An uncomfortable feeling grew in my stomach. Clearly, this

was too overwhelming for him. Emotions were high and he didn't know what he was saying. The sooner he left this place, the better.

"We should join the others. They've probably secured the exit by now and are wondering where we are."

"Alright," he sighed, and gave me a sorrowful smile, "can I see the stone before we go? I never got a good look at it last time."

I hesitated, though I couldn't explain why. Alto was my friend. He was confused and grieving, like I was. But I'd learned to trust the warning bells in my head, so I tightened my fist around the gemstone as I turned to open the door.

"It's better if we—"

The blow hit me from behind, a kick to the back of my knees. I went down hard, but I managed to keep my grip on the stone in my hands.

Before I could comprehend what happened, I was pressed into the rocky floor. A foot came down hard on my wrist. My scream echoed throughout the cavern as Alto plucked the gemstone from my hand.

31

I scrambled away the moment I felt the pressure release my back. I could hear shouting on the other side of the door, but my focus was wholly on the man in front of me. Hoarfrost covered my hands, though my conscious mind hadn't yet processed the fact that I should attack.

Alto ignored me, gazing at the gemstone with hunger in his eyes.

"What are you doing?!"

He raised a finger in my direction, though he kept his focus on the gem. The stone floor around me melted into mud. Shocked and off balance, I put my hands down to steady myself. Between one blink and the next, the floor resolidified, encasing my hands and feet completely. I cried out at the pressure on my injured wrist.

My mind reeled. Alto had never been powerful enough to manipulate stone. And my friend would never hurt me.

"Who are you?!" I shouted. "How did you infiltrate our group??"

The cries on the other side of the door became frantic. The man before me closed his eyes and took an exasperated breath.

"That's easier for you to believe, isn't it? That I'm someone else. That I'm Zaletor in disguise, or one of his constructs. It helps you preserve the narrative you've created where you're the hero in all this." He looked at me then, and the hate burning in his eyes sent a chill up my spine. "But you're not the hero. You're just another monster. And I'm finally strong enough to stop you."

Goddesses above, what was happening?

I swallowed. I couldn't tell if the nausea that threatened to overwhelm me was from the pain in my wrist or Alto's words. Casting a quick glance at the door, I realized chips of stone had grown out around it, keeping it sealed no matter how much my friends pounded on it.

My voice cracked as I pleaded, unsure what else to do. "I can see you're angry, and we should talk through this. But Alto please! We need to get the gemstone to Mercury now, before Zaletor shows up and takes it!"

He sighed again, his face darkening with disappointment.

"I never understood why The Goddesses chose you. You're so fucking stupid." He crossed the space and crouched before me, and I cringed as he reached into his coat.

From within the folds of cloth, Alto pulled a golden crown. It gleamed just as bright as the day I'd taken it from Zaletor's tower, with a gaping hole where we'd pried out the stone.

"Zaletor is dead, Phoebe," he said, his voice full of mock pity. "You killed him twenty years ago."

The world went quiet as I stared at the crown. "But the monsters...the attacks?"

He groaned with impatience. "With only the base of the crown, they were not nearly as useful as I'd hoped. Without souls to infuse into them, I had to rely on my Terra Gift to control them, and I could only manage a dozen at a time. Still, I only needed them to cause enough chaos and destruction to get some attention. I must say, you caught on much sooner than I'd anticipated."

I felt my mind go silent for a moment, and when I spoke, my words were thick. "I don't—I don't understand."

"I know you don't. You were never much of anything without the rest of us propping you up. But that didn't stop you from taking all the credit. Her Majesty Queen Phoebe Blessed-Heart." Alto sneered as if the words were vile, then rose to stand over me. "What a joke. But I was willing to let it go, willing to be pushed aside. Until you killed Becca."

My mouth went dry, but Alto began pacing. "Oh sure, maybe you didn't know about the storm, but you didn't need to. It could have just as easily been the pirates, or a rogue wave, or an injury aboard the ship, miles from any help. You sent her out *time and again*, knowing at some point she wouldn't come back. Jax and Tristan might not have seen it, your master plan, but I did!"

"Were you trying to keep us apart? You knew it was over with Tristan and didn't want anyone else to be happy?" He scoffed. "And then the little performance just now, with the tears and the sad words? Pathetic. Even now, in this place, you had to make it about you."

He twirled the crown around his finger. "But none of that matters now, because I'm finally strong enough to make you pay."

My head swam, and I was overcome with the sensation that none of this was real. My guilt and despair threatened to swallow me whole, and I felt I must be hallucinating, because nothing made sense. Alto continued to spin the crown in triumph, and I grabbed the first question that came to mind like a lifeline.

"How did you even get it?"

He laughed, the sound tinged with madness. "That was the easiest part. All I had to do was follow you. I admit, that was before you killed Becca, but I knew that someday the crown could be useful again. And you were so wrapped up in yourself you didn't even notice me follow you into the catacombs. Not that you ever noticed me. By the way, I took it *years* ago! I assumed you knew it was missing and were trying to keep it quiet, or simply didn't care! Instead, you never even realized it was gone!"

The intensity in his eyes was terrifying as he looked at the golden circle. "And the power it holds! Even without the stone, the crown has made me the most powerful Terra alive!" His face filled with resolve. "But it wasn't enough. I needed the gemstone to make it whole."

My wrist throbbed from where it was trapped, anchoring me to reality. Gritting my teeth, I tried to free myself. To move the stone the way I'd widened the tunnel opening less than an hour before. But my heart thundered in my chest, and I simply couldn't focus. I was too afraid.

I hate being afraid. So I channeled the fear into rage.

"Why not just kill me?! Why this whole charade?"

"Because I wanted to destroy the only thing that actually mattered to you: your image. You care SO MUCH about how people see you! You'll do anything to have them worship you, to treat you like their savior. If I'd simply killed you, it would have made you immortal. People would have mourned you for eternity! But if I could convince everyone that you'd failed, that Zaletor was alive, and you'd been a liar all this time, I knew they'd all hate you just as much as I did."

"You rebuilt the tower," I realized.

"Finally!" Alto cried. "You're catching on!" He shook his head in disgust. "The day you showed up at the bookstore, it took every ounce of my willpower not to strangle you on the spot. But I knew the reward would be so much sweeter if I waited. I'll admit, there were a few things I didn't foresee. Mercury's return was unfortunate, and no doubt they're how you picked up on my Gladiators so quickly. And that Ignis girl was unexpected and forced me to adjust. I've had to fireproof my robes after that incident on the road. But overall, you behaved *exactly* as I knew you would. And, if I'm honest, I think this new plan is going to work out so much better."

There was a crackle behind me, and a wisp of smoke curled past. Ness must be burning the door down, I realized, but in that moment I didn't care.

"Let me guess," I spat, "you're going to name yourself king."

Alto scoffed. "I have no desire to rule. But there is someone who deserves the title of queen far more than you." He smiled with satisfaction and returned his focus to the gemstone. His eyes seemed to glow red from the light reflecting off it. "This started as simple revenge: to humiliate and destroy you. But she's given me a better idea, Phoebe."

Despite the growing heat at my back from the door, my body went cold. "Who's given you a better idea?"

"She knows I'm strong enough. All I have to do is open a portal to her prison in the Ethereal Plane. Once I've freed her, and she has access to her remaining essence, she'll return Becca to me."

The sliver of Kalexia's essence. Fear froze me in place. He was going to release her.

My thoughts were somehow a jumble of chaos and quiet at the same time. Becca couldn't be brought back, could she? The Goddesses had brought me back to life, but that was immediate. I was dead for barely a second. Could someone be revived after thirteen years? Was there even a body to heal? The thought made me sick, but I realized I didn't actually know.

But it didn't matter. Even if it were possible, I knew it would never happen.

"Kalexia is lying to you" I insisted, my voice quivering. "She won't bring Becca back! Once the portal is open and she's free, she'll destroy the world to spite her sisters!"

It was exactly what Mercury had feared once we'd realized what the crown truly was.

"Nonsense," Alto waved. "She only wants to be free of her prison. Besides, *I* won't be doing anything." There was a swish of movement as he flipped his coat around, revealing black robes. His voice dropped, becoming cold and eerie. The exact voice I'd heard him use when he'd attacked. "Zaletor is alive, remember? He'll be the one unleashing hell on earth. All because you failed to stop him, and you kept that fact to yourself."

There was another crack behind me, and I heard Mercury screaming my name.

"Becca was always loved," Alto went on, his voice returning to normal. "And once she 'defeats' Zaletor and people realize she's come back from death to save them, they'll discard you like the trash you are and hand her the throne. Becca will be a much better ruler, and I will be by her side to help. And I know the perfect stage for Zaletor's return," Alto grinned, his features ghastly in the shadows of the hood. "You wanted this year's Commemoration Festival to be bigger than ever. I'll grant you that final wish."

With a swirl of robes and a final laugh, Alto vanished right as Ness burst through the charred door.

Everyone was talking at once, making it impossible for me to concentrate on freeing my hands.

"It can't have been him!" Jax argued for the millionth time. "It was a construct, or he was brainwashed!"

"I heard it from his own mouth, Jax," Ness countered, "it was him."

She and Kitt had broken through the door with a spray of splinters and burning shards of wood right as Alto had fled. They must have overhead him monologuing through the weakened door. At least I didn't have to worry about them believing me. Kitt crouched beside me where I was still trapped, looking for a way to help.

"Maybe there's something else going on," Tennian offered, "something we're not seeing?"

"What's happening?!" Mercury called from the tunnel's entrance. "Phoebe? Are you alright?!"

"I don't believe it," Jax insisted. But I could see the pain on his face.

"Everybody shut up!" I shouted, "I'm trying to focus!"

They all jumped to face me as though they'd forgotten I was there. Taking a few deep breaths, I tried using the same technique that had allowed me to widen the tunnel's opening: picturing the rock as sand or clay. It took a bit longer than before, but eventually my hands came free with a sucking sound.

I was *so sick* of getting trapped in the ground.

My right wrist ached, and an angry red patch bloomed where Alto had stomped on it. I whimpered as I rolled it from side to side, but relief filled me all the same. It would certainly bruise, but at least nothing was broken. Forcing myself up, I opened and closed my stiff fingers as I stalked to the exit and left without a second glance. Becca's special room now felt tainted.

"Thank The Goddesses," Mercury sighed as I maneuvered my way down the tunnel. "What happened? Where's the gemstone?"

"Gone."

The tunnel filled with light as Ness and the others followed me, and I could see fear and confusion on Mercury's face. But I pushed past them, scrambling out the tunnel's exit into the night air.

Mercury glided out, following me.

"Gone where? Did Zaletor—"

"There is no Zaletor!" Even the wind couldn't dampen my voice as I shouted into the night. Ice stung my fingers, colder than I'd ever felt it. "Zaletor is DEAD! He has been this whole time. Alto played all of us for fools. He took the crown from the crypts and now he has the gemstone."

I could hear the others making their way toward us, but I kept walking. I didn't know which direction the house was, but I didn't care. The Ethereal kept pace in the air beside me. "Why?"

"Revenge. He blames me for what happened to Becca, and he wants to humiliate me." My voice hitched as I struggled to breathe.

"Ok," Mercury sputtered, "we need to regroup, and—um, we'll figure something out." They were floundering and falling back on old habits. Analyze, plan, action. It had always worked for us in the past. But I couldn't do that right now.

"Stay with the others," I said, not slowing down, "I need some space."

"If you think I'm leaving you again after what just happened—"

"Mercury, for once in your miserable existence, listen to me!"

Turning, I sprinted off into the night.

My body was screaming when I finally came to stop, not because I was tired, but because the magic raging inside me could no longer be contained.

It was tied to my emotions, that's what Mercury had said. Fear made it weak. Anger made it unpredictable. This was neither of those.

What I felt now was unbridled rage.

Throwing my hands in front of me, I released it all. Ice poured out of me like an avalanche, turning the rocks into a frozen wasteland, but I didn't stop. The ground trembled, cracking in jagged lines out into the distance, while flames licked up my arms. My sleeves burned away, and the heat seared my skin. Only the ice in my veins kept my flesh from burning.

How had I not seen it? I'd known Zaletor was dead! I'd watched him crumble right in front of me. But I'd let everyone else's uncertainty creep in, making me doubt myself. Making me question my own eyes.

Alto had controlled me from the very beginning.

Would I have suspected him if I'd never doubted myself? If I hadn't been so easy to trick? Would I have been on the lookout for another option, instead of focusing so blindly on the enemy from my past?

The stone softened beneath my feet, sucking me down, even as I unleashed hell with my hands. It was more power than I'd ever used, even on the day I'd defeated Zaletor. But it wasn't enough. I screamed, adding my voice to the cacophony of elemental rage.

I'd failed. Again.

I'd failed the kingdom. I'd failed my friends. I'd failed Becca.

Becca.

Despite all his other madness, Alto had understood one thing clearly. Hells, I'm sure *everyone* knew it. This was simply the first time I'd heard someone else speak the truth aloud. I was responsible for Becca's death. The storm may have killed her, but I was the one who'd sent her to her doom.

Everything below my knees was submerged in the frozen earth, but I didn't care. If the ground swallowed me whole, that would be less than I deserved.

But in the light of my raging flames, a flash of orange caught my eye.

I looked down and found Pumpkin still tucked into my belt.

I immediately stopped sinking.

My outpouring of fire and ice slowed. I could have carried on all night, but instead I pulled myself stiffly from the earth. Suddenly exhausted, I sank to my knees, ignoring the shards of ice and broken rock that bit into my legs.

No matter what harm I was willing to bring on myself, I

wouldn't risk damaging Becca's favorite toy. Thank The Goddesses nothing had happened to it during the attack. Pulling it free, I hugged the thread-worn rabbit to my chest. The silver locket was cool against my skin, and I rubbed my thumb over its tarnished surface. An abrasive texture caught my attention, and I frowned. On the back, what had once been a blank silver disk was now etched with an elegant script.

Sisters Always

Though I hadn't seen the locket in ages, I was certain that the inscription wasn't there before. Reverently, I opened the locket, expecting to find the images of her parents on each side, as it had been every other time I'd seen it. But her parent's faces were gone, completely painted over. My eyes stung with tears when I found different faces staring up at me.

Now, in stunning, minute detail, there were portraits of the two of us. Both smiling.

I gasped for breath. An ache twisted in my gut that I couldn't put a name to. For a brief second, I thought a wisp of gold drifted from my mouth, but when I looked again, it was gone.

Clearly, I was losing my mind. Not that it mattered. I ran a finger along the locket's edge, studying the portrait. They were beautifully done. Even though they were small, the joy in our eyes was obvious.

When had she done this? Becca had said the necklace was no longer necessary. I'd assumed she meant her vengeance had been achieved. But what if she no longer needed to carry a reminder of what was important, because her most cherished thing was with her every day?

And I'd let her die.

My heart cracked open as I hugged the tattered stuffed rabbit to my chest and sobbed.

33

———

The entrance to the tunnel was empty, so I assumed the group had gone back to the mansion. I followed the track of stones back, having just enough energy to keep a small flame to light the path ahead until the glow of the house was visible.

I found Mercury waiting for me.

The Ethereal sat on the stoop facing the night, watching me approach. But rather than swooping out to meet me, they waited still as a statue until I reached them. I couldn't read their expression, but something like hurt danced in their eternal eyes.

"That was quite the impressive display," they said. "I could see the flames from here."

I sat beside them. My throat was raw from screaming and crying, but I forced the words out. "I'm sorry I yelled. I was angry and confused, but I know you were worried about me."

They remained stoically facing the night, but their eyes darted my direction. We were silent for a time, and when they spoke again, it was barely a whisper.

"I hated not being able to follow you into that tunnel. And then I could hear you scream, and knew you were in pain, but I couldn't do a damn thing. I couldn't even blast the door for your friends to get through. I felt so helpless, just like I did the day you died."

I stilled. We'd spoken about that day when we first started this adventure, but I didn't realize there was more to it.

They shifted uncomfortably, not looking at me directly. "That day was terrible, for so many reasons, but mostly because I knew how it had to end. How, even if you were victorious, you wouldn't win. I'd begged The Goddesses to bring you back after —after it happened, but I didn't know if they'd listen. And, even if they did, I still hated that you had to do it at all. I might be immortal, but even I was aware that, for all your strength and bravado, you were a child walking to your death."

Finally, Mercury faced me. The stars in their eyes glowed with a life of their own, but their cat-like face was filled with sorrow.

"I care for you a great deal. I always have. I know that when I found you in your castle, I commented that you are not the same person I helped all those years ago. Then, I meant it as an insult, but now, I see it's not. And it's not entirely true. All the qualities that made you amazing back then, your warmth and determination and willingness to fail over and over and over again, those are all still there. You're simply more now. A more complete version of the 'you' that I knew. And I like this version very much. I don't want you to suffer anymore."

My throat closed at their words. The emotion in their face was overwhelming, and I longed to throw my arms around them, but refrained.

"I love you too, friend," I croaked. "Though I wouldn't call my propensity for failure a positive trait."

Their ears perked forward. "On the contrary. If you're failing, it means you're still trying. That's always better than doing nothing."

Even though their statement went against everything I'd believed, I felt the sentiment settle in my bones.

"I'm afraid," I whispered. "I can't lose anyone else."

A smoky wing brushed my back. The sensation was cold, yet comforting. "I know, and fear isn't always bad. But everyone will suffer if we don't do something."

Together, we looked up at the stars. Like that day in the grass, I again imagined my fear as a living thing. It wasn't a terrifying goblin this time, crouched and dangerous.

It was me. Standing alone, paralyzed by insecurity.

There was a lot I'd done wrong over the years. But if I didn't do *something*, Alto was going to unleash a dark Goddess and destroy the world. I didn't like failing, but I'd gotten incredibly good at it. And sitting here, waiting for the end, was not an option.

I nodded to myself, and the fear-image dissolved. My lips twitched in the smallest of smiles.

"Okay. Let's get the others and figure out how to destroy that son of a bitch."

Inside, everyone was packing up except Jax, who sat slumped on the stairs. His face was lined with sadness and defeat.

"On your feet, Jax!"

Everyone snapped to attention at my words. Jax leapt up, more out of surprise than any desire to follow orders, but I took it as good enough. My friends clustered around me.

"How long till we can get back to the ship?" I asked Tennian.

She didn't hesitate. "We're almost finished packing. If we

leave as soon as we're done, we'll reach the rowboat right before low tide. It will carry us back to the ship quickly."

"Perfect. We need to make that tide."

"Where are we going?" Ness asked as she stacked bedrolls near the door. "We only caught the end of what was said in the cavern."

Right. I took a breath.

"Zaletor is dead."

Everyone stopped.

As succinctly as possible, I told them all what had happened in the cavern. I was amazed that my voice didn't tremble.

"Alto's plan is to open the portal to the Ethereal Plane during the Commemoration Festival while disguised as Zaletor. Since his main goal is to turn everyone against me, he'll want a big audience. That means his target will be the parade. It draws the biggest crowd of any event, and this year it's going to be grander than ever."

At least, I hoped that was his plan. I realized he could have lied to throw me off, then carry out his actual plan in peace. He'd been two steps ahead this whole time. But this was the best option I had.

"Are we sailing back to the capitol then?" Kitt asked from where he was packing books into an old trunk. I realized they were the books Becca had left behind in the tunnel.

Jax shook his head. "The festival starts in three days. Even with good winds, there's no way we can get to Glassleaf by then."

"We can," I corrected, and turned to Mercury.

The Ethereal looked at me, then Jax, then me again. "What?"

"You can teleport us there!" I cried. "You told me once you can carry someone with you!"

Mercury scoffed. "Yes, and that doing so would use a dangerous amount of dark energy, which is why we've never done it! It's not worth the risk."

"It is now. We need to get back or the world will end."

Ness jumped in. "If we're teleporting back, then why do we need to return to the ship?"

"We're not teleporting!" Mercury insisted.

"Because," I turned to Tennian, "you need to get back to the ship and you can't row around the rocks by yourself."

Our captain frowned. "Why would I need to go back? If you're all teleporting to Glassleaf, then I'm coming too."

"No one. Is. Teleporting!!!" Mercury flew into the air in front of me, but I stepped aside.

"You need to return to Salt Winds."

Tennian's shock transformed to anger. "I might not have magic, but I can fight. You need all the help you can get!"

"I do," I nodded, "but if we fail, or if Alto misled me and has some whole other scheme planned, the world needs to know what really happened. You need to tell Tristan and everyone else about Alto's treachery."

Not that it would matter, since if we failed there was an uncomfortably high likelihood that the world would be destroyed, but that was secondary. Thanks to the current, the return journey would be shorter than our trip here. If the weather was good, it would take three days to reach Salt Wind which, if things went bad on our end, would at least give Tennian a chance to be with her family one last time. She deserved that.

Tennian must have seen the true intention in my eyes and chewed her lip. "But I can help."

"You are helping." I smiled, taking her hand. It was small, but I could feel her strength as I gave it a squeeze. "This is important."

She held my gaze for a moment, her brown eyes shining, and finally nodded.

"If we're going to make the tide, we need to leave now."

We left the mansion minutes later. I was the last one out and shut the door behind me. The warped wood groaned in protest, but I pulled until it closed.

The cavern where Becca had hidden all her treasures was a precious, almost sacred space. The mansion was merely a shell. A tomb that deserved to be forgotten. If my strength weren't still depleted from my outburst the night before, I would have razed the whole thing to the ground, no matter what Becca had wanted all those years ago.

As I followed my friends toward the beach, I didn't look back at it once.

It took three of us to manage the rowboat while Mercury flew alongside, leaving Jax and Ness to sit quietly while we struggled.

"I still don't understand how he could have done this," Jax muttered, more to himself than any of us. "Even if he was obsessed all these years, how could he have gone this far?"

"It wasn't entirely him," Mercury corrected, bounding in the air beside us. "The crown contains a sliver of Kalexia's essence. The moment Alto used it to become more powerful, she began poisoning his mind. He might not even realize how far he's taken things."

I gritted my teeth as I struggled with an oar. "The Dark Lady might be pulling the strings now, but Alto set all this in motion. He took the crown of his own free will with the intent to make me suffer."

Jax wrapped his coat tighter around himself and stared vacantly at the waves.

We made it to the ship in good time, thanks to Tennian's expert direction, and scrambled on board. She paused only long enough to wish us luck, her face a mixture of fear and resolve, then took charge of the crew, preparing to set sail for Salt Wind. Meanwhile, the rest of us gathered around Mercury on the deck. I had given Tennian a way out of this mess, and I felt it was only fair to do the same for the others.

"Anyone who wishes is welcome to return with Tennian," I said, looking at Jax, Ness and Kitt. "I know you all have family and friends, and I won't begrudge you returning to them. Mercury and I had planned to do this ourselves in the beginning, and we are still prepared to do just that."

Mercury moved to sit beside me, their head high.

Ness smiled. "My family always wanted me to devote my life to The Goddesses. This seems like a good way to do that. Besides," she winked, "if you die, you'll never be able to rebuild my glass studio."

Jax scratched his chin. "Mary would be furious if I let the world end and her tavern got destroyed. And my family is right here."

Kitt met my gaze. "I go where you go."

My heart swelled to the point that I thought my chest would burst apart. While I hated to let them walk into danger, I nodded.

"Alright then. Let's do this."

"This is a stupid plan," Mercury said, "but if you don't die in the process, I think I can get you to the castle. Just you."

"No," I said, "it needs to be all of us. Alto's final challenge was 'stop me if you can.' He expects me to come and fight him alone. To face him myself the way I once would have." I ignored the pit in my stomach. "Our advantage here is in our numbers."

Pride glowed in Ness's eyes.

But Mercury shook their head. "I'm sorry. I can't get that far with all of you. We'll need a different plan."

Jax groaned. "Alto is dead to me, but no one can deny he was the best at coming up with well thought out, serious plans! I guarantee the rat has already considered every logical move we could make."

Kitt cleared his throat. "It sounds like we need a plan that's so random and ridiculous, he'll never see it coming."

I saw the glint in his eyes. "You've got an idea."

He smiled. "I've got an idea." He looked at Mercury. "You can't get us all the way to Glassleaf, but could you get us close to Narism?"

The Ethereal did some mental calculations. "That sounds more reasonable, but again, I want to reiterate that there are no guarantees, and that this is a terrible idea!"

"Narism it is," I said, then turned to Kitt. "You can fill us in on the details once we get there."

Because if we didn't leave now, we'd lose our nerve.

Mercury instructed us to hold hands. The Ethereal's wings were tucked in tight, and their tail flicked nervously.

"I don't know that holding hands will help," they admitted as we clustered together, "but it sure as Hells can't hurt. And I don't want anyone getting separated and winding up in the middle of the ocean."

"It will work," I assured them. I took Kitt's hand to my right, and Ness's to my left, with Jax between them opposite me. Mercury stood in the center of our little circle, and I smiled at them. "We believe in you."

"That's assuming we don't all get sucked into the Ethereal Plane, doomed to a violent and suffocating death," Jax muttered.

"We'll call that the 'worst case scenario,' I said, hoping to lighten the mood.

Mercury took a breath and their tail stilled. A gust of wind swirled about us. "Actually 'worst case' would be you all getting ripped apart, *and* something creeping through from the Ethereal Plane to wreak havoc on your unsuspecting world."

I blanched, nearly dropping my friends' hands as I realized they weren't joking, but the Ethereal gave me a wicked smile.

"It's your dumb plan, remember. Now, away we go!"

And then we were falling.

34

I was surrounded by swirls of color and shadow. It felt like someone had tied a rope to the base of my spine and was pulling me backwards, down, and sideways at the same time. I couldn't see my friends except in flashes. Hells, I couldn't even tell if I was corporeal or not, but I could feel their hands in mine and gripped them tight. They both squeezed back just as strong.

The most upsetting part was the lack of sound. I'd been expecting it to sound like being stuck in a windstorm, or even horrific screaming. Instead, there was a complete absence of sound, like being underwater in a still pond. I considered screaming, simply to prove sound still existed, but refrained in case I was wrong.

The sheer terror of it all made the trip feel hours long, but I knew it was only a fraction of a second. When I finally felt solid ground beneath me, I sighed aloud with relief.

And promptly vomited everywhere.

I'd managed to let go of my friends' hands before crouching down, too dizzy to remain upright. Tears blurred my vision as I expelled the contents of my stomach, but I could hear my companions were all in a similar state. Still, the retching sounds were music to my ears after that nerve-wracking silence.

Unconcerned with our digestive struggles, Mercury gave a loud whoop.

"I did it! Not that I ever doubted for an instant, of course. But I do love proving how great I am!"

"Excellent work," I mumbled, spitting out the last of the bile. "You're truly a marvel."

The Ethereal, too excited to perceive my sarcasm, preened happily.

"Are we close to Narism?" Ness had remained standing during her ordeal and was looking around between burps.

Meanwhile, Jax lay flat on the ground, groaning. "I think we died."

Kitt was taking deep breaths, hands on his knees. "For once, I agree with Jax."

Pushing myself to my knees, I took in our surroundings. The grass around us was wilted and dead, sacrificed to the dark energy Mercury had just used. My heart stuttered at the sight, but I pushed the discomfort aside, knowing what Alto had planned would be far worse. The sun was shining, which was a good sign because it meant we were out of the Crescent Sea. We appeared to be in the middle of a field, and there were a few buildings on the horizon to the north. My disorientation was evaporating quickly, and I took a deep breath to help steady myself.

We did it, I realized. We were alive.

Whimpering slightly, Jax lifted his head off the ground. "I—urp, that's Narism all right."

I shook my head, driving away the last of the dizziness, and stood.

"Alright," I said to Kitt, "what next?"

His cheeks were bright red beneath his beard, but his eyes were clear as he gave a slight smile.

"Next, we go to the theater."

~

"Remind me again why we aren't charging straight to the castle?" Mercury grumbled. Their voice was muffled from within the canvas wagon that shielded them from view.

A steady crowd flooded the road from Narism to Glassleaf, and there was a celebratory feeling in the air. I strolled beside the wagon casually, just another stagehand managing the supplies, and resisted the urge to scratch my head. "If we run in making a scene, he'll know immediately and start his plan. This way, we have the element of surprise to get as close as possible."

"But if his plan is to free Kalexia, why not do it immediately?" The Ethereal sounded stressed. I couldn't blame them.

My scalp itched furiously from the blond wig I was wearing, but I curled my fingers into fists. "Because he wants me there when it happens. He wants me to see that I failed, to see everyone's faces when he tells them I've been lying all these years."

"Would you two stop mumbling!" Jax snapped from where he sat at the front of the wagon. "We're almost to the city, now get into character!"

He turned back, hunching forward beneath his shawl, and I couldn't help but smile. Kitt sat at his right, a broad hat shielding his face from the sun as he steered the two horses, while Ness, dressed in the black leggings and tunic of a puppeteer, walked near the front of our procession with the actors of The Russell Theater.

I still marveled at the genius of Kitt's plan: sneak into the city in plain sight, with the acting troupe as a cover. Their show hadn't been scheduled to perform at the Commencement Festival, but the stage director and actors had all been more than happy to help once they learned who was asking.

I was used to shocked faces when I entered a room, but I don't think I'd ever seen an entire room literally stop breathing only to burst with joy. The actress who portrayed me had rushed forward, tears in her eyes, with a million questions about my life. I'd promised her to sit down and discuss whatever she wanted to know once this was all over, and the girl had nearly fainted.

We hadn't told them the whole story, thinking it was best if the potential apocalypse was kept under wraps, but I'd told the assembled cast and crew how I'd been traveling in disguise for the past few weeks investigating corruption within my court and needed to return to the city without anyone knowing. I'd also explained how Jax had left the production to assist me, which made everyone look at him in awe. Jax, who hadn't known I'd be endorsing him, had feigned modesty while the stage director had practically groveled at his feet.

But the star of the group, as usual, had been Mercury. The Ethereal had made the crew promise to burn the "blasphemous puppet" when they returned from the capitol, and even posed for sketches while the rest of us prepared so a better replica could be produced.

My biggest fear had been that our traveling companions would give us away. I worried about their enthusiasm, that they would send too many casual glances my direction or begin to giggle at the excitement of our quest. But to my eternal relief, everyone had adopted their role of secret transport with the utmost professionalism. I was merely "stagehand number three," and they treated me as such. I made a mental note to ensure The Russell Theater was funded in perpetuity.

It had taken a day of preparation and a full night of travel to reach the city's edge, but I knew we'd made the right choice when we arrived at the outskirts of Glassleaf to find a statue waiting.

It didn't move, standing like a scarecrow by the roadside, but I knew what it was the instant I laid eyes on it. Alto's newfound power was clear in the detailed, lifelike appearance of the stone figure, though it remained inanimate. But it didn't resemble Zaletor. While the Dark Wizard's Gladiators had borne his face, Alto must have known setting up similar figures throughout the city would cause alarm and show his hand too soon. So he'd chosen a different likeness.

It was me.

Or rather, it was Alto's version of me. My face was smiling unnaturally wide, while my hands were stretched high to the heavens, ready to receive The Goddesses blessing. Lifelike eyes gazed out at the crowd.

I saw it as a mockery, but everyone else saw a shrine. I watched as people stopped to brush the creature's feet with their fingertips or pile flowers where it stood.

"What's out there?" Mercury whispered. "It reeks of dark energy."

"It's a statue," I replied. "Now shut up."

My stomach clenched at the sight of people getting so close to it, but it made no move to attack. Alto had said he could only control a dozen monsters at a time. He might be more powerful with the crown complete, but without human souls to animate them, he'd have to control the movements of every single statue using his Terra Gift. Were these statues simply waiting to be useful? Or did they serve a different purpose?

For all I knew, he could see through their eyes.

The trek into the city was surreal, like a broken mirror version of my flight from the castle weeks before. Once again, I was traveling in disguise, worried every second my true identity would be discovered and questioning whether I was pursuing the correct course of action. But this time I was surrounded by my friends, sneaking back into the home I'd dreamed of escaping for so long.

And, unlike a few weeks ago, this time I knew who the enemy was.

The statues grew in number as we entered the city proper. By the time we reached the Merchant's District, I counted one on every corner, each with the same pose and wearing my face. The people here didn't seem quite as enthused by their presence, as even off to the sides they interrupted the flow of traffic, but everyone delighted in the mystery of them. I overheard a shopkeeper tell someone that they'd all shown up overnight two days prior. He seemed to think several Terras employed by the castle had put them up as a stunt.

I kept close to the wagon, but I was even more thankful we'd gone with Kitt's plan. If the statues had appeared two nights ago then Alto had created them the instant he'd appeared in the city. Even if I'd come straight here when he'd vanished, I would have been caught the second I'd set foot on the streets. The element of surprise would have been impossible.

The parade was scheduled to start tomorrow morning, and I could see my advisors had taken Mercury's assurance that I'd return before the festival seriously. Banners and swags decorated every available post, and several food vendors had already staked out the best spots along the route. The whole city buzzed with activity.

The troupe entered the Theater District, heading to the Citadel's theater. They weren't performing, but no one else needed to know that. The Citadel Theater was as close to the castle as our group could get without raising suspicion. I needed to find out what was happening inside the castle.

"How are we going to figure out where he is?" Jax whispered as we loitered outside the theater. The crowded street felt like the safest place to be. With so many people milling about, no one stopped to notice a group of stagehands stretching before a performance.

Even with my disguise, I didn't like the idea of going into the castle myself. At least, not until I knew whether Alto was there waiting for us. I considered sending Ness or Kitt, who were both unknown to the castle staff and unlikely to be reported back to Alto, but if the statues had been told to keep an eye out for them, or worse, Alto himself was watching through them, they'd be caught in an instant.

"I could teleport in," Mercury offered. "We don't seem to care about the dark energy it takes to do so anymore, so—"

I shook my head. "I'm not going to risk it. And you drifting through the halls as a mist would be way too conspicuous."

Their ears flattened, and I knew they'd been about to suggest exactly that.

"I need someone Alto won't recognize to get a message to Vena," I grumbled. While I was still suspicious of the members of my Council after Mayfield's betrayal, the castle steward had been the only one to ask after my well-being when Mercury had appeared. That, and the fact that she and Mayfield had always hated each other, made her the only person in the castle I was willing to trust. "She could tell us if Alto's there. But who—"

The answer struck like lighting to my brain.

"Wait here!"

I didn't bother to see if they listened but turned and hurried back the way we'd come. Not wanting to get lost in the already crowded city, I didn't attempt any shortcuts, but made my way as quickly as possible through the throng of people. Soon the grand buildings gave way to beautiful storefronts. If anything, the Merchant District was more crowded than the Theater District, and I could barely see through the crush.

This wouldn't work, I realized, not if I couldn't find her. I needed a better view.

Before I could question the wisdom of my actions, I pushed my way to the nearest building. Hopefully the statues wouldn't pay attention to a clumsy blond woman making a fool of herself. My hands started trembling before I even touched the drainpipe, but I didn't let myself pause as I began to climb. I kept my focus on the wall in front of me, rather than on the growing space between my feet and the ground, and each exhale was accompanied by a curse word. Eventually I scrambled over the ledge, sweat sticking the wig to my scalp. As I crouched to gulp down air, a choked laugh escaped me.

I'd climbed a building! Even in my youth, when everything had seemed easier, I hadn't been able to do that.

Still smiling, I made sure my wig was in place, then stood to look into the street below. My exhilaration faded as a wave of dizziness overtook me.

"This is what you came here to do," I hissed to myself. Crouching as low as possible, I gripped the edge of the building and scanned the crowd below. Hundreds of people crisscrossed the street, but not the one I was searching for.

What if she wasn't here? I'd told her to go to the Citadel and seek refuge, but I figured she wouldn't have listened. Because what child listens to a grown up? But as the seconds passed, my heart sank.

A cloud of red hair caught my eye.

Barely daring to hope, I looked down.

And nearly cried in relief as Poppy darted across the street below.

35

———

"It's been too long," Jax muttered.

"It's barely been an hour!" I argued, even as my own anxiety made my heart race.

We stood in the crowd outside the castle, waiting for any sign of Poppy. After giving the girl detailed instructions on who to ask for and what to say, I'd handed her a note for Vena. I wasn't concerned about Poppy reading it, she seemed far too dedicated to her new task, but even if she had, nothing I'd written would be noteworthy to anyone except the castle steward.

The girl had been running through the Merchant District when I'd caught up with her, a diamond necklace in her hand and two men on her tail.

"What did I tell you about stealing?" I'd whispered, grabbing her by the hand. Turning quickly, I had surreptitiously coated the pavement behind us with ice, sending the two men sliding into a fruit stall.

She'd started at my voice, studying me for a moment before a toothy grin broke across her face.

"I did better this time, honest," she'd insisted, swinging my hand in hers as if we were merely out for a stroll. "The jeweler didn't see me nick it or anything!"

"Uh huh. Then why were they chasing you?"

She'd frowned. "The jeweler didn't see, but someone else did, and they started yelling. I didn't know the guards were standing right outside."

I'd sighed to hide my smile. "The second lesson of being a thief is when you're stealing something high value, always have a lookout."

She'd grinned again, nodding with earnestness, but I'd stopped. I knew there was no way I was going to convince her to go to the castle without telling her. Ducking into an empty doorway, I'd crouched to face her.

"Poppy, I need to tell you who I am because I need you." Turning my back to the road to hide it from view, I'd summoned a small flame to my hand. The girl's eyes had grown wide with wonder as she gazed at me, meeting my eyes.

"It's you," she whispered.

"I've been on a secret mission, and now I need your help."

The smile that had appeared on her face could outshine the sun. And that was that. She'd gone to the castle without any hesitation. Leaving us to await her return. Jax resumed pacing.

"What if she got caught? Or she told someone you're here?"

"Give her time. I imagine the castle is in chaos with all the guests and the preparations for my return. It might take her a while to find Vena, and—"

"There she is!" Ness pointed to where red hair bobbed amongst the crowd.

"Thank the stars," I cried. I'd been ready to storm in there myself, secrecy be damned.

Poppy skipped up to where we loitered, beaming with pride. She thrust a crumpled missive into my hand. "Here!"

I saw Kitt and Ness searching for any sign of someone following the girl, but I smiled back. "You were so quick!"

She nodded, dancing in place. "That castle is HUGE! There were so many flowers, and I could smell some pastries baking, but I didn't see where the smell was coming from. Can I go back and find them?"

"Let me read this first, then we'll get you all the pastries you want."

I smoothed out the note. Vena's tight script covered the page. I scanned it quickly, my heart sinking with each line.

"Well?" Mercury whispered from the bag where they hid.

"He's here, in the castle."

"That's good news," Jax nodded. "We know where he is at least."

"He arrived early this morning, saying he was here for the festival and had important news for me. Vena says he's been waiting in the throne room all day, asking not to be disturbed and insisting on being the first to know when I get back to the city."

"Again, isn't this a good thing?" Jax glanced around the group.

I scrubbed at my face with my hands, mind racing. "The throne room is in the center of the castle. It will be impossible to get to it without being spotted, and while Vena will keep our arrival a secret, the rest of the staff won't. People are anxious for me to return before morning, so the second someone sees me, word will spread. And if Alto has more monsters throughout the castle, that will make it even worse."

"He knows you're on your way," Ness mused, "even if you've slipped into the city without his minions seeing. If your suspicion is correct, that he expects you to face him alone, he'll be waiting for you to walk through the door to the throne room."

"Let's just send Ness in to torch him, then," Jax suggested.

He shrugged at the frowning Ignis. "You nearly killed him last time."

I shook my head. "He told me he'd fireproofed his robes, and there's probably more he didn't mention. He's too calculating to let himself be burned again."

Kitt rubbed his chin, and even now it was distracting. "We need to get him off balance. Do something he won't expect."

I imagined the layout of the castle as only I knew it. "There's a secret tunnel in the throne room on the left of the dais. I'm positive Alto doesn't know it's there."

"How are you so sure?" Ness frowned.

"I found it when the castle was being rebuilt. No one knows it's there but me. The entrance is near the kitchens, so we could get through most of the castle without being seen. But, shit," I grimaced, "he would certainly see us as we emerged."

"I can handle that," Mercury stated. "Just get me in the room, and I can wind blast the damned crown right off his head. It will be back in the Ethereal Plane before the sniveling traitor even knows what happened."

An uneasy feeling curled in my gut. "I still don't like it. There's too many 'ifs.' For all we know, he's got the throne room filled with monsters, ready to ambush us."

A feral grin spread on Jax's face as he rubbed his hands together. "Sounds like you need a distraction."

I hated this plan so much.

It wasn't the stupidest plan we'd ever done. That honor belonged to Mercury teleporting the four of us through the Ethereal Plane without knowing whether we'd survive. But even though that plan had carried the threat of annihilation, I hated this plan more. Because in this plan, we were going to have to split up, and in this plan, my friends were going to be in danger.

But this was our best shot at beating Alto.

Mercury, Kitt, Ness and I made our way to the secret exit that led straight to my bedchamber. I'd sent Poppy back to Vena with some final instructions and the request to keep the girl safe. With any luck, Poppy was stuffing her face with pastries while the steward finished clearing the staff out of the residential wing, giving us the best chance of creeping into my bedroom undetected.

Getting in was tricky, as the door to the secret stairwell was only meant to open from the inside, but I was able to force the wall open with my Terra magic. We all held our breath as we climbed the circular stairs, but we didn't encounter a single soul. When we emerged into my bedroom, the others sighed with relief. I'd sighed with regret.

Mere weeks before, this room had been as close to a refuge as I'd had, and even then, it wasn't totally mine. Now I saw it as the glittering cage it was. But we didn't have time to linger. I shoved stacks of dresses and pillows into my friends' arms and grabbed a vase of fresh cut flowers, and we were on our way.

The entrance to the secret passage that led to the throne room was in a utility closet near the kitchen. The exit by the dais was concealed by a wood screen carved with birds, making it invisible to anyone who didn't know it was there.

Our luck held until we neared the kitchens, where a smiling statue waited. It was off to the side of the main hallway, leaving plenty of room to maneuver around it. The creature wasn't facing us, and I'd kept my horrid wig on to better conceal myself, but I still wanted a moment to reassess. I dipped my chin in the slightest nod.

With a cry, Ness tripped over her own feet, spilling dresses around us as she splayed out across the hallway.

"Oh!" Kitt exclaimed. "Let us help you."

He and I set aside our own supplies to assist her, while Ness cursed her own clumsiness. Mercury was gone in a blink, evaporating and curling inside the vase I'd set down. Once the Ethereal was out of sight, the others looked at me, questioning. I considered all the routes to our destination, searching for any way around. Frowning, I shook my head. This hallway was the only way to access the secret tunnel to the throne room.

Kitt pulled Ness to her feet while I grabbed the now significantly heavier vase. Ignoring the effort it took to carry the damn thing, I plastered a doe-eyed smile on my face.

Ness continued murmuring apologies as we proceeded toward the statue. Its hands were extended high to the heavens like the others', but its eyes were trained on the door opposite where it stood. I realized the door was one staff used to come and go throughout the day. Alto must have placed one at every entrance and exit he knew of, keeping watch for my arrival.

I tried not to look at it, tried to keep my steps light. But this close, I could see how truly horrifying the monstrosity was. The grin was so wide it looked like a snarl, and the eyes were too lifelike, too aware. They seemed to follow us as we approached. Magic roiled under my skin in response. More than anything, I wanted to smash the creature to bits. But I couldn't risk alerting Alto to our presence. If he was connected to each statue the way he was connected to his monsters, he'd know the second I laid a hand on one. I gritted my teeth behind my smile and kept my grip on the vase loose.

I am unimportant, I repeated again and again in my head. *I am not a threat.*

Still, I didn't know if I was breathing as we breezed past the statue.

One step.

Two steps.

Five steps.

I didn't have to look to know the eyes were still following us. Around a corner.

I exhaled as softly as possible, not daring to say a word. But a look at Ness and Kitt revealed a similar hesitant relief.

We arrived at the utility closet seconds later.

I ripped off the wig before the door was even closed, scratching my liberated scalp as I assessed the room. The small space had several rickety shelves of crates and buckets, and the layer of dust on everything led me to believe it wasn't used often.

"We'll have to block the door behind us or it will cause a draft in the throne room," I said. "That's how I discovered it last time, and I don't want Alto doing the same."

It was a tight squeeze with all of us in the closet, but Ness shoved rolled-up dresses under the crack in the door while Kitt and I moved a shelf aside as quietly as possible. Mercury floated above us, trying to stay out of the way for once. There wasn't enough space to pull the shelf out completely, but we shifted it enough to reveal the wall behind. The raw wood didn't look different from the other walls, but I remembered where to look for a seam in the boards. I'd replaced the planks myself all those years ago, and now as I pried the covering away to reveal a low passage, I was grateful I'd made the effort.

The opening was covered in cobwebs, but I took that as a good sign. Ness blocked the door as much as possible with crates to prevent anyone else from entering and discovering the mess we'd made. Still, after we all crowded into the narrow tunnel, we pulled the false panel back over the passage's entrance as much as possible. Crouching to fit, I began groping my way in the dark, not daring a light. I could hear the others following, but I didn't have enough space to turn and see how they were managing. I wanted to ask, to check in. Trust them to be alright, I reminded myself.

I remembered the passage would snake around several rooms before arriving at the throne room, and led the way as much as possible, getting a face full of cobwebs every few seconds. It was nerve-racking. Without any light, there was no way to know how far we'd gone. I didn't recall any offshoots, but the fear that we were somehow going the wrong way began to fill my mind.

I forced myself to keep going, refusing to give the fear an inch of my energy. Finally, the tunnel took a sharp right turn, and a glow appeared ahead.

36

The passage stopped at a small opening disguised by the wood screen. There was enough room for all of us to cluster at it and look out at the throne room beyond, though it was a tight squeeze. Mercury was practically hanging over my shoulder, trying to get a better view.

With the afternoon sun streaming in from windows high above, the throne room was cast in a golden hue. The throne itself glowed in the light, the white marble turning a pale pink. It was exactly what the artists had envisioned when they'd created the blasted thing.

Except someone else sat upon it.

Alto had plunked his traitorous ass in *my* chair. While I wasn't fond of the throne, seeing him sitting in it so imperiously made my blood boil.

"Doesn't want to be king" my ass.

The only consolation was that, even from my current angle, I could see Alto shifting uncomfortably. He arched his back, then twisted side to side, trying to find a less painful position. Based on his deep frown, he was unsuccessful.

Good. I was suddenly glad I'd never gotten a cushion.

Mercury shifted. "Something's not right."

Their words were hushed; even with their face next to my head, I barely heard them. I scanned the room as much as I was able. The elaborate design carved into the screen offered few openings large enough to offer an unobstructed view, but from our vantage point, nothing seemed amiss. The crown was nowhere to be seen.

I kept my voice just as low. "What do you mean?"

They gazed at the room beyond, giving the slightest shake of their head. "I can't place it, but something is different. Something is wrong."

Before I could ask them to elaborate, the door to the throne room opened, and Vena breezed in. Right on schedule. Her eyes widened at the sight of Alto in the throne, her mouth forming a tight, angry line, but she kept her thoughts to herself. While I hadn't explained the extent of the disaster that was unfolding around us, I'd stressed to her the importance of keeping him happy. As much as I wanted to believe there was still good in him, I had to accept the fact that I didn't know anything about the man Alto had become. If he was willing to bring the Dark Lady into the world, he was likely willing to hurt as many people as necessary to get his revenge.

"Has there been any word from Phoebe?" Alto's voice was light, deceptive.

"Not yet, sir," Vena lied, smooth as silk. "I wanted to inform you that your room will need a few hours to be prepared. We didn't think you were coming, so some of the rooms in the family quarter were opened to our visiting guests. We're relocating them now, and once your room has been cleaned, I'll—"

"All of our rooms were given away?" Alto had stopped shifting.

"No, sir. Her Majesty requested Becca's room to remain sealed."

"Wonderful. Keep the guests where they are. I'll stay in Becca's room."

It took every ounce of self-control not to gag. Vena merely nodded. She said something about having the room aired out and cleaned.

"Just let me know when it's ready. And I need to be informed the moment Phoebe is spotted."

"Of course, sir. You'll be the first to know." Despite Vena's rigid nature, she came across as sincere. I made a mental note to pay her more.

After being assured nothing else was needed, Vena excused herself.

Using the momentary distraction of Vena's exit, I shifted as much as I was able with the weight of the Ethereal pushing down on me but didn't dare try to reposition. Kitt and Ness were pressed tight to my sides, both hardly daring to breathe. For all we knew, these were our last moments together before the world split open. Despite the cramped conditions, being surrounded by my friends bolstered me, calming my fraying patience, and I settled in to wait. Vena's arrival had been our signal that Jax would be in soon.

"No," Alto said suddenly, his voice echoing in the empty room. "Not yet."

Every muscle in my body tensed at the intensity in his voice and Ness instinctively grabbed my hand. But Alto's attention was on his hands, as he pulled the crown and gemstone from beneath his robes.

"Because she's not here yet! There's no point starting until she arrives. Make sure Becca is ready."

The four of us glanced at one another in confusion.

"Why is he talking to himself?" Kitt whispered.

"He's not," Mercury said. They curled their body tighter around mine. "He's talking to her."

None of us needed to ask who "her" was. I swallowed as a cold wash of fear returned. Back in Becca's hiding place, Alto had said Kalexia had given him a better plan. I hadn't realized she'd been speaking to him directly. No wonder his mind had become so twisted. But the crown wasn't whole yet, which meant there was still time.

Silence filled the room again. Alto's face went vacant, his attention far away. We waited, not daring to move, until the door finally banged open.

"There you are, you son of a bitch!" Jax barked, an accusatory finger already raised.

Alto jumped out of his seat, holding the crown and gemstone dangerously close together. "Jax?

"Yes 'Jax.' I've got a bone to pick with you." The swordsman slammed the door shut behind him and stormed into the room. "How *dare* you leave me behind!"

"I—what??" Even from across the room, I could see Alto's eyes darting about, as if I would emerge from every shadow. Which, I supposed, wasn't far off.

"You left me with *them*! You could have brought me along this whole time, and you didn't! That really hurts!"

"Where are the others? How did you get here so qui—"

"And to find out that *you* were the one who embarrassed me out in the fields was the cherry on top! I admit I was afraid, because I thought you really were Zaletor, but of course Phoebe jumped in and had to save me. Now I'll never get a chance to prove myself! Everyone is going to hear that story and think I can't fight my own battles. I've built my reputation on being capable and not needing *that woman* to get by in life. Do you know how hard I'll have to work to rebuild that?"

The confused shock on Alto's face was almost comical. "That's why you're upset?"

"Damn right! I'm furious! Honestly man, if you'd wanted help destroying Phoebe, you should have just asked!"

A beat of silence. My heart thudded in my chest.

But Alto focused on Jax with a new intensity. "What?"

Shedding the dramatic flair, Jax leveled a gaze at him that was somehow both wrathful and anguished. "You aren't the only one who has suffered from her actions, you know."

"I thought you were happy with your life."

"Happy? My life is in *shambles*. I didn't 'leave' the castle, she kicked me out. Said I wasn't pulling my weight. Pulling my weight! After everything I did for her! But it didn't matter once she was queen." His voice cracked, and I watched Jax smooth his jacket, struggling to regain his composure. "Do you know what they call me, out there in the world? 'The One Without Magic.' As if that's all that matters. I was famous enough that people knew me, but not famous enough for them to want me around. You know I didn't even want to be an actor? But I wasn't going to come back here, groveling for scraps. I've been living in the damned theater basement and blackmailing directors for years to keep my role, all so I wouldn't end up sleeping in the streets."

Alto remained standing beside the throne, but his face softened a fraction. "Why didn't you come to me? Talk to me?"

"Oh, the way you came and talked to me about all this?" Jax gave a vague wave of his hand, and Alto grimaced. "I heard you were happy with your shop. I didn't want you to see how far I'd fallen. I—I was ashamed."

Even from my place behind the screen, I could see Alto's eyes were shining.

"She's ruined both of us," he whispered.

"She ruins *everything*," Jax corrected, "when you took the

gemstone and left, I knew what I had to do. While they hopped on the ship to sail straight here, I said I'd ride west to retrieve Tristan. Phoebe wanted him to bring Salt Wind's forces down to press you out. I raced here instead, to help you in any way I can, *my king.*"

He bowed. Jax actually bowed.

With a terrifying smile, Alto placed the base of the crown atop his head.

My insides had gone cold. Jax was meant to distract Alto, to strike the first blow. But his words, his pain, were all so real. Too real.

Was I being betrayed again?

"So, what now?" Jax asked, arms spread wide.

"Now we wait for Phoebe to come to us. I've been watching for her through my stone Sentinels. As soon as she is spotted approaching the city, I'll resume my role as Zaletor and make the crown whole again, unlocking its full power."

"Why wait? Why not become the Dark Wizard and combine the pieces now?"

I cursed Jax to eternal damnation. *Stop giving him ideas!*

Alto considered the gemstone still in his hand. "I want Phoebe to see her people's fear. To hear their cries for mercy. To witness the realization dawn upon them that she's betrayed them all along. Then, when all their hope is lost, I'll open a portal to the Dark Lady. Once she's free, she will return Becca, and all will be set right."

Jax nodded, looking around by his feet. "Is that why there's all these swirlies on the floor?"

My breath caught as Alto nodded. "In a way. This is a safety measure, in case things go badly. The last thing I need is for Mercury to get involved."

I felt the Ethereal bristle as I held in a curse. Alto must have recreated the sigils Becca had inscribed in the tunnel to prevent

Mercury from approaching the throne. That's why they felt something was wrong. They wouldn't be able to enter the room or use their magic to get the crown away from Alto. Mercury and I looked at each other, their starry eyes panicked. But I felt only relief. Jax was still on our side. He was warning us about the sigils so we could formulate a new plan. He strode around the room, examining the markings.

"Skies, I haven't been in this room in years. Aside from your *artistic additions,* nothing has changed."

Rather than climbing back onto the throne, Alto leaned against it, arms crossed. "Of course. Why would Phoebe bother changing it when she had everything she wanted?"

"True. Whole portions of this castle were built to her specifications, you know?" Jax shook his head, but I noticed his wanderings took him in the opposite direction of our hiding place. Alto had to turn to continue the conversation.

"Of course she did. The walls were painted her favorite colors, everything was decorated to her tastes, and she got the biggest, grandest bedroom. Oh, your room is occupied, by the way. She needed more space for her precious guests visiting for the festival, so she gave away all of ours except Becca's."

Jax snorted. "Of course she did. At least she respected the sanctity of Becca's room. That's something, I suppose."

"It wasn't about respect! It was jealousy and hatred and pride! She didn't want to share Becca's memory with anyone, like always. She probably thought Becca's room wasn't good enough for other people."

Jax was almost directly opposite from our hiding place. A few more paces, and Alto would have to turn completely to see him. We would be able to sneak out and into the throne room without detection.

I couldn't see Alto's face anymore, but he gave a derisive snort. "I don't think she ever cared for Becca. Not like we did."

Jax froze. "We?"

I heard it then; the barest hint of tension in Jax's voice. It was different from the anger he presented when he first walked in, and I realized this was real.

Oh shit.

Alto didn't seem to hear the change. "We both loved her. It may have caused tension back then, but it's fitting that we are united now, in our vengeance."

Jax's face had drained of color. "Our feelings were not the same."

Alto sighed. "Yes, I know your interest was more physical, whereas Becca and I were soul bonded, but that doesn't matter now. We can both—"

"Stop."

I could see Jax shaking. I wanted to call out to him, to tell him to stay calm and it was all an act. But I couldn't, not without ruining our advantage.

Noticing the shift for the first time, Alto stood straight. "Excuse me?"

"Get ready," Mercury said.

Whether this had been his plan all along or not, Jax now had Alto's undivided attention. I tensed as the Ethereal shifted off my shoulders. Beside me, Kitt and Ness crouched forward while I threaded my fingers through the screen.

"Don't compare us!" Jax snapped. "You make it sound like my feelings were trivial. Yes, I fall in love easily. I admit it. But that doesn't mean my feelings were purely carnal or untrue."

As gently as possible, I pushed the screen forward. It didn't budge.

"I meant no offense," Alto countered, "but even if she had returned your feelings, I don't believe your love would have lasted. Eventually, you would have grown bored and moved on, leaving Becca heartbroken. Then I would have had to pick up the pieces." His voice was calm, as though he'd considered this many times before.

Praying to The Goddesses for the first time in decades, I pushed harder.

"Which I'm sure was exactly what you wanted. For her to come crying to you, vulnerable and alone. But it never would have happened, you know. She never would have turned to you. She despised you."

Alto began descending the dais toward Jax. "Jealousy doesn't suit you, *brother*. You never cared for her like I did."

Ness and Kitt gripped the screen as well, adding their weight to mine.

Jax didn't cower. Instead, he glared at Alto, letting venom drip from his words. "I stopped being your brother a long time ago. But you're right, our feelings weren't the same. I loved her enough to be her friend."

Alto gave a snort. "We'll see how cocky you are when you're in a tomb."

I was going to have to burn out the screen. Surprise be damned, I couldn't let Jax get hurt. But before I could blink, Alto raised his hand. Everyone paused, tense, waiting to see what wrath he would rain down.

Nothing happened. When he looked around in confusion, Jax laughed.

"You probably shouldn't have warded the entire floor, dumbass. It's like Mercury said, as powerful as you are, even you can't wield this stone."

I saw what was coming, even if Jax didn't. *No no no no.*

Alto sneered, the base of the crown glittering on his brow. "I don't need to."

<h1 style="text-align:center">37</h1>

They moved at the same time: Alto thrust his empty hand into the air as Jax drew his sword. But Jax was faster. With the fluidity of a dancer, he darted forward, slashing high then low in one smooth motion. Alto cried out in pain, the scream echoing around the room.

"You always did underestimate me," Jax grinned, holding up his sword. A thin line of blood gleamed on the blade. "You should have learned how to fight instead of how to scheme."

Alto staggered back. His robes appeared to have protected his torso from Jax's blade, but he clutched his right hand to his chest.

"You SHIT!"

Jax smirked again. But even though he'd been slower, Alto's intent was already manifesting. I watched in horror as my throne rippled, then melted, transforming into three glittering stone statues. "Sentinels" Alto had called them, except these didn't look like me. They looked like him, right down to the crown on his head.

"Kill him!" Alto commanded, pointing his good hand at Jax.

Leaning back as much as possible, I braced my legs on the screen and kicked. It popped out, clattering to the floor with a crash. Kitt, Ness and I didn't hesitate, all of us leaping out into the throne room.

Alto whipped toward the source of the noise, and our eyes locked. His face crumpled in rage as I beheld his damaged hand.

His *empty* hand.

Blood flowed in a steady stream from the stumps of his second and third fingers. The gemstone must have fallen when Jax attacked.

"Help Jax!" I told the others.

Sure enough, the three Sentinels had advanced on the swordsman. While he might have been skilled, he couldn't kill stone.

Trusting them to handle it, I climbed onto the dais to face Alto.

"Surrender. I won't ask again."

I knew the request was folly. It would only give him time to attack or flee. But I had to give him one final chance to make the right decision. I wouldn't be able to live with myself if I didn't.

"Are you going to kill me, Phoebe? Are you going to suck the soul from my body the way you did Zaletor?" Alto smiled, but his eyes darted about. To use my Specter Gift, I'd have to touch him. He examined wall after wall, looking for more stone to use against me.

The sounds of battle echoed as my friends fought the stone Sentinels, but I didn't blink. "I could. But your soul is so rotted, I'd hate to have to touch it. So, I thought of a better plan."

He braced for an attack, but I didn't raise my hands. I didn't need to.

"Surprise, asshole," Ness whispered.

Alto didn't have time to turn before the Ignis unleashed hell upon him. I threw myself out of the way to avoid the blast of flame that engulfed the dais. My shoulder screamed in pain, but I ignored it as I rolled to my feet.

The Sentinels all froze mid step, solidifying into inanimate statues. Alto's focus must have shattered, which made sense, considering he was on fucking fire. Panting and bloody, Kitt and Jax retreated from the figures as much as possible.

"Damnit!" Ness hissed. Her barrage ceased, filling the room with an eerie silence.

Alto was gone.

"He must have teleported out again." I rolled my aching shoulder to ensure it was still in the socket. "We need to find the gemstone before he returns. It's somewhere on the floor."

"Be careful!" Mercury shouted. They paced in the narrow opening of the passage, wings flared in agitation. "He could reappear anywhere!"

"Whoever finds it, take it straight to Mercury," I added. "Everyone else, provide cover."

I knew Alto couldn't have gone far. No matter how injured he was, he wouldn't let his plans crumble.

We scrambled around the room. It should have been easy to find the dark, glittering stone against the pale tiles, but the room was massive. And the dark swirls of paint were distracting. There was no telling how far the gemstone had slid when it was cut free of Alto's hand. All the while, Mercury offered suggestions.

"Check under those curtains! Don't lose track of it if you kick it! Oh, I see something red by the statues! Just blood? Gross."

I knew they were trying to help the only way they could. But as the seconds ticked by, panic built in my chest.

It had to be here somewhere, I reminded myself.

A glint of red caught my eye.

There, wedged into the step of the dais, was the gemstone.

I didn't say a word. I couldn't. A lump had appeared in my throat, formed by panic and relief and hope. Keeping my movements natural, I crouched, miming the act of getting a better view of the floor, and grabbed it.

The stone was cool in my fingers, just as it had been the last time. But I didn't look at it, or acknowledge it in any way.

I needed to get it to Mercury.

I knew I was trembling, but I forced myself to walk. Forced my head from side to side as though I was still searching. Step by step, I moved toward the hidden tunnel. I didn't look at them, but I noticed Mercury had stopped shouting instructions. Glancing up, I saw their eyes locked on me. Waiting.

So close. Only a few more steps, then this would all be over. Alto still had the crown, but he could never make it whole.

"That's far enough I think."

Though I couldn't see him, Alto's words echoed through the room. In an instant, the Sentinels came to life, grabbing Ness, Kitt and Jax, who'd all been looking around their feet. My friends were grappled around their waists or necks, and no amount of fire or steel could free them. Mercury let out a snarl, and I spun to find Alto had reappeared directly between me and the Ethereal. A cloud of black smoke still lingered in the air around him, and I could see his face was oozing from a myriad of burns, but his eyes gleamed clear.

"Throw me the gemstone, Phoebe."

I heard a cry and a strangled choke behind me, but I didn't take my eyes off Alto. Thanks to the crown, which rested undamaged on his head despite Ness's blast, his burns were already healing. Most had scabbed over, the holes in his flesh filling before my eyes. But the scent of charred skin and hair still stuffed itself up my nose.

"My Sentinels are going to squeeze until I tell them to stop. And if you come any closer to me or try to harm me in any way, your friends will be dead before my body can hit the ground. Your only choice is to give me what I want."

"Don't do it!" Kitt choked. "Get it to Mercury."

Alto didn't bother silencing him. He smiled at me, his lipless grin revealing too many teeth. And I knew in that moment that even if I did exactly as Alto asked, he'd kill my friends for spite. In his mind, I'd taken Becca from him. He'd never let me have happiness again.

I knew my course of action. Alto wouldn't let me touch him, so if I pressed forward, he would retreat. I could get the gemstone to Mercury. As much as it pained me, I, of all people, should know that sometimes a sacrifice is required to defeat evil. My friends might die, but the world would be safe. Wasn't that an acceptable trade?

I can't lose anyone else.

Sensing my indecision, Alto held out a hand. "None of your Gifts can save you now."

Ness cried out as she was squeezed tighter.

My mind raced. When Alto had been consumed by Ness's fire, he'd lost concentration on his Sentinels, and they'd stopped attacking. If he were forced to relinquish control of the statues, maybe I could free my friends. I needed another distraction, something big, to catch his focus. Something that would scare him enough to freeze him in place. What was Alto afraid of?

The stone in my hand seemed to pulse in response. I felt an unfamiliar tug in my stomach.

Most Spectors could only see spirits. To pull the soul from another person, a truly powerful Specter needed to place a hand on their victim. It's how I'd killed Zaletor, releasing the dozens of souls trapped inside his body. This felt...different.

Like my own soul was trying to escape. It was a totally foreign sensation, something Becca had never mentioned in her Anima training, but it felt somehow right.

"Quickly now!" Alto shouted, his eyes burning with madness. "We don't want to keep our guests waiting!"

I gripped the gemstone tight, connecting with the malice and greed that saturated it. I felt the tug in my belly, stronger this time, and finally understood.

"You want to resurrect the boogeyman so badly?" I asked, as tendrils of golden mist began curling from my mouth. "Allow me to oblige."

38

"What are you—" Alto started, but he stopped as golden mist began pouring from my mouth.

Anima was always beautiful to see, which I thought strange as it was widely considered a power of death. When I closed my mouth, I watched the golden cloud float before me. It condensed into a column, then into a figure. It was frightening—I'd never heard of Anima performing in this way before—but didn't try to stop it or control it.

I knew whose figure would appear and steeled myself to face it.

It only took a second for the mist to congeal and take shape. The figure that finally solidified between us was twisted and thin. Even though the form glittered with golden light, it was not beautiful.

Alto paled. His exuberance was gone as he watched the horror before him stretch its limbs. "Zaletor."

The figure snapped its head toward him, and Alto stumbled several steps back.

"What is this?" Zaletor hissed, with a voice like a tomb lid cracking. His head wobbled on a too-frail neck, gazing around the room.

To my surprise, I felt no fear. I'd been preparing myself for weeks to face my old enemy, with the dread of anticipation always present in my gut. But now that he stood before me, now that I saw what his soul had been reduced to, I felt only revulsion.

"You never saw what he looked like without all those souls trapped inside him, keeping him alive and strong." I waved, gesturing to the wretched figure. "This is what Kalexia does to her servants."

"It's a trick," Alto insisted, "some Specter ploy." He touched the crown on his head like a talisman.

Zaletor's golden gaze found mine, and he growled. "You."

"Me. Again. I'm glad to see the afterlife is treating you poorly. I thought you'd like to see the man who claims to be your successor."

Again, he turned to Alto, and again Alto flinched.

I listened and found the Sentinels behind me had gone silent. There was the occasional grunt of frustration or the scratch nails on stone, so hopefully my friends were still alive. But I didn't turn, didn't risk drawing Alto's attention back to me.

"My crown," Zaletor rasped. His gravelly voice was dripping with desire as he reached a thin, golden arm toward Alto.

I'd never wielded Anima and another element at the same time. This wasn't an ideal time to experiment, but there was no other option. I allowed my free hand to drift behind my back, and I visualized the statues as I'd last seen them. Alto was speaking again, giving some sort of excuse or command, but I ignored him. He had dropped his control of the Sentinels, and I struggled to reclaim them with my Terra magic. It would have been easier if I could see them, but that would give away my intent. Instead, I focused on how they felt. They were rigid and monstrous, created by vengeance and greed. I gritted my teeth, struggling to move the stone arms that held my friends.

It was no good. Alto's magic lingered in the statues that all bore his face.

"You know nothing of true power!" Zaletor shouted, drawing my attention back.

Alto sneered. I could see his shock at Zaletor's sudden return was quickly giving way to his desire to dominate. I was out of time. Zaletor might be corporeal, but he couldn't use his old Gifts. Soon, Alto would blast him away and resume his plan to free Kalexia with the hope of returning Becca and putting her on the throne.

My pulse quickened. The throne.

My throne.

Alto may have transformed it to make his Sentinels, but the stone was the same. I'd spent hours sitting upon it, my back aching and legs numb. I'd run my hands over the velvet smooth armrests. It was where I'd made decisions that had changed the kingdom. It was where I'd been sitting when I'd made the decree that no child would go hungry. It was where I'd announced Becca's death. So many good and terrible memories were tied to that throne. And it was mine.

I reached for the stone again, and Alto's control gave way like paper. I didn't need to look to know they were mine. With a thought, I set my friends free, and stood all three statues to attention.

Refocusing in front of me, I realized Alto hadn't even noticed my friends gasping and choking for breath. Zaletor had advanced on him, and they were grappling for the base of the crown. The golden mist of Anima was starting to fade at the Sorcerer's edges, but that didn't matter. He'd served his purpose.

"Enough," I commanded. Both figures froze. "It's over."

Alto seethed, but the expression vanished when he realized what I'd done. His eyebrows raised, though rage still burned in his eyes as he opened his mouth to speak. But he never got the chance, as Zaletor's hand wrapped around Alto's throat.

"You don't deserve her gifts," the dead Sorcerer hissed. Then Alto was flying across the room. He landed in a heap near where Ness had finally been able to stand. She didn't give him a moment to rise, jumping onto his prone form. Kitt scrambled over to add his strength to hers, and together they struggled to keep Alto flat to the ground. I smiled, but when Zaletor crowed in triumph, my heart went cold. Turning, I saw he held the base of the crown in his hands.

"My Lady," he sobbed, "I have returned to you."

Shit! I tried to pull the Anima back into my body, but to my horror, Zaletor's form was solidifying before my eyes. The crown was healing him, I realized. I tried to rush him, to tackle him to the ground, but I stumbled. The world seemed to lurch as I fell sideways. For a moment, I thought Zaletor had regained his Terra Gifts, but when I hit the floor, I realized how weakened I'd become. Fear flooded through me as I understood: the power of the crown was allowing Zaletor to steal my Anima. If he wasn't stopped soon then I would die, and he would become unstoppable.

"Stop," I mumbled, but already I was too weak to cry out. My friends were too busy restraining Alto to realize the danger we were all in. Except Mercury, who was screaming.

With the crown atop his head, Zaletor strolled over to me. I gripped the gemstone as tightly as I could, but my strength was failing. My vision swam, but I blinked to find Zaletor standing above me, a hungry grin on his face. He leisurely bent down and pulled the gemstone from my loose fingers. I let out the softest of sobs as he joined the two pieces together.

The room trembled, and this time I knew it had nothing to do with me.

"Your soul will keep me alive forever," he boasted as an invisible wind whirled around him. "And I will destroy—"

A hiss cut through the air, and Zaletor's eyes went wide.

"You'll go back to hell where you belong," Jax grunted, as he twisted his sword.

Zaletor shuddered, his mouth open in a soundless cry, before he burst apart in a snow of golden dust.

39

—————

For the second time in my life, I heard the glorious sound of a crown hitting the floor.

But this time, I couldn't stop and appreciate the beauty of it. The golden Anima was seeping back into my body, but behind me I heard a struggle. Jax cursed and ran to where I suspected Alto was working free. My strength was recovering as the last of the soul magic quickly returned to me, but I felt disjointed, like my body didn't fit correctly in my skin. Still, as the shouts behind me grew louder, I forced myself to rise. The now intact crown lay at my feet, and while the thought of touching it made my jaw clench, I snatched it off the floor before Alto could recover and claim it.

"No!" Mercury shouted.

Immediately, a purring female voice filled my head.

I know of you. Thank you for saving me from the whelp. I explained the errors of his plan, but he refused to listen."

Surprised, I gripped the crown tighter, my eyes darting

around the throne room, but I didn't see the speaker. A strange pressure filled the space around me.

"What is this?" I demanded as the pressure grew. The air tingled with electricity and the smell of ozone filled my nostrils.

"Phoebe! Bring it to me!" I could hear the edge of terror in Mercury's voice.

> "He was never deserving of my gifts – his mind is poisoned by imagined slights and malice. This power can be yours, if you want it."

My stomach dropped. Kalexia was speaking to me through the crown. I shook my head, hoping to dislodge her melodious voice.

"I already have power, thanks."

"What's going on?" Ness grunted, just before Alto elbowed her in the gut.

> "Do you? The worm told me all about you. You were stuck here, in this castle, trying your best to keep everyone else happy. I know what it's like to feel trapped, hopeless."

An immortal trapped in an eternal prison. I hated that I believed her.

> "My sisters wronged you as well – another thing we have in common. They think they can meddle in the lives of others, use them and discard them, without any repercussions."

"Why is her face doing that?" Jax was staring at me even as he scrambled to hold Alto's legs, and I was taken aback by the terror I saw in his eyes.

Of course, I realized. No one else could hear her.

"We can help each other. You may have magic, but I can give you true power. No one will ever challenge or manipulate you again."

Visions of Mayfield and Renis floated through my mind. I couldn't tell if she caused them, or if they were purely from my imagination, but a pang of anger went through my stomach.

"You would have their respect. But you'd also have their love. Anyone you wanted would be honored to be at your side, loving you unconditionally. And no one would say anything against it."

More flashes. Kitt. Tristan. Kalexia must have been doing this, because I didn't want Tristan anymore. Did I? Not his love, surely, but his recognition? His empathy for all I'd endured when he'd left?

"You are worthy. You are strong. You are *queen*. Remind them of that."

Would it be better, being queen, if I actually ruled? Not the democratic, everyone has an opinion, we're all in this together nonsense I'd created. If I *ruled*? I could eliminate corruption instantly. Every child would have food and shelter. Because I commanded it.

"You were created with the gifts of four Goddesses. If I add my power, you will be invincible. All you have to do is embrace it and open the portal, and you will never fail again."

The voice was almost a whisper now, and gentle as a caress.

I could picture it as clearly as if it was happening before me. I'd absorb the power of the crown, becoming practically a Goddess myself. All my friends would bow, enraptured by my presence. With a wave of my hand, I'd open a portal to the Ethereal Plane and cross through. I'd be the first human to enter, impervious to any damage or undoing, thanks to Kalexia's sliver of essence. And by pressing that sliver against her prison, her bonds would shatter in an eruption of darkness and chaos. Once freed, the two of us would work together to destroy her sisters for all the damage they'd wrought upon the world. Then, Kalexia could claim the Ethereal Plane for herself, while I'd return here to rule over the human world. Unchallenged and immortal.

Two queens. Equals. Forever.

"Shall we begin?"

The illusion faded, and I stared at the crown in my hands. The pressure around me was nearly unbearable, trying to force its way into my skin. A drop of blood dripped from my nose, staining the pale floor.

I nodded.

"I am ready to begin. And this time, things will be different."

Kalexia laughed, the sound reverberating through my brain.

Until I pried the gemstone from the crown.

My body was heavy as I staggered across the throne room to Mercury. With the crown broken, the pressure had eased but not vanished. Kalexia's presence was still here. But not for long.

I heard the struggle continue behind me but ignored it. It took all my determination to simply put one foot in front of the other. I kept my eyes locked on Mercury, who watched me anxiously, shifting on their feet with impatience.

Someone was shouting now, crying with rage and pain. Only a few more steps.

Finally, I reached the hidden panel. I placed the crown around Mercury's neck, while they took the gemstone in their paw. Once the cursed items were out of my hands, I crumpled to the floor in exhaustion. Mercury's eyes widened.

"Are you—

"Go!" I grumbled. I didn't want the Dark Lady's presence in this world a moment longer.

My Ethereal gave me one final look, filled with concern and pride and love. For the briefest of moments, they pressed their forehead to mine. I closed my eyes, ignoring the tears that sprang up at the gesture. Then, they vanished in a curl of mist.

Behind me there was another cry, this one a shout of warning followed by quickly approaching steps and a snarl. I looked up and found Alto barreling toward me, his arms raised in violence and hatred burning in his eyes, and I didn't hesitate.

He'd made his choice.

I opened my hand and shot ice across the floor. But this wasn't my normal ice, which would have merely coated the floor and caused a slipping hazard. Despite my exhaustion, I opened the part of myself that was full of grief and anger and poured it into my hands. When the ice reached Alto, it snaked up his body. His scream of anger twisted into one of panic and pain as his feet froze to the floor.

"Agh! What are you doing?!" His brow creased in confusion, he looked from his feet to me, then back. Trapped in place, he pulled at his legs, but the ice spread up to his ankles.

"What is this?? What's happening?!"

I knew why he was confused. The ice was so cold, he wouldn't be able to feel anything. He had no idea how dire the situation was. Because this ice wasn't merely on the outside of his body.

It was on the inside.

In a matter of seconds, his legs had frozen solid.

"Stop!" he cried.

But I didn't stop as the ice consumed his hips.

His stomach.

"Have mercy!"

His ribcage.

Alto let out a final cry before I froze his lungs.

And his heart.

He reached his hands out toward me, the fingers hooked like claws.

I think he was dead before the ice spread up his neck, but I didn't stop.

His face contorted into a mask of pain as the ice glazed his eyes.

Only when his entire body was frozen solid did I stop.

"This is not a day for mercy."

The room was painfully quiet as my friends huddled around me, all three of them holding me tight. No one spoke. There were no words that were appropriate. I don't know how long we stayed like that before Vena peered in through the door. To her credit, the Steward didn't scream at the sight of Alto's frozen body. Though she did vomit quietly in the corner.

Rallying the last of my strength, I gave everyone a final squeeze before stepping forward. I rested a supportive hand on Vena's back as she spat the last of the bile from her mouth. Finally, she nodded, her face proper and impassive once more. I wanted nothing more than to sleep for a week, but there was too much to do.

"I need you to gather the Council," I said. "There is much to discuss."

~

The only available room in the entire castle aside from my own was Becca's. Ness offered to sleep on a couch somewhere or find a room in town. But I marched her to the spacious room, which had been freshly cleaned due to Alto's demands.

"I guarantee there are no rooms in town, and you will not sleep on the floor when there's a perfectly good bed available here," I instructed, walking about the room. I hadn't been in Becca's bedroom in years, and it was exactly as it had been the last time I'd seen it. The bed, dresser, lounge chair and book-shelf were pristine, but seeing them no longer brought me sorrow.

We'd spent hours with the Council going over the truth of my travels, and it was well past midnight. Kitt had nearly fallen asleep in his empty plate by the time I'd ended the meeting, and Ness was currently swaying on her feet. But she looked around the room nervously.

"I just—I don't want to take up her space."

I paused from where I stood by the dresser and smiled, recalling Becca's hidden cave. "It's alright. This is just a room. Your staying here does not erase her."

"Does that mean there's room in there for me as well?" Jax asked as he sauntered through the door. His right arm was in a sling, and there were fresh bandages on his forehead. He saw Ness and I frown and held up his good hand. "I wasn't flirting, I promise. But there's some Duchess sleeping in my room, and I don't know where else to go."

Before I could answer, Ness sighed. "You can sleep on the chair. But if you try anything, I will literally destroy you."

Jax gave a salute. "Understood."

I paused by the door. Something had been weighing on my

mind since the throne room, and I needed it sorted before I could do anything else.

"Jax, the things you said to Alto, about being unhappy with how your life is going—" I didn't know how to end my question, and found myself trailing off.

With a kind smile, Jax took my hand.

"Dearest, as far as I'm concerned, I've got the best life of all of you. That theater is my kingdom, and I relish the opportunity to rule with an iron fist. But I'm flattered you found my performance so convincing."

I burst out laughing, even as Ness chucked a pillow at him. They began arguing over blankets, and I hastily bid them goodnight, leaving them to sort it out. My leaden feet wanted to go straight to my bed, where I knew Kitt was waiting, but I couldn't yet. With only a few hours until the start of the parade, I had one last thing to do before I could attempt sleep.

It took a while to find an empty room. At least there was little chance of being disturbed this late at night. Settling in on the floor, I steadied my breathing and pushed aside the events of the day. Pumpkin sat in my lap, the silver locket glinting in the candlelight.

When the moment felt right, I let out an audible exhale, watching as a cloud of golden mist poured out. Like in the throne room, I didn't try to control it, trusting the magic to know what to do. The features solidified, growing clearer, and though the misty form remained a pearlescent gold, I knew exactly who it was.

"Wow, Phebs," Becca smirked, hand on her hip. "You look like shit."

40

When Mercury had appeared in my room weeks before, I'd been amazed and overjoyed, at least, until they'd spoken, because I'd assumed I would never see them again. But I'd always been comforted by the knowledge they were out there somewhere, soaring around the Ethereal Plane, causing trouble until the end of time.

This was different. Now, with Becca giving me a sly grin and hearing her voice, both of which I'd assumed were lost to the sea, my face crumpled. I'd been prepared for her to look as she had in death: with bloated flesh and vacant eyes. Instead, she was beautiful and strong, as she'd been the last day I saw her.

Even through my grief, even though I hadn't seen her in years and thought I wouldn't see her again until death claimed me as well, my instinct to sass back when Becca spoke overcame everything else.

"Are you going to tell me I've gained weight, too?" I choked through the tears. "Because that's what happened the last time someone from my past appeared out of nowhere."

Becca's smile softened. "I think it suits you. To be honest, aside from the matted hair and layer of what I'm hoping is dirt, you look healthier than ever. And I bet your boobs look amazing!"

I couldn't help but laugh as she took in the world around her. Her eyes swept the room, taking in each detail, before finally settling on Pumpkin.

"You went looking for the gemstone? Things must have gone very, very wrong."

I nodded. "That's an understatement. But how are you here?"

She smiled at the stuffed rabbit clutched in my grip. "Magic."

"But you've been...gone...for thirteen years."

"That long?"

"Too long. My Specter gifts shouldn't be able to reach you anymore."

She rolled her golden eyes. "Gee, it's almost like you're super powerful and when you let the magic guide you rather than fight it, it shows you things no one has ever thought to do before. Weird."

Wiping away the tears, I chuckled again. "Hells, Becks, I miss what an asshole you are." My smile wavered. "I'm... I'm so..."

I couldn't even say it. I'd been responsible for her death. Any apology I could offer was pitifully insufficient.

With silent steps, Becca crossed to plop down across from me. "What happened, Phebs?"

I shook my head, unsure of where to even begin. "You died. Then everything went to shit."

She waited patiently, and forced myself to breathe.

"Alto. He betrayed us all." The tears started again as I told her everything that had happened. How the group of us had all fallen out, how I'd hid in the castle like a helpless princess, how

Mercury had reappeared and set a new adventure in motion, how the world was going to end, all of it. She listened impassively, but got to the events in the throne room, her face fell.

"You don't seem surprised," I noticed.

"I never would have guessed he'd take things this far," she clarified, then sighed. "But no, I'm not surprised."

"Why not?! Because I was fucking shocked!"

Becca's brows creased as sorrow filled her eyes. "Think back, Phoebe. Even when we were young, Alto never took "no" for an answer. He saw rejection as an obstacle, a challenge for him to puzzle out. It made him an excellent battle strategist, but a kind of shitty friend and a terrible romantic prospect."

I considered her words and saw she was right. Whenever anyone said something couldn't be done, Alto was the first to disagree, insisting we merely needed the right plan to make it work. I'd never realized he'd used this trait in all aspects of life, but now that she said it, more memories came flooding back.

Alto, staring at a map for hours to figure out the correct angle of attack, and, once decided, explaining there was no other option.

Alto, arguing that we shouldn't hide the crown, insisting we might need it someday, then sulking when Becca and I did it anyway.

Alto, glaring at me, and only me, in the carriage the night after Becca and I had slipped out of the party in Linipa.

Alto, always two steps behind Becca wherever she went.

"He was harassing you," I realized.

She considered, discomfort clear on her face. "He never outright propositioned me after the first time I rejected him. But he was always hovering behind me, trying to make himself useful or finding ways for us to be alone together. Sometimes he'd talk about how smart our child would be and other weird shit like that. I knew he was waiting for me to change my mind.

I chose to avoid him rather than deal with it. Hells, if anyone is to blame for me volunteering for missions away from the capitol, it's him."

I couldn't imagine how that must have felt. "I'm sorry," I said again. "I should have stepped in, or sent him away, or—"

"Stop Phoebe!" Becca snapped. The fierceness in her ghostly eyes startled me. "Stop taking responsibility for every single thing that went wrong!"

"But I *am* responsible! I was supposed to keep all of you safe. It was my job to protect you, and I let you down." I shook my head. "In so many ways, I let you down."

"No! I'm not excusing anything Alto did back then, but I also made the choice to avoid it rather than come to you. I excused it as annoying and awkward, and decided it wasn't worth making a deal out of it. I was wrong, and I know now I should have told him to shove it rather than always feeling uncomfortable, but at no point were you at fault!"

My head was pounding and I clutched her toy rabbit as though my life depended on it. "I am, though. I'm the reason you died."

"You had nothing to do with what happened to me." Becca's voice was angrier than I'd ever heard it, but it didn't absolve the ache in my heart.

"I sent you away."

"Yeah, to do my job. No one was responsible for the storm; it was just a thing that happened."

"But if I hadn't –"

"If you hadn't what, Phoebe? If you hadn't sent me to deal with the pirates? Guess what, I would have gone anyway! I know you're the queen and all, but keeping people safe wasn't your job alone. I would have disobeyed you if I'd had to!" She looked at the ceiling, taking a deep breath. When she spoke again, her fury had melted. She smiled, the soft, contented smile that so few people had ever seen. "You always were the strongest of us, and the problem is, you *knew* that. We were a team, but you felt you had to protect us from the worst of it. Hells, Phebs, you were willing to die for all of us when we were only kids."

"Because I needed to die! I'm the fucking Chosen One after all! And once you're the Chosen One, you're always the Chosen One. What other purpose do I have?!"

The thought settled in my stomach like a stone.

Great skies, what other purpose did I have? Yes, I was queen, but considering how many mistakes I'd made over the years, how easily I'd been fooled, it was clear I didn't deserve that title. I was never qualified to rule, people simply named me because they were desperate. Considering the nightmare of Zaletor's reign, anything I did would have been seen as a vast improvement. But that didn't make me a good ruler.

A cool sensation spread down my left side as Becca sat beside me. Though it had been ages since we'd sat this close, I instinctively leaned my head onto her shoulder. I shuddered at the pleasant chill as she rested her head atop mine.

"You told me once what the afterlife was like. How calm it was before The Goddesses brought you back. That knowledge comforted me in those final moments. And I wasn't alone. We're sisters, Phebs, as true as any born by blood. And you were with me then, just as I'm always with you. You are never alone."

Tears rolled down my face as I squeezed her hand. Though it was cool to the touch, it was solid and strong. We sat together, and I felt the broken pieces inside my heart shifting. The sharp edges became less painful, less heavy, as they fused together. Finally, I smiled, feeling more complete than I had in years. My heart wasn't the same as before, there were still lines where the cracks had been, but it was whole again. New.

"So, do you live inside me now?" I asked, thinking of absorbing the mist back into my body. "It's going to make sex super awkward."

Becca cackled. "Unfortunately, no. The energy is yours. I'm just visiting."

"Does that mean I can call you back whenever I want?"

Her smile turned sad as her gaze drifted to the locket still looped around Pumpkin's neck. "I love you, Phebs, but we're on different paths now. Enjoy your life. Get laid. Besides," she winked, "once you've experienced eternal rest, the living world feels kind of shitty."

Her meaning was clear: while I might be capable of summoning her spirit again, she didn't want me to. I nodded, my heart heavy, until a thought struck.

"Oh shit! Speaking of which, you know Kitt! He's the guy who tried to rob you on the road when you first hid the stone! You're the reason he was able to get help for his sister and make a life for himself."

Becca beamed. "Well, I happily take full credit for your relationship then."

My strength was fading. Unlike with Zaletor, Becca wasn't trying to steal my Anima, so wisps of soul energy drifted back to me with every inhale. I knew I would have to let the magic go, let Becca go, but I held on for one more minute.

"I love you, Becks. Thank you."

Her form was blurring at the edges, but her smile was clear.

"I love you too." Becca kissed my forehead, the cool sensation filling me with warmth. "And remember: your friends don't need you to die anymore, Phebs. We need you to live."

EPILOGUE

Three Months Later

Sitting tucked back against the wall of the upper balcony, I basked in the evening sun as the sounds of the city below filled the air. A few months ago, I never would have set foot on the balcony, which jutted out from the castle, seeming to float above the city. But while I still couldn't go near the railing that ran along the structure's edge, I'd recently found this to be the best place to watch the sunset over Glassleaf.

Somehow, the city was still cleaning up from the Commemoration Festival. It had been a drawn-out, wild affair, especially once everyone learned it would be the last one of its kind. My decree had come as a shock to everyone, but I'd explained in my speech after the parade that the future of the kingdom required everyone to look forward instead of back. Plans were already being made for how to make next year's "Bearnel Festival" an appropriate replacement, but I'd made it clear that I was no longer the focus, and I was done with the dozens of events that had become expected of me. If every-thing went as planned, I might not even be in the city. Jax had hoped to open his new production around that time, and I'd promised I'd be at the premiere, in the front row. He'd given me his word that the new play would be a heavily edited version of events. I'd warned him that it had better be, or I would find out who decided to make him The Russell Theater's new Assistant Director and make them rescind the position.

Truthfully, I was happy for my brother. He'd graciously stepped down from his role in *The Great Victory*, which was still traveling the country to sold-out venues, allowing his talented understudy to take the reins while he focused on his new duties. And, of course, worked on his masterpiece.

"I'll call it *The Secret Victory: Zaletor's Return*," he'd said, waving his hand through the air like he was framing a banner.

Ness had chuckled. "I can't explain why, but something about that sounds…salacious?"

"Oh, it will be," Jax had nodded, "it's all part of the editorial liberties I'm taking."

I'd glared at him, the threat of violence in my eyes. "Under no circumstances will you have my character be naked on stage." Ness adamantly agreed.

But Jax had waved us off. "Oh please, as if anyone would be interested in a romance story about either of you. It will be about *me*, and the love I found on our quest with the tragically handsome blacksmith, Cameron." He scratched his chin. "I'll have to find someone who can match my energy on stage."

I'd winced. "Oh, please tell me you're not—"

"Starring as myself!" Jax had finished, grinning like a madman.

Readjusting my position on the stone floor, I smiled at the memory. It was strange, to be reconnected to everyone again, but in a way that made me feel whole. For the first time in ages, I knew where all my friends were, and how they were doing.

Tristan and Tennian had arrived a few days after the parade with a contingent from Salt Wind. Tristan had assured me the city was in good hands while they were away, and I noticed he didn't complain about his mayoral duties nearly as much as he'd promised. When he'd walked away to chat with Jax, Tennian had confided that he'd actually been enjoying the work. Setting the city to rights had given her husband a new purpose, and the improvements to the lives of the citizens had been instantaneous.

"He's hesitant to tell you how much he's enjoying it," Tennian had smiled, "because he knows you'll gloat."

I'd cackled with joy as I'd hugged her. "Oh, I'll *definitely* gloat!"

Thankfully, ours hadn't been the only reunion, as Boss had been among the visitors from the port city. Kitt had inspected every inch of the horse who, despite traveling for several days, appeared well rested.

"No more monsters," I'd promised the stallion as I'd rubbed a hand along his head. He'd responded with a snort of appreciation and took the apple I'd slipped from my pocket.

Kitt was probably with the horse now, I reasoned as the sky bloomed pink, preparing for our journey. I should be doing the same, but instead I closed my eyes, soaking up the final rays of sunlight on my face. It was so peaceful, until a throat cleared behind me.

"You'll have to figure it out, Vena," I called, not bothering to open my eyes. "You'll need to run this place in my absence, so I figure you should start handling the decisions now."

Despite her rigid, commanding nature, the Castle Steward was having trouble adjusting to her new role as Head of the expanded Advisory Council. I had no doubt she'd adapt quickly, but with new Council members arriving every day from the various cities, she was overwhelmed with the sudden power.

Rather than Vena's crisp requests, a different voice replied.

"There's the laziness I've been wanting to see."

Whipping around, I found Mercury grinning at me.

I squealed in delight. "I thought you'd gone for good... again."

They sauntered over to where I sat. "I informed The Goddesses there were a few things to wrap up here. You're looking comfy," they said, eyeing my trousers.

"There was a new decree a few weeks back," I beamed, crossing my ankles. "No dresses for the queen, except when she wants to."

"Glad to hear it. You're still the queen then?" I sensed the hesitation in their voice and couldn't fault them for it.

"For now. I'm considering a transition in the future. But I'm not the same queen I was before."

As quickly as possible, I explained that I was leaving at first light to begin visiting cities and interviewing the mayors. After Mayfield's treachery, Vena and Captain Inniual had conducted an investigation and discovered three additional council members had been in league with my former Secretary. They'd spent years concealing corruption in various cities, all while taking a hefty profit. While I doubted anywhere could be as bad as Salt Wind, I needed to know for myself. Word of Renis's imprisonment had spread, which was good because now all of the mayors knew what was at stake.

When I finished, they let out a whistle. "That sounds like a long trip."

"I certainly hope so. And that doesn't even include all the stops I want to make."

There was a lot of lost time to make up for. I was most excited to see what progress Ness had made on her new studio. When the main events from the festival had wrapped up, I'd gone with her back to Beeson to survey what damage remained. People had been overjoyed at her return, as they had assumed she'd perished after following the monsters into the night. She was shocked by the warm reception, admitting to me later that she never knew her neighbors cared so much. But a fierce, kindhearted person like her is easy to spot, and I was pleased to see her get the welcome she deserved. Most of the homes that had been damaged had been rebuilt by that point, but despite her eagerness to begin on her shop, Ness had insisted the market and inns be repaired first.

Mercury nodded in approval. "And you trust this new expanded council to rule righteously in your absence?"

"I do. Mostly, because I promised to come back and unleash hell if I hear they're doing anything less."

They'd taken the threat seriously, since by that point rumors had spread that a frozen body had needed to be removed from the throne room.

"Good. And the trapper?"

Butterflies danced about my ribcage. "Kitt's coming with me. I may know facts about the various cities, but he has first-hand knowledge. Besides, it's no fun traveling alone."

There was a wicked gleam in Mercury's eyes. "Is he your true love, then?"

I smiled. Kitt and I had been spending most of our days, and nights, together, but I also knew we'd just been through a rather exhilarating and traumatic experience. I wasn't about to rush into something serious based on that again.

"I don't know, but I'm excited to find out."

We sat in silence, watching the first of the lamps to be lit below. The sun wouldn't be fully set for another hour, but the flickering lights were already popping up throughout the city as people prepared for nightfall.

"Why didn't you take Kalexia's offer?"

I started at the question, and found Mercury studying me.

"I mean, I'm glad you didn't!" the Ethereal insisted. "But... how did you resist?"

Returning my gaze to the city, I suppressed a shudder. The memory of the Dark Lady's voice in my head was still painfully fresh. "I realized all the things I wanted in life were already within my grasp. I simply had to be brave enough to get them. The things Kalexia was offering wouldn't have made me happy. Not truly." I shrugged. "Besides, in the vision she showed me, I still had the powers given by the crown. But that power comes from her essence, and once she was freed from her prison, she'd have no use for me anymore, so why let me keep it?"

"Both honorable and practical," Mercury nodded. Then added, "I'm very proud of you."

My heart swelled at their words. "How did everything go on your end?"

The Ethereal sighed. "The Goddesses were less than pleased to learn Kalexia had a viable exit strategy. But they were able to bind the crown to her prison, ensuring she can never be free, and are grateful the threat is passed. I hope you don't mind, but when I recounted what happened, I made it sound like I did most of the work."

I hummed. "You know, there are more dangers in this world than The Goddesses realize. Maybe you should come back from time to time, to keep an eye on us."

Their tail swished back and forth. "I think an argument could be made for that. But now I need to return. I've got very important work to do, you know."

My heart sank. Though they'd only been back for a few minutes, I'd already begun to hope they'd come with me to travel the world. But I nodded. "Thank you for everything. For training me, for yelling at me. And, most important, for reminding me who I am, and believing in who I could be. Thank you for being on my side."

Their starry eyes gazed at me, glittering like dark rainbows in the setting sun. "Always."

They turned, but before they could leave, I called out. "Oh, and promise me one thing." The Ethereal looked over their shoulder at me, an eyebrow raised. "Promise me you won't return in another twenty years, needing me to save the world."

Mercury shrugged, the casual gesture at odds with the wicked grin that spread across their face.

"We'll see," they replied, and vanished in a cloud of silver smoke.

REVIEW REQUEST

Thank you so much for reading my book! I truly hope you enjoyed it!

As an indie author, I rely heavily on word of mouth and reviews to let people know about my books. If you enjoyed reading *Still Chosen* please consider leaving a review on your favorite online retail site. It will only take a minute and I pinky promise you will feel soooooo good knowing you helped me.

ACKNOWLEDGMENTS

I still can't believe this book is finally real. So many people helped it see the light of day!

To my editor Brouge Ramos, we both know this book would not be anywhere near this good without your help! Thank you for taking a chance on me and for believing in this project. Your notes made all the difference.

To my fabulous beta readers, Brieta, Gail, and Shaunie, your feedback and encouragement meant everything to me!

To Sarah, my proofreader, thank you for your eagle-eye. I'm still little concerned by how quickly you read this, but you're the best!

To Melissa, your industry knowledge made this possible. Also, for formatting and editing and walking me through uploading and everything else you did to make this happen. Thank you for helping in any way you could.

To Greta Sandquist, thank you for the incredible art! I know this was your first time working on a book as well, so I'm glad we got to figure this out together.

To my YA Lit professor, Lise Kildegaard. Thank you for letting me write a short story for my final project instead of an essay all those years ago. I'd always loved writing, but you kicked this whole thing off with your encouragement.

To Donna, thank you for being the best babysitter ever and always encouraging my creativity. I truly think my love of character-driven stories stems from watching *Days of Our Lives* with you.

Thank you to Jason Norman at The Paper Prophet for your help with the title and cover design! I greatly appreciate your help!

To Robbie, the *Ghost Wax* team, and the *Passages Podcast* team, thank you for letting me write stupid things and telling me they were awesome. Even though these projects didn't overlap, you all helped keep me inspired.

To the Brunch Coven, for your unending support. I cannot explain how grateful I am to have found my group of weirdos who thought my book sounded cool. To celebrate this accomplishment, I suggest we all watch *Deep Blue Sea*...again.

To Jill, Theresa, and every friend (and occasional stranger) who listened to me describe this project and demanded to read it. Thank you for your enthusiasm and helping me realize I'm not the only person who wants a female fantasy protagonist in her 30s.

To my parents and my sisters, thank you for always being there for me and supporting me. And thank you for letting me watch Labyrinth over and over and over again.

Finally, Colton. I have so many things to thank you for, it would fill its own book. Thank you for loving me as I am and supporting my crazy dreams. Thank you for pushing me to write, even when I thought everything I did was garbage. Thank you for recording my mid-sleep ramblings that night I bolted upright and started spouting the idea for this book, ensuring I wouldn't forget. And thank you for being a loving partner. I mean it when I say this book, and the person I am today, would not exist without you. Through this life and whatever happens next, platypus bear.

ABOUT THE AUTHOR

Stephanie Olson (she/her) is a writer, horror movie enthusiast (especially the bad ones), and Halloween-all-year person. She is also a writer for the Audioverse Award-winning horror podcast, *Ghost Wax*. When she's not writing, she enjoys watching *Bob's Burgers*, cosplay, and stress-baking. She lives in Minnesota with her equally talented husband and chaos gremlin of a dog. *Still Chosen* is her first novel.

You can sign up for Stephanie's ~~dog photos~~ newsletter at www.StephanieGOlson.com, and follow Stephanie on Instagram @stephaniewritesstuff.